**G T Philips**

# TERRAPODS
## THE
## INVASION BEGINS

Terrapods The Invasion Begins, is the first book in the Science Fiction series of books called The Tricerapod Trilogy by G T P Butters under the pen name of G T Philips

Published by G T P Butters 2013
Email: gtphilipsbooks@gmail.com

**ISBN** 978 0 9927954 0 5

## Acknowledgements

Many thanks to NASA for the front cover image of Earth and the invaluable information to help write this novel. Cover designed by G T P Butters.

## ABOUT THE AUTHOR

The author G T P Butters was born in London, England in 1962 and writes under the name of G T Philips. He worked as an engineer in the British aerospace industry. Before moving into the motor racing industry, and working on components for World Rally Cars, Sports Cars, D. T. M., Touring Cars and Champ Cars, then moving on to work for top Formula One Racing Teams known all over the world. Terrapods, The Invasion Begins is the first book in The Tricerapod Science Fiction Trilogy. After having a lifelong interest in science fiction G T P Butters has been inspired to write this novel. The author still resides in Surrey, England with his close family and ties to London.

******

## Dedicated to

This book is dedicated to Nicola for her love and support throughout the creation of this novel. Your support and guidance has been invaluable, along with your amazing patience and tolerance. I also dedicate this book to my children for their constant inspiration. Additionally I dedicate this book in memory of Paula, who could not be here to finally see my vision realised

# Contents

## CHAPTER 1

## HEAVENLY COLLISION

As human beings, we have enjoyed a rich and prosperous evolutionary lifestyle on this lush blue planet of ours, with our ever increasing hunger for knowledge and technology, moving us ahead of every other species, in an ever changing world. Humanity has overcome climates both hot and cold, and inhabited even the most hostile of environments, including the space station, now orbiting Earth. As human beings, our only shortfall has been of our own making, fighting endless wars against our fellow men and women throughout the ages for greed, religion, politics, territory, freedom and that liquid gold commodity oil. The only other species to rule these fresh beautiful green lands of planet Earth so dominantly were the dinosaurs. Who knows where they would be now, if it wasn't for a huge asteroid some sixty five millions years ago finding its way down to Earth's holy ground, and wiping out almost an entire race in a single catastrophic blow. After all, it could be them in the driving seat now, and not man!

As for Mother Earth, she is in danger every now and then from asteroids finding their way to ground and causing mayhem. Even a small asteroid, if travelling fast enough, could cause colossal devastation, if by chance it landed on a large city. Many larger asteroids are thankfully now mapped and the world could possibly react to a collision, if there was enough time! The super powers might be able to work together to stop a catastrophic collision, but what would happen if a rogue asteroid caught humanity out? Could we survive?

\*\*\*\*\*\*

## Arecibo, Observatory, Puerto Rico, June 1st 5 pm

Inside the main viewing gallery of the observatory, new images had arrived of the asteroid Apophis. After travelling close to the sun, it was now on a path that would take it near planet Earth, but most astronomers thought it harmless, and unlikely to be troublesome. Astronomers estimated it would be due in 2036, and it would miss the planet by a small margin, but they were keeping an eye on it just as a precaution, as it was a large asteroid, with a low level threat to humanity.

There were many astronomers inside the observatory, using varying types of 3D imaging software, plotting the paths of all the large known solar system asteroids. Astronomers came from all over the world to work in the prestigious observatory.

In the middle of the observatory were four computers, with two men standing over them studying the images of the asteroid Apophis. The first Rafael Gonzales is a local astronomer, who is thirty eight with receding straight black hair, just long enough to hide his ears. The second Chad Benson is a white American of some fifty years, with grey straggly hair, brown eyes and very large ears. His nose was smaller and broader than Rafael's, and his mouth was partially hidden by a stout grey beard.

Both men studied the images on screen closely, scanning from the middle outwards. Rafael, put his finger on the screen and said "Chad, I think I can see another object behind Apophis" Chad moved in a little closer, seeking a better view then said "You could be right, let's blow it up and put it on the large wall screen" Chad turned the switch on beneath the table, then clicked on the computer screen, minimizing the image. He quickly loaded the images of Apophis onto the wall, enlarging them by four times as he did so. Both men could see that the first object was clearly the asteroid Apophis, but on the lower right behind it, was a second object. It was considerably smaller than Apophis, but on a similar trajectory. Chad said "There definitely looks like another object behind Apophis, I think we need to look into this" Chad loaded a second image then said "This image was taken the day before" Both men studied the image, before Rafael said "The second object can barely be seen" Chad said "If that's the case, it must be moving considerably faster than Apophis" Chad

8

loaded the preceding image from two days ago. Again, both Rafael and Chad studied the image closely, but only the asteroid Apophis could be seen. Rafael was feeling a little uncomfortable as he said "Chad, the other object can't be seen here, it's moving very fast indeed. Where has it originated from, and is there any chance of it hitting Apophis?" Chad replied "I don't know, but if it does hit Apophis it's likely to be destroyed. I wonder what effect it would have on Apophis?" Chad loaded the final image from three days ago. The second object could not be seen, but Apophis had been partially blocked out by the glare of the sun. Rafael said "Chad, we need more images to find out what is going on here. I'll set the telescope up to track it, then we can take more pictures, but it will still be a day before we can view them" Chad said "Yes, the sooner the better, we need to know more about this situation and if there is a possible problem on the horizon, that the world may need to know about" Rafael immediately emailed engineer Pedro Martinez with the message "Pedro, get the telescope up and running urgently please, we need images from Apophis daily. We have a possible situation that needs attention. Send images to Chad and myself as soon as they are available. Best regards, Rafael" Rafael sent his email then turned to Chad and said "The next images will be back in twenty four hours, then every twenty four hours afterwards. We should then have a better idea of what we are dealing with" Both men then prepared to leave for home, as there was nothing more to be achieved and it was getting late.

Twenty three hours later, Chad received an email from Pedro "Rafael, your pictures are ready to view, regards Pedro" Chad called to Rafael "They've arrived Rafael! I'll put them on the large screen" Rafael walked over to him from the opposite side of the room, as Chad uploaded the new images onto the screen. Both men scrutinised the first image of Apophis. It showed the large asteroid Apophis, about to be hit by the smaller object. Rafael said "This is clearly another asteroid" Chad replied "Yes, and judging by this image, it will collide with Apophis. We need to put the next image on screen" Chad loaded the next view showing the second asteroid, after it had hit Apophis, but unlike Chad's expectation, it had not been destroyed by the impact. Chad said "I don't believe it! Both asteroids have survived the impact. Have we got any more information?" "Yes!" replied Rafael, and he followed on with "They've both survived the impact, but the second asteroid, of which I believe is Sekhmet, is riding on Apophis's back, and it's pushing Apophis along at incredible speed. We now need to find out if it will still miss planet Earth, and when it's likely to arrive" Chad put the next image up, with both asteroids looking very unstable, as they wobbled, unpredictably through space. Chad said "This is the last image we have!" Rafael looked at it then said "This concurs with our plotted path for both asteroids. Between this view, and the previous image, they are moving at break neck speed, and wobbling around in an unpredictable manner" Chad said "We need to get more images, before alerting the world's governments to a possible problem. In the meantime monitor their paths, and let's hope, it has not altered either of the asteroids trajectories" Rafael acknowledged Chad, then after a short pause suggested "I'll get in touch with Cornell University in New York State and give them all the information we have, so they can come up with precise predictions for both asteroid paths, whether good or bad. They will be able to simulate different scenarios, and my old friend Josh Leonard will keep us informed" Chad said "That's settled then" Both men went about their business, making a point to meet and discuss the phenomenon every day, at four in the afternoon, after viewing the new images of the day. Afterwards, they would inform the necessary authorities of any occurring changes, coming to light.

Rafael notified Josh, at Cornell University in America, he was very interested in the phenomenon occurring within the solar system. He thought it was an amazing find, which had likely started over thirty thousand years ago. He was impressed that his old friend had also requested his help in the matter. He asked Rafael to send as many details as possible, so he could plot several possible paths for both of the asteroids. Then make simulated predictions of what might happen in the near future, with the known facts. Josh also insisted on passing the information on to the United States government. Josh did so, but the President was only mildly concerned. Nonetheless, he did ask to be kept informed, promising to convey the data to other governments worldwide. However, he wanted more solid proof before considering going public, especially as it may never happen, whilst he was in office.

Eight days later, Rafael and Chad met up for their usual four o'clock meeting by the imaging computers to view the latest pictures. Little had changed over the previous days, but today there was a change. The first image appeared to show both asteroids breaking free of each other. Rafael said "Chad, it appears Sekhmet is trying to move away from Apophis" Chad said "I believe you're right Rafael. Sekhmet appears to be moving to the right of Apophis, but they are still moving quickly" Chad changed to the next image. In this view, Sekhmet was free and appeared to be in front of Apophis to its right. Rafael said "Sekhmet has broken free and overtaken Apophis in this view Chad. When I talked to Josh, he said there was very little danger of the asteroids impacting Earth, but now things have changed dramatically. I'd better let him know then get an updated simulation for both asteroids" The next image appeared on screen, with Sekhmet now a long way in front of Apophis, to its left. Chad said "They appear to be crossing paths as they go about their way, but still they both are following the same Earth bound trajectory" Chad added "There is damage to both asteroids! This is probably the reason for their unpredictable paths. They could be attracted to each other by Apophis's gravitational pull" The final image confirmed exactly what both men thought was happening to the asteroids. Rafael said "Josh's simulation had both asteroids locked together and eventually missing Earth by a narrow margin. I think it will change now Sekhmet has accelerated the pair of them and broken away. I predict they will likely get very close to Earth in July of this year, but I will need to confirm it" Chad said "Pardon, did you say this year!" Rafael said "Yes, they are travelling fast, but it could change, so I'll get in touch with Josh as soon as possible and get new trajectories" Chad said "If either of them hit Earth, there will be very little time for the world to react, let alone prepare for the consequences. We need plotted paths for both asteroids, to find out where they might impact on Earth. We'll need to estimate the asteroid sizes, to calculate the scale of any possible damage" Rafael finished the four o'clock meeting, promising to inform the United States government, along with as many other authorities as he could get to listen to him. First, he needed Josh to simulate fresh predictions for proof, because there was no point in worrying the world, without concrete evidence of a real impact possibility.

The following day at four o'clock, both Chad and Rafael viewed more images of the asteroids. But the only changes coming to light were of the different velocities that both asteroids were travelling through space at. The new images of Sekhmet, showed it moving quicker than Apophis and getting further ahead as each day passed. However, Sekhmet had settled down to a much smoother trajectory, making it easier to predict its future path. Apophis however was still moving unpredictably, as it pin balled through space.

Rafael said "Chad I've got a path for Sekhmet from Josh. He has estimated it will hit Earth on the fourteenth of July this year. It's about sixty metres wide and expected to break up, while entering Earth's atmosphere, but some large pieces may get through, causing minor damage to property. It will enter the atmosphere around the Isle of Wight in England, and we may have some minor fragments scattered around other parts of the world, over a two day period" He added "There's not enough data for Apophis to get a definite path, so Josh will continue collecting data from us and give us a path, as soon as possible" Chad replied "We'll inform the authorities, and let them decide the best course of action. Sekhmet will be a minor problem, but if Apophis impacts Earth, it will change everything we know, and take for granted. It will be a major catastrophe" Both men, continued their business, whilst collating as much data as possible.

******

## The Pentagon, Washington DC, June 11<sup>th</sup> 2 pm

The president, George Booth and his advisers, Ed Bernstein and Corey Nicholson, were deciding the best course of action after conversing with Rafael. They had been briefed about the asteroid Sekhmet impacting Earth's atmosphere on the fourteenth of July, along with the many possible outcomes. By the time America received the fall out, it would be several days later, with only small showers of rocks, causing virtually no damage to the United States.

George said "Ed, do we need to inform the people about this low level threat, or shall we just dismiss it as a problem for Europe?" Ed replied "This won't affect us. Why don't we offer the British help tracking the asteroids, and some financial aid, but limit what we can do, after all this is not our problem, and we don't have billions of dollars, to throw at exterior countries. Especially, as we have enough internal expenditure and this won't have any bearing on us" Corey butted in with "This asteroid may cause damage to Europe, and may or may not affect the United States, but don't forget the threat of Apophis, which is a much larger asteroid, and it could be coming our way" Ed said "These astronomers in Puerto Rico, don't have a clue where Apophis is heading, it's likely to have been thrown away from Earth. So until they have a definite impact position on the planet, I think we should just dismiss it and only inform Britain, Russia and China, as these countries will have been monitoring these asteroids anyway" George was sceptical, but both men had good arguments. There was no point worrying the people, as it might cause chaos for no reason, making him look like a worry monger, but if the second asteroid did impact, no one would be prepared, and depending on where it landed it could be a major catastrophe. George addressed both Ed and Corey "Gentlemen, we don't want to cause mass panic within our nation, so we won't inform them of the second asteroid's coming yet! However, we will notify them of the asteroid Sekhmet, especially as it will appear as glitter in the sky at night, and questions will be asked. Notify the British government of the second asteroid, but pressurize them into not broadcasting it, unless we have more concrete evidence. Inform China and Russia, and leave it to their discretion as to what they want to do. We'll need to be kept updated daily as events unfold" George concluded the meeting, by ensuring they all convened again in two weeks, unless events dictated otherwise.

As promised, they informed the relevant governments, playing down any possible impact, so as not to cause mass hysteria. Other governments, Britain included decided to broadcast a warning of Sekhmet's arrival into Earth's atmosphere on the fourteenth of July, but it would only be a low key affair, as the United States had watered down the consequences. The possibility of the second asteroid impacting Earth was not to be broadcast, because the United States deemed it to be missing the Earth, as would have happened normally, when following its original plotted path.

\*\*\*\*\*\*

**Arecibo, Observatory, Puerto Rico, July 13th 10 am**

Back at the observatory, Rafael and Chad were viewing the previous day's images of the asteroid Sekhmet. It was now only one day from

Earth, and the images were very clear. The asteroid itself could also be seen high within the sky by the naked eye.

Whilst studying the asteroid, Chad remarked "I can see light patches on the surface of the asteroid, amongst the backdrop of the dark rock. I wonder what it is!" Rafael said "Could it be ice accumulated upon it over its long journey, but where has the moisture come from? No, it must be metals, forced to the surface, when it collided with Apophis" They both agreed, that the latter was indeed the reason for the discolouration on its surface. Chad said "Has Josh estimated where Sekhmet will enter Earth's atmosphere, and at what time?" Rafael replied "Yes, it will enter Earth's atmosphere, near Portsmouth, England at 9pm GMT. Then it will fragment, as it breaks through, causing small pieces to find their way to the ground, although some may be large enough to cause minor damage to property. The asteroid will continue spreading minor fragments around the globe, in the form of microscopic particles, hanging in the atmosphere for several days, before dropping to ground" Chad said "What about Apophis?" Rafael looking very optimistic said "Josh simulated several outcomes for Apophis, and believes it will get close to Earth, but will luckily miss. On every single simulation, it will be travelling past Earth on the thirty first of December, close enough to be seen by the naked eye. It will however fly by safely" Both men concluded the meeting on an optimistic note, and it was left to Rafael, to inform the United States government, of the better news ahead.

By the time the news from Washington reached the British government and Europe, it had been played down. Only a display of flashing bright lights would be seen in the night sky, as the asteroid broke through the atmosphere. The news that Apophis would miss the Earth came as a huge relief, although there were many sceptics, who believed it would still impact, with its path being so erratic.

******

## Arecibo, Observatory, Puerto Rico, July 14th 2 pm

Both Rafael and Chad, were viewing the latest images of both asteroids inside the observatory. Only an hour to go, before the asteroid Sekhmet would begin it's descent into Earth's atmosphere, and drop to ground, near Portsmouth. These will be the last images ever seen of Sekhmet, and despite the asteroid being very small, the latest images showed the clearest and most detailed pictures of any asteroid ever taken. Rafael said to Chad "This is the closest we have ever got to detailed pictures of an asteroid about to impact our planet. Those lighter areas are scattered all over the faces now. Before, there was more darker areas, but the lighter sections have now expanded outwards, covering sixty per cent of the asteroids exterior surface" Chad said "Yes, it will be interesting to see what the scientists make of it when they get their hands on a piece of this rock" Chad added "Only an hour to go now, seems a shame you found this asteroid, only to see its demise Rafael" Rafael said "Never mind, it might hopefully change the worlds thinking about asteroids in the future" He paused then added "Our job on Sekhmet is now done, best we keep an eye on our friend Apophis for now, and make sure he does not vary from his expected course" Chad said "Let's hope no one gets hurt when Sekhmet breaks through, showering Portsmouth. I bet the sky will be an awesome sight to behold!" Both men were in good spirits, as they returned to work. If everything continued as estimated, they would be happy onlookers, as the asteroid Apophis, flew over in late December. Both men were thinking of the amazing images they would collect, because Apophis was much larger than Sekhmet.

## CHAPTER 2

## DUSTING THE FIELDS

It's now 9pm in Portsmouth, England and high in the night sky, within the realms of space heading towards Earth's atmosphere, is Sekhmet. It's an asteroid of sixty metres wide, and twenty metres in length, travelling at an astronomical speed. But this will change when it attempts to enter Earth's protective barrier, the atmosphere. The asteroid with its flattened walnut shaped hard space rock starts to bear down on Earth. Its smooth appearance, only broken by several small craters, likely to have been caused by smaller asteroids impacting it when it began life in the asteroid belt, between Mars and Jupiter, millions of years previous. The rest of the asteroid, with its light grey colouring, appears fairly smooth in texture. This part had impacted Apophis and had been smashed open, revealing the inner fruits of Sekhmet. Inside the central impact area, there was a much darker grey recess, hinting that this indeed, was the central impact area. The grey impact area appeared like a dirty grey carpet, sweeping across the asteroids face. However, when viewed from afar, it took on the appearance of a frozen black pond, especially when the sunlight glanced across it.

Although Earth's gravity was affecting the asteroid, it was still travelling at fifty thousand miles an hour, but this would come to an abrupt and rapid slow down, as it tried forcing its way through Earth's protective life giving shell. Its path would take it directly into Earth's atmosphere at a very steep angle, before the asteroid swiftly met its violent end.

The asteroid approached Russian airspace, getting ready to start its rapid, violent slow down. Mother Earth will not allow anything to enter her life supporting cocoon easily. Sekhmet broke free of the asteroid belt, some thirty thousand years earlier. It's now on the final leg of its journey, ready to light up Earth's sky, with a large firework display of its valuable possessions. Sekhmet will take just thirty minutes to break through, but the last five minutes will seal the glorious fate of the asteroid.

Appearing motionless, the asteroid navigates rapidly into the breach. In space, Earth appears teasingly inviting, especially after a long perilous journey across the solar system. The frozen voids of space, can't match the warm tranquillity offered by Earth, as the asteroid sits on the edge of the beautiful, blue hazy atmospheric halo. Sekhmet could almost reach out, and touch this warm and bountiful world. Sekhmet admires the planets serenity, but to touch down, it must first venture into the atmosphere, that holds the glorious finale it was made for. The first hints of descent are upon Sekhmet, as it skims the atmosphere, gently bouncing, as if surfing a wave. The first stage will see the asteroid break the outer skin of Earth, while poking its nose underneath for a quick glimpse below. This will start Mother Earth's rejection of this heavenly celestial body. Sekhmet bounces gently upon Earth's outer breath. Now and then, it tries pushing its nose further underneath, as if trying to get a sneaky peek at the beautiful place beneath, that it wants to call home. Every sinful peak at Mother Earth enrages her fury even more, and she buffets the asteroid violently, shaking it sideways and forcefully pushing it upwards, nose first. Every time Sekhmet loses valuable speed, it makes it more difficult to push back with enough force, to enter into the Earth's warm cocoon of life. Another push, a little harder this time, much more testing of Mother Earth's convictions. Sekhmet soon pushed a quarter of its body beneath the planets outer skin. Mother Earth fights back again, with an even bigger vengeful counter blow that smashes the asteroid, causing it to shudder. Then with an almighty push, she rejects the beast. Sekhmet shows signs of battle wounds, as the stress fractures become apparent across the top of the asteroid. Sekhmet will not give up easy on its dreams. It wants valuable time on this beautiful sacred land below, even if its time will be but a few minutes. One more downwards push into the breach, and Sekhmet is forced vertical once more. It dives through the outer skin, forcing the beast through the outer layer. Chards of rock loosen then cling desperately to the main body. There's no stopping Sekhmet now, destiny, and the gravitational pull of the Earth, now make these small fragments a worthy price to pay, to enter the next stage of descent.

Rock slithers clung to the main asteroid body, in an attempt to show defiance and unity. Mother Earth again violently tries to halt the asteroids passage, shaking more chards of rock off in all directions in the process. These will later explode into smithereens, dusting the globe over several days, after being blown around on the world's weather systems. Most will drop to ground, blending in to the background, as just another piece of Earth's landscape. The pushing has now finished, and Sekhmet can rest for a minute, before taking on its next task.

Sekhmet has succeeded in getting through the first stage into Earth's sweet atmosphere, but now it has to endure a rapid free fall, in a swift second stage. Mother Earth has not finished unleashing her fury yet, and this will be a much sterner test of Sekhmet's endurance, and convictions. The battered asteroid accelerates once again in a free fall, whilst Earth's atmosphere does its utmost to reject it once again, causing the asteroid to drop at a steep angle. As the speed rapidly builds up on the nose of the asteroid, it glows red from the friction. The red hot nose protects the rest of the asteroid from the dangerous heat, shielding the grey colouring around its mid-rift, and the rear of the beast. Mother Earth bides her time, as she waits for the right moment to finish the job she started in stage one. The superheated asteroid's front expands quickly as the friction pounds it, but the rear still retains a cool core temperature. Visible stress fractures appear, these were rooted within the first stage of entry, the crack's creep slowly along deadly paths. It will not be long now before the end is in sight, for this heavenly body.

The crack of death appears on the red hot nose of Sekhmet. It quickly changes from red to white. Then the crack suddenly, but slowly peels open the asteroid, revealing a glimpse into the universe's past life. It takes just a split second for the crack to extend rearwards, riding through the centre of the asteroid to its tail. Then "Bang!" in a fraction of a second, the past millions of years, are laid bare to the world. The asteroid has split in two, revealing the solar systems early secrets. The two huge chards barrel-roll over and over as they collide. The impacting rocks crash hard against each other, causing several loud sonic bangs, until small fragments are spewed out all over the sky. Several large chunks continue downwards, on their chosen paths, heading directly towards Portsmouth in England. They are far too high to be seen at the moment, but as they drop they will light up the evening skies within the next few minutes. Other suspended fragments, will eventually fall to ground slowly over Russia, Europe and eventually America over a two day period. Suspended tiny fragmented rocks are all that is left of Sekhmet, most are held airborne, in a large floating dusty cloud in the night sky, as if a storm was brewing on the horizon.

Over the next few days, the dusty remnants will eventually find their way downwards dropping on Earth's sacred ground, concluding the last stage. Sekhmet lost its battle with Mother Earth, but it will at least reach its final destination, and win the war, albeit in millions of minute pieces, scattered around the globe.

## CHAPTER 3

## ON THE FERRY

Tuesday evening, cars and trucks were waiting to board the nine thirty roll on, roll off ferry from Portsmouth, destined for Fishbourne in the Isle of Wight. It's a warm clear summer July night, and the air is very still. This will be the last ferry until the morning, and with money being tight this year, it will only be half full. The cars were lined up neatly in rows, with only three of the seven rows completely full, with the forth having but two queuing cars parked up.

To the far right, sit two trucks, the first, a large dark green arctic with J McIntire, the drivers name written on the cab and trailer. Underneath his name, written in small lettering is "Haulage you can depend on" Behind the arctic was another smaller red truck, it was clearly the post, ready to be sent over to the island for distribution in the morning, because it has "Mail" written on it and "We deliver by the next day"

In the ferry car park, many people could be seen standing by their cars, some talking, whilst others were having their last cigarette, before boarding the ferry. The first car waiting within the first row was a white saloon, with a couple in their mid-twenties inside, waiting patiently. Behind them was a red hatchback with a family of four inside, about to start their holiday in the Isle of Wight. In the rear, two young boys are sat wearing jeans and T-shirts, and they are playing on their game consoles. Thomas now five, with short blonde hair and blue eyes is sat behind the driver. His gaze was glued to his hand held portable console. Next to him is his eight year old brother Joe, with brown curly hair and blue eyes. He has linked his console to his brother's, enabling them to play together. In the front passenger seat sits Mary, the boy's mother with long blonde hair and blue eyes. She has her seat tilted back slightly, and has drifted off to a light sleep. Next to her, sitting within the driver's seat is Mary's husband, and the boy's father Dave. He has short brown hair, clean shaven and is slightly taller than Mary. This is the Ellis family, and after driving for a few hours, they are now looking forward to boarding the ferry and having a short break, before completing their journey.

Dave looked forwards, checking to see if the ferry gate was going to lift soon, enabling him to embark the boat. The gate master was standing beside the gate, but he made no attempt to lift it. After all, it was still a few minutes to go until nine thirty, when they were due to board. Dave looked sideways towards his wife Mary. Her eyes were tightly closed, as she sat silently. They had been travelling for several hours, and Mary usually dozed off from the boredom of not driving. Dave peered up to the rear view mirror, quickly checking on Joe and Thomas in the rear. They were happy enough playing against each other. Happy now they may be, he thought, but it was only a matter of time, before they would begin arguing, then a fight would break out, as kids do. Now however, he was enjoying the peace and quiet.

His eyes searched the dashboard then he reached out, turning the radio on, lowering the volume as he did so. He again looked towards Mary, making sure she had not woken. She stirred, but settled back down immediately. A woman's voice came across the radio "This is Deborah Carr, with the news on Tuesday the fourteenth of July, at nine thirty in the evening. Here's the main news. Another six hundred redundancies in the retail sector have been announced today, along with a further two thousand jobs going in the city, due to the down turn of the economy, and the credit crunch. It looks like a very bleak second half of the year for most house holders" Dave was not very keen on hearing of the doom and gloom in the world, because he had been out of work the previous year for several months. It had taken a year to recover financially, with his wife and him working many long hours for several months. They were looking forward to a family holiday, because they had been unable to afford one last year.

He was about to turn the radio off, when the newsreader said something of more interest to him, and Dave found himself drawn to the rest of the broadcast. She said "On a good note! England, that is Portsmouth and the Isle of Wight, might see the sky light up tonight, when the asteroid Sekhmet, enters Earth's atmosphere around ten o'clock. It should present no danger, as it will burn up high in the atmosphere, but if you are lucky enough to be in the area, you may see it light up the night sky, with a bright dazzling firework display. This is the end of tonight's news with Deborah Carr. There will be more reports at eleven tonight, goodnight" Dave turned the radio off then looked up to the heavens, but nothing could be seen, save a stagnant murky grey cloud.

Dave turned briefly back towards the gate, before turning his head to his right, and looking through the driver's window. He watched the driver in the green arctic, open the door to his cab, and climb out. As he did so, Dave heard the clunk of another door being closed, coming from behind the arctic. He turned his head to face where the noise had originated from. Then he watched a slim man in a red and grey uniform, walking to the front of the arctic and heading towards the cab. It was clear, he had come from the red truck behind the arctic, because the truck had "Mail" written on it, and so did his uniform pocket. The man was wearing a cap, that hid most of his hair, any on show was very grey and straggly. Dave could not see a great deal of his face, but he appeared to be in his late forties, and in need of a good shave. The man reached into his right hand top pocket, then pulled out a packet of chewing gum. He immediately offered it to the other man, who by now had exited his cab. The arctic driver was a lot larger than the mail man. He had broad shoulders, a large gut, bald head and a clean shaven face, making him look a little younger than the slimmer man. The arctic driver proceeded to take the gum, unwrap it then chew it. It was clear these two men knew each other well, and had probably done this trip many times before. Dave could hear them having a conversation, but their voices were too far away to make out what they were saying.

Then a loud grating noise, and an unusually loud "Bang!" was heard, making Dave turn quickly to his left, immediately looking towards the gate master. He was lifting the gate up, but he also briefly stopped, while he tried to find out where the loud noise had come from. He looked up to the sky, before continuing to lift the gate upwards until it was vertical. He then faced the ferry, waving at the cars waiting to disembark. One by one, the engines started, and the cars disembarked the ferry then drove past Dave, and all the other waiting cars. Only twelve cars disembarked, so when the last car drove by the gate master, he waved at the trucks, allowing them to board.

After the trucks boarded, the gate master waved towards the couple in front of Dave, allowing them to embark. Dave started his engine in anticipation, and Mary suddenly sprang to life, acting as if she had never been asleep. The car in front drove off then Dave duly followed on, he past the gate master and boarded the ferry. He followed the white car, until they neared the end of the ferry, where he found both trucks already parked at the rear of the ferry. The green arctic was on the left with the cab by the ferry exit doors. The mail truck sat on the right, with its front just over lapping the cab of the arctic. The white car parked at rear of the arctic, then Dave slotted in behind it. He turned to his wife and said "At last we can get out and stretch our legs Mary" He turned to Joe and Thomas and said "Pack your consoles up, and get ready to get out boy's, but wait until the other cars have parked up first, or you may get hurt" Dave and Mary prepared to exit in the meantime. Joe and Thomas were very keen to get out and go up the stairs to the top of the ferry, as it was their first time travelling on a boat. Thomas said excitedly "Can I go outside and watch the ferry pull out of the harbour?" "Of course you can, dad will take you outside, while I get us some drinks" said Mary.

They exited the car and made their way through the tightly penned in cars, then headed for the middle of the ferry, to where the stairs were situated. They climbed two floors, until it opened out into the restaurant area. Mary looked towards the food service area. It was quiet, with only the arctic driver getting served. Mary said to Dave "Take the boy's outside, and I'll get some coffees for us and fruit juices for the boy's, then find some seats by the window" "Okay" said Dave. He turned to the rear of the ferry then said "C'mon boy's, let's go outside and watch the ferry pull away" He barely had time to finish his words, before Joe and Thomas sprinted past him, on their way to the glass door at the rear of the ferry. They opened it and went through to the outer deck. Mary said "You better get after them. Don't be outside too long or your coffee will be cold" Dave hurriedly walked to the glass doors, pushing them open, then caught up with Joe and Thomas. All three of them continued walking to the end of the decking, where a two tier protective white fenced railing, surrounding the edge of the deck stood. They put their arms forward and lent on the rails, mirroring each other's stance. Dave lent on the top rail, Joe and Thomas rested on the bottom rail, then they looked downwards.

The cars could be seen tightly packed together, keeping the weight evenly distributed. They peered to the back of the ferry, to where the boarding doors had now been closed, and watched the boat being readied to set off from port.

The ferry made a loud chugging noise, before drifting to the left. The chug, quickly turned into a continuous drone of engine noise, and they prepared to depart the harbour. The engine noise increased rapidly, as the ferry shuddered and moved away from its moorings, building up speed. It soon chugged past the boat yards on the left side of the ferry.

Thomas was excited, as he said to Dave "Lift me up, so I can see" Dave lifted him saying "I'll lift you up, but when we clear the boat yards ,you won't be able to see much, because it's too dark" He held him high in the direction of the boat yards. After reaching the last yard, the ferry began turning, whilst entering into open water. This was to avoid the concrete gun emplacements, between Portsmouth and the Isle of Wight that were left over from previous wars of a bygone age.

Once past the emplacements, only a few lights were on view from the shore. Thomas was still keen to stay outside and watch, but Dave was now struggling to hold him. So it came as a welcome relief, when Thomas said "I need the toilet dad" Dave replied "Okay, we'll all go back inside to mum and I'll take you to the toilet Thomas" Dave put Thomas down on the deck. Then all three walked back towards the glass doors, leading into the restaurant.

They reach the doors, just as the large arctic driver arrived on the other side, now holding a hot drink in his hand, and with the mail man following closely behind. He courteously pulled the door towards him, allowing Dave, Joe and Thomas through first. Joe stepped through, followed by Thomas, pulling Dave through by his hand. Dave walked through and said "Thanks" The large man said "No problem!" in a strong Scottish accent.

Dave searched for his wife, who was by now sitting on a table for four beside the window. As they drew closer to Mary, Dave said "I've just got to take Thomas to the toilet, then we'll be back" "Okay, do you want to go Joe? We'll only be on the ferry for another twenty minutes" asked Mary. "No thanks mum" replied Joe. Dave and Thomas walked past Mary and Joe and headed towards the centre of the ferry.

They walked beyond the stairs, then past the canteen and in to the toilets. Mary watched them as they disappeared through the toilet door, then she continued sipping her coffee.

Meanwhile, both truck drivers had exited the glass doors and were now standing in the same place that Dave, Joe and Thomas had once stood. The arctic driver, John McIntire nicknamed Mac, looked up towards the darkened sky, and said to the other man, in his strong accent "Sure is a clear warm night Ian" Ian replied "It certainly is Mac! I heard on the radio that an asteroid will be coming down over Portsmouth tonight, causing a big firework display for us all. Where are you delivering to today Mac?" Mac said "I've supplies for St Mary's hospital in Newport, I'll drop the truck off later then I'm booked into my usual hotel, hopefully the truck will be unloaded by the morning, so I can get the eight thirty ferry back" Ian said "I'll see you in the morning at eight thirty then, as I'm also booked in on the return trip" Both men stood quietly, thinking for a while then Ian jokingly remarked "Best keep an eye out for that asteroid, might get a piece of it on the ferry, perhaps we can sell it on the internet" Mac replied. "Chance would be a fine thing!" Ian said. Mac then proceeded to remove a packet of gum from his trouser pocket and offer one to Ian. Ian took one then Mac removed one for himself, as Ian thanked him. Then they proceeded to unwrap and eat their gum.

Both men stared skywards as they chewed their gum then waited expectantly for a firework display to happen. They had both heard the loud bang earlier as they waited to board the ferry, but had not realised it was the asteroid. Instead, they presumed the ferry had hit its moorings. They looked upwards, but the only thing seen in the clear night sky, was a small grey cloud.

Meanwhile, back inside the ferry, Mary and Joe were sat at a table near the window. Mary was by the window, facing the rear of the ferry with Joe sat opposite her. They were looking out into the dark night sky. Mary slowly sipped her coffee, while turning to look towards the toilet door. The door opened slowly then quickly closed tightly afterwards. Immediately, Mary guessed it was Thomas, because he was not strong enough to open the door by himself, but he would be determined to try. The door flung open again, and out came little Thomas with Dave chasing him. Thomas arrived at the table and said "Mum have I got a drink please?" Mary replied "Yes, it's on the table Thomas" Dave finally arrived at the table, as Thomas climbed over Mary, to get a better view. He gently pushed Mary aside, to attain a good position by the window. Mary said "Your coffees on the table Dave!" Dave replied "Cheers!" Both Joe and Thomas sat quietly, peering out through the window, which was very unusual for them. As they both stared towards the many bright sparkling lights high in the evening sky. Dave said "Did you hear that bang in the car park earlier Mary?" "No" She replied, turning to look at Joe and Thomas. Then she added "You two are very quiet, what are you watching?" Thomas said "Look over there mum, someone's letting off fireworks" Thomas pointed through the window, towards the flashes of light as they brightened the dark sky. The showers of light fell from the heavens to the sea without any sound, until they splashed down. Dave said "I know what it is. It's the asteroid breaking up in the atmosphere. It was on the radio earlier" Dave and Mary turned to each other and continued drinking their coffees in unison. Joe remarked "Hey! Some of the rocks are falling into the sea, and making huge splashes" Mary and Dave gazed back through the window, watching them fall into the sea. These were very large rocks indeed, and the ferry was sailing straight towards them. Mary said "I don't like the look of this Dave!" She shouted at Joe and Thomas, in a nervous frightened voice "Get away from the windows boys!" Dave said "We'll move to the centre of the ferry" He rose from his seat, then pulled Joe away from the window, just as Mary grabbed Thomas, pulling him to her. Thomas was reluctant to move, and was more interested in watching the rocks dropping outside the ferry.

They all moved clear of the window and stood next to the central staircase. Here, they stared through the window at the falling rocks splash landing into the sea. The ferry ebbed closer to the noisy crashing rocks. Dave said "They mentioned the asteroid on the radio, but they said it would disintegrate through Earth's atmosphere" Mary replied "They were wrong!" Mary cuddled Thomas, as he started shaking with fear. Her arms gently wrapped around him, like a warm protective blanket, making him feel safe.

Outside the ferry, Mac and Ian stood holding the top rail, as they watched the rocks falling either side of the ferry. They ignored the danger, whilst admiring their once in a life time asteroid experience. They shuffled along the rails, to acquire a better view of the rocks as they pounded the side of the boat. They watched the rocks getting ever closer, until a loud crash was heard on the front of the ferry. A large chunk of rock hit the bow. Then there was another loud bang, followed by several more in quick succession.

Suddenly, there was a hollow thudding sound, and a hand size rock pounded the deck near Mac and Ian. Fortunately it bounced away from them, hitting the glass door to the restaurant. The glass immediately shattered into small pieces, most of which ended up inside the ferry. Then a shower of smaller rocks fell onto the ferry, making a continuous tapping sound, as they rattled against the cars on the open deck.

Mac looked up, catching a glimpse of a very large fragment of rock coming directly towards both men. Momentarily stunned, he watched the bench size rock falling towards them. He quickly came to his senses, and launched himself at Ian, pushing him away from the object's path, thinking it was the last thing both of them would ever do on this planet. They both slipped sideways along the rail with the momentum, until Ian lost his balance and they both fell to the deck.

The rock sped past, catching Mac's bicep, tearing through his shirt, whilst grazing his skin beneath. The rock continued onwards, smashing through the railings, taking some of the decking along with it. This left Mac and Ian close to falling thirty feet to the car deck below, and a certain death. The rock continued falling, ploughing into the car deck below, landing on top of a four by four truck. It tore through the roof like paper, crushing the interior down to floor height, eventually stopping when the underside of the truck rested on the deck. Cars either side of the damaged four by four survived the impact, but their windows shattered in the violent halting of the rock.

Ian ended up lying on his back with Mac crushing him, making it impossible for him to move. Ian looked to his left, only to find a missing security railing. The rail that had once stood beside them, stopping them falling to the deck below, had now disappeared. The crumpled remains, were sitting in front of the ferry loading doors. He quickly noticed that both he and Mac were very close to toppling over the edge, with Mac's right leg dangling over the deck edge into mid-air. Mac was barely moving, and was very quiet. Ian in a strained voice said "You okay Mac?" Mac made a grunting noise. Ian spoke again, but louder, and with more urgency, due to Mac's weight crushing him "Mac, you okay? You're squashing me. Can you move?" Mac replied "I'm alright, but my left arm hurts like hell. Hang on, I'll try to get off" Ian replied "Move towards the doors, we're close to falling off the edge" "Okay!" said Mac. Mac had damaged his left arm, so was unable to help himself, and his right leg was of little use dangling over the top deck. So he rolled to his left and in doing so, gave out a yell as all his weight transferred onto his painful left arm. Now Ian was free of Mac and could move freely.

Ian's thoughts rapidly turned to getting back inside, and away from the fragments of rock bombarding the ferry. Ian said "We need to go inside Mac. Do you need help?" Mac was in pain, as he began shaking, and entering into shock. Mac said "You go in, then I'll follow" Ian was unable to get Mac in by himself. He also knew Mac could not get himself inside, but Ian could not leave him outside at the mercy of the falling rocks.

Dave was watching as the large rock caught Mac's arm, before smashing through the railings. He had seen the men fall out of his sight, but he thought the rock had taken them to their graves. He moved towards the broken door, and heard what he thought, was voices. He stared outside and to his astonishment, both men were very much alive, despite the larger man having a nasty gash on his left arm, and blood trickling down. It was clear they needed help to return to the safety of the ferry, before more rocks rained down upon them. That would not be an easy task, with the larger man on the floor injured and small asteroid fragments still showering the ferry.

Dave opened the smashed glass door in time to see the slim built man, trying to move Mac in on his own. Dave shouted over to him "I'm coming to help you, grab his left arm and I'll race over and grab the other!" Dave rushed to the men. On arrival, both men bent downwards, lifting Mac's arms up. One big effort from both men, and they pulled Mac to his feet, then all three of them slowly headed towards the door. Mac in extreme pain understood the urgency of getting under cover quickly. Mary watched Dave helping the men, and as they neared the glass door, she quickly swung it wide open, allowing them to seek shelter from the bombardment.

All three men, shuffled away from the door, carefully avoiding the broken glass on the floor. Then Dave and Ian gently lay Mac on the floor, giving all three men a well-earned rest, but Mac seemed extremely lethargic. Mac had struggled to move his legs, and Dave and Ian had been very surprised when he was unable to help them return inside. They put it down to shock, because after all he had just saved Ian's life, and nearly ended up on the deck below.

Shortly afterwards, a crew member arrived on the scene to help. He was holding a first aid kit as he knelt down beside Mac, and said "Hi, I'm Neil Bennett the medical officer, please don't move Sir. Can you tell me your name Sir?" No answer was forthcoming, and Mac looked confused. Ian said "It's Mac, John McIntire! But everyone calls him Mac" Neil then looked to Dave before turning back to Ian and said "Could you help support your friend, while I clean his wound. My colleague should be here shortly with a wheelchair then we'll take Mac to the first aid room" Looking towards Mac, Neil continued with "If you don't mind Mac!" Mac looking extremely tired did not answer. Neil cleaned up the wound as best he could, then said to all three men "I've instructed my colleague to arrange for an ambulance to be waiting for us in Fishbourne, to take Mac to hospital" A few seconds later a female crew member arrived to help. She came pushing a wheelchair and said "Neil, do you need any help?" Neil replied "Yes please Danielle. This is Mac, he's been struck by a piece of rock, and we need to transport him to the first aid room. After docking, the ambulance will pick him up and take him to St Mary's hospital in Newport" Danielle said "I've already informed the hospital, the ambulance will be waiting when we arrive. They mentioned that many more similar rocks have fallen all over the island and on the mainland" Neil turned to Mac then said "Are you okay to get up on the wheelchair Mac, or do you need help?" Mac was silent, but did try getting up on to the wheelchair. However, he was unable to rise to his feet, let alone climb on to the wheelchair. Neil said "Stay there Mac! Let me and your friends help you" So Neil, Dave and Ian helped Mac onto the wheelchair. Neil then strapped Mac in securely and said "Danielle and I will take Mac to the first aid room and look after him there, until we arrive in Fishbourne. On arrival, he'll leave the ferry first and an ambulance will transport him onto Newport hospital" Ian said "I'll stay with Mac if you don't mind Neil, then I'll inform his family in Scotland. If Mac's truck is blocking the ferry doors, I'll park it safely in the port car park after docking, allowing everyone to disembark" "Thank you!" said Neil. Afterwards, Neil and Danielle began pushing Mac towards the first aid room situated near the restaurant.

Ian turned to Dave and said "I'm Ian, and my mates name is Mac, as I expect you know by now. Thanks for your help, we both appreciate it. I don't know how I would have got him in on my own. What's your name?" Dave said "No problem, my name's Dave, I thought both of you had followed the rock down to the deck below" Ian said "We nearly did! I'd better go now, thanks again Dave" Ian shook Dave's hand then turned to catch up with Mac, Neil and Danielle, in the first aid room.

Mary put her arms around Dave then said "You're either brave or stupid, going out there to help those men" Dave replied "Ian was never going to get Mac in on his own. It took a split second to help them back inside. After all, if it had happened a few minutes earlier, it would have been Joe, Thomas and me out there. I would like to have thought, that someone would have helped us back inside" Joe and Thomas grabbed Dave and Mary, seeking the security of their parents embrace.

They all turned to face the ferry windows, listening to the sound of the pounding rocks, as they gradually subsided. After a minute, the noise stopped completely, so they ventured a little closer to the windows. Outside, the air went clear, as they watched the stars glistening serenely in the night sky. Dave said "Mary are the boy's okay?" Mary replied "Yes, Joe's fine and Thomas just wanted his dad to come back inside, far away from the stones. He was fine after watching you enter the door, along with the other men" Dave said "Five more minutes, and we'll be in Fishbourne, heading to the cottage in Sandown. Hope Mac's okay, that was one hell of a rock that hit him" Mary said "I'm grateful no one was seriously hurt, it could have crashed through the ferry roof, injuring many more people inside"

A male voice announced across the ferry speakers "This is Captain Nigel James! I hope everyone on the ferry is okay, after our chance encounter with the asteroid. Apparently it was supposed to break up before reaching the ground, but obviously this was not so! We have one casualty on board, and he will be disembarking first. If anyone else has been injured, can they please report to the first aid room on the second floor, near the restaurant? We've sustained minor damage to the ferry, but this won't cause any major problems. Anyone with damage to their vehicles should remain behind, and someone will arrange transport to help you on your way, and to help remove your vehicles from the ferry. May I remind you that we will shortly be arriving at Fishbourne. I'm sorry for the delay in getting you off the ferry, but the injured must be a dealt with first. Hope you enjoy the rest of your stay on the island, thank you!"

Five minutes later, the ferry docked at the quiet, lifeless port of Fishbourne. A gentle bump was felt as the ferry position itself and quickly moored. The doors of the loading bay lowered, but no one hurried to release the cars. The medical officer, Neil Bennett soon came into view, as he walked towards the open bay doors. He had a brief conversation with another crew member then continued on his way to a small building, just inside the ferry port.

Through the building window, a silhouetted man could be seen talking on the phone. Neil arrived at the building, as the man slid the window along its rail, fully opening it. The man immediately put down his phone then said "Are you Neil Bennett?" Neil replied "Yes, I requested an ambulance, has it arrived yet?" The man said "I've just opened the gate for them. Do you want to tell them where to go, as they will only be a moment" Before the man finished his sentence, the ambulance was heard nearing the building. Neil turned to face it, just as it came to a stop, with the driver's door aligned to him. "Alright Neil, what you got for me then?" said the chirpy voice of the driver. It was a friend Neil knew well, called Roy Stoner. They had trained together in London, but later chose to follow different paths. They found themselves frequently bumping into each other every now and then, especially when Roy was called to assist at the ferry port. Neil said "Can you reverse onto the ferry as far as you can Roy. We've got a man called John McIntire with a nasty gash on his left arm. The wound has been cleaned and dressed, there doesn't seem to be any bleeding to the local area. He's confused, and possibly in shock. He prefers to be called Mac. The gash was caused by the remnants of the asteroid catching his arm" Roy said "Okay mate, there's lots of tiny asteroid pieces scattered all over the island" Roy then proceeded to reverse the ambulance onto the ferry.

Neil returned to the ferry doors, finding his assistant Danielle waiting, along with another crew member and Mac. Roy repositioned the ambulance close to the party, then exited the cab and joined them. Mac was indeed looking slightly dazed, and showed signs of shock, and he was in considerable pain. Roy said "Hello Mac, I'm Roy, I'm going to put you in the ambulance, then take you on to St Mary's hospital in Newport" He opened the ambulances rear doors, whilst speaking. A woman appeared from inside, as the doors sprung open, and Roy added "This is Jane, she will look after you Mac, until we arrive at the hospital" He paused a while, whilst waiting for a response. Mac looking bewildered, eventually said "Okay" Roy, with the help of Neil, loaded Mac into the ambulance, and settled him onto a bed. They all said goodbye and Roy returned to the cab, and prepared to leave. Roy, unhappy with Mac's lack of response, asked Jane to keep a close eye on him, as they drove off towards the hospital.

Neil returned to the ferry, as the ambulance drove away in the distance. He walked towards the stairs leading up to the restaurant, then stopped, and unlocked a small metal door at chest height, then pulled it open. Behind it, sat a phone, which he duly picked up. He informed the Captain, that the injured man had been safely removed from the ferry, so all passengers could now disembark. He returned the phone, then locked the door and walked towards Mac's truck.

Ian was sat inside waiting, with the keys in the ignition as Neil approached the cab. Neil said "Are you okay to drive the truck?" Ian said "Yes I used to drive these things years ago, before I was made redundant. I'll put it in the car park, near the terminal building over there, until Mac's ready to collect it" Neil said "Okay, go when you're ready, if you need assistance sound your horn" Ian carefully drove Mac's truck off the ferry, releasing his truck and all the other cars.

Meanwhile, Captain Nigel James made an announcement to the remaining passengers, allowing them to return to their vehicles and disembark. The Ellis family gathered their belongings, and followed the relieved passengers, down the stairs to their waiting cars. By the time the Ellis family arrived at their car, most of the other vehicles had disembarked, leaving them free to drive away. They got in their car then set off from the ferry port, to their holiday cottage in Sandown, just ten miles away, on the islands south eastern coast.

Left back on the ferry, were the few remaining passengers, with damage to their vehicles. The crew were now frantically trying to sort out alternative arrangements, to get them on their way. This would take a while, with the stricken four by four and its passengers, because a hire car and tow truck was required.

## CHAPTER 4

## THROUGH THE NIGHT

The first signs of the asteroid breaking up were seen over the Isle of Wight, but the true extent of the damage would not be clear for several days. Tiny particles would continue dispersing their contents all over the world. The asteroid should have disintegrated on entry into Earth's atmosphere, but it had partly survived, to fall as minute unnoticeable fragments. The first of the larger remnants were dumped on the south coast over the Isle of Wight. These larger pieces caused widespread damage to property, injuring many people. The brown coloured fragments, also had small light grey areas upon them. Other particles were suspended on the top of the atmosphere, just awaiting their final destinations. These particles caught high in the turbulent air, fell down gradually overnight over England and reached as far afield as southern Europe. More would wander the winds, eventually dropping to ground over the rest of the world. Whatever the size of fragment, they all carried a new life form that had travelled millions of miles to find its new resting place. The Earth might just be the perfect place to settle. Only time would tell!

In a very short time, the fragmented rocks had scattered themselves all over the Isle of Wight. The warm moist air obviously suited this new life, and it was quick to take advantage of its new surroundings. During the night, thousands of tiny fragments settled, blowing a breath of fresh air into the new alien inhabitants.

The rock dwelling creatures appeared as tiny mushrooms, with heads no bigger than the tip of a pen. Some had fallen off the rock fragments on landing, then attached to the local plant life, or found sanctuary on grass verges in small grey communes. Any alien attached to a plant thrived, growing twice their original size within an hour of landing. The ones left on the rock fragments hardly changed size, but nonetheless were still very much alive.

As each hour passed, more fragments settled around Europe, along with the new species they carried. The alien took a firm hold, cementing roots wherever it landed. As for humans, they took no notice of this new being, after all, the asteroid entering Earth was of more interest, because it was a larger than life event, and a rarity for one of Sekhmet's size, to break through Earth's protective barrier. There was now a far more pressing concern for the British government, with reports of the asteroid causing damage to people and property, in the proximity of Portsmouth, and the Isle of Wight. After all, the American government had informed Europe that there was no danger at all from any asteroid fallout. So the last thing on the British governments mind was of any life form being transported aboard the asteroid, but more of saving face with their voters. The country was in deep recession, so getting another prediction wrong, did not stand well with their ever increasing critical public.

As the hours rolled on, the fall out gradually spread its winged dusty cloud across Ireland, then onwards, over the Atlantic sea. On land it was the same story with the settling aliens, but in the sea, it was totally different story. The heavier fragments of rocks carried their new life to the bottom of the deep dark cold waters. The new plants could not survive in the bottom of the deep blue abyss, with the lack of light and no heat to support them. The asteroid had a good source of heat on its turbulent journey, with the sun providing it with plenty of light along its long journey. This was perfect to keep the plants alive, but not for them to flourish. The alien life form falling into the cold black depths, met a watery grave, changing colour from grey to a bright red. However, any aliens floating on the sea on the dusty asteroid particles might survive, if lucky enough to have a light source. However, they still required a source of heat, if they are to last until the new day. Moving across the sea, the majority of the aliens will die, even while on the top of the sea, due to the lack of light and the waves constantly drenching them in ice cold water.

Where the fallout crosses the big pond, and reaches the United States and Canada, it will again be close to the artificial lights of the coastlines. Here, the aliens will have a chance of survival, but it will be difficult with the sun soon preparing to set, for the evening. The only saving grace will be the warmth of the night, and the bright lights of the busy nonstop cities. Any aliens finding sanctuary on land will survive and flourish, especially if they make the lush green areas. After the United States and Canada, the cloud will move on in turn to Japan, China and Russia. The majority of the fallout will be deposited over a twenty four hour period, with the exception some smaller particles, caught in the trade winds. They will take a further two to three days, to find their final resting places.

\*\*\*\*\*\*

Back in the Isle of Wight, it's now four o'clock in the morning and still dark. In an hour or so the sun will rise, and a new day will dawn, bringing a bright warm summers day. The first aliens to take up residence had already grown to an inch long, in and around the grass verges of Fishbourne. The light and heat would soon arrive, bringing the beginning of the aliens first day on a lush planet, holding a promising future for this new species.

Five fifteen in the morning, day breaks over the Isle of Wight, as the shadows are being pushed back by the advancing sunlight, beating down on the pretty little island. In the port, the ferry awaits idly silent, with its damage rendering it unusable, because its condition is worse than first thought. All vehicles had been cleared from the ferry decks, along with the large piece of asteroid, as this was now sitting on a flatbed truck within the car park, along with the remains of the four by four. These were to be taken away and examined by scientists at London University.

There was a large indentation on the ferry, caused by the rock impact, where it had finally come to rest on the car deck. The ferry also had several broken windows, and any exposed woodwork had small grey buds growing on it. The new aliens obviously liked the wood, so the Captain had ordered the ferry to be replaced by a refurbished one from the old fleet. He had decided this one needed repairing, and he had ordered the removal of any unwanted space debris to be cleared off at Portsmouth. So he made arrangements, to return it to Portsmouth later that day.

Outside the ferry port through to Fishbourne village, then onto Ryde, many patches of dark grey mushroom like buds, resembling grey rugs, were scattered along the verges. The mushrooms had increased in size, as the sunshine warmed them through, whilst their tips quietly followed the heat source. Moving on to the many small cottages, scattered along the main road, the aliens had settled not only in the gardens, but also on some of the thatched rooftops. Inland, fewer aliens settled, unlike the majority of the buds close to port and seaside resorts. It was the same story on the mainland near Portsmouth, with the port also taking most of the brunt from the fallout.

Six thirty in morning, the day had truly broken over Fishbourne, with many people preparing to rise and go about their business. Outside the ferry port and onto the main road to Ryde, the mailman was delivering letters to the last cottage in the row. He knocked on a cottage door and an elderly gentleman opened it, wearing a dressing gown. The mailman said "Morning Bernard, here's your mail?" "Thanks!" was the reply. He then added "Have you seen those grey plants everywhere? They've sprouted up overnight" Bernard said "Yes, I noticed them when I first got up Mike, they're all over my lawn, I'll have to weed them out later, it will take ages. I wonder what they are!" Mike tidied his mail bag then said "See ya Bernard, happy weeding!" "Goodbye Mike" Bernard said standing back and closing the door behind him. Mike turned, and duly walked away. Above Bernard's rooftop, a small grey patch of mushrooms, sat menacingly, by the guttering, unseen by both men.

Mac was now in St Mary's hospital in Newport, where there was little sign of any alien mushrooms within the hospital grounds, despite only being a short distance from the initial asteroid fallout. Overnight in the emergency department, the staff had treated only a few minor injuries, mostly from the ferry. They consisted of small lacerations, caused by broken glass from the asteroid chards, shattering the ferry windows and cutting people. Mac was the only major casualty admitted during the night.

Mac was admitted into the emergency department, with a large gash on his left arm. The night duty doctor considered it to be a deep laceration, so he administered pain relief after checking, cleaning and dressing the wound. The doctor was unhappy with Mac's general health, as he appeared lethargic and confused. In his opinion, Mac should have been over the initial shock after a few hours, and his body would normally have started on its road to recovery. As a precaution, he put Mac in a side room in the Newchurch ward then he requested the nurses kept a close eye on him throughout the night. Any changes to his condition were to be communicated to Doctor

John Arnold on the day shift, when he arrived at eight in the morning. Two nurses, Jane and Kate were working the nightshift, they monitored Mac frequently, checking him once an hour, but there had been very little change in his condition. Mac was nonresponsive throughout the night and they were now waiting to inform the day shift nurses of any changes. They would usually drift in around seven thirty for the hand over.

The two night nurses, began handing over to the day nurses Angela and Jo, who both had short dark hair, with Jo's being slightly curlier. They wore the traditional uniforms associated with their chosen profession. They approached the nurse station and Jo said "Kate, what have we got today then?" Kate replied "It's been a quiet night, with only minor injuries coming in overnight, mostly from the asteroid fallout. Doctor Brown has asked us to keep an eye on John McIntire in the isolation room, and to inform Doctor Arnold of any change, when he arrives" Jo said "Okay!" They finished handing over, then Jane and Kate made their way out of the ward, homeward bound.

Angela and Jo checked through the ward patient's paperwork, before deciding to get a coffee, then continuing their rounds. They walked past Mac's isolation room on the left, checking his door was fully closed, as they did so. After Mac's room, they walked through an open door, leading into the staff kitchen.

When inside, Angela made them both a drink then handed one to Jo and said "The asteroid was big news last night" Jo said "Yes the guy in the room next door was hit by it. Better check on him after we've finished our coffee, then let Doctor Arnold know his condition" Jo's gaze was drawn to the clock, above Angela's head, as she said "Nearly eight o'clock, we better finish up Angela, then check on the wounded. We can fill in the early morning reports later, before Doctor Arnold gets in" Angela said with a smile "No rest for the wicked, and we are wicked!" They quickly finished their coffees then headed towards the open door, returning to the nurse station.

On arrival, they both picked up clipboards and Jo said "Angela you sort the ward patients out, we've only got four today. Make sure they're awake, and have taken their medication. I'll check on John in the side room" Angela said "Okay" Then she walked towards the nurse station and entered the ward.

There were eight beds inside, four either side of the ward walls. Only the nearest and furthest beds were being used, giving the patients more privacy, as it was quiet. Angela walked down the middle of the row of beds, and shouted in a perky voice "Wake up, breakfast will be here soon!" She arrived at the last bed then pulled open the curtains, revealing a large window and a bright summer morning. A head appeared from under the left hand bed cover, and a young man looking a bit sleepy said "About time! A full English, if you please waitress" Angela smiling at him said "You've got no chance Jack, you're nil by mouth, until you stop being so cheeky" She then returned to the ward entrance and wheeled over a monitor, then began checking an elderly gentleman's blood pressure on her right, called Wilf.

Meanwhile, Jo opened the door to Mac's room, and stepped inside. Mac was very still as she neared him, despite being awake and sweating. She peered into his eyes. He was aware of her, but made no effort to move or say anything. His eyes however, gave the impression that he wanted to communicate something. Jo said "I'll check your vitals John, or can I call you Mac, like your friends?" Jo proceeded to read Mac's notes, whilst collating his information. She pulled a monitor over to the bed then wrapped the blood pressure band around Mac's arm. After checking Mac's blood pressure, she wrote down the results, while putting a thermometer into his mouth, checking his temperature. She removed it after a few minutes then filled in the results, but she paused, looking very puzzled and concerned. Jo looked at Mac and said "Your temperature's a bit high Mac, and your blood pressure's low. Do you feel okay?" Jo knew this would usually only happen, if the patient was in pain, but Mac was not showing any sign of distress. Mac stayed very still and no reply was forthcoming. Jo said "I'll get Doctor Arnold to have a look at you on arrival Mac. In the meantime, I'll remove your bandage then clean and redress your wound" Jo however, was unsure how much Mac had understood. She finished her checks then moved the monitor away, before returning to the nurse station.

Jo wheeled the trolley out, from behind the nurse station, along with equipment required to sterilise and redress wounds. She returned to Mac's room, sliding it next to him. Jo said "I'm going to take your bandage off and clean the wound Mac" Jo lifted Mac's arm by his wrist, then carefully began removing his bandage from his wound. After removing part of the bandage, she checked Mac for a reaction. His facial expression showed more emotion, as he screwed his face up, as if in pain. Jo stopped and said "Are you okay Mac?" His eyes pointed towards his arm, and she thought Mac had made a quiet groaning noise. Jo said "Are you in pain Mac?" Mac cleared his throat and whispered quietly to Jo "My arm's hurting, it's sore inside, stop the vibrating" Jo was shocked when Mac actually, unexpectedly spoke, but she was even more surprised at his muttered words. Jo lent close to him then said "I'll get Doctor Arnold in here, before I go any further Mac. He'll issue painkillers to ease the pain. I'll just go and get him" Jo rested Mac's arm on the bed then walked out of the room, watching him as she did so.

After exiting Mac's room, Jo almost bumped into Angela in the corridor. Jo said "You made me jump!" Angela laughed then said "Did I hear you say you needed Doctor Arnold, because he's standing by the nurse station, ready to do his rounds" Jo said "Good, can you keep an eye on Mac for a few minutes, whilst I get him. Mac's awake now, but in pain" Angela said "No problem, I'm finished in the ward" Angela left Jo, and headed for Mac's room.

Jo turned towards the nurse's station, where indeed Doctor Arnold was stood, in his white coat and dark hair, with his back to her. Jo said in a raised voice "Doctor Arnold, can you look at Mac first in the side room please!" Doctor Arnold was stood bent over reading, when Jo asked him to look at Mac first, so he stood bolt upright and turned to look at her. He replied in a pleasant formal voice "Of course Jo" He walked towards her, then they both continued through the door and on to Mac's bedside, as she explained what had happened earlier.

Angela, now positioned at the head of Mac's bed said "He seems a little better now Jo" Then Angela turned to Doctor Arnold and said "Hello Doctor" in a suggestive and cheeky manner. Doctor Arnold said hello back, but Angela's cheekiness went unnoticed by him, but not by Jo, who had a smirk on her face. Doctor Arnold moved round to view Mac and check his arm. He said "Do you mind if I have a look at your arm Mac?" Mac turned his head to face him then said "No, I was in a lot of pain earlier, but my arm's better now, albeit a little sore. Is there any chance of something for the soreness?" Doctor Arnold said "Of course, Jo will get you painkillers, after we have examined your arm thoroughly" Jo quickly proceeded to remove the rest of the bandage from Mac's arm.

As the last piece of bandage was unravelled, Jo, Angela and Doctor Arnold's facial expression changed. They were shocked and speechless for a moment, until Doctor Arnold said "Jo can you get some painkillers, then prepare a new dressing for Mac please" Jo walked away saying nothing, as she fetched the painkillers. Doctor Arnold said "Mac you seem to have an infection on your arm of some kind. We'll take a sample, and get it checked out in the lab. I'm going to have a closer look at it, if you don't mind" Mac said "Go ahead doctor" although he could not see the infection.

Doctor Arnold put on rubber gloves then bent over Mac's arm, to get a closer look. He held Mac's arm up, scanning the outline of the gash, caused by the asteroid remnant. He expected to see an open wound, with blood seeping from it, or an infected wound, outwardly oozing pus. What he actually found was a blood free wound, with skin and muscle tissue having receded into his arm, causing an indent. The indent was filled with a thin covering of grey buds, like the ones found on the grass verges near Fishbourne. However, they were smaller, because the bandage had blocked out the light. The doctor asked Mac "Does your arm hurt at the moment Mac?" Mac replied "No doctor it's fine, but why can't I move any part of my body, except my head?" Doctor Arnold replied "I don't know, perhaps your body is in shock, although I would have thought you would be fine by now. We'll analyse the infection in your arm, and check for toxins affecting your body" Doctor Arnold continued checking the external wound area, by pressing around the area then waiting for a reaction from Mac.

Jo returned, holding painkillers and a glass of water for Mac. Doctor Arnold said "We don't need them at the moment Jo, Mac's not in pain, but keep them here for now, as things might change" Jo put them inside Mac's bedside cabinet. Doctor Arnold said to Mac "I'm going to check inside the wound, and take a swab for the lab, if it hurts too much tell me to stop" Mac replied "Okay" Doctor Arnold removed a sample bottle, along with a scraper from the trolley next to the bed. He unscrewed the lid of the bottle. Then held both the lid, and bottle in his left hand, while holding the scraper in the right hand. He bent over Mac and tried scraping a sample of the grey mushroom buds from the wound. He pressed down lightly at first, but when they would not loosen, he applied even more force, but they still would not budge. He moved away from Mac then threw the scraper into the clinical waste bin, then returned to the trolley. This time he picked up a pair of tweezers. He bent over Mac's arm once again, and tried gripping a single bud. Holding it tight within the tweezers jaws, he then lifted it away from Mac's arm. It immediately propelled itself back into Mac's arm, taking the doctor by surprise. The doctor gripped it again, this time he was more forceful, and with a mixture of a strong grip and speed, he wrestled it into the bottle, quickly closing the lid. He said "These things are slippery suckers!" In time, he managed to remove three more buds, putting them inside bottles, and closing them tight afterwards. When finished, he put the tweezers in a plastic bag, then placed it in the bottom of the trolley, to be sterilised. Mac hardly felt a thing, and was unconcerned with the doctor's removal techniques.

Afterwards, Doctor Arnold studied the buds within the bottles, and then said to Jo, Angela and Mac "They could be some sort of tick. I expect the lab technicians will find out in due course" He wrote on the bottle labels "Handle with caution, could be contagious!" Then handed them to Angela and said "Can you take them to the lab and ask for them to be checked urgently please" "Yes Doctor Arnold" She replied, then she proceeded to walk out the room, to transport the bottles to the lab.

The doctor soon returned his attention to Mac's arm, pressing on the outside of the wound once more. There was no reaction from Mac, so he peered deeper inside the wound. There was now a small gap, where the four buds had been removed. There was no sign of any blood, but Mac's bone was clearly visible. The doctor pushed gently on the grey buds, near the wound rim. He felt the buds pushing and vibrating through his fingertips. He tried nearer the centre of the wound, where again he felt the vibration, before receiving a sharp pin prick and rapidly pulling his finger away. The doctor watched Mac feel something, but it definitely wasn't pain. The doctor said "What can you feel Mac?" Mac said "I can feel vibrating, and it's almost tickling me" The doctor said "Jo, can you dress his wound, and we'll check the results from the lab later. I'll pop back at eleven thirty, hopefully a bit more enlightened" The doctor removed his gloves then put them in the clinical waste. He handed Jo new gloves and said "Best use these until we know what these things are. Can you ensure no one comes in this room, unless authorised" Doctor Arnold turned towards Mac and said "I'll be back later to see you Mac"

Doctor Arnold turned away from Mac then exited the room, to continue his rounds. As he headed down the corridor, he felt a slight numbing sensation on his fingertip, where he had been pricked by the buds.

Jo finished dressing Mac's wound, then tidied everything up and said to Mac "Before I go, do you want a drink or some breakfast Mac" Mac said "No thanks, I'm okay at the moment" Jo finished up and exited the room, moving the "Authorised personnel only" sign over Mac's door, ensuring it was in clear view. Then she headed for the nurse station, wondering what the infection was on Mac's arm.

At the nurse station, Jo filled in her report sheet then carried on her daily routine. Jo being mindful of the infection on Mac's arm, made sure she used the antibacterial gel on the walls. She was grateful Mac was in a side room, so the infection could at least be kept under control.

## CHAPTER 5

## CHRYSALIS OF LIFE

Starting from Sandown's pier, the road climbs up steeply, cutting through the high street at right angles then continues for another hundred yards, passing hotels on either side of the road. At the end of the road, on top of the hillside overlooking the village, stands a quant detached white cottage, called Carisbrooke Heights. It is a symmetrical two storey house, with windows either side of the white front door.

The beach road narrows into a single lane on the approach to the cottage, where several large conifers hugged the edges of the driveway. On the first conifer to the right of the driveway, there is a small white sign which reads "Carisbrooke Heights" The driveway then rises steeply upwards a further thirty yards, until you reach the house frontage. Here the driveway extends out like a letter "T" so vehicles can be parked either side of the house doorway. The cottage has a manicured lawn extending all around the house, to large conifers, giving the lower floor of the house a good deal of seclusion and peaceful tranquillity, away from the bustling busy working seaside resort of Sandown.

The exterior of the cottage is of a typical two hundred year old English seaside residence. The inside however, has been converted into modern living quarters, perfect for the holiday market. The kitchen at the rear, leads into the open plan dining area on the left, which has French doors opening out, into the secluded back garden. The study, situated at the front, to the right of the entrance hall is sparsely furnished. The only thing left from days gone past, is the two foot oil painting of Carisbrooke Castle in the living room, from which the house originally derived its name.

The Ellis family had arrived and drove up the driveway of Carisbrooke Heights, yesterday evening. They soon found it was eleven o'clock in the evening, before they had a chance to unload their luggage from the car. They were so tired, they just slung a few items inside the house, and made their way off to bed as quickly as possible. The boys were so tired they did not even want to stay up any longer, which was unlike Thomas, as he always wanted to drag out extra time. Dave and Mary sorted the boys out first then made a quick coffee and followed them up to bed, talking about the night's activities from the ferry, until they both drifted off to sleep.

Both young boys were sleeping in their beds in the back bedroom. Thomas woke first on Wednesday morning, at seven thirty. He excitedly woke Joe, by jumping on the end of his bed. The sunlight was shining through the curtains, and Joe could feel the heat warming the room. Joe slowly focused on the room then watched Thomas go to the window, draw back the curtains, and drench him with unwanted sunlight that was far too much, first thing after waking. Joe hid under the covers mumbling to Thomas to close the curtains, until he was ready. Thomas ignored his mumbles and continued to look down into the garden that they had on loan for the week, trying to work out where to explore first. The garden below had a small area of concrete paving reaching out from the back of the house. It stretched outwards for twenty feet until it met the short freshly cut lawn. There was also a brick barbeque at the rear of the cottage, with a white table and four chairs sitting in front of it. The lawn stretched back a further fifty feet to a large hedge of conifers, climbing upwards some thirty feet, then extended out enclosing the whole of the rear and sides of the garden. On the right to the rear, sitting on some hard standing concrete, was a small wooden shed. This looked an ideal place for Thomas to begin exploring a little later in the day. Thomas also noticed a strange grey area, sitting at the top of the conifer hedge, but he dismissed after a short while, as it was of no consequence to him.

Thomas turned to Joe and said "Let's go downstairs and have some breakfast then explore the garden" Although Joe was still half asleep, he was keen to venture outside and see where they were going to spend their holiday. He said "You go down Thomas, I'll follow soon" So Thomas quickly got dressed, using yesterday's clothes then went down stairs to find breakfast.

Thomas opened the kitchen door then entered through the doorway. He found a modern kitchen with oak units and black marble tops, directly in front of him. In front was the fridge and freezer, with the sink to the right, beneath a large window. The units stretched round to the right, passing the oven and extending around the corner, to where Thomas stood. Here it finished with a curve, and two open shelves. To the left of Thomas, the stairs protruded into the kitchen. The wall from the kitchen into the dining room had been removed, allowing the wooden flooring to flow neatly into the dining area, giving the impression of space. In the dining area a wooden oak table sat, with four chairs, all neatly placed, ready for the newcomers.

Thomas was eager to have breakfast, and Mary had placed food inside cupboards ready for him, but first he had to hunt for it. He eventually found a bowl and his usual flakes, and drowned them in milk from the fridge, spilling some on the top, as he did so. He then headed off with his bowl to the dining table, pulled out a chair and sat down, ready to eat his breakfast.

Joe turned up ten minutes later, dressed and ready for breakfast. Thomas told him where to find everything, so he prepared his breakfast, whilst clearing up after Thomas. He knew Mum and Dad would not be very happy, if they were greeted with Thomas's mess, first thing in the morning. Both boys finished breakfast and decided that next on their agenda was to venture outside and explore.

Joe opened the French doors leading into the garden, and Thomas and he walked through, glancing upwards at the gleaming sun, as it shone through the rear conifers. Thomas looked towards the barbeque area then made a bee line towards it. He first encountered the table and chairs then sat on the nearest one, pretending to be lord of the manor.

Joe meanwhile, was more interested in going down to the rear of the garden, and checking the contents of the wooden shed. He arrived at the shed door, finding it padlocked, so he gave the lock a wiggle, to see if it would open, allowing him to see the contents inside. This did not work, so he moved down the side of the shed, peering into the side window. There were a few gardening tools inside, but nothing out of the ordinary. He moved on to the rear of the shed, where the conifers stood thirty feet high. He looked up to the top of the conifers. His gaze moved slowly from right to left, until at half way, he could see a small grey area. There was a fungus eating away the top of the conifer, and it had already carved out an indentation of several inches. It seemed a little out of place, to see fungus in the middle of summer, so he stared at it for a few minutes. He thought the fungus was vibrating, where it contacted the bush.

Thomas called to Joe, and his focus was drawn back to the patio area, where Thomas was now stood, stroking a black and white cat. Thomas said "He's called Chester Joe! It's written on his name tag, and he's so friendly" Joe walked towards Thomas, as the cat gently brushed up against his leg, and purred. Joe said "Best leave Chester here for now and go back inside. Mum and Dad will be up soon" Joe began walking back towards the house. Thomas disappointed, gave Chester one final stroke, then followed his brother into the house.

The boys entered the dining room, through the patio doors, finding Dave and Mary in the kitchen. Mary was waiting for the toaster to eject their breakfast. She opened the fridge door, removing the butter. Dave poured water into two cups, to make a refreshing cup of tea then said "Good morning boys!" as they appeared in sight of the kitchen "Do you want some toast?" Joe replied "No thanks, we've eaten Dad" Joe then asked if they could watch television. Reluctantly Mary said "Yes" knowing it would be easier, if Joe and Thomas were out of the way, while they sifted through the rest of their belongings after breakfast. After breakfast, Mary thought they could all explore their surroundings, with a quiet walk to the village then have a bite to eat, as they gazed on the beautiful sandy beach and pier.

Meanwhile, on top of the conifers, the sun heated the grey fungus, breathing new life into the alien life form. At a distance, the creatures appeared like a grey blanket, but when moving closer, it became apparent that there were many individual buds, basking in the sunlight. The buds stillness hid the underbelly contact areas, where the vibrating teeth were destroying the sweet juicy flesh of the conifers. They had attached themselves to their prey by two pincers, one at the top and the other beneath. In between the pincers, sat a fearsome teeth infested orifice, and anything unlucky enough to find itself pulled inside, was duly pulverised into a pulp, then digested. It was a slow steady affair, which left no waste, as all was ground down. The buds had grown steadily on their diet of conifers, reaching twice the size they had originally started from, after landing on the previous night.

Underneath the slowly descending buds, sat a small bird's nest, a mere foot below the fungus, but well hidden, within the heart of the conifers. It was clear the buds were heading straight for it. Three young chicks lived inside the nest, able to fly, but not quite ready to leave to start their own lives. The alien buds were heading directly for the nest, but was it a coincidence, or an instinct of this new species?

The chick's parents frequently flew in and out of the nest, clearly uninterested in the slow moving buds. The young chicks were vulnerable to danger being so small, but danger only presented itself when the older birds encountered Chester the cat, or when they foraged for food and nesting materials near the ground. However, the bird's natural instinct made them steer clear of the buds, which was just as well, because these small buds seemed to be at home on animals, as well as plant life.

Chester the cat stood statuesque beneath the conifers. He knew where the family of birds nested, but despite them being well protected inside the conifers, he was always looking for a way that would allow him to hunt his prey. The young birds were vulnerable and unwise to their surroundings, and Chester knew it. So far however, he had only managed to get twenty feet up inside the conifers, not close enough to reach the nest. He was nonetheless a master at hunting on his own turf, and he could see a change occurring at the top of the conifers. He knew that if he jumped onto the shed roof, he could climb to the top of the conifers, then work his way along to the centre, until he was above the nest. The close knit branches would still resist him, keeping the nest well protected, so there would be no way he could surprise the young ones, and lure them into his domain for now.

This morning was different, because a recess had been carved out by the alien buds, and Chester had spotted it. He made his usual climb to the shed top, before straddling along to the conifer recess. He could see a path through to the nest, where the buds had destroyed the conifers. This could give him a way to the nest, and a tasty snack. The nesting birds were not expecting him to arrive from the top, so he waited beside the alien buds, for the birds to settle. He hoped an unsuspecting chick would stray over to him, so he could surprise it.

After waiting patiently for ten minutes, it was clear a young chick would not approach him unwittingly, so he began creeping closer to the nest. He avoided the buds, by carefully negotiating around them, because instinct told him they should not be touched. He crept as close to the nest as he dared, before moving downwards. He then struggled to grip the outer part of the conifer. He was now within a paws length of the nest. Chester went unnoticed by the birds, but he could not achieve a decent grip, whilst getting his claw deep into the nest at the same time. It was either a safe grip, or risk losing his balance, and falling to the ground. The smell of the kill was too much of a tease to him, so he tried reaching out anyway. He slipped, immediately his claws reflexed outwards, as he tried gripping the surrounding branches, to prevent his fall.

This alerted the nesting family, so straight away the adults flew out, to protect the nest, and ward Chester off. They flew close to Chester, being mindful of his sharp claws. This was fun for Chester, as he swiped outwards towards the birds, in the hope of catching one with a lucky shot. The male bird dived close to Chester, catching him on the right side of his head with his wing. Chester's reaction was to try and claw him, but the momentum took him close to the alien buds, then he slipped. His front leg grazed the outer ring of buds. The contact, paralysed Chester's leg, so when he tried to put his leg on the branch above to get a grip, it failed to hold his weight. He then abruptly plummeted to the ground below, landing awkwardly on three legs.

He was luckily unscathed, but keen to try again another day. The paralysis in his right leg inhibited his walking for a short period, before wearing off after an hour. Then Chester returned to the same place beneath the conifers. Chester was now weary of the grey buds, but his instincts made him want the spoils he could gain inside the nest, even more. So he would bide his time, and try again on another occasion. The birds watched Chester closely, whenever he ventured near the nest, immediately circling him, to warn him off.

Eleven o'clock in the morning at the cottage, the Ellis family had already unloaded their luggage. Dave and Mary needed a rest, so they decided to have a drink and a five minute sit down with the boys in the lounge. Then a stroll to the beach, where they could have some lunch, while the boys played on the sand.

After a drink and a sit down for a while, Dave rose to his feet and said "Come on then, get your shoes on boys, we'll go down to the beach. If you're good, we'll have ice creams after lunch" Mary followed Dave, by encouraging the boys to get a move on, hurrying them into the hall. They all soon exited the front door, leaving Dave to lock up then catch Mary and the boys up, halfway down the drive.

Meanwhile, near the conifers sat Chester, he was keeping a vigil on the nesting birds. The chick's parents had left him alone, and returned to the nest. Time to go up again, thought Chester the chancer, so once more he climbed onto shed then swiftly continued up to the top of the conifers. He arrived slowly to the edge of the alien buds then stopped. Changes had occurred to the buds, they were developing into a greyish brown chrysalis, with each individual bud separating, leaving a small gap between each other. The two pincers still held firmly on to the conifers woody flesh, but the continuous vibrating had ceased. There was now a large opaque tulip shaped blanket, covering the rest of the bud, with the top flaring outwards. Chester's curiosity made him move closer towards the buds. He then put his nose against the nearest bud, peering inside the opaque tulip. He moved his head above the top and looked in. He could see a silky greyish black fleshy bulge, so he put his nose in closer, to have a smell. A pungent smell of rotten bananas hit his nose, making him screw his eyes up, and he moved away rapidly. The smell was so strong it quenched any thoughts Chester had of infiltrating the nest that day. So he duly scarpered back the same way he had arrived, deciding to get his dinner from home today.

******

The buds were developing towards the next stage of their evolution. They had been set free from their restrictive prison on the asteroid, and were now allowed to fully develop into their natural adult form. The chrysalis moved into a hibernating state, so they could develop from a parasitic mushroom, into a more mobile creature. Over the next several days, they would begin to evolve into a more formidable creature, growing several inches in size.

On the island as well as the mainland, buds took on the chrysalis state, moving on to the next stage of their evolution, as long as they had a victim, be it plant or animal to feed on. Even on the woodwork of the ferry, buds were seen moving into a chrysalis. The same pattern began happening all over the globe. In areas where nutrients were scarce, these small buds clung to each other and the strongest survived, as nature would have intended. The buds then continued

51

the process into a chrysalis and then onto forming a young adult, whatever that may be.

## CHAPTER 6

## A NEW CYCLE BEGINS

Nearly eleven thirty at the hospital. Jo had kept Mac under close observation all morning, despite him being quiet. She was concerned for his health, and was checking him every thirty minutes. He drifted in and out of consciousness, but showed no sign of pain. His vital signs were good, but there was still no news from the lab, to give the staff a clue as to what the infection was on Mac's arm.

Jo went to Mac's bedside for the eleven thirty check and waited for Doctor Arnold to arrive. Doctor Arnold duly turned up dead on time. On walking through the doorway, he asked Jo if there were any changes. Jo said "He's been drifting in and out of sleep, but no real change" Doctor Arnold replied "I've not heard back from the lab yet, I presume they do not know what we are dealing with. I'm not keen on prescribing anything until we ascertain the cause of this infection, but it won't hurt to give Mac some more antibiotics and painkillers" He looked towards Mac then said "Do you want more painkillers Mac?" Mac's semiconscious state prevented him from answering. Doctor Arnold turned back towards Jo "I'll give the lab a ring after my rounds, to see they have any developments. They should have something for us soon. If Mac's suffering, just give him painkillers for now" Jo replied "Okay doctor, is there anything else you want me to do?" "No, just change his dressing at twelve then give me a call, so I can view the wound again, to see how it is healing" He then walked back through the door and continued his rounds. Jo filled in Mac's notes at the end of the bed. Then she checked on him, before promptly following the doctor outside. She then made her way to the kitchen for a drink, before coming back to start Mac's dressing.

The lab was conveniently situated at the rear of the hospital, it searched for infections that were usually known and quick to recognise. New infections turned up in test tubes on a trolley with name of the patient, the ward and how urgent they were, graded from a one to five on them, with one being the most urgent. The trolley arrived early this morning, with Mac's marked very urgent. The trolley had now passed through, into the lab.

The lab was twenty five feet wide and forty feet long, and absolutely spotless. Inside, on the left was a six foot square clean-up room, especially for the two staff members, and when not in use the door was always tightly closed. Past the clean-up room, benches ran the whole length of both sides of the lab. Another long bench ran through the centre, with microscopes situated every five feet, in order to evaluate different types of infections.

Inside the clean-up room, putting on his rubber gloves was a gentleman called Richard Heard, who was of medium height, fairly bald with a distinguishing mole on his left cheek. He had worked for the hospital since passing his degree in the mid-seventies, and had been in charge for some twenty years.

Eleven forty in the morning, Richard knew Doctor Arnold required the results from a patient called John McIntyre, because he had received the hurry up call from the ward. So he thought he had best talk to his younger associate, to see how he was getting on. He exited the clean-up room then approached the first bench in the middle of the room, where Darren Kennedy was sat looking into a petri-dish, studying the results from one of his tests. Darren was younger than Richard, a typical twenty year old student. He had worked with Richard for two years and they got on very well, with him learning a great deal from his mentor.

Richard spoke in a friendly, but hoarse voice "How are you getting on Darren? Doctor Arnold is very interested in the results of this one?" Darren replied "I'm not sure! It's not like any infection I've encountered. It has attributes of a plant, but seems to cling on to its host like a tick, and it's very strong. It reacts like a bug, but it's more like an animal in other ways. It's resistant to all antibiotics that I've used so far and is able to continue living, even after being partially dissected. The one thing I have noticed is its need for sunlight, and a host to grow on. It then grows very quickly indeed" Darren moved a small glass jar from his right, towards Richard "This was blacked out with a dark top covering it" He removed the black covering, by sliding it over the top of the glass container. The small grey parasites size had stagnated and was motionless. Darren reached to his right for another clear jar. The parasite within, was attached to a rat by two pincers and it had grown to five inches. The rat was dead still, while being slowly digested by the parasite gripping the rat by its back. The rat showed no signs of distress from the parasites actions. It simply allowed the parasite to feast on its flesh. Darren said "The rat has been partially paralysed, ensuring it does not escape its hunter. Every now and then it will make a brief sound. The last parasite was put into another jar with no prey. I've allowed it to receive just sunlight and it has also grown, but not as quickly as when they have to a host to consume. It's now three inches in size, so the parasite must be able to survive on sunlight, or perhaps it's taking nutrients from the air, possibly as microbes around it" Richard asked "What's the best way to kill the parasite Darren? Doctor Arnold will be asking me soon" Darren's reply was swift, and to the point "Carefully, and surgically, but the one thing I've noticed with the parasite on the rat, is that it is starting to make a cocoon like substance on its base, close to the host. So I'll watch it, but surgery seems the best way" "Thanks Darren! I'll pass the information on to Doctor Arnold" said Richard. Richard immediately returned to the clean-up room, and proceeded to call the ward, to inform Doctor Arnold of his conversation.

Doctor Arnold had just recently finished the first half of his rounds, when he was called to the phone by Jo. She passed the phone over to him then waited before entering Mac's room, to change his dressing. Doctor Arnold finished on the phone then Jo requested he attended Mac, alongside her.

Walking through the doorway, he watched Jo removing Mac's dressing from his arm. Doctor Arnold said "Be careful Jo! I've just heard back from the lab, and it was an interesting conversation. It seems these things on Mac may be parasites, so don't touch them! We don't know how they attach to a host. I don't want you to touch them, or allow them a chance to contact you" Jo now felt slightly nervous, whilst removing Mac's dressing, but nonetheless she continued her duty.

Beside Jo, was a trolley with a new dressing and some forceps sitting on top. She opted for caution, picking the forceps up then slowly removing the dressing from Mac's arm, revealing the true extent of the parasite damage. The parasites had devoured the muscle tissue from Mac's arm, with him being completely oblivious to parasites attentions. Half of Mac's arm tissue had been lost to the parasites, but they had ceased activities for now. The parasites had entered into a chrysalis state and were now dormant.

Doctor Arnold moved closer, scrutinising the parasites in their dormant state. There were ten entering the chrysalis stage, with another two smaller dead parasites. The live ones had grown in size, filling the void where the flesh of Mac's arm had once been. The dead ones had turned red, and were partially eaten by their fellow parasites.

Taking the forceps from Jo, Doctor Arnold tried removing the nearest live parasite, but it would not budge. After wrestling with it for a short while, it moved, and the two pincers released their grip from their host. He pulled it away from the wound. Then saw a change in the parasites behaviour, as the pincers moved wider then retracted backwards, leaving a small amount of the tips on show. The rear of the parasite flattened its back then stayed in position for a brief second. Suddenly, it powered straight back into Mac's arm, so quickly that the doctor was unable to stop it. On reaching its host, a reflex action propelled the pincers back into the remainder of Mac's arm, this time they pushed in ever deeper than before, to put off any thoughts of removal.

The force from the parasites action, made Doctor Arnold fall backwards, as he tried holding back the parasite. He muttered "God almighty!" He was shocked at the parasites brute strength. He added "I think we'll have to consider surgery to remove these blighters! I'm worried they may try to reattach to something, or someone if removed this way!" Mac was unconcerned with events, but now was regaining consciousness. His eyes looked towards his arm. Although paralysed, it was clear he could see what the parasites had done to his flesh. He was speechless, but fear was clearly seen through his eyes. Jo said "Don't worry Mac, we're going to get you well as quick as possible" She looked towards Doctor Arnold, knowing this would not be an easy task, but nonetheless Mac needed reassurance that his injuries could be addressed. Doctor Arnold said "Mac, we're going to dress your wound for now, then I'll arrange for the surgical team to get you in theatre, to remove the infection" Doctor Arnold was being diplomatic, he knew Mac would at least lose part of the use of his arm, but more likely his arm would be sacrificed to save his life, especially if the lab could not find a quick solution to his infestation.

Carefully, the doctor and Jo redressed Mac's arm using the forceps, ensuring he was comfortable. They both moved the trolley away from Mac's bedside then informed him they would return soon to discuss what could be done, as soon as the surgical team had been notified.

Jo and Doctor Arnold exited Mac's side room then the doctor commented "Make sure no one enters Mac's room, unless accompanied and do not get too close to the parasite. I'll ring the surgical department to check if anyone is free immediately. Then recheck with the lab, to see if they have any news that could help the surgeons" Doctor Arnold then walked back to the nurse station to ring the lab again.

It was now two thirty in the afternoon, Doctor Arnold had spoken to Andy Price on the phone about Mac's unwanted pests. Andy would be the surgeon, who would be in charge of proceedings due to be carried out on Mac, at three o'clock.

Andy's team had assembled outside the operating theatre, ready for a briefing and scrub up. All five of them, of which included nurses Angela and Karen, the anaesthetist Tim, a student doctor called Brian and himself, were going through what they knew about the parasite. They talked through the procedure that would be required to remove the pests. Andy made it clear, that no one was allowed to contact, or to get close to the parasite. Special buckets were provided to enable them to put the pest inside, but not allow it to escape. These were clear, so the parasite was always in view at all times while inside the bucket. Andy informed everyone that a delayed visual phone contact to the lab with Richard Heard on the other end was there, to aid them through the procedure. This was in case the lab came up with any useful information that could be used. Also, outside the theatre, Doctor Arnold was on hand, because he had managed to release a parasite, albeit briefly from Mac's arm, despite it being to no avail, but he had seen what they were capable of.

When ready, Andy moved to the operating table, checking he had all the tools required for the job in hand. Then he asked each everyone inside, if they were ready. After everyone acknowledged, he turned on the screen to his left. This was a camera view fixed to one of the tools he used, enabling him to see inside the patient while they worked on him. On the right hand side was a second monitor. Andy also turned it on and a view of the clean-up room appeared, with Richard looking into the monitor. They both greeted each other warmly, while preparing for the job in hand. It was a new experience for Richard, as he had never been asked to be involved before, but he hoped to learn more about the creatures and help Andy with his patient throughout the procedure.

There was a knock on the theatre door to let the team know, their patient was ready. Nearly three o'clock, as Andy raised his voice so he could be heard behind the doors. He said "Okay stand clear, they're coming through!" The anaesthetist and Andy opened the doors, first glimpsing two nurses with their patient having already been prepped ready for the theatre. Mac was subdued and hooked up with lines, ready to be put out completely when required. His gown hid all, but the area of his arm to be worked on.

The nearest nurse to Andy released the drip line from the hospital bed. Andy immediately moved out of her away then checked all was well. He said "We're good to go! Let's get you in Mac, then we'll put you out and you'll be back in the ward in no time. Have you been told of all the possible outcomes Mac?" Mac did not answer, so Tim the anaesthetist turned to the nurse and said "Has Mac been advised of the procedure, and all outcomes?" He emphasized "Outcomes" as he spoke. The nurse replied "Yes, he's signed a disclaimer, although he was not always coherent" Andy said "Let's go then, we need to get these parasites of him"

They pushed Mac to the operating table then Andy asked the nurses that had accompanied him to leave the theatre, and stay away from the doorways for a few hours. Then only come inside when called, in order to reduce any risk of the parasites infecting them.

The nurses exited through the theatre doors then locked them, ensuring no one could enter, but more importantly to stop parasites escaping. Tim said "Right to your positions, we'll move Mac over, but don't touch his infected arm! Ready one, two three go!" They moved Mac onto the operating table together. Then Tim monitored Mac, while Karen the nurse put a tube into his mouth, to aid his breathing "All yours Andy!" Tim said as he put Mac to sleep. Mac lost consciousness then Andy proceeded to uncover the dressing, from his arm. The parasites were still in a dormant chrysalis state. Andy pulled a trolley towards him and removed a scalpel then he moved towards Mac's arm, he immediately started slicing through the first parasite. Andy said "As soon as the parasite's free, move the bucket towards me Angela" Angela was the nearest nurse to Andy and she was holding the bucket.

The bucket possessed a special guard to protect Angela's hands from any parasite deciding to attack her. Andy said "I'll cut the parasite three quarters of the way down, removing the large section first. Then I'll remove the final section with the pincers attached to it afterwards. This will be dangerous, but hopefully most of the power of the beast will be in the bucket, leaving it severely weakened" Andy's knife sliced deep into the parasite. Despite struggling to start with, it eventually sunk down with little resistance from the parasite. Andy pushed the knife across the thick flesh very slowly, ensuring it cut cleanly and precisely. When almost reaching the start point, the flesh quickly began reattaching itself, to Andy's astonishment. He continued cutting round to the beginning, the section should have been sliced off then fallen downwards. Instead it continued mending itself, in front of its audience. Andy said "Did you see that!" He then returned the scalpel to the trolley, before removing a larger knife then announced "I'll slice off the section in one go this time" He indeed sliced deep into the beast, this time it came off as planned, then he quickly hurried the section into bucket using the forceps. Andy proceeded to return to the pincer end, and said "Are you ready! I don't believe this will be as easy" He tried slicing into the last section, and removing the top pincer's grip from Mac's arm. It was met by a solid hard bony substance, with the scalpel unable to cut through it. He tried several times, but eventually gave up. He searched the trolley, quickly finding a pair of surgical pliers, this was he thought, the way to break the parasites grip. He picked them up, gripped the pincer tight then began squeezing slowly to start, then much harder, until it cracked and the pincer broke into half, leaving one piece stuck within Mac and the other attached to the beast. The parasite moved closer to Mac trying to regain its grip. Andy see its plan, then used the pliers to push it away "Quick, Angela take my forceps and pull it away from Mac, I'll cut the lower pincer off" She took the forceps and held the parasite as best she could, while Andy hurriedly snapped the second pincer off. Then Angela shoved the parasite away from Mac, forcing it downwards towards the bucket. The parasite struggled, then retracted its broken pincers and catapulted outwards, making it difficult to get it into the bucket. Andy picked another set of forceps up, and between them they pushed the parasite into the bucket, locking it inside. Andy returned to Mac's arm then pulled out the remainder of the lower pincer. He then went back for the rest of the top pincer, which had a large hole running through it.

Andy looked towards the lab monitor, and commented "Looks like our friend is putting some sort of nerve agent into Mac, ensuring he's compliant, I'll get you to look into it Richard" Richard replied "Yes please, I'd love to send it to me as soon as possible Andy" There were still another nine parasites on Mac's arm, so Andy first removed the two dead ones, noting they had been partially eaten by the surviving parasites. He then continued removing the next live parasite from the lower part of Mac's arm. Another three were quickly removed, and by now it was becoming obvious that these parasites were not only feasting on Mac, but were also keeping him compliant and symptomless. Three parasites were now left on Mac, and his vital signs were starting to fail as his body entered shock. Andy turned to Tim and said "If I remove any more, we could lose him from shock. He may be better off losing his arm with there being so little muscle tissue left, otherwise it could be his life" Tim replied "The parasites are keeping him alive, but they have eaten most of his bicep away, it won't recover. What do you want to do Andy?" Andy's reply was quick, and to the point "Removing his arm is the only option! Let's go for it and save his life" Andy then went about securing Mac's arm, ready for the first incision. The strap was tightened, stopping the blood flow to Mac's arm. All three remaining parasites, began releasing their grip and retracting their lower pincers.

Andy watched the parasites reaction, while reaching for the forceps and attempting to grab the lowest parasite. It came away easily, but once in the grip of the forceps, it was impossible to hold. Andy tried as hard as he could to get the beast into the bucket, but it flattened its back, curled upwards then pounced towards him. Andy quickly moved out of its way, as the parasite landed on the floor next to him. Andy shouted "Clear the area everyone!" Then he moved towards the theatre doors. The doors were closed tight, as they all stood huddled together, waiting for an eternity for them to be unlocked from the outside.

They stood watching and waiting, to see what the next move would be from the parasite. Nothing happened for a minute, until Andy decided to check on the situation against the others best judgement. He picked up a bucket, removed the lid as quietly as possible and began moving towards the operating table, searching for the parasite. Andy needed to find out if any parasites were still clinging to Mac's arm.

He arrived at the table, and looked closely at Mac's arm. The other two parasites clinging to Mac's arm had moved. They had detached themselves, and were now retracting their pincers. Not a good place to be, thought Andy, but he had to find the one that had landed on the floor. He moved to the left of the table. Suddenly, a distressed sound of "Argh, help me!" came from Mac on the table, quick as a flash, the parasite from the floor, flew past Andy with pincers at the ready. It missed him, but he was not its intended victim, it landed back on Mac's chest. Mac struggled for a brief moment, trying to remove it with his good arm, until the other two parasites moved in onto him. One latched onto his pelvis, the other on his neck, and Mac returned to a subdued state within a minute. It was clear the parasites were controlling their victim again, but this time it would be more difficult to remove any of them, without consequences that would likely be fatal to Mac.

Andy told the others to leave the theatre immediately, while he rechecked the positions of all three parasites in more detail, albeit from a distance. He talked to Richard on the monitor with a despondent voice "Any ideas Richard? If we leave him with these things on, he'll die, but if we remove them I'm not sure I'm able to keep my staff safe, let alone save the patient" Richard said "We'll work on the problem with the three specimens we have here Andy. No promises but...." Andy stopped him there and said "I know you'll let me know if you come up with anything" Andy checked Mac again, before exiting the theatre doors ensuring they were locked behind him. He did not want to leave Mac on his own, but safety must prevail, while he talked to his team and discussed another plan.

## CHAPTER 7

## A PROBLEM TO SOLVE

Richard watched the frightening events unfold through the eye of the monitor, knowing it was imperative a solution was found quickly to the parasite problem, but how? They were alien to Earth, an unknown creature that had become obviously very dangerous. Surgery was dangerous, unless the parasite could be disabled during removal from the host.

Richard stepped outside the door of the clean-up room then walked towards Darren, who had been watching his mentor from his bench, inside the lab. Darren knew things had not gone to plan, by Richard's demeanour, as he walked towards him. This meant that urgency had now been bestowed on them both. On arrival, Richard hurriedly explained the events that had occurred, but a few moments ago inside the theatre to Darren, who was totally bewildered and speechless. Darren's next thoughts turned to just how safe they were from the parasites, and how could they protect themselves from also becoming a victim. They needed to solve the parasite problem presented to them quickly to save Mac's life. However, this would be a massive challenge in the short time they had.

Richard finished briefly explaining the theatre events then said "We need to get these things under control for the surgeons Darren. I'm not sure how, but time is important, because the patient is locked inside the theatre with parasites attached to him. Andy and his team can't touch the patient, until we manage to disable these things" Darren looked straight at Richard's worried face, then said "I guessed it wasn't good news, how long have we got?" Richard's reply was not of optimism, but he said "We need to find a solution within the hour if possible, or it may be the end for the patient. The theatre is at present a no go area. I watched Andy dissect a parasite in half, but he did not kill it! We need to find a way to kill them quickly, with little or no danger to the patient or staff" Richard paused then said "Right let's get these things out, and have a look at one, but don't release it from the container. We'll try as many things as possible to disable, and destroy it. We'll try burning the first one then watch the reaction we get" Darren reached over and moved a glass container with the parasite attached to the rat, towards him. He then scrutinised it closely. He immediately stood up then went into the clean-up room, returning after a short time with a metal wire cage, that he fitted over the container. He removed the glass container through the top, closing the wire lid afterwards, preventing the parasite from escaping.

Darren removed a metal gas torch attached to a rubber pipe, along with a box of matches from the cupboard below. He connected the torch to the gas supply on the rear of the bench, resting it near the metal cage. He immediately lit the torch with the matches then adjusted the flame. Then he pulled the rat with the parasite attached, towards him, removing the top of the metal cage, enabling the torch to be pushed through the opening and onto the parasite. Darren said "I'm not sure if this will work Richard" Darren inserted the torch deeper into the opening, aiming the tip of the flame at the parasites back. The parasite just ignored the flame, so Darren forced the flame closer and slid it along to the beast's pincers.

After five minutes of constant heat, the parasite was left undamaged, forcing Darren to remove the flame. He said "This is pointless it's having absolutely no effect! We need to try something else" Richard replied "Perhaps we can try freezing it Darren" Darren extinguished the flame then moved the torch away, closing the top of the cage. Darren said "Don't want to leave that off!" Richard replied "Definitely not"

Richard walked away and entered the clean-up room. He returned, wheeling out a bottle of liquid nitrogen on a trolley. He picked up two pairs of gloves from the top rack then handed a pair to Darren. After fitting his gloves, he said "I'll freeze the parasite through the opening Darren, so you can get the grips through the other hole, and we'll see if we can prize the pest off. If we lock the parasite in position, we can try to remove the rat completely from the container, using the small forceps inserted through another hole. It may mean removing the top completely" Risky, they thought, but they would still have the liquid nitrogen attached to the parasite to fall back on, if it required another dose.

Richard inserted the nitrogen nozzle into the cage, aligning it on to the parasite as close to the pincer end, as possible. He hoped this would not give the rat a harmful dose of the cold nitrogen, at the same time. Darren then picked up a pair of forceps, manoeuvring them through a hole within the cage. He then positioned them, ready to prize the rat away. Richard looked at Darren then said "Ready, nitrogen going in, wait until the parasite goes solid then I'll say now! Then pull the rat away Darren" Darren acknowledged with a nod of his head then Richard started turning the freezing nitrogen valve on, releasing the cold liquid onto the flesh of the parasite.

As the cold nitrogen touched the parasite, it became clear it did not like it. It tried moving away from the source, changing its shape, to avoid the main stream of nitrogen. Richard, quick to notice increased the flow, moving the nozzle ever closer to the parasite, ensuring it was unable to avoid the freezing nitrogen. The parasite retaliated by curling its back then crashing into the nozzle, trying to knock it backwards. Richard held firm, moving the nozzle even closer to the parasite, giving it as much dose as possible. Slowly the cold nitrogen rendered the parasite to a complete standstill, and its gripping pincers released. Richard kept the nozzle trained on the parasite for a while longer, before he said "Darren, grab the rat and see if you can release it from the parasite, but be careful I've no idea how long this effect will last. It may be dead, or may just unfreeze, returning to its parasitic nature" Darren managed to secure a good grip on the rat. Then he began pulling the rat away from the parasite. Slowly, the pincers slid out, until the rat was almost free.

Suddenly, the rat began to move, albeit clearly in pain as with Mac earlier. The rat immediately sent out a high pitched shriek. Darren jumped, whilst holding the rat tight within the forceps. He then pulled outwards, away from the cage. The rat and forceps flew towards him. The cage lid fell down onto the bench. The parasite followed the lid and landed on the bench, close to the freezing liquid blowing nitrogen nozzle. However, the nozzle was too far away from the parasite to have any effect on it. Richard thinking quickly, shoved the lid towards the parasite, but he was too slow. It jumped up at him, hitting the lid. In a flash, the parasite altered course, moving sideways as it tried to snare Darren. Darren immediately dropped the rat and forceps to the floor, while ducking downwards avoiding the parasite. The parasite ended up on the floor next to him. Richard shoved the cage lid over the parasite with his hands, then stood on it, holding it down, then shouted "Darren turn the nitrogen up and freeze it to death, before it gets loose again" Darren moved the nitrogen nozzle close to the parasite and increased the cold nitrogen, aiming it at the centre of the parasite. The parasite was again rendered to a standstill, but this time the nitrogen was allowed to completely freeze it, without a host being present. However, Richard could feel the cold seeping upwards, through his shoes.

Darren moved away from the nitrogen bottle then grabbed the glass container from the bench. He lowered it to the floor then looked towards Richard, and said "I'm not sure how I'm going to get it in here, should it come back to life Richard, but you can't stay there forever" Darren searched around to see what he could use. The forceps nearby were the obvious weapon of choice, but they would not stop an attack from the parasite. Darren was sure he could not avoid the parasite for a second time. He turned the container on its side then rested it next to the metal lid. He held the forceps as close to the lid as he dared, then said "After three Richard, let's get it right! Don't miss with the lid we may not get another chance. One, two three" Richard stepped off the lid then reached down with his hands, rapidly lifting it up. Darren quickly picked up the parasite with the forceps, shoving it into the container. The parasite flexed its back then moved into attack mode. Richard immediately slammed the lid down hard, locking the parasite in. Afterwards, the parasite propelled itself upwards, hitting the container lid, to no avail.

Both men looked relieved, as Darren replaced the container back on the bench, and Richard turned off the nitrogen. Richard said "Let's have a look at the rat now Darren" Darren picked up the limp rat from the floor, it had not survived its ordeal. This was not good news for Mac. They swiftly realised that even if they managed to remove the parasites from him, he would likely fall victim to shock. Richard said "Fire didn't work Darren and the cold slows them down, but we need something more potent to kill these things!" Darren said "What are they? Where have they come from? It may help if we knew!" Richard remarked "They start off as a plant like land pod, then evolve into an animal, that's terrifyingly prehistoric in nature. They are not easily neutralized, we need to find another way to help the patient, because he has more on him" Darren said "But how can we kill these things? These…" He paused then blurted out "Terrapods!"

Darren again reviewed the rat, studying how the terrapod had slowly devoured its host. Darren viewed the terrapod, mumbling under his breath "Where have you come from? Tell me? How can we bring you to your knees? I won't give up until I find a cure!" Richard overheard him and said "We need an answer soon Darren, let's try other chemicals. Try injecting each one of the three terrapods, as you've now called them in turn with a dose of the chemicals, to see where it leads. We have less than thirty minutes left now, so you work from one end of the bench and I'll work from the other" Both men set about their task, by using different types of chemicals and gases, but nothing seemed to have an effect. Freezing was the only thing that had come anywhere near to controlling the terrapods for any length of time.

Darren soon noticed one of the terrapods had not grown as quickly as the others. The terrapod was starved of food and sunlight, so it made sense that these factors alone would have had an influenced on the parasites stunted growth. Darren deduced that perhaps a mixture of freezing and the removal of the light source, could aid the removal of the terrapod from its host. Any surgeons performing the removal of terrapods in the dark, would however, be blind and at the parasites mercy, especially if it failed. It would be very risky for the patient, but he had nothing to lose, and everything to gain, but the medical staff would face the wrath of the terrapods, if they escaped. Richard instructed Darren to continue looking for more answers. Then he went into the clean-up room, to phone the surgical team of their findings, giving their patient some hope.

Andy finished his conversation with Richard from the lab. He now knew that although there was not a definitive fool proof method to disable and destroy the parasites, but he had been offered a lifeline for his patient. Andy addressed his team then said "These terrapods do have a weakness to the cold and dark, and I intend to go back inside and exploit this, and possibly help our patient. It's risky for whoever follows me in, but I will be the first to enter. I intend to remove these parasites one by one, and rid the patient of them. The parasites will be dangerous when removed from the patient, especially if the dark and cold does not work. If we can't imprison them quickly, they will want a new host and they'll be gunning for one of us, if opportunity arises. Richard and Darren have given us a small amount of knowledge, but these terrapods are very resistant to drugs and the usual approach to parasite removal" Andy paused, then

Tim said "I'll help, you will need me, but how do we protect ourselves against these terrapods, as you call them! Have we any way of keeping them off us?" Andy replied "Not at this time, but if anyone has any ideas, I'm listening. Gowns will keep us sterile, but we will need to be close to the parasites to remove them" Nurse Karen said "Terrapods! Who called them that, and why?" Andy replied "Darren from the lab has nicknamed them terrapods, because of their pod like appearance and qualities. It certainly has been a terrifying experience so far, making the first part of the name very meaningful" Karen said "Yes, I don't want to be dinner for one of these things, but I'll help. Will we be receiving protection from security?" Andy nodded indicating no then said "Unfortunately the authorities are limited in what they can do, and time is running out for Mac. It will be a matter of freezing them one at a time, then using the forceps to put them into containers, before they defrost and come looking for us. We know what to expect from them, so if they do get loose, get out, and leave them to it, they will likely reattach to the patient. Not ideal, but it won't change the situation, but I don't want any of us put in danger. The patient is our priority, but time is not on his side" They all agreed that it was worth another try, after all, they had removed several parasites, with little knowledge of the beasts. Andy instructed Angela to stay beside the theatre door and if the worse happened, and the terrapods escaped, she was to seal the doors preventing any further infection.

All three prepared themselves for a second attempt, while Andy again rang Richard, letting him know they were going back in, using the liquid nitrogen. He insisted Richard stayed in touch as before.

They were all nervous as they approached the theatre, but after going through the door, their attentions turned swiftly to their patient. Andy and Tim first approached the operating table. Tim checked the equipment was still okay, while Andy checked on the patient, making sure the three remaining terrapods were still on him, where he had previously left them. The terrapods were still in the same position on the subdued patient. The terrapods took no interest in the medical team's activity. Tim moved the liquid nitrogen towards his patient, securing it in a position that meant he could easily administer it. Tim and Andy put on their safety gloves then Tim said "I'm ready when you are!" Andy checked Karen was ready and replied "Let's remove the one from his pelvis first Tim. Be careful, and don't take risks!" Tim positioned the nitrogen nozzle over the body of the terrapod, then looked towards Andy "Put the forceps on it Andy, make sure you have a container ready Karen, we may only get one chance with each of these things" Tim slowly turned the valve, releasing the freezing nitrogen onto the terrapod. At first, the terrapod edged away from the cold nitrogen spray, but Tim forced it closer, making sure it could not escape the freezing nozzle.

Three minutes later, the terrapod was motionless as Tim said "Another two minutes Andy then go for it! I'll keep the nozzle as close as I can to the parasite, giving you more time to put it in the container" Andy replied "Okay"

Two minutes later, Andy gripped the first terrapod "Good to go!" he said, looking first at Karen then towards Tim. Finally, he focused fully on the terrapod. He pulled the terrapod backwards, attempting to release the pincers from the patient, but this was futile. He then tried moving it sideways, but again this had very little effect. Finally out of frustration he pushed the terrapod inwards, towards his patient, forcing the pincers deeper. A reflex action, made the terrapod's pincers retract. Andy immediately pulled the terrapod out of the patient, while Tim kept the ice cold nitrogen on it. He rapidly shoved it towards the container. Karen quickly opened the container and the terrapod duly fell in, without any fuss. Andy said "One down, two more to go! Let's hope the other two are as easy" Tim replied "Getting them out may be easier this time, if we can keep them subdued, but the next problem will be to keep the patient alive afterwards" Tim moved the nitrogen nozzle onto the next terrapod residing on the patient's chest, then waited for it to freeze. The same method was used to remove this terrapod and it worked very well. This resulted in making them feel more confident with the last terrapod, perched on the patient's neck. Andy checked the terrapod on the patients neck then said "Tim, make sure you're ready afterwards, because the patient is likely to wake and will want pain relief as quick as possible" Tim nodded, with a sign of acknowledgement then moved the nitrogen nozzle onto the last terrapod. Three minutes later, it started to freeze and again the parasite tried moving away from the cold source, until finally it could not move any further. The nitrogen did its job, and the terrapod was soon subdued. This was perfect for removal of the parasite, but it meant the patient was now regaining consciousness, and feeling pain. Andy recognised this from before and said "We need to do this quickly! Before the patient gains full consciousness, or we will all be in danger" He pushed the terrapod inwards, then pulled it out quickly. Tim struggled keeping the cold nitrogen on the terrapod, thus enabling it to warm up. Karen moved the container in front of the terrapod. The terrapod pounced in Andy's direction, but Karen's reflexes were quicker, and she caught it near the edge of the container, by the open cap. Quickly, her other hand pushed the cap over the top of the opening, forcing the terrapod deep into the container, capturing it safely. The sweat dripping from Andy's forehead was clear to see, as he said "Thank you Karen, can you get all of these contained terrapods over to the entrance, then keep an eye on them, while we concentrate on the patient" She replied "Yes!" then continued the job of moving all the containers to a safe distance.

Andy and Tim watched their patient gaining consciousness. So Tim set about anaesthetising him, while they discussed all available options. They managed to stabilise their patient, but the only option left, meant him losing his arm. Afterwards, they could deal with the damage the terrapods had caused to his pelvis, chest and neck.

After working on their patient for an hour, they finally finished removing his arm and repairing the damage, caused by the terrapods on the soft tissue. Andy repaired the damage, but he concluded that more operations would follow, to rectify any further problems. All that was left was to remove the terrapod containers, and get the patient to intensive care to monitor his progress in a safe environment, away from other patients. Andy turned to the monitor and addressed Richard "These parasites are yours now, come and collect them please! Please destroy them, before they cause any more damage to life" Richard replied "My pleasure! I'll fetch them personally. I'll be five minutes and I'll bring security" The monitor went black and both Tim and Andy unhooked the lines from their Patient, with the exception of the heart monitor and pain relief drip. Andy shouted "Angela your patient's good to go!" Angela opened the theatre doors and entered, pushing a hospital bed inside and putting it next to the operating table. Between them they moved the patient onto the bed, keeping all monitoring attachments safe. Andy said "Take him to intensive care, but put him in isolation afterwards, until we are sure he is safe. Do not take any chances!" Angela replied "Okay Andy!" Angela then quickly checked all was okay with the patient.

Karen now standing beside the captured parasites said "Andy I'll help to remove the patient" Andy said "Okay, you carry on" Karen cleaned herself up then moved to the other end of the bed. Then both nurses removed the patient from the theatre, leaving the two men together, along with the terrapod containers. After leaving the theatre, Angela pushed the door button, ensuring the theatre was locked, keeping the parasites confined inside.

As promised, five minutes later, Richard arrived at the theatre doors, with two security guards and a trolley, with a large square metal box on the top. Richard shouted "Andy! Tim! I'm here, are you ready for me?" Tim shouted back "Yes!" then added "It's safe to come in Richard. Please remove these containers, so we can clean the theatre, and get it back in use" Richard replied "No problem, I'm opening the doors now then I'll take them away" Richard pushed the button, opening the doors then walked into the theatre.

Richard turned to the security guards, asking them to load the containers onto the large metal container on the trolley, emphasizing to be careful with them and not to allow the containers to be opened, at any costs.

Afterwards, he walked towards Andy and Tim, and conversed with them about the terrapods, checking to see if they had more information that could be of use to him when combating these strange creatures. The guards finished loading the terrapods, while Richard said his goodbyes to Andy and Tim. He then took the terrapods away to be analysed, with the aid of the security guards, escorting him.

## CHAPTER 8

## TIME TO LEAVE

Five thirty in the afternoon arrived, in beautiful sunny Sandown. The Ellis family had finished eating in the restaurant near the beach, after spending most of the afternoon on the sand, enjoying the hot sunshine, with only a brief venture into the arcades, to escape the heat of the hot afternoon sun. They were now ready to return to the cottage, to rest from the busy day and recharge their batteries, by cooling down far away from the busy life in the popular beach village.

Dave stood up from his restaurant chair, then said "Mary are we all finished? I need to return to the cottage to cool down, and if you don't mind, I'll go to the hospital to see how Mac is getting on later" Mary said with a smile "Yes it's been a busy afternoon, the boy's will be tired later. I'll give them a shower and settle them down to bed early tonight" Dave, with a grin on his face, added "I'll pay the bill then we can make our way back to the cottage. Thomas! Joe! Are you ready to go?" "Yes dad" Joe and Thomas replied, in tired voices. Dave caught the waiter's eye and asked him for the bill, while Mary sorted Thomas and Joe out, then began making a move back. Dave settled the bill, then after leaving a tip, he followed Mary and the boys out of the restaurant. They immediately turned left after exiting the restaurant door, taking them away from the pier and up the steep hill, towards the town centre.

At the top of the hill, they encountered the crossroads, where Dave looked instinctively upwards, towards the rooftops of the souvenir shops on the other side of the road. Several patches of grey could be seen on the ridge tiles of two of the shops. They appeared to be moving slowly downwards, towards the guttering. He dismissed it, thinking the heat was playing tricks with his eyes, causing an illusion, or it was more likely nesting seagulls on the rooftops. Dave grabbed Thomas's hand, whilst Mary held Joe's, then they all crossed the road, and continued towards the cottage.

They arrived at the cottage, passing the lion statues on guard above the gates then walked to the cottage door. Dave opened it and they stepped through, with Dave being last to enter. Mary headed for the kitchen and began making a drink, asking the boy's what they wanted in the process. She received no answer, because they had disappeared into the living room, and were resting. Joe and Thomas immediately started their games consoles, and began playing against each other. So Mary decided to make everyone cold drinks.

It's now seven thirty, with everyone relaxing in the living room, with the television on. Mary, rose from the sofa, and said "Boys get showered and ready for bed. You can stay up a little longer as we're on holiday, if you're quick!" She turned to Dave, and said "Do you want to go and see how Mac is Dave?" Dave replied "Yes, I'll leave it until later. Why don't you give your parents a ring after the boys have settled down" Mary said "Okay, I think I'll ring them on my mobile. It's been an interesting and eventful holiday so far, but I do hope Mac's okay" She turned away from Dave then walked out the living room, heading upstairs to the bathroom to prepare the boys for a shower. Dave followed her through the living room door, but he headed towards the kitchen to do chores.

Dave finished up in the kitchen then entered the dining room, briefly peering into the rear garden, where he watched the evening drawing to a close. He noticed a dark greyish area within the middle of the conifers, causing an indentation in the crest of the bushes. It looked surprisingly similar to what he had seen above the rooftops of the souvenir shops, in the town centre. He opened the dining room door leading to the garden, and walked over to the greyish area above the conifers. Standing beneath it, he looked straight upwards, viewing the area more clearly. It resembled a row of grey carpet like pods, and they were held on to the conifers by a pair of pincers. They appeared to be gnawing at the conifer branches below. He stood puzzled for a minute or so, while he studied them for a while longer. After ten minutes, he convinced himself that these were bird's nests, or a kind of native bat to the island.

Dave returned to the dining room door and stepped inside, locking the door behind him. He made his way to the kitchen then opened the window, allowing a cool fresh breeze to travel through the house. He continued through the kitchen door and up the stairs, to say goodbye to Thomas, Joe and Mary. He kissed Mary then said "I've got my phone with me if you need me!" He quickly turned towards the boy's bedroom then said loudly "Be good boys!" Both boys were clearly tired, and more interested in getting dressed and settling down to sleep, so they did not reply. So Dave immediately disappeared down stairs.

He reached the front door, put on his shoes and checked his car keys were in his pocket, then shouted "See you later Mary!" He duly opened the door and walked through, closing it firmly behind him. The moving grey patches on the conifers crest, crossed his mind once more as he walked, causing him to pause briefly. What were those strange creatures, and why had he not seen them anywhere before? Dave's attention soon turned to Mac's predicament, as he climbed into his car, then drove off, in search of Newport hospital.

As Dave approached the hospital entrance, he turned left into the car park, and searched for a parking space. The car park was almost full, so he ended up driving to the furthest point of the car park, before finding a space. After parking, he exited his car, locking the door then searched for the hospital entrance. He spotted it on his right, fifty yards ahead, so he walked towards it, looking for a sign to indicate where the reception was situated.

After finding the entrance doorway, he stepped through then went up to the reception desk. Directly in front of him, sat a blonde haired lady in her thirties, her eyes looked Dave up and down, then she asked "Can I help you Sir?" Dave said "Yes thank you, I'm looking for a man who came in last night, his name is John McIntire" The receptionist looked at the computer screen, while typing in his name. After a few seconds, Mac's whereabouts came up "Ah ha, here he is! He's currently in intensive care, but you will have to see the doctor, before being allowed to see him" She paused then pointed to her right and said "If you go straight down the corridor, then through the double doors, and take the second door on the left, it will take you to the intensive care unit. Just talk to reception there, and ask for Mr McIntire" Dave said "Thank you" then headed off down the corridor.

Dave arrived at the intensive care unit and approached the nurse behind the reception desk. She asked politely "Hi sir, can I help you?" Noticing the nurse was in charge, Dave's asked "I'm looking for a John McIntire, I was told he is here" She replied "Yes he is. He's in an isolation room at present. Who are you to him sir?" Dave answered "I was present when the asteroid caught him last night. I helped him away from the falling debris" The nurse picked up the phone then rang Andy, the doctor in charge. As she waited for Andy to answer she said "I think the doctor would like a word with you before you go in, to see if you can help with the infection on his arm" Dave looked puzzled, he hadn't seen any infection on Mac's arm when he left him on the ferry. He did have a nasty gash on his arm, so he presumed the wound must have become infected. The nurse then asked Dave to sit in the waiting area, while she informed the doctor of his arrival.

Dave walked over to the waiting area, and sat down on a chair, picking up a magazine to read, to kill time. He waited patiently, wondering what was so important, that the doctor needed to speak to him, before he could see Mac.

Shortly after Dave sitting down, a familiar figure walked through the door, and made his way to the reception desk then spoke to the nurse. Dave recognised him, as Ian, Mac's friend! Dave overheard the nurse telling Ian exactly the same thing as him, then shortly afterwards, Ian walked over to join Dave.

They both greeted each other warmly, questioning why they could not see Mac straight away. Ian commented on the grey buds that had sprouted up, along the roads near the ferry port, and he also mentioned that some had been reported on the mainland. Ian said he had decided to stay on the island today, to see how Mac was recovering, before leaving for the mainland.

Suddenly, there was a thud, Andy walked through the door, and his gaze was automatically drawn towards the two men. He momentarily turned his head, acknowledging the nurse then said "Sophie, I'm going to speak to these gentlemen in a side room, before we see Mr McIntire" Sophie said "Okay, I'll make sure you're not disturbed doctor" Andy then continued towards both men, as they automatically stood up, to greet him. Andy said "Can you follow me please gentlemen, I just want to discuss a few things with you both" He led them to a side room, holding the door open for both men, as they entered the room. Then they all sat down to talk about Mac.

Andy started asking questions about Mac and his chance encounter with the asteroid. Soon he moved on, asking if there had been any grey buds, or chrysalis type creatures on the asteroid remnants. This made Dave a little uneasy, because he remembered seeing many grey creatures around the cottage, and had wondered what they were.

Andy did not tell them why he was so interested in the creatures, but the two men did not push for the reason why, despite Dave's worries. Andy said "Before you see Mac, I need to tell you about an infection that was found on his wound, we think he received it from the asteroid. We couldn't control it, so eventually we had to remove his arm. He's very unwell, but stable at present" Ian and Dave thought momentarily about Mac, and the gash on his arm. How could he end up losing his arm, surely, they could have saved it, as it was only a minor injury. Dave was now getting worried, and asked Andy "When we left Mac he was very ill, but it did not look as if he may have to lose his arm. What sort of infection spreads so quickly, that within a day or so, it's necessary to amputate his arm?" Andy had no choice, but to give an explanation to both men, so he replied "We found some grey buds, nesting on his arm, and they were slowly munching through his flesh and bone. They were very difficult to remove, and seem to be very resistant to drugs. When we tried to physically remove them, they tried reattaching themselves to him" He paused then added "They are some sort of parasite" Ian asked "Can we see Mac, if it's safe to do so?" Andy replied "It is now safe to see him, but he's very unwell. All the terrapods have been removed and stored safely" Andy let slip the name of the parasites, and now both men wanted to know more after seeing Mac.

Andy escorted both men out of the side room, and into intensive care, where Mac was now recovering. Inside, they cleaned their hands then Andy led them to Mac's personal quarantine room, and opened the door. They entered through, closing the door behind them.

Mac lay quietly on his bed with his nurse sitting beside him, keeping a close vigil. It was clear, his arm had been removed, and he was subdued with painkillers. Andy moved closer to Mac and said "Hello Mac, how are you?" He received no response, so repeated his greeting, but still received no answer. Andy said to the nurse "How is he Karen?" She replied "He has not gained consciousness yet, and he's very quiet. He should be more lively by now, so I've been staying with him full time, making sure he's on the way to recovery" Both Dave and Ian were taken back by Mac's poor condition. He had indeed lost his arm, but this subdued quiet man, was not the man, Ian knew from before the incident on the ferry, it was very much out of character for him.

Dave studied Mac, before asking "These terrapods, what do they look like, and are they dangerous?" Andy replied "I think they are very dangerous indeed, that's why I asked you questions about them. We nearly lost your friend trying to remove them, and they tried attaching to the medical staff, after being given drugs to freeze them. They are greyish in colour with two pincers and they are similar to a tick" Ian and Dave, struggled to take on board Andy's information.

Dave's thoughts eventually changed to the cottage, and his vulnerable family. The terrapods were very dangerous, and there were many of them near the house. Who was to say, they wouldn't come looking for Mary, Joe and Thomas. Dave said "How did they get on Mac? How can they transfer to another person?" Andy replied "I think they start out as buds, developing via a chrysalis. They mature into a tick like creature, using pincers to attach to their victim. They can jump very quickly, up to several feet onto their prey, after emerging from their chrysalis state" Dave moved from being just concerned for his family, to wanting urgently to inform Mary to lock all the cottage doors and windows. Dave said "Andy there's some of these things by the cottage where I'm staying, with my wife and children, and they are likely to come in contact with them. I need to get in touch with them, right now!" Andy had not realised there were more terrapods outside. He assumed that Mac's infestation was an isolated case. This made him think very differently about the situation, because the surgical team had struggled to remove ten terrapods. If there were more outside, then the public was in grave danger. Ian said "There are hundreds of these things, scattered all along the ferry route" Andy responded with "Oh my god! I need to inform the police, they think this is an isolated problem. If these creatures start preying on the public in large numbers, we will never be able to cope in the hospital" Dave said "I'm sorry gentlemen, but I do need to go now" Dave shook their hands, and wished Mac well, then headed for the door, quickly exiting Mac's room. Andy said hurriedly "Okay, if you can think of anything to help us, please get in touch, thanks for your time" Andy continued talking to Ian afterwards.

Dave exited intensive care, then passing reception and walked into the corridor. He pulled out his phone from his pocket, as he walked quickly through the hospital entrance, towards his car. Unable to get a signal, he continued frantically into the car park. The lack of phone signal, made him more anxious, as he hurriedly opened his car and got inside.

After starting his car, he hastily drove it out the car park, and continued speeding towards the cottage. It was now nearly nine o'clock and Dave although hurrying back, knew it would take thirty minutes to get home. This was thirty minutes too long for him!

After fifteen minutes, he stopped the car, and tried the phone again, this time he had a signal, but he received the engaged tone. He thought, Mary was likely to be talking to her parents, as he had told her to do so earlier. So he continued on his journey, eventually reaching the gates of the cottage.

It was still light, as he drove up the drive, and found himself looking high into the conifers, surrounding the cottage. He could see many grey areas, but they were much larger and appeared to be moving eerily down through the branches. He hurriedly stopped, got out the car then ran towards the cottage door shouting "Mary, Mary!" He quickly arrived at the front door. Then in a Panic, he put the key into the lock. Suddenly, a cold shiver shot down his neck, as instinct made him look to his right. Ten feet away, sat a terrapod, curling its back readying itself to pounce. The door clicked, it then opened abruptly. Dave fell to the hall floor, in front of Mary. The terrapod immediately pounced, hitting the door before ricocheting back onto the grass. Dave shut the door then said "Mary, are you okay? Are the boys safe?" Mary bewildered said "Yes, we're all fine, what was that?" Dave said "I've just been to see Mac in hospital. The asteroid seems to have left some type of parasite on him, called a terrapod! These things attach to you and eat you, Mac has lost his arm from them" After a short breath, he added "Are the boys windows open?" Mary's answer was a nervous "Yes!" Dave said "You close all the doors and windows downstairs. I'll close the windows upstairs. We can't take a chance with these things getting inside!" Mary looked very frightened, but quickly did as Dave asked.

After closing every opening, they both settled down on the sofa, inside the living room and Dave explained in detail, what Andy had told him, inside the hospital. He mentioned that they had a lot of trouble removing them from Mac, and he was still gravely ill. Dave's thoughts then turned to all of their safety. They were on an island, possibly with hundreds of developing terrapods on, if Ian was correct. They both concluded it would be best to cut short their holiday, and leave for home tomorrow. In the morning, Dave would ring the ferry port, to book the earliest available ferry home, to the relative safety of the mainland.

Morning came, and Dave woke at seven o'clock. Straight away, he left Mary in bed and went into the bathroom then showered. He returned shortly, with Mary still sleeping, so he quietly proceeded to get dressed. Afterwards, he carefully made his way downstairs to the kitchen, for breakfast and coffee.

Dave stood in the kitchen with everyone still fast asleep. He thought it beneficial, to attempt ringing the ferry port, to see if he could get them aboard a ferry today for the mainland. He removed his phone from his pocket then rang the port booking office. He waited patiently, while the phone rang in the port. He received no answer, so Dave went to the kitchen sink, reached over, and pulled the blind up with his other hand, whilst waiting.

A few minutes passed, and still no answer, so Dave peered through the window at the garden, to check the weather. He soon began searching for any grey areas around the garden, for anything looking suspicious. He scoured the conifers thoroughly, where there were indeed small areas of grey, sitting within the middle of the bush. He could also see another small grey area on the grass, near the barbeque. So he walked into the dining room, to acquire a better view through the patio doors. There he had a complete view of the rear garden, with the exception of a small patio area, partially hidden by the barbeque furniture.

Suddenly, an answer came back from the ferry port, making Dave jump. Dave calmed down then enquired about getting a place on a ferry sometime today. The male voice on the end of the phone was very apologetic, but said he could not fit them in today, the earliest he could do, was the following morning, on Thursday the sixteenth, at ten. It was not what Dave wanted to hear, but he took the offer anyway, and booked the ferry home. After finishing the call, he returned the phone to his pocket. Then he continued finishing his breakfast in the dining room, peering out through the patio doors regularly, keeping a watchful eye on the moving grey areas, within the conifers.

It was nearly eight in the morning, when Joe and Thomas opened the kitchen door, wanting their breakfast. Joe started to fetch his own, knowing exactly where to find it. Dave stood up, and moved towards Thomas, to assist him with his breakfast then told both boys to eat at the table, while he made them a drink. Mary followed them through the door soon afterwards, with the words "Don't go out in the garden today boys, as there are some nasty bugs around. Only go out with me or Dad!" She emphasised the last part of her sentence. The boys were disappointed and only half listening whilst eating, so just said "Yes" to please Mum. Mary knew she was getting the brush off, and knowing how dangerous it was outside, she decided to keep one eye on them throughout their time on the island.

After they finished breakfast, things settled down, with Dave and Mary telling the boys to stay inside the house again, with the doors and windows closed tight. She made sure they were very clear about the earlier message. Mary continued to make sure the boys were always amused during the day, while Dave kept a constant vigil on the doors and windows.

Meanwhile, beneath the patio table, Chester the cat, kept his eye on the nesting birds, unperturbed by his misfortune on the previous day. His instincts were far too strong to ignore, and the nesting birds were fair game. So once again, he sprinted across the grass, swiftly missing the five inch terrapod that was sitting dormant in the middle of the lawn. The terrapod was too slow to react, and although it moved slightly, it just made Chester flinch, as he sped past it, but not enough to break his stride. He made his way up the shed then on to the conifers, the same way as the previous day, but as he neared the top of the indented conifer, eaten away by the budding terrapods, he was a touch more cautious. Their nasty smelly defence was the reason why! He wanted to sneak up on the birds nest quietly, but it would be more difficult now, as the nest had been moved deeper into the heart of the conifer. It confused him at first, as it was unlike birds to move it away, because it had been well protected in its original position. It was likely that it had been moved, because the buds had eaten part of the bush away, leaving the nest exposed.

Chester approached the nest very carefully, but the chicks did see him coming, and gave out a loud shriek, letting their parents know he was around. Within seconds, both parents arrived on the scene, in no mood to just fly close to Chester. Chester was so close, that both birds took turns in flying into him, hitting him hard, trying to get him to retreat from the nest. Chester however, was strong and fearless, and continued to move inwards, until he could see his first chick facing him. The end was in sight for the chick, and the fruits of Chester's endeavour, were but a paw away. He reached forward to the first chick, extended his sharp claws outwards. Then he clipped the chick, making it fall out of the nest, and closer to him.

He wanted to remove it completely from the bush, and get it onto the ground, where he would be in complete control, with it far away from its protective parents. His next swipe pushed the bird out of the bush, sending it spinning to the ground. The parent birds went into full attack mode on Chester, hitting him harder and harder, but they knew the chick was lost. On the floor, Chester would toy and torment the youngster, until he decided to end its agony, and kill the poor bird. However, the adult male bird ploughed into Chester, sending the cat instantly out of the bush, and following the young chick downwards.

Both the chick, and Chester were now on the ground, and the chick's fate was sealed. It had no hope of rescue, or any way back to the nest even after surviving the fall.

Chester however, as with all cats, just landed on his feet, and after finding his bearings, sprinted over to the chick and started to toy with the young bird, flicking it up into the air. However, Chester was not ready for the kill just yet.

Meanwhile, the parent birds gave up on the chick and circled above Chester, making sure he did not come back for the other chicks inside the nest. Chester continued playing with the chick for several minutes, moving it around the lawn at will.

Inside the house, Dave watched events happening from behind the safety of the patio doors. He was going to go outside and save the chick, but something inside, told him it was not safe to do so. He soon noticed a stationary terrapod, sitting on part of the lawn close to Chester. The terrapod flattened its back, while Chester edged closer and closer to it, as he played with the chick. Dave guessed the terrapod was about to show its true colours and pounce, on either the bird or the cat. He wondered how it would achieve this, with no limbs. It had been too slow to react to Chester running past it earlier, so Dave's gaze fixated on the beast, to see what was about to unfold.

Chester came within two feet of the terrapod, along with the chick. He immediately stopped, as his instincts took over. He sensed danger, but as he looked around, nothing was obviously threatening him. The chick next to him completely froze, hoping Chester would think it was dead, and lose interest in it. Chester peered at the dark greyish terrapod on the lawn waiting for it to move, but nothing happened. He sniffed around, where soon the pungent smell of rotten bananas again came to his notice. This gave him cause for concern, as he remembered what had happened with the buds on the conifer crest, the previous day.

The chick took its chance to make an escape. It hopped away from Chester, back in the direction of the bush, without Chester seeing it. Then another hop, and afterwards another soon followed. Chester suddenly caught a glimpse of the chick making a bid for freedom, so he turned quickly, watching it getting closer to the conifers. He fully engaged his hind legs, pouncing in the direction of the chick. By this time, he had already made his mind up to go in for the kill, then take his spoils away to a quiet spot, and enjoy it. The terrapod catapulted itself towards the bush near the chick. It caught Chester in mid-flight, connecting with his lower rib cage, bringing him down to ground, with a thump.

After landing, Chester tried to wriggle free of his captor, but within a second, the pincers of the terrapod closed in on Chester's ribs. The top pincer immediately began injecting a nerve agent deep into him. Chester became subdued, and just lay resting upon the grass, allowing the terrapod to slowly devour him.

The chick scuttled away to the relative safety of the bush, but in reality its days would be numbered, without the safety of the nest, and the many deadly parasites waiting for an easy meal.

Dave watched everything unfolding in front of his eyes, and now knew how dangerous these beasts were. He remembered Ian's words, inside the hospital, when he mentioned seeing many grey areas of buds all over the island, whilst driving from the ferry to the hospital. It also crossed his mind, that there were many buds on Sandown's rooftops, so the whole town would be crawling with these dangerous creatures soon. Dave knew it was imperative they crossed the waters of the Solent, to the mainland, to escape the danger that these parasites posed.

Dave ran around the house on a mission, rechecking windows and doors were closed, then he informed his family of the dangers of going outside, with these predators lurking. The ferry home could not come quick enough for Dave and his family.

## CHAPTER 9

## ISLAND INVADERS

Thursday morning on the island, with the sun shining, and clear blue skies, stretching as far as the eye could see. In Sandown, along many of the roof tops and grass verges, the dormant terrapods were waking from their chrysalis state, and beginning to use their new mobility. Small animals, such as unsuspecting birds and rodents, were easy prey for the terrapods. They first moved slowly towards their prey, creeping up on them, or pretending to be dead, staying dead still, whilst waiting for their prey to come to them. They knew their sudden lightening pounce, would capture their victims, rendering them paralysed, and it would be totally unexpected on this new home, called Earth. They could then feed on their victims, at their convenience, after being captured.

Inside the local newsagent on Sandown high street, the owner Ron James, in his early forties with a receding hairline, was busy working. His white shirt and jeans were partially hidden by a brown leather pinafore, as he leant over, stacking papers on the shelves underneath his shop window, near the doorway.

A man walked towards him in his twenties, with short cropped hair and wearing blue overalls. He was clearly a painter, by the amount of stains on his clothes. "Good morning Ron" He said, then paused and added "Can you pass me the Sandown Times, please Ron" Ron handed a paper to him then said "Morning, there you are. How are you today Pete?" Pete said "Not too bad, I'm on my last day at Bill's. I've just finished painting the outside of his shop, I'm in this morning to finish the sign above then pick my money up. Then I'm off to a new job on Monday, in Cowes" Ron said "You've done a good job for Bill on his shop, can you pop round later and give me a quote please? This old place could do with a lick of paint before the winter arrives" Pete paid Ron then said "I can do that. I'll be finished about two. Then I'll pop in afterwards. See you later Ron!" Ron replied "Cheers Pete!" Pete walked off towards the souvenir shop, another forty yards along the same side of the road. Meanwhile, Ron went about his business, making his papers look neat and tidy, in order to attract customers. As he finished tidying the papers, he turned his head, glimpsing Pete entering the front door of Bill's shop.

Pete opened the door of the newly painted souvenir shop then walked through. He was immediately greeted by Bill, an old man with straggly grey hair. Bill's untidy hair made him look older than his sixty years, despite being smartly dressed in a suit. He believed it should be worn at all times, when selling to the public, despite the scorching hot day that lay in front of them. Bill said "Morning Pete, the paints all dry, just need to touch up the red and gold on the lettering above the door. You've made a fine job as usual" Pete replied "Yes it does look smart now! I'll go round the back and pick up the red paint I left there. Then finish the red letters first, by the time I've done that, I'll be able to highlight the outside of the lettering, with the gold you asked for Bill" Bill admired the paintwork again, then said "I'm closing for lunch at one o'clock today, so I'll pick up some cash and pay you the money I owe you, if that's okay Pete" Pete said "That will be perfect Bill, I've got to give Ron a quote at the newsagent at two, so it's perfect for me" Bill said "I'll leave you to it then Pete, let me know if you need me for anything" Bill then went about his usual business, of tending his shop.

Pete was halfway through painting the red letters, when something above him, caught his eye. He looked along the tiled roof, until his eyes stopped near the chimney breast. He viewed a large greyish object, about a foot in diameter. He was unsure what it was, but found himself watching it move slowly towards him. He studied the creature in detail, almost in a trancelike state. Pete was confused by its shape, because it looked like a small seal or marine ray, but at this height, he thought it must surely have been some sort of wounded bird. He scanned for any wings. Whilst wondering how it had managed to get up onto the rooftop? At the front, he could see two small pincers, with the top one slightly longer and thicker than the lower one. This, he thought must be its beak, but it must be a mutated bird of some kind. Throughout all his years on the island, he had never seen any creature like it. Pete climbed up the ladder, to get nearer to the creature, but he was still too far away, to see it clearly.

Suddenly a loud noise came from behind Pete, making him jump! He turned rearwards, nearly falling off the ladder. "Hi Pete" Came a woman's voice. Pete recognised the voice, as his neighbour Jan, from Newport, where they both lived. She was tall, blonde and very pretty and in her thirties. The loud noise Pete recognised was Jan's dog barking, to say hello to him. The dog, called Bentley was named after a place Jan once live in, on the main land. Pete said "Hi Jan what brings you and Bentley to Sandown then?" She replied "I'm just visiting an old friend, who runs the Victoria hotel, on the beach front. I thought I'd get my friend a little something, before I popped in to see her. Nice paint job!" Jan winked at Pete, whilst pulling the dogs lead tight, moving him closer to her. Then they both walked slowly on, as Jan smiled back towards Pete. Pete smiled back and said "Bye my lovely" then added "See you Bentley. If you need any painting Jan, let me know"

Bentley suddenly barked very loudly, pulling Jan back towards Pete. He barked again, pulling even harder, hurting Jan's wrist. This time, he wrenched at the lead so hard, Jan could no longer hold Bentley. Pete watched Bentley and shouted "Stop Bentley, it's only me, you know me!" Bentley however, continued running towards the bottom of the ladder that Pete was perched on. Then he tried climbing the ladder rungs with no luck. Bentley continued barking towards Pete, scratching at the ladder. This made Pete quite nervous of Bentley's behaviour, wondering why he was acting this way, as he had never been aggressive towards him before.

Jan eventually caught up with Bentley, picking his lead up then she tried calming him down. Bentley however, tried even harder to climb the first rung of the ladder. Jan said "I don't know what's wrong with him Pete, he's never done this before" Jan looked up towards Pete, trying to reassure him, making sure he knew she was sorry for Bentley's behaviour.

Behind Pete, a silhouetted shape became visible on the rooftop. It was round, with the sun shining directly from behind it. Jan could see it perched behind him, with its rear flattened downwards. She caught a glimpse of two pincers on the front of the creature, as they started extending outwards. Jan shouted "Pete!" but before she could finish her sentence, Bentley pulled on the ladder, bringing it crashing downwards. Pete lost his grip, and followed the ladder downwards.

The terrapod above, pounced towards Pete, but it hadn't bargained for the dog bringing the ladder down, along with Pete.

Pete fell, landing with bent knees onto his feet, unhurt. The terrapod came to rest on the floor, very close to Pete, but trapped beneath the ladder, caught between two of the rungs. Bentley immediately broke free of Jan and pounced towards it, barking as he did so. Jan went to Pete's aid, helping him to his feet then said "Are you okay? What is that thing?" Pete regained his bearings then said "I haven't got a clue, it was by the chimney breast just now" As they talked, the terrapod slowly tried breaking free of its constraints, but Bentley barked louder at it, whilst keeping the beast at a safe distance. Pete watched the terrapod trying to move, so he jumped on the ladder, stopping it from escaping. Pete said "Quick Jan, my tool box it's in the back of the shop. I left it there yesterday, get the hammer and a sharp knife and I'll kill it!"

Jan ran inside the shop, returning with hammer in hand, a knife and Bill the owner. She handed the hammer to Pete. He forcefully tried smashing the creature, by striking between the ladder rungs at it. This had little effect, so he asked Jan for the knife then plunged it deep into the flesh of the creature. Again and again, the knife sliced into the creatures flesh, with no effect on beast's mobility.

The terrapod flattened its body, powering upwards, pushing both the ladder and Pete skywards, as if paper. Pete dropped the knife in the process. Bentley began barking again, whilst Pete, Jan and Bill moved hurriedly away from the beast, worried about what it would do next.

Suddenly, a ringing noise sounded along the roadside, a young man was riding towards them. He had no clue of the events that had just happened. Pete shouted "Stay away from here!" It was too late, as the terrapod pounced once again, but not towards the three on the pavement, or the dog, but at the man arriving on the cycle. The cyclist stood no chance, as the terrapod knock him clean over and onto the floor. Once on him, the reflex action on the pincers clamped the man, piercing slowly downwards, through the man's skin, rendering him paralysed. Pete, Jan and Bill watched on, unsure of what to do. They moved slowly towards the man, to see if anything could be done to help him. Then Bill finally worked up the courage and tried removing the beast from him, but after grappling at the flesh of the beast, he found it had a nasty sting to its tail, leaving his hands sore and burnt and him in agony. The parasite stayed glued in position, and did not budge from its prey.

Pete moved closer to the ensnared man, despite being weary of the terrapod. He studied it carefully from several angles, searching for a safe way of removing it. The terrapods pincers had sunk deep into the man's chest, and a clear fluid was now leaking from the top one. Pete said "There must be a way of getting it off!" He searched around, eventually picking up his hammer once again. He tried smashing the beast as before, but after this failed, he tried using the claw of the hammer. He forced the top pincer between the hammers claw, then pulled it towards him, as hard as he could. Bill and Jan kept a good distance from Pete, in case the beast come off, and was launched towards them. Pete wrenched the beast with the hammer, eventually releasing the top pincer, and sliding it out of the man's chest. Pete could see the pincer was bent, and partially broken. This made Pete pull even harder. The beast retracted the top pincer completely into its round body then flattened down, preparing to catapult itself back into its prey. Pete pulled even harder, but the beast was extremely strong, and Pete's arm muscles started aching. Pete finally released the lower pincer from his chest, only to reveal a bloody, open wound that had been gnawed away, by the tiny razor sharp teeth, lying between the terrapods pincers.

The man began regaining consciousness, and feeling pain. Shock took hold, as he looked deep into the beast's mouth then straight back into Pete's eyes, with fear filling his mind, and adrenaline filling his veins. He quickly pulled away from the beast. Rose to his feet, and ran back towards the centre of the road. The terrapod catapulted towards the man, ripping the hammer from Pete's hand. The man collapsed downwards from exhaustion, before reaching the centre of the road. The terrapod stopped shy of the man's foot. Now very weak, he froze, while watching the terrapod flatten its back, readying for another assault on him. Pete, Jan and Bill would only be onlookers, unable to help this time. Bentley ran out the shop towards the terrapod, barking at it, but the beast took no notice, as it flew towards the man. As it closed in on him, another terrapod, from a neighbouring rooftop came plunging downwards sinking its pincers into the airborne terrapod. It quickly subdued it on landing.

Pete, Jan and Bill instinctively looked up towards the roof tops afterwards. There were three more terrapods, poised to pounce downwards. Two came down together, the first missing the dog and the second one going straight into the man face, taking him back to ground, for his final time. The third pounced, narrowly missing Jan. It immediately prepared to pounce again. Pete shouted "Get inside everyone!" He smartly grabbed her hand, hurrying her towards the door of the souvenir shop. He returned to help Bill, but it was too late, a terrapod fell from the rooftop, plunging down into Bill's leg. Pete ran back towards him, only to watch Bill's strength, being sapped away, as he was quickly subdued. Bill said "Save your selves! I won't make it" Pete was reluctant to give up and continued moving towards him, but another terrapod hit Bill on his shoulder, sealing his fate.

Pete then began scanning the rooftops, spotting many more parasites, waiting in line, to come down on any passing prey. Pete moved backwards then said "Sorry Bill!" Although he knew by this time, Bill was unconscious and doomed, no matter what he did. Pete then shouted to the dog "Bentley, here boy!" Bentley looked at him briefly, before dashing towards him, amidst several terrapods, trying to latch onto him, but the dog's instinct, and speed, helped him negotiate his way back to Pete. Bentley burst through the doorway, as Jan slammed the door shut.

A terrapod, immediately slammed into the outside framework of the door. Then they watched it drop slowly down to ground. Moments later, they stood peering out the shop window, completely unharmed, but could only look on, as terrapods began to lay further hosts to waste outside.

A few minutes passed, and a car engine was heard approaching. An open top sports car neared the shop, slowing down near the man lying on the roadside. Pete and Jan shouted and waved at the driver, trying to make sure, he stayed inside the car, but he continued onwards, stopping next to the man's lifeless body. The driver looked over to the shop, thinking the inhabitants needed help, but he did not hear their warning pleas.

After getting out of the car, he proceeded to walk towards the man on the roadside. He soon caught a glimpse of Bill, also lying on the floor nearby. Terrapods were feasting on both men, as he wondered what the creatures were, so he continued moving closer to them. The first man was clearly dead, and he could do nothing for him. The terrapod on Bill's shoulder however, was now gnawing through his flesh and bone, causing his head and neck to jolt up and down. The car driver presumed Bill was still alive, and in need of help, so he moved towards him. He bent down beside him, quickly realising Bill was also dead. A chill shot down his neck, as his attention was drawn down the road. Astonished, he watched several people being attacked by marauding terrapods. First, a young man on the opposite side of the road, then an elderly couple, as they walked out of Ron's newsagent, followed by Ron himself, as he exited his shop, checking on the commotion. One by one, they were attacked and picked off by the feasting terrapods.

Fear filled the man's eyes, as he looked back at the souvenir shop, towards Pete and Jan. It suddenly dawned on him, that exiting his car was a huge mistake. Adrenaline took over, as he ran towards the door of the shop. Pete and Jan tried desperately to warn him off, and get him to move away from the door, but he arrived at the shop door anyway. He looked through the glazing into Jan's eyes, expecting the door to be opened for him. Jan was unable to open it, because the terrapod was sitting on the floor, blocking it. Pete and Jan, could only look in horror, as the man slowly looked downwards, and was duly met by the terrapod, as it pounced up to meet him. It clung firmly to his face, pulling him down to his grisly fate. Pete and Jan wondered how they would ever escape the beasts, and were resigned to following in the man's footsteps very soon.

Jan tried phoning the police, but received an engaged signal, due to the many calls made from the terrapod attacks. She worked along her phone list, trying each number in turn, to see if she could get any help, but all numbers were either engaged or not answering.

******

It was not long before terrapods, began swamping most the island, actively taking their prey unexpected. Some people managed to seek safety away from the beasts, inside their houses. The hospital was getting inundated with calls from people with loved ones, and friends that had been attacked by the parasites. On grass verges, terrapods could be seen making their way slowly towards the occupants of cars. Many people were caught in traffic jams, waiting to enter the hospital, whilst holding injured loved ones, with parasites attached to them. Panic soon set in, leading to people carrying their injured or in some cases, dragging them by any means possible, to escape more marauding terrapods. The hospital car park was full with cars queuing up along the nearby roads for miles. Fights broke out with occupants of the cars, arguing over who should be first in line to enter the car park, or to be seen in hospital.

Inside the hospital, things were no better, as chaos was the word of the day, with as many as six people in a cubicle, waiting to be seen by a medic, most with terrapods clinging to them on all parts of their anatomies. Moving along the corridors, some patients waited on mobile beds, while some were even slumped against the walls. Many of the hospital staff had been unable to help the patient's, as they had no clue in how to deal with the strange parasites. Being short staffed, the only option was to just make them comfortable and safe from further injury. Two nurses showed signs of trying to remove terrapods from patients, because despite wearing gloves, to try and extract the beasts from patients, they had torn, resulting in allowing their hands to contact the outer flesh of the terrapods, making their hands sore. One medic was panicking frantically, whilst going round trying to ascertain if any of the patients, or staff could be easily treated. He soon realised it was a lost cause with no knowledge of the parasite. He had already told the remaining staff, to avoid contact with patients, if it could be helped, as he could no longer afford to lose any more staff.

Suddenly, the accident and emergency doors slid open, as a mass of people rushed through, barging each other out of the way, making their way over to the reception desk, trying to get the attention of the nearest medic. Lots of arguments broke out, then a big scuffle, as two men attacked each other, knocking over chairs, drinks and patients alike.

A security guard came running down the corridor, trying to get between both men, but he ended up, being pushed to the floor. He tried climbing back to his feet, as the doors reopened, and a second wave of screaming, panic stricken people, came running in. They pushed past the two fighters, knocking them out of their path. Then the hordes pushed the guard back down to the floor, trampling across him. Most headed towards the corridors, but a few managed to jump over the reception desk. The crowd finally began to thin out and the guard gradually stooped back up, and on to his knees, by putting his hand on the top of the nearest chair, and lifting himself to his feet. He then rested for a brief moment, while he regained his breath.

A woman came running through the open doors screaming. The guard turned to find out why, in time to see a terrapod leap on her arm. Fear gripped him, as he turned and greeted two more terrapods, sitting beside him. The perspiration ran down his forehead, as he quickly tried scrambling away, but it was too late. Both terrapods pounced on him simultaneously, attaching to his back, bringing him down to the hard floor. Other people, hurriedly vacated the doors, as screams were heard when the terrapods caught up with their defenceless prey, in the car park outside. After a few minutes, a deathly quiet entailed, and the sliding doors ceased opening.

Ten minutes later, a doctor appeared along the corridor heading towards the entrance doors. He ebbed carefully towards the sliding doors, but kept his distance from the sensors. This prevented the doors from opening automatically. Peering through the glass doors, he scoured the local area, beyond the entrance. No visible terrapods were within the door vicinity, so he looked further afield. It was clear, many people had not made the doors, falling victim to parasites, within the car park and the preceding roads.

He stared towards the parked cars, watching for any apparent movement. He presumed that many people had managed to survive the onslaught of terrapods, but were now in hiding. There was no way of knowing how many parasites were stalking the occupants, just waiting for them to make a break for a safer haven, before pouncing. He made a difficult decision to protect the people inside the department, so he turned off the door sensor, stopping the doors opening. Afterwards, he turned to the people behind him, who were by now beginning to calm down, and said "Help me, we need to get the guard and woman into the corridor, safely away from the entrance" No one was immediately forthcoming. Then after a short silence, the two previously fighting men, agreed to help. They followed the doctor's orders, moving them into the corridor.

Afterwards, a short solemn stillness engulfed the department, as the realisation slowly dawned on everyone, on just how grave their predicament actually was. It was likely they would now be hostages inside the hospital indefinitely, while being extremely worried that terrapods might eventually find a way inside. The doctor now turned his attention to phoning each department in turn, advising them to secure all doors and windows. Afterwards, he requested a meeting with all the managers on site, discussing a plan, or a possible solution to the terrapod problem.

The doctor's next port of call was to the local police department, but they had been overrun by calls for help. It soon became clear the police station was also under siege, and in dire need of help themselves. The local police station, was not prepared for anything like the full on terrapod invasion, they were experiencing. They were more accustomed to dealing with holiday makers losing belongings, small pickpocket gangs from the mainland, or tourists asking for directions. The last murder had been over thirty years ago, and as a result, they had just five available commissioned firearms, three pistols and two rifles, with limited ammunition held on site. After all, if armed police officers were required, they would have been called in from Portsmouth, on the mainland.

The Sargent in charge, Bob Horton, had already been in touch with Portsmouth constabulary. The message he received back was not good. No officers free at the moment, as they were drafting in extra help from neighbouring counties, because of a problem around the harbour areas of Portsmouth. Although the problem was not as bad as on the island, they needed to clear Portsmouth harbour area, before they could do anything about the island invasion. This was not the message Bob wanted to hear, he knew that outside the station, there were at least twenty terrapods in view, and they did not have the fire power to repel them all.

He gave permission for his officers to fetch a gun each from the armoury, and to use deadly force against the invaders. He only had five officers on site, so it was an easy decision. He offered each one a weapon, leaving it up to his men to choose what they were comfortable with. He would use the weapon left, which ended up being a revolver, but he was happy with this, as it was more practical. Bob had last used a weapon when first training, more than twenty years previous.

Bob assembled his officers together, giving them each a key to the armoury, so they could get more ammunition, when they ran out. Then together, they discussed plans on how to best combat the immediate terrapod threat, outside the station.

After thirty minutes, a plan was finally manufactured, with Bryan Tompkins leading two other officers, to clear a way to the car park, where two police cars were situated. They would then return both cars to the station doors, so they could stock them up with ammunition. The officers would then go out, helping people in the local area, after finding a safe house. The safe house was discussed at length, and they all agreed that the local shopping mall would be perfect, as it held plenty of food and water needed, to hold many people safe, for a considerable amount of time, whilst keeping the intruders out. The officers felt sure help would soon arrive from the mainland, whether from police or possibly the army, if the problem was too big for the constabulary to handle.

Bryan armed with a revolver, took two officers with rifles, outside the station doors. The car park was on the left of the station entrance, with the police cars, parked directly in front of them, some fifty feet away, near several shrubs and trees. Once outside, the officers made their way down the six steps, heading towards the car park. It was a short distance to cover, and clear of terrapods for now. They were still worried there could be a nasty surprise waiting for them behind the shrubs, while they approached the vehicles. They crept forward, keeping a vigil on the bushes for any hint of movement, or glimpses of lurking terrapods.

Nothing stirred in the local area, as they neared their first patrol car. Bryan walked forward, with his officers following carefully behind. Both Bryan and the officer immediately behind him, removed the car keys from their pockets, and pushed the fob buttons. They watched two cars flash their lights, while unlocking their doors. The officers paused briefly, looking round to see if any terrapod had taken notice. Nothing stirred, so they made a decision to enter the cars. Bryan opened the nearest car, then clambered inside, with a sense of relief radiating through his body, from the security of having a door between him, and any terrapod. He waited inside the car, while the other two officers moved on to the next patrol car.

Bob signalled to the other officers to quickly enter the second car. Both men gingerly approached the car and the officers slowly opened its door. The first officer slipped inside, then after getting seated, he put the keys into the ignition. The second officer quickly entered the rear door of the car, sliding quietly into the seat. The first part of their plan had now been achieved.

Now, they needed to transport both cars safely to the station entrance. Both drivers turned towards each other, and in tandem, they started both cars. They slowly reverse the cars away from their parked positions, then steered the cars towards the station entrance. It was then, that the two officers in the second patrol car glimpsed a terrapod, sitting in front of them. It had clearly been hidden beneath the first car, unable to pounce, while trapped beneath the car's underbelly. Bryan in the front car continued driving away, clueless of the terrapod beneath his car. He rapidly parked up, near the station entrance.

The second driver, unsure of what action to take, continued reversing. He hesitated briefly, before making a final decision. He said to his fellow officer "Keep your gun ready, I'm going to drive through it!" He heard the click of the safety catch release, from his fellow officer's gun then he floored the accelerator pedal, and the car moved rapidly forward. He veered sharply, to avoid the terrapod. As he drew near the beast, it flinched. Then it flew up at the car, breaking the rear passenger window, leaving the parasite, partly suspended inside the car. The parasites top pincer had pierced the roof of the car, leaving it dangling. The bottom half of the beast had finally came to rest on the headrest, leaving it unable to free itself. The rear officer shoved his rifle, to within a few inches of the beast then shot it, expecting it to be propelled out of the car. The bullet entered the hard flesh of the beast, causing it to jolt from the impact. The beast then flattened its body, and tried breaking free of the roof, that was trapping the top pincer. The officer was totally stunned for a second, before hitting the body of the beast repeatedly, with the gun butt. The violent force broke his wrist, but it was to no avail.

Suddenly the car stopped outside the doors to the station entrance. Both officers heard Bryan shout "Leave it, just get inside!" So they leapt out the car and looked up to Bryan, who was by now, holding the station door open, ready for them. They rapidly moved up the six steps towards him.

The driver ran up the steps, straight into a descending terrapod, as it arrived from the entrance rooftop. His momentum took him rolling back down the steps, leaving him face down on the paving slabs, with the terrapod claiming his broken body.

The second officer hesitated, as he looked searchingly above the roof, where another five terrapods sat in waiting for him, to make his deadly dash to safety. He loaded his gun, and rattled off several rounds towards the parasites. Several direct hits had little effect on the beasts. One answered, by dropping from the rooftop, landing in front of him. He paused, then panicked and said "I won't be your next meal, you parasitic bugs!" He returned to the patrol car, opened the driver's door, and sat down inside, firmly closing the door behind.

He quickly realised the other officer still held the keys he needed, so decided to retrieve them. Sweat rolled down his forehead, as he began opening the door handle. Suddenly a "Cracking" sound came from behind him. Then he slowly turned round, to find out what had made the noise. The once hanging terrapod was no longer there! He slowly and deliberately moved his head, peering down into the back of the car, to the rear seats. Then he caught a flashing glimpse of grey, as he was duly pounced on by the terrapod. His hand continued grabbing the door handle, trying to open it, to aid his escape, but within a few seconds, he slumped forward, falling onto the steering wheel, and setting the horn off.

Bryan watched the gruesome event unfold, completely helpless, and he was annoyed with his inability to save at least one of his men. He momentarily thought about rescuing the keys from the officer nearest him, but the terrapod outside quickly turn its attentions onto him, so he closed the door keeping his distance from the beast.

There were now only three surviving officers inside the station, as they waited a few minutes, before looking back through the glass door, at the prowling terrapod. It clearly had no intentions of moving, so the men knew another plan was needed. Guns were pointless against these beings, and now there were only three officers with revolvers. They knew it would be unlikely they would survive long, if the terrapods breached the entrance. Bob called his last two officers over then said "Block the doors and windows up, we don't want these things getting in" The officers needed no pushing to go about the task ordered.

After finishing, the officers stood by the front reception desk, discussing their plight. It was soon decided to stay put for now. Afterwards, Bob rang Portsmouth constabulary again, but it took several minutes for him to get an answer, then a man's voice said "Portsmouth constabulary here, if you require help, we suggest you stay inside your house. When we have the situation under control, we'll make our way to you" Bob said "This is Bob Horton, from the Isle of Wight police station, we are under attack from some sort of parasite. We are desperately in need of help now please! There are three of us locked inside the station, with two officers down outside with parasites on them. I don't think they are still alive" The voice replied "I'm sorry mate, but I'm just the cleaner, most of the officers are either on call, trying to tackle some nasty pests that have invaded the harbour, or defending the station from being overrun, by some type of parasite" He paused then continued with "You have no chance of getting help here, you'll have to deal with the problem on your own, I'm sorry!" Bob was very unhappy with his response and said "Put someone on, with some authority will you please!" He nearly finished his sentence, when he heard another faint voice say "No! How did they get inside" Bob heard a "Thud" as the man on the other end dropped the phone. Then the man moved hastily away from the scene. A door was hurriedly heard opening. Then another loud "Thud" sounded as if someone or something had fallen to ground.

 Bob's heart sank, along with any hope, he guessed the man had been a parasite victim, and knew no help would be coming to their aid, in the near future. His two officers Phil and Carl, also heard the phone call and knew they should protect themselves as best they could, as it could be a very long wait, before any help arrived.

## CHAPTER 10

## PANIC IN THE COTTAGE

Afternoon arrived at Carisbrooke cottage. The Ellis family were all sitting down in the dining room, having lunch. They had discussed the terrapod threat at length, with Dave informing Mary that he had booked the ferry home. They finished lunch and Mary assembled the crockery in the kitchen, then neatly stacked it, inside the dishwasher, and started a wash cycle. Joe and Thomas returned to the living room, turning the television on then continued watching the cartoons. Dave rose from his chair, and looked out the patio doors, gazing on Chester the cat, lying motionless on the lawn. The cat was now dead from its trauma, as the terrapod continued munching away at its juicy flesh.

Dave searched along the patio, towards the table, where two more terrapods sat within three feet of each other. Dave could not move his gaze away from the nearest one, as it flatten ready to pounce. The one behind, soon followed suit. Suddenly, Dave moved backwards, realising he was their intended victim. The front terrapod pounced towards him. The second one followed on very quickly. The first one slammed into the glass door in front of Dave very hard, but fortunately it did not breach it. The second terrapod followed closely behind the first, but Dave was not its intended target. Its target was the first terrapod, as it landed on its back, taking it quickly to ground. It made short work of bringing the parasite under its control. Dave's eyes searched the area for more lurking creatures, quickly spotting another two terrapods, parked beneath the shaded conifers. He presumed they were dormant, or had not seen him inside the house yet, so he decided they posed no immediate threat for now.

The sound of the terrapod hitting the window went virtually unnoticed by Mary, with the background drone of the dishwasher washing it out. She turned to Dave and said "I'm done now, let's go sit with the boys" Dave replied "Okay love, did you see that just now? One of those things tried to get me, it ended up sat on its mate instead" Mary replied "No" Dave however could tell by the tone of her voice, she wasn't concentrating on his remark. She was clearly worried about the boys being left on their own. Mary headed towards the living room to join Joe and Thomas as Dave followed her, while he pondered a way of stopping, and killing the parasites.

The Ellis family were now gathered inside the living room, with children's programs on the television. Mary stood up and picked up the television control and said "Right, about time we watched something more interesting on the television" She turned the channel over, catching the news.

On the screen, people were seen fleeing from the centre of Portsmouth, and the surrounding areas. The view swiftly switched to the ferry port at Portsmouth, where the Ellis family had previously left for the Isle of Wight, when beginning their holiday. The camera panned towards the ferry sitting in the harbour under repairs. Terrapods were visible all over the ferry, as many workmen lay on the decks, having fallen victim to the creatures. Mary said "That was our ferry Dave! That's where we were, oh my god!" She pointed towards the ferry restaurant, where they had been seated, and very close to where Dave had helped Mac return inside away from the falling rocks.

This was live television in the modern era, with the cameraman zooming in close to one of the unlucky victims, by the passenger steps. Most of the male victim's torso had been consumed, with the terrapod now devouring his hip. The cameraman, desperately wanting a better shot, moved from his safe distance, ebbing ever dangerously closer to the victim, to get a better shot. A female voice could be heard in the background behind the camera "Not too close Mike" Mike moved nearer, before concentrating his lens on the terrapod attached to the victim. He kept his camera firmly trained on the victim's hip, as it was being gnawed away. The terrapod stopped momentarily, flattening its back. Mike unperturbed kept his lens firmly aimed at the terrapod for the perfect media shot. He said on camera "This will make for an amazing picture" Suddenly, he rapidly felt an impending doom, as a shiver rolled down his back. Too late, the terrapod catapulted straight into the Mike, knocking the camera out of his hands. The camera dropped to ground, finishing up on its side. The parasite finished up resting on Mike's face, as he fell in unison with it.

The camera now faced directly towards Mike, who was by now lying awkwardly on the floor. Live television now broadcast the terrapod attacking his face, as he struggled briefly, before succumbing quietly to the beasts paralysing charms. The terrapod, and the motionless Mike, were now both stars, as he lost the unfair fight. The female voice could be heard close by, screaming then briefly stopping, as she cried "Why Mike, why?" The camera then broadcast to the nation, the grisly sight of Mike's demise, while the parasites razor teeth, began grinding through his face, for all to see.

The television broadcast then skipped to another camera, further away from the ferry, in time to catch another terrapod pouncing. It launched itself onto the woman, near the stranded cameraman. She fell over screaming, while trying to release the beasts grip. Panic, quickly consumed the complete ferry area, as many people involved with the outside broadcast, began making a hasty retreat. The television screen broadcast the many people fleeing. The camera lens panned back to the ferry again, broadcasting the hordes of marauding terrapods, appearing from the ferry decks.

Terrapods jumped off the ferry on to dry land, searching for new prey. Dave said "Oh my god, those poor people" He added "We're travelling back through there tomorrow morning" The Ellis family continued watching the report, until presenter Carol Gardner said "I'm sorry if some of the pictures were disturbing, unfortunately, they were beyond our control. We will be monitoring the situation and we'll give you more information when we have it. A spokesman for the ferry port said that all ferry crossings from Portsmouth have been suspended for now" She then continued reading the rest of the news.

Mary stared at Dave in total shock, after viewing the news pictures. They had banked on getting home through Portsmouth, but another way would now have to be found. Dave immediately phoned around trying to find an alternative route home, but the ferry ports at Ryde and Cowes were locked down due to the parasite infestation on the mainland. Another way needed to be found, and that would not be easy.

Meanwhile, Mary changed the television channel back to the cartoons, whilst signalling to Dave to exit the room. He duly followed her lead, as they both went through to the kitchen. Mary closed the door tightly behind her then said "What are we going to do?" Dave said "I'm not sure! If we can get a boat to Southampton we might be okay, but we'll have no car even if we can get there" Dave was unsure how they could leave the island, but it was clear, they could not stay in Sandown. After finishing their discussion, they both returned to the living room, keeping their worries secret from Joe and Thomas.

At the rear of the cottage, the terrapod had devoured most of the cat and increased in size, while basking in the sunshine. Only a handful of edible flesh was left of the cat. The parasite was now unable to grip what was left of the flesh. The terrapod left the remnants, and rested on the lawn for an hour, before moving towards the house in small leaps.

The terrapod cannibalising the second parasite near the doorway, sensed the larger one's presence, it immediately gave up its half-eaten prey and moved away. The larger terrapod flattened its back several times, in a threatening display of superiority then pounced on the carcass, taking advantage of its dominating size. The smaller terrapod moved backwards, out of pouncing range and froze.

There were many terrapods appearing around the cottage, varying in size, depending on their feasting habits, and food availability. Most of their food source was made up of small animals, such as birds, rodents and domestic pets. As their size increased, so had their appetites, so a bigger food source was now needed, humans were perfect, but not the easiest of prey. They surrounded the house, waiting for a chance to pounce on one of the Ellis family members. They were not fast, but they were prepared to wait and bide their time.

It was five in the evening at the cottage, and the children were very hungry. Joe asked "Can I have a drink please mum? I'm hungry, when will dinner be ready?" Thomas added "And me!" Mary replied "You can have some juice, and a biscuit from the cupboard then I'll start dinner in a minute" Both Joe and Thomas made their way to the kitchen.

On arrival, Joe fetched them both an orange squash. He then went to the kitchen sink, adding water to the first glass of squash. He offered it to Thomas, who immediately guzzled it down. Joe then made his own juice, drinking it while standing at the sink. Joe said "Do you want a cookie Thomas?" "Yes please!" was the keen reply. Joe rested his glass beside the kitchen drainer, careful not to spill any. Suddenly a flash of grey hit the window, making a loud bang. Joe jumped, quickly looking towards the window, in time to catch a brief glimpse of the terrapod, as it slid down the pane of glass. A small crack appeared half way down the window, on the outer glazing.

Joe was curious, so he bent over the sink towards the window, and peered gingerly through it. His eyes looked slowly towards the ground. He could just make out the shape of a small grey terrapod. He felt frightened, as a cold shiver slid down his back and the beast pounced. Instinctively, Joe blurted out "Thomas move away from the window" Thomas did as he was told as Joe tracked the beast with his eyes. Then shouted "Dad something has hit the window!" Dave shouted back "Get back in here both of you, stay away from the doors and windows" Joe moved to the left of the window, grabbing Thomas's hand as he did so. A second terrapod hit the window, breaking through the outer glazing, cracking the inner glass. Joe panicked and moved further to the left, dragging Thomas with him. This action distanced them from the kitchen door, leading back to the hallway.

Another crash sounded, as a third terrapod smashed hard into the window. This time it breached the window and continued inwards, until it crashed into the kitchen door. It impacted the door, pushing it closed. Then the terrapod came to rest on the floor.

The boys found themselves trapped in the kitchen with the parasite. Exiting through the dining room patio doors would only take them straight into the path of more oncoming terrapods. Adding to their problem, the breached window presented an open house, to any terrapod wanting to enter.

Joe held Thomas tight as he said "Dad! Mum! We're trapped, and there's one of those things in here. Dave and Mary arrived at the kitchen door, pushing like crazy trying to force it open. The terrapod was a mere twelve inches in size, but it was extremely heavy, with its flattened back gripping the floor well, making it impossible to move. Dave and Mary pushed as hard as they could. Dave even tried kicking the door, but it would not budge. Mary shouted "Keep away from the parasite boys" but her voice was noticeably croaky and she was close to crying. She had seen what the parasites could do, and knew Joe and Thomas were defenceless against the beasts. Dave shouted "We're on our way don't give up! Hide behind the table if you need to" Dave knew if they could not wrestle the door open, they would lose the boys, but if they did manage to open it, they would all be at risk. Thomas said "Mum, its back is going down!" Thomas then began crying. Joe said "What shall we do dad? I'm frightened!" Joe pulled Thomas back towards the window as the terrapod set its sights on them. This ensured the beast had to readjust its position, in order to pounce on them.

Thomas pulled open the cupboard door behind, picking items up at random then throwing them at the terrapod. The effect was minimal on the beast, but nonetheless, Joe joined in out of desperation. He picked up a plastic container with cooking oil inside, throwing it at the terrapod, hitting it on its right hand side. The container split open and the oil spilled out, running down the side of the beast. The oil managed to creep underneath its body, reducing its grip on the floor. This resulted in the parasite being unable to stabilise itself, despite trying several times to maintain a good grip. Joe said "It does not like oil dad, it can't jump" Dave shouted "Good" Dave and Mary pushed even harder against the door, thinking it would be easier to get the beast away now.

Joe found a vinegar bottle then he had an idea. He unscrewed the lid letting it drop to the floor, the bottle he threw at the terrapod hitting its back. The contents spewed out and immediately began burning the terrapod, with a noticeably pungent smell. The terrapod retracted its back to the floor, in a last vain attempt to propel itself at the boys. It launched from the floor, only pushing from the left side of its body. It flew slow and low as it veered to the right. It quickly unleashed both pincers, extending them out to full attack mode, but it was very pedestrian. Joe reacted quickly, by opening the fridge door beside him. He quickly manoeuvred out of the parasites way, whilst watching it fly directly into the fridge. Joe slammed the door shut on the beast just as Dave came through the kitchen door, falling face down onto the floor. Dave looked up and said "Are you two okay?" Then he checked to see where the beast was. Thomas replied "Yes we're okay the bugs in the fridge. Joe put it there!" Dave went to the fridge and pushed against the door, in case it tried freeing itself. He immediately told Joe and Thomas to go into the hall with Mary. Then he searched around, trying to find something he could use, to keep the door shut. He soon spotted the table in the dining room.

Dave hurriedly ran to the table, throwing the chairs out of his way, on arrival. Grabbing the table, he dragged it against the fridge door, wedging it tightly against the handle. Then he rested for a short while, whilst regaining his breath.

Shortly afterwards, his eyes were drawn to the smashed window, this needed attention quickly if he was to keep terrapods at bay. Looking around, he decided the only option was to use a cupboard door. He pulled a door off from under the sink unit, leaving the hinges dangling. Then he wedged it against the open hole, to cover the gap. This would stop terrapods getting through the opening, but it needed something else to keep it held securely in place. He fetched a chair from the dining room then positioned one leg in the sink bowl, with the other placed in the waste disposal bowl. The back of the chair he forced tightly into the top of the window opening. He knew it would hold temporary, but would not last long if terrapods continually battered it.

Dave closed the kitchen door behind him then caught up with Mary, Joe and Thomas, inside the living room. He was tired and relieved from the whole ordeal. He peered out the living room window, checking outside, before sitting down with his family. After catching his breath, he thought about their situation, before saying abruptly "We need to get out of here and back to the mainland, as quick as possible. I suggest we only pack what we need, some clothes and food to get us home" A sense of panic came through Dave's words, because he knew the infestation in Sandown was unknown. Even if they managed to get to a port, they had no reservations to travel. So they may be unable to return to the mainland. Dave added "If we can get out of town and head to Ryde or Cowes, we might be able to get home by ferry or the hovercraft, what do you think Mary?" Mary knew Dave was right, but she pointed out that they needed to get to the car, before finding a safe route out of town. However, the media had mentioned that all ferries had been cancelled, and this was of great concern to them both.

Dave and Mary made haste, as they sorted basic items out to take on their journey home. They took turns, checking on the boys as they worked, because it was no longer safe to leave them alone, with the parasites beyond the cottage walls. After finally assembling everything together, they were ready to go, despite knowing it would be a challenge to get safely into the car, with the uncertain whereabouts of terrapods. They presumed they were at the rear, far away from the car.

Everything needed, was now sitting inside the front door of the cottage, ready to be loaded into the car. Joe and Thomas stood back from the door, well out of pouncing range, for any nearby terrapod, or so they thought. Dave was peering through the living room window, scanning the external vicinity by the doorway. He scrutinised the area carefully, beginning from the doorway and working his way over to the car. There were no terrapods visible at the moment.

Dave moved back into the hall then opened the front door, ensuring Mary was behind him, ready to close it should any trouble appear. He opened the door just wide enough for him to slip through. Then he checked outside making sure all was okay. Nothing obvious presented itself, so he moved towards the car. He arrived at the car, unlocking it with the key fob. Mary pulled the door ajar behind him narrowing the gap, but leaving just enough room for her to see what was happening. Dave searched inside the car, checking all was safe. Next he slowly bent downwards, checking nervously beneath its underbelly. He searched the front wheels thoroughly then moved back along the chassis, towards the rear bumper. It was very dark, but fortunately appeared clear of terrapods. Dave's attention quickly returned to the car door. After regaining his feet he started opening it. He pulled the handle, allowing the door to move away from the latch and gradually open. He continued slowly increasing the door gap. Suddenly a dull "clonk" came from inside the door. Then a loud "Thudding" noise followed as something hit the ground, frightening him. A reflex action caused Dave to slam the door shut tightly. He worriedly looked downwards, only to find a damaged cola can, sat on the floor, squirting its contents out all over the ground, and the car's underbelly.

Dave now relieved, reopened the car door and climbed in then started the car. He reversed backwards slowly, trying to keep the noise to a minimum. He came to a halt outside the cottage door, ensuring it was in line with the middle of the car, to aid a quick departure. He waved over to Mary, urging her to quickly load the bags into the car. The boys would enter the car at the last moment, so they would not be put in any unnecessary danger. Mary turned to the boys and told them to pick up their rucksacks then wait. She would then take the rest of the bags to the car, with Dave's help.

She picked up the first suitcase then continued through the doorway, pushing the door almost to a close. Dave exited the car and opened the boot, whilst Mary struggled with the suitcase. When she arrived, Dave hurriedly lifted the case into the boot. Afterwards, they returned for the last cases, picking them up and negotiated their way back out of the doorway. Dave first, then Mary followed, but she caught the bottom of the door with the suitcase. The door was gently pulled along, allowing it to click shut, leaving the boys alone inside. The shut door went unnoticed, as she continued catching Dave up. After loading the cases into the car, they returned for the boys to ensure they got into the car.

When Mary arrived at the door, she tried opening it, but found it locked. She shouted at the boys, begging them to open it and come out. The closing action of the door, had jammed its lock, making it difficult to open and Joe could not see why he was unable open the door, despite his best efforts.

Meanwhile at the rear of the cottage, three terrapods gathered by the kitchen window. Two smaller terrapods, jumped repeatedly at window, breaking the glass further and dislodging the chair. After a while, a small gap appeared. One terrapod jumped through the gap, settling near the kitchen door and a second quickly followed, sending the chair crashing away from the sink, and onto the kitchen floor.

Joe and Thomas heard a faint noise coming from behind them, in the kitchen, but they ignored it, choosing to carry on trying to open the door. Mary pushed hard on the door, while Dave gripped the letterbox, in the hope it would open. Joe attempted to twist the door knob back and forth, but although the door moved, it would not open far enough to allow them to exit the cottage.

At the rear of the cottage, a third larger terrapod readied itself to leap inside the kitchen window. It leapt upwards, smashing through the remainder of the glass. Its momentum took it flying into the kitchen door. On impact, the lower wooden pane exploded outwards into the hallway, leaving a gaping hole. Suddenly, Joe and Thomas turned to see a large terrapod, perched halfway through the broken door. Two smaller terrapods also sat menacingly behind it. Fortunately, the smaller terrapods were unable to pass by the larger one. Joe and Thomas screamed at Dave and Mary "They're in here, get us out!" Dave and Mary pushed for all their worth, but still the door would not budge. After a lengthy ten seconds, Dave shouted "Go into the living room boys, and open the window!" Both boys sprinted into the living room and opened the window then Thomas was forcefully shoved through by Joe, straight into Dave's waiting arms. Dave passed Thomas to Mary and she transported him to the car.

A loud crack came from the hallway, as the larger terrapod broke free of its constraints, clouting the wall close to Joe. Joe panicked, and jumped clean through the window, rushing past Dave, in his haste to escape. They both ran back to the car, with Dave rapidly closing the car door, after being sure Joe was safely inside. Mary checked all was okay then said "Dave let's get out of here!"

Dave was in his hurry to vacate the cottage area and found he was unsure of where to go. He drove out the gates of the cottage, quickly heading down towards the crossroads, in the heart of the town. Meanwhile Mary kept a close eye on any threatening terrapods nearby.

Dave cautiously approached the crossroads in front of him. Then he viewed the road carefully, as it meandered downwards to the pier, mindful of terrapods taking down their prey by the promenade. They came to a standstill at the crossroads, as they both pondered the safest way to go. On Dave's right, the road led to Shanklin, an old English village with thatched cottages. To the left the road made its way to Cowes, through Sandown's high street, then onwards to the ferry port.

Ron's newsagent on the corner had several bodies in front of the doorway, receiving the attentions of terrapods. Dave and Mary looked right, noticing an oddly lifeless quiet about the streets. Further down the road, several body parts lay on the ground, along with many feasting parasites. Mary turned to Joe and Thomas and said "Keep your heads down boys, it's not safe here" This was just an excuse to keep them from seeing the true horror, that had been bestowed upon these unfortunates.

Dave stared into the open door of the shop to his right. An elderly woman was slumped over the counter, with two terrapods feasting on her. In front of the shop counter, sat another terrapod and Dave fixated on it for a while. Suddenly, it leapt out of the shop, parking itself a short distance from the car. Mary said "Dave! Go quickly to the left!" Dave accelerated rapidly, spinning the wheels, sending the car sliding sideways as it shot off down the road.

After a short distance, they encountered the stranded car outside the souvenir shop. Dave slowed down avoiding the first body then steered carefully around the parked car. Both of them peeked over to the shop window. Two people were moving inside, clearly unable to escape through the front of the shop, due to a terrapod blocking the entrance. There were other poor souls, lain across the nearby floor, but they were beyond help.

They continued driving away very slowly, until Dave said "We should help them Mary" Mary was not keen, she felt they were extremely lucky to be alive, and it would be suicide trying to get the people out of the shop. Mary replied nervously "Is that wise?" Dave replied "We can't leave them to die. They don't stand a chance inside there. It's only a matter of time, before those things break in" Dave stopped the car, and looked back towards the shop.

He spotted two people, and it was obvious they had seen him. The couple inside the shop waved at Dave, warning him to leave. Surely they were not prepared to die in the shop, he thought. Dave guessed the reason for the warning, was the many terrapods scattered outside. Dave began driving away unhappy, but what could he do? Mary also felt guilty, as they pulled off. Dave continued driving for half a mile, thinking of the two people waiting in the shop, for what fate would bring them.

They passed a small van parked on a grass verge, on the other side of the road with the driver's door wide open. There was no one to be seen anywhere near it, so Dave slowed down then turned around to check it out. He pulled up next to it and shouted "Is anyone there?" No answer was forthcoming, so Dave continued searching for any nearby terrapods. He exited his car then took a look around. He peered inside the van and found the keys, still parked in the ignition. His eyes scrutinised the van, noting the boarded screen between the cab and rear compartment.

Dave walked around to the other side, checking to see if the driver was in the nearby bushes. His eyes searched down the grass verge, until he found a man with a terrapod eating away his flesh, making light work of his lifeless body. It was clear the van was of no further use to him. Dave thought he could utilise the van, perhaps to aid the couples escape from the shop. He returned to Mary and the boys, and said "The driver's dead Mary. The van has a dividing screen between the cargo bay and the cab. Why don't I go back and help the couple out of the shop" She replied "It's too risky Dave! How will you manage it? We need you with us to get us home" Dave thought long and hard then said "I'm not sure Mary maybe if I drive up to the shop door, they could make their own way to me. The choice will be theirs, but I won't be in any danger" Mary replied "If you are going to try it, why don't you reverse with the rear doors open, they can climb in the back. If one of those things does get in, you will have something between you and the parasite. Then you can drive off safely" Dave resumed his seat in their car, and drove into a layby a little further along the road.

After chatting briefly, Dave got Mary to agree to the plan. He hugged and kissed her, before exiting the car and making his way to the van. He shouted "If I'm not back in an hour, don't wait, find your way home and I'll find you, somehow!" Mary watched Dave walking to the van and told the boys to wave, while doing her best to hold back her watering eyes. On arrival to the van, he got inside then started it up. He checked around thoroughly then headed back to the shop.

Dave shortly arrived at his intended destination, stopping short of the shop entrance. He checked thoroughly for terrapods, then exited the van and opened the rear doors. After returning inside the cab, he drove off and approached the shop. He manoeuvred around the parked car, by mounted the kerb and driving as close as he could to the shop entrance.

Inside the shop, Pete and Jan stood stunned, wondering why anyone would bother coming back to help them. They watched Dave for a split second, before Pete shouted "Leave us we can't get out!" Dave replied "I'll reverse back with the rear doors open, climb in and bang on the inside of the van when you're inside, then I'll drive off" Jan shouted "One of these things is preventing us getting out, it's stuck on the dead man by the doorway" Dave looked at the body on the floor, no help was required for him, he thought. He drove forward slightly, adjusting the angle of his car, enabling him to reverse directly into the shop door. He reversed backwards slightly then waited for a while.

Pete and Jan pushed, with all their combined might, but still could not move the door. Dave watched, as a terrapod jumped out in front of him, trapping itself beneath his van. It repeatedly flattened its back catapulting upwards, but just hit the underneath of the chassis, unable to escape. An idea shot across Dave's mind. If he trapped the terrapod by the doorway beneath the van, he could reverse through the shop door, with the parasite unable to attack anyone.

Dave reversed, then shouted at Pete and Jan, explaining his knew plan, he insisted they stood well back when he was about to crash through the shop door. They would have to get in as quickly as possible, because he would not hang about afterwards. He watched them move clear of the door through his door mirror, and quickly pulled forward as far as he dared. Then keeping the van straight, he aimed towards the door. Checking his door mirror once more, he rapidly reversed, pulverising the shop door. The rear of the van crushed the door, along with its frame, leaving a mixture of shattered glass, wooden splinters, and broken souvenirs, scattered about the floor and a large gaping hole, for them to climb through.

The terrapod however, sat dangerously beside the left hand rear wheel. Pete shouted "That thing is by the rear wheel mate!" Dave checked in his door mirror. The terrapod lay stunned, but still loose, and it would certainly soon make a leap for a new victim. Dave drove forward again. Then rapidly reversed and manoeuvred the rear wheel over the terrapod, trapping it beneath the tyre.

Pete shoved Jan towards the van doors and immediately followed in her footsteps. He pulled the van doors fully open and they both climbed inside. Pete shouted at Bentley the dog. Bentley promptly arrived, jumping straight in the van, as Pete pulled the doors tightly shut, just as a terrapod jumped down from the rooftop and bounced off the rear doors.

Inside the van, it was full of dust and very messy, but it was a very welcome site, to its human cargo. Pete and Jan slammed their fists hard on the board of the cab. Dave instantly sped away from the scene, heading back towards the road and his worried family.

Dave pulled up gently into the layby near Mary, Joe and Thomas. The relief on Mary's face was clear to see, as she rushed out of the car to greet Dave, as he opened his door. When out, he received a big hug and kiss from Mary.

Pete and Jan pushed open the rear doors, bursting out of the van and taking a big gulp of fresh air. It was a welcome relief to enjoy the open space, without any threat from the parasites, strewn around the town. Ten minutes previous, their fates sat waiting for them outside the shop, but now a big debt was owed to a brave unselfish man and his family.

Pete, Jan and Bentley went to the front of the van towards Dave. Pete shook Dave's hand firmly, introducing Jan, Bentley and himself to him. Pete then kissed Mary on the cheek and said "Thank you, I felt sure you would have to leave us there" Dave replied "It was hard to drive off. It was a difficult decision, but it was Mary's idea to use the van and with a little improvisation, we pulled it off" They then continued talking about how they came to be in the situation.

Shortly afterwards, the subject turned to everyone's future plans. Pete and Jan wanted to head home and stay there, until someone came, as they felt sure the army would be called in to cleanse the area of parasites. The Ellis family needed to find a ferry, so they would be heading to Cowes in the hope of crossing the waters of the Solent and going home.

Mary switched on the car radio, and waited to see if there was any updated news. The local radio was on air, with bulletins every hour, reporting on the terrapod invasion sweeping through the island, and infecting the mainland. The news bulletins advised not to approach terrapods, as they were dangerous and difficult to kill, insisting people avoided them at all costs. By the sound of the newsreader, it became apparent, there were many casualties, and help would not be available for a considerable amount of time on the island. Refuge inside houses was advised, and people were to avoid going outside. The newsreader then listed all the infected areas, including Blackgang Chine, Newport, Ryde, Sandown and the most northern parts of the island, including the now infested ferry ports. She informed everybody of all ferries having been cancelled, in order to stop more people from the mainland becoming infested. She then gave out the telephone numbers of all ferry port operators for customers to ring. This dampened the spirits of Dave and his family, as they realised they could be stuck on the island indefinitely.

Dave immediately rang the ferry operator, but when he eventually got through, the news was not good. He was informed that the terrapods had infested the ferry terminals on both sides of the Solent. They were scattered along the grass verges along the roads, making it impossible to get in or out of the ferry ports. Dave dejectedly, returned the phone to its holder.

After the call, Dave reluctantly informed every one of the bad news. Reality hit home hard, as they searched their thoughts for a safe place to stay on island. Pete said "No point going back to my place in Newport, as it sounds like we would just be fodder for the parasites" Jan thought quietly then said "There might be a way of getting you back to the mainland Dave. If the terrapods have not infected my friend's boat in the marina" Pete said "We can't go back to your friends place in Sandown Jan. She'll be locked up in her hotel, if she's heard the warnings, I expect she managed to escape somewhere safe" Jan knew Pete was being optimistic, because it was likely her friend had become a parasite victim, as the hotel was open at the front to encourage passing trade. Jan said "My friend has a small boat to the west of Ryde. She used to go cruising a lot when she was younger, but now it just sits idly on the quayside, only being used when her family come over. She lets them use it for sightseeing around the island shores" Dave had no idea how to handle a boat, but it could be a way home for them. Dave asked "Will your friend mind? Is it far?" Jan replied "It's a short drive outside Ryde. I hope it's not overrun with those things. My friend won't mind, she's always telling me to borrow it anytime I like. You can leave her a note saying you borrowed it, and where you're heading" Dave asked "Are you coming with us to the mainland?" Both Pete and Jan said they would be staying put on the island, but offered to get them to the boat and show them how to use it the best they could, because Pete had some knowledge of sailing from when he was a young boy. His grandfather had once been a small time fisherman on the island.

They set out on their perilous journey, expecting a thirty minute drive, lined with a dangerous array of terrapods waiting for them. Dave and his family followed Pete, Jan and Bentley in the van.

Pete and Jan talked continually along the journey getting to know each other, laughing and joking, to relieve the tension of the situation. When they neared Ryde, Jan began giving Pete directions towards the quayside marina, where the boat was moored.

## CHAPTER 11

## THE INFECTION GOES GLOBAL

It was seven o'clock in the evening, when they arrived at the approach road, to the marina. Pete stopped on the top of the hill overlooking the quay then looked down the long winding road, searching for any signs of terrapods strewn along the tree lines. It was five hundred yards to where the first boat was moored, but at least the road looked clear. Pete said "Which one is your friend's boat Jan?" Jan replied "I'm not sure, all I know is that it is at the back of the marina somewhere, so we may have to walk down to it" Jan eyes scanned the marina trying to find her friends boat, but it was not in clear view.

Meanwhile, the Ellis family came to a stop behind the van. Dave got out the car then walked over to the van. He knocked on the window and Pete wound it down. Dave asked "Where do we go from here?" Pete answered "We'll drive down as far as we can, then walk the rest of the way to the boat. Jan knows roughly where it is" Dave returned to his car then shortly afterwards, they all drove slowly down the hill, towards the marina.

They stopped near the marina boardwalk, and Pete and Jan exited the van, allowing Bentley to jump out for some fresh air. They walked towards the Ellis's car, with Mary exiting their car in time to meet them. Pete said "If you all stay inside, we'll look for the boat, then come back and get you. Bentley will stay with us in case there are more parasites lurking around. If you get any trouble, sound your horn and drive away" Mary re-entered her car, then conveyed the message to the others. Meanwhile, Pete, Jan and Bentley went to find the boat moored within the marina.

After passing several boats, Pete said "Does this boat have a name Jan?" Jan replied "It's called Bluebelle, it's only a small cabin cruiser, suitable for four people. My friend was always telling me to settle down and find a nice man then we could go out together, I've not found him yet!" Jan's eyes opened wide, as she smiled, and spoke the last part of her sentence. She hesitated, while waiting for a compliment from Pete. It duly came when Pete said "I can't believe you haven't found someone special yet, you always look lovely" Jan's face lit up, as she smiled again, asking another searching question "Have you someone in your eye then Pete?" Pete said "No" Jan subtly pushed against Pete, but he was a touch slow to recognise her womanly hint. Jan said "Perhaps we may find someone together, very soon!" Pete blushed, as he finally got the hint. Then his hand accidently found Jan's, as they walked along the boardwalk, with their fingers entwined.

A small blue and white cabin boat came into view, and Jan said "Here it is!" She moved in closer checking the name was correct then proceeded to climb aboard, with Pete holding her steady. Pete pulled himself aboard the vessel, as Jan scampered over to the rear of the boat. She lifted the engine compartment, searching for the keys, hidden on a shelf inside. After picking up the keys, she proceeded to the captain's chair.

After inserting the key and several turns, the engine eventually sprang into life, then Jan checked the fuel and instrument gauges and said "I can start it Pete and go for a Sunday cruise, but I don't know how to navigate to Portsmouth" Pete said "Don't worry, they can use the GPS on their phones to guide them to the mainland" Jan said "Best get the others now, as they only have a few hours of light left. They won't want to get caught in the waters of the Solent, unable to see" Pete immediately headed back to the others, while Bentley jumped on the boat.

Pete arrived back at the car and Dave lowered the window, ready to greet him. Pete said "You need to move quickly, so you can navigate in the daylight to the mainland. You don't want to make land in the dark straight into a parasite nest" Dave told Joe and Thomas to pick their belongings up, and follow Pete to the boat, then he would follow on shortly.

Both boys grabbed all they could manage, leaving Dave to bring the suitcases with Mary's help. Dave handed the first case to Mary then watched as she walked away and followed the boys. He continued lifting his case out of the rear of the car. However, his case jammed awkwardly on the boot lip as he lifted it. Dave pulled it up hard then had a feeling of being watched. A cold shiver immediately shot down his back. He deliberately turned slowly backwards. A terrapod complete with flattened back, sat facing him ready to pounce. He momentarily froze, as his life flashed before him.

Dave, wondered which one of them would move first. Suddenly, it rapidly pounced at him. In a split second, Dave regained his senses. He pulled the boot of the car upwards using it as a shield. The beast slammed into it, dropping inside the boot, taking his suitcase along with it. Dave slammed the boot shut, trapping both the terrapod and his suitcase. His case and vital food were lost to the parasite, but better that, than his life. He locked the car with the key fob then left the scene. Quickly, he caught the rest up, as they headed down towards the boat.

On reaching the boat, one by one they embarked with their belongings. It was a bit tight for space, but they all managed to fit in. Pete, Jan and Bentley readied to leave, but as they disembarked terrapods came hopping down the boardwalk. Jan and Pete searched for another route out, but eventually found they had no choice other than to return to the boat, and accompany the Ellis family. Jan called Bentley back and he duly returned inside the boat, while barking at the parasites.

They were ready to set off in the nick of time, just as terrapods began jumping on the boats and catching people unaware. Pete sitting on the Captain's seat said "Hold on tight, we're off!" Dave unmoored the boat, and they drifted away from their moorings. Pete throttled up, piloting the craft towards deeper water, passing through the marina of moored crafts.

The Bluebelle crew looked on completely helpless, as one by one, terrapods made light work of the stranded victims. One man broke free, he ran along the boardwalk, only to be ambushed by three terrapods waiting for him. All three took him down at the end, with each taking their spoils of flesh. Pete and Dave shouted at the remaining boat occupants, warning anyone still alive to get out, but no one took up the challenge and most were simply trapped fodder for the parasites. Dave noticed that the parasites never once entered the water when chasing victims. He commented to Mary "They seem to clearly be landlubbers, as the beasts have made no attempt to board any boat by swimming through the water" Mary turned to the children then guarded their eyes, against the ensuing horror happening around the marina.

The boat crept out the marina, making its way into the open waters before heading north, towards Portsmouth. The occupants knew it would be a slow journey, as they made themselves comfortable within their tight confines.

The Ellis family huddled together with the dog at the rear of the boat, talking about what they would likely find on arrival to Portsmouth. Pete was at the helm, accompanied by Jan, with her arms around him, squeezing him tight for comfort. Pete looked directly into Jan's eyes and smiled. She clearly only had eyes for him. Jan moved closer until their lips touched, and they gently kissed. Jan hugged Pete tighter and they both felt very secure in their embrace. Both had thought they were homeward bound to Newport, but now found they were sailing to the mainland, with absolutely no idea where it would lead, but at least they were secure in their love for each other.

The cruiser travelled through the silent Solent waters, as they discussed what to do after landing. Mooring the cruiser was mentioned in their conversation, because the state of the parasitic infestation on the mainland was uncertain. The conversation fell quickly quiet, as they continued through the light tidal waters, wondering what their fate would hold.

******

Meanwhile, on the mainland, the roaming terrapods began expanding outwards from the ferry port. They were running riot around the heavily populated housing estates. Hundreds of parasites now found a massive new food source, in the human race. Increased food source, meant many terrapods would grew to several feet in size. Their appetites would soon make them search further in land for fresh prey, where hundreds of people were now inside their cars, seeking safety further in land from neighbouring towns and villages.

On the main road, cars queued up for mile upon mile, trying to join the road headed north. Unfortunately, there was a six car accident and the resulting carnage, was blocking the northbound carriageway. Many disgruntled drivers were now causing trouble, mostly arguing with each other.

The police arrived on scene, but struggled getting things under control and the traffic came to a total standstill. People started sounding their horns, getting impatient. Meanwhile, the parasites were only a few miles away in the distance, closing in on the incident.

Sitting at the tail end of cars, was a young couple in a bright blue sports car. They had queued for several minutes, and were now getting frustrated with waiting. Kira, a slim blonde welsh girl, sat in the passenger seat, with Ray her boyfriend next to her. They listened intently to the radio, trying to find out why there was a traffic problem. The couple had finished their holiday and were heading home to London, with no knowledge of the parasitic problem approaching from behind.

Eight o'clock came, and a voice announced on the radio "This is Deborah Carr, with the news at eight. There has been an infestation of bugs around the south coast. They have appeared around Portsmouth, along with sporadic outbursts around Southampton. The Isle of Wight is also under siege from these parasites, with some being reported to be up to two feet in size, although this has not been confirmed officially yet. The Isle of Wight has been cut off from the mainland, with all ferry ports now closed. It's thought that the breakout of terrapods originated from there. The terrapods are considered very dangerous, and people are advised to avoid contact with them" The young couple looked worried as Kira said "My god, how are we going to get out of here Ray?" Ray said "I don't know Kira, let's listen to the rest of the news, to find out what's happening" Kira turned the volume up then listened to the newsreader again "There are more reports from several other European countries including France, Holland, Germany and the Republic of Ireland of similar outbreaks. There are unconfirmed reports in Russia of breakouts near St Petersburg that are getting out of hand, and the army has been called in to deal with it. New York has confirmed breakouts, around Brooklyn and New Jersey. We'll keep you updated on those! Washington has a small outbreak, and the National Guard has been called in there. The president has reportedly said "Everything is under control" and has made no intentions of leaving office at present, or changing his plans. Now the rest of the news" Kira said "Oh my god! Ray we need to get out of this queue" Ray answered "Have a look around, to see if we can get through anywhere" They searched either side of the car, but the road was crammed tight with cars on their side of the carriageway, and the steel barrier was preventing them from crossing to the opposite side.

Ray exited his car and searched by foot, but after walking several feet between parked cars he could not see a way out. A truck driver, stuck in traffic further down, was talking to a second man beside his cab. Ray approached him then asked if he knew what was going on. The answer received, was of the carriageway being closed for two hours, while the wreckage was being cleared and the injured driver was airlifted to hospital.

Ray thought they would have to either wait until the road was cleared, or leave the car and go somewhere for a coffee, returning later. The truck driver said "There's a broken stretch of barrier in front, possibly where the accident started. Maybe the police could remove it. We could escape to the other carriageway, and get off at the next junction" Ray dismissed the thought, then walked back towards the waiting Kira.

Ray returned to his car and looked back down the carriageway. He noticed several cars parked erratically. It seemed strange they had not queued behind them in the jam. His eyes were quickly drawn to a woman, running from one of the cars, as she headed towards the grass verge. Suddenly, a large animal pounced on her and she fell to ground. He thought he was seeing things, because he had never seen anything like it before. Then it suddenly dawned on him, this was one of these bugs. He scrutinised the other cars more closely, noticing other people strewn across the carriageway, with parasites attached to various parts of their anatomies. Panic filled his head as he realized, they needed to escape the beasts. Ray rushed into the car and said "Kira, we need to get out of here now!" While watching the panic in Ray's eyes, she turned backwards, looking through the rear window. Terrapods were making their way towards them. It was a daunting sight as she said "Ray what are those things?" Ray said "I don't know!"

Everyone in front of Ray and Kira, suddenly began starting their engines, attempting to turn round, as the panic gripped them. Many headed straight back into the oncoming terrapod army, only to find they needed to slow down to pass the snake of stricken cars. Terrapods took full advantage, catapulting themselves at the slow weave of cars, using their weight and speed, to launch through the windscreens and into their defenceless victims. This resulted in more stricken cars, and an even larger amount of casualties. Eventually the carriageway became completely blocked, leaving many motorists queuing to die. When the stricken occupants realised they were sitting ducks, the car doors were flung open, and the inhabitants ran towards the grass verges. There, they were duly ambushed by a gauntlet of terrapods, lying in wait for them.

Only one car lay between Ray and the truck, because most people were meeting their grisly fates, at the hands of the ravenous terrapods. Suddenly, Ray remembered his conversation with the truck driver earlier, and had a brainstorming thought. He reversed his car then pulled forward, passing the car in front and driving up to the truck. Clambering out of his car he said "Stay here Kira. I've got an idea, I'm not sure it will work, but we'll die here if it doesn't" He rushed up to the cab then hurriedly knocked on its door. The driver lowered the window then while poking his head outside said abruptly "What do you want? I'm getting my things, I'm off! I suggest you do the same!" Ray somewhat taken back, blurted out "We're dead if we stay here. I've got an idea, if you're willing to help. It may mean the loss of your truck, but it might save many lives" The truck driver took little interest, while picking up his phone, but he did take time to partially listen to Ray and said "What's your plan then mate?" Ray said "Reverse your truck, and drive it through the broken barrier, the cars can then escape to other side of the carriageway. Besides, if we run away from these things on foot, they will catch us up eventually and ambush us" The trucker viewed the broken barrier, noting it was only secured properly at one end, and the bolts on the other end had sheared off, leaving it resting on the floor. The barrier was strong enough to stop an arctic, but with one end broken, he might be able to condemn it to scrap if he rammed hard enough, or it could become his steel tomb otherwise. The trucker said "It might work, but it might wreck my truck, but I suppose it's worth a try" Ray said "When you break through, jump in with us" "Ok" he replied. Ray shouted "Good luck!" Then proceeded to get back in his car and reverse clear, giving the trucker plenty of room to position his truck.

The trucker reversed his truck and positioned it square to the barrier. He selected first gear then truck rushed forward. The truck ploughed into the central reservation, bending the barrier round, making a small opening. It was a good start, but not large enough to allow a car to drive through. The truck stopped, and the trucker looked out of his cab at the approaching terrapods. They were travelling directly towards him, but there was still enough time to allow him a second run. Once more, he reversed, a little further this time then realigned the cab. After selecting first gear, he accelerated hard and quickly gained speed. He crashed into the barrier again, further widening the gap. However, another run was needed, so he drove backwards dragging the barrier attached to the front bumper, this partially closed the gap until the truck broke free of it. The trucker reversed and repositioned for a final run as the terrapods closed in. On this charge, he quickly engaged second gear, carrying more speed, whilst colliding with the barrier. A large section of the barrier was sent skywards, clear of the central reservation. A smaller steel slither slid underneath the cab, finding its way through and into the engine bay. The truck continued forward with the engine running, despite slowly dying from internal damage, incurred by the deadly foreign object.

After coming to a rest, the driver disembarked and walked over to Ray and said "The engines knackered. I'll ride with you if you don't mind" Ray said "No problem jump in" The trucker thought for a second, then said "Wait a minute, I need to do something first" He returned to his truck, reversing it back through the opening, parking it diagonally across the carriageway. Terrapods could be seen, just thirty feet away, behind the opening heading towards the truck. The trucker sounded his horns loudly, ensuring everyone knew there was an escape route through the barrier. He watched several cars drive through the gap, escaping the terrapods. He exited the door, rushed to the rear of the cab and removed the fuel cap. After removing matches from his pocket, he lit one and stared admiringly at his glorious truck, then peered behind him, towards the advancing terrapod colony. Then he stared back at the flame, before closing his eyes and then he said "Annabelle, you've been a good truck to me, sorry!" He dropped the match inside the fuel tank. It immediately ignited the fumes, as it fell down the funnelled filler. He sprinted away, and caught up with Ray and Kira. Kira pushed open the car door, allowing him to enter then they all drove off, in haste.

Soon flames erupted upwards, and shot along the length of the trailer, setting the flammable curtain alight. Ray remarked "Why did you set it alight?" The trucker replied "Three reasons, the first was to hopefully attract those beasts to their deaths, in the hot flames allowing more cars to escape. The second was to slow them down, as it is a big hot object to negotiate and the last is because my insurance will now pay out, due to the fire damage" He smiled and winked as he said the last comment jokingly. Then said "Thanks for the lift, the name's Terry" They continued introducing themselves to each other as they drove along the road and escaped the Terrapods.

The burning truck sent arid black flames high into the sky, and across both carriageways. This gave many cars the one chance of escaping the marauding parasites, saving many lives as planned. The parasites were drawn to the heat, jumping directly into the fire, perhaps mistaking the heat for fresh live food.

It was not long before terrapods navigated the truck and a picked off a motorist, as he drove through the narrow gap. Another victim quickly fell by the wayside then a third, who crashed his car, causing the gap to narrow even further.

One woman tried to make it through, but she was easily picked off. She panicked, ploughing into the right hand barrier, completely blocking the escape route and rendering it impossible for anyone else to pass. The car quickly ignited into flames as onlookers watched on, until the engulfing flames swallowed everything inside. Occupants inside the remaining cars were unable to get through the abandoned metallic mess. Most opted, to escape their vehicles and run for their lives.

Many jumped across the central reservation, and were picked up by drivers having already negotiated the gap. Soon the taxi cars were full to the brim, but it did not stop the masses from attempting to clamber on to the overloaded cars. Chaos arose, as fights broke out with people being wrenched out of slower vehicles, and left by the roadside at the mercy of terrapods.

As two cars sped along the carriageway, they colliding together, crushing a man between them, while he clung helplessly between them. Another man fell beneath a car as it hurriedly drove away. One driver's obscured view, caused him to panic, knocking down a woman in a bid to escape the marauding people, trying to mount his car. Many cars became unable to move from the extreme weight of people crammed on every available space. The approaching terrapods swamped many unsuspecting victims, while they attempted seeking the safety offered by the motorists. Most people ignored the danger coming from behind, and were easily caught. They soon found themselves looking terrapods in the eye, before meeting their deaths.

Mass hysteria engulfed the area, as the hungry terrapods enslaved their large food source. People died flagging down cars, when the drivers failed to stop, driving straight through them, in their haste to escape the desperate insane carjackers. Insanity reigned, as the crowd began throwing the feeble and weak minded, out of any available car.

A couple sat in their car, awaiting their inevitable fate. A terrapod pounced onto the bonnet in front of them with such a force it caused a huge dent to appear. The windscreen immediately shattered into tiny fragments. The couple unable to see anything, pushed the glass fragments outwards with their bare hands. The large terrapod sat supremely on their bonnet and claimed its spoils. It flattened its back, ready to pounce with the couple watching. It pounced into the car, through the broken screen. The man reacted instantly, putting his arm over his wife's face to protect her. The terrapod landed on her, trapping his forearm, then forcing it hard into his wife's face. He then watched in horror, as the terrapod's top pincer slowly extended past his arm, piercing into his wife's eye. In a fraction of a second, it released a paralysing nerve agent into her head. The lower pincer then pinned his arm to her lower jaw, ensuring he was unable to escape. The parasite then set about devouring his arm, leaving him in excruciating pain, while leaving her paralysed. Both watched his arm slowly being eaten, despite his desperate efforts to rescue his arm, amongst his pain.

Several minutes later, the terrapod released his blood soaked, half eaten arm, leaving him in shock. While his blood dripped over his wife's paralysed face. He watched speechless for a brief second, as the terrapod continued gnawing into his wife's face. Suddenly the realisation of the situation dawned on him. He tried removing the beast, burning his remaining hand on the outer skin of the beast. Finally he ran out of ideas, and could no longer watch his wife meet her gruesome end. He turned away, clambered out of the car with a degree of difficulty.

His eyes quickly scanned through the stranded cars, catching glimpses of many victims along the roadside. He turned to face his wife as her life ebb away and the parasite slowly munched deep into her forehead. Then he looked skywards, with tears streaming down his cheeks.

A large terrapod dropped down before him, blocking his escape. He simply offered himself to it, with a complete lack of fear. The beast pounced onto his chest, pushing him back against the car. He slowly slid down the door, joining his wife, in a slow mutual death.

Meanwhile, Ray, Kira and Terry, were unaware of the events unfolding behind them. They passed many motionless cars, sitting on the opposite side of the road stuck in the traffic jam. Then they quickly approached the initial crash area. Many cars were strewn across the carriageway, with the carnage clear to see. Briefly stopping, they warned police and public alike of the peril that lay behind them. They advised them to shove cars out of the way, clear the road, then vacate the area as quickly as possible. The uninterested authorities were focusing on the injured casualties around the crash site. Despite Terry insisting on the extreme urgency of clearing the route, the police would not be persuaded, and waived the good advice away. They tried informing other onlookers of the perils behind, but again it fell on deaf ears.

Ray reluctantly drove off, annoyed at the response received from the authorities, but there was nothing more they could do. They resumed their journey to London, with Kira turning the radio on, listening to the latest report. She said "I expect it will be all over the news shortly" A newsflash soon claimed "A disturbance has been reported on the main route out of Portsmouth, with a crash causing a huge traffic tail back. A helicopter has been sent to view the situation, as police are unable to attend due to another accident blocking the northbound carriageway" Kira said "That's rubbish! No one's going to help those people, until it's too late" Ray said "Yes, we've done all we can do, perhaps the helicopter will hurry the police along and clear the route quicker" The atmosphere was very solemn, as they continued driving.

A short time elapsed, before Kira said "We're off to London near Kennington, where are you headed Terry?" Terry said "I live in Oxford. If it's okay, I'll ride with you as far as I can, then catch a train home. I'm not expected home until tomorrow, as I had another drop to make. I should have slept at a hotel tonight, before heading home in the morning" He paused and added "I'd ring my wife, but I left my phone in the cab in the confusion" Ray offered Terry his phone. Terry said "Thanks" He took the phone then rang home, explaining to his wife, what had happened.

\*\*\*\*\*\*

Meanwhile back at the crash site, a helicopter arrived and set down on the southbound carriageway. Two paramedics emerged then ran over to the central reservation, checking on the condition of the casualties. The officer that had recently sent Ray, Kira and Terry away met the medics. He briefly explained that they had one man seriously injured near the centre lane with concussion, and three further casualties with minor cuts and bruises.

The medics discussed the injured, then opted to remove the seriously injured man by helicopter first. One medic jumped over the barrier then went to the patient, who was being prepared for a stretcher.

Meanwhile, the remaining medic returned to the helicopter and prepared the craft to receive the patient, he then fetched the stretcher from the rear of the craft. Then he made his way to the patient after negotiating the barrier. The fire service finished their job so they permitted the medics to remove the patient. Both medics checked all was well with the patient then manoeuvred him into the helicopter, with a helping police officer manipulating him over the barrier. The paramedics then strapped the patient into the helicopter, ready for lift off.

The pilot made his usual take off checks, but before he had finished, a red car caught his eye as it sped erratically towards him. It drove straight past the helicopter, forcing the policeman on the other side of the barrier to jump backwards. The pilot then peered down the road at the many cars swerving around the helicopter. He rubbed his eyes in disbelief, because the road should have been closed to all traffic. So where were they coming from, he thought? As several more cars weaved speedily past.

The police officer leapt over the barrier, waving two cars down. The first stopped briefly and a woman shouted "Run, run for your lives they're coming!" She then accelerated away, leaving him perplexed. Who was, he thought? The next car slowed, to avoid the helicopter then sped up, after negotiating it.

Soon, a steady stream of cars drove towards the helicopter, but at a more leisurely speed. Most were overloaded, with people hanging on to any available part of the car. The policeman, unable to stem the flow of cars, panicked and shouted to the pilot "Lift off now!" The officer's words went unheard by the pilot. So he used hand gestures to signal to the pilot to take off, but this took time for the pilot to comprehend his message. Many of the cars just avoided colliding with the helicopter at the last moment. The pilot increased the rotor speed, and attempted to lift off.

A large meandering green car was hurtling along the carriageway, as it carried nine people inside, while approaching the helicopter. One man was on the roof, with two others clambering to the front, partially blocking the driver's view. The driver swerved several times along the carriageway, occasionally sticking his head out the side window to see where he was headed. On the rear of the car sat a large terrapod, along with a man clinging to the roof, having already spotted it. He shuffled towards the front of the car, to avoid the attentions of the terrapod. Meanwhile, the terrapod tried desperately to attain a firm grip to pounce on a victim, but it struggled as the car weaved around erratically. The man slid down the front of the car, completely blocking the driver's sight. The driver automatically slowed down, enabling the terrapod to acquire a firm grip. It quickly catapulted forward, latching onto the man blocking the windscreen. The man's head dropped suddenly, smashing through the screen, sending glass everywhere. The driver panicked when the terrapod appeared in sight. He presumed they had been caught by the invading terrapod pack. He drifted towards the left side of the carriageway, on a collision course with the helicopter.

The police officer tried warning the driver of the car, by running in front of him. The car hit him, knocking him swiftly downwards to ground. The driver responded by accelerating, thinking he had hit a terrapod. He ploughed on, out of control, with the dead officer being dragged along beneath the under tray of the car, and headed straight towards the helicopter.

The helicopter pilot watched the approaching car, before managing to leap out of his aircraft, avoiding the impact. The trapped patient and medics had no chance of escaping, as the car careered into the landing skid, resulting in tipping the helicopter over, towards the car. The rotors spun, until slicing deep into the road surface, then one by one, they sheared outwards and headed directly into the parked cars on the opposite carriageway. They damaged several cars, as they sliced through the bodywork, fatally injuring the occupants in the process.

The medics survived the initial crash impact then tried freeing themselves from the wreckage. They manage to attain their freedom, but were unable to help their patient. Both medics eventually clambered out the opposite side of the helicopter, quickly running to check on the crashed car to see if help was needed.

They arrived to find the blood soaked driver appearing to be dead. The passenger next to him sported a terrapod on his shoulder, while being slumped over the dashboard. Other people had jumped off the car, moments before impacting the helicopter and were littered about the roadside, all with minor injuries. Another man left in the rear of the car was still conscious, with blood over his face and in desperate need of help. The medics asked him if he was okay, but received a muted response.

Both medics began checking him over, with a view to removing him from the car. One medic checked to see if he could reverse the vehicle away from the helicopter, to help release the door to the patient. He began searching the wreckage, but quickly found the helicopter fuel tank leaking. The fuel was running down the car front, coming to rest on the road surface, along with drenching the dead mutilated police officer. He quickly turned to his colleague and said, with major urgency "Hurry up Jack, get him out quickly, then we'll worry about his injuries afterwards"

Suddenly, the driver made a noise, making it clear, he was not dead. He muttered "Got to get out of here! We must leave now!" The nearest medic said "Don't move, we'll get the man behind you out then work on you, please don't move" He touched the man's shoulder, trying to reassure him. Afterwards, he turned and continued helping his colleague to move the man in the rear. They manoeuvred him out through the partially open door. Then they lifted him away from the car, setting him down a short distance away on the roadside.

The driver reached down to the ignition keys, trying to restart the engine. The engine turned over, but did not start. One of the medics rapidly rose to his feet and run towards him, shouting "No don't start the car!" On the second attempt however, it started, with one cylinder not firing. The damaged plug lead, sent a stray high powered spark directly onto the underside of the car bonnet, the liquid fuel immediately ignited. The flame shot along the bonnet and followed the fuel, as it trickled down to ground via the dead officer. The searing heat began burning the helicopter floor. As the heat got hotter, the flame began following the bonnet in the opposite direction, until meeting the dripping fuel source, from the helicopter's tank. There, the flame streaked upwards, disappearing down into the fuel tank. Here it briefly gasped for air, before combusting into one large fireball, consuming the cab in a fraction of a second. Afterwards, the flames quickly died down, to a black acrid, suffocating smoke.

The medics watch on, as the helicopter made a loud hissing noise. Then a brief quiet entailed, before it exploded with an almighty bang, sending flames out in all directions along with twisted metallic shrapnel. The flames then rapidly engulfed the crashed car, setting everything alight. The driver's screams were consumed by the roar of the flames in a flash, until he fell deadly silent.

Chaos reigned down on the area, with many people in severe pain from burns and shrapnel wounds. Two officers were fatally injured, along with the two medics near the helicopter. Civilians lay dying from blood loss and their wounds. Quickly the crackling flames from the helicopter and the moans of the dying were the only sounds heard.

The quiet soon changed, as a voice behind shouted "Run, run, run, run" A man in his thirties, came running towards the wreckage, with a woman and young boy. All three, ran past the crashed cars, risking injury from the burning wreckage. Several survivors wondered why they were running so fast and not offering any help. They looked between the many damaged stationary cars. The terrapod army had arrived, claiming anyone unable to escape.

A mass exodus rushed through the cars, in a bid to escape the terrapods. Anyone attempting to exit cars was left trapped inside by the stampeding hordes. Anyone falling to ground was duly trampled on, and many met their deaths at the hands of the stampede. Anyone unable to exit the cars was easy fodder for the marauding terrapods, along with the injured, including the two medics and their patients. Many people, unable to outrun the beasts said their goodbyes to loved ones, via their mobile phones. Some even recorded their last moments, uploading the images as they were being attacked. The uploaded pictures, quickly found their way onto the various internet media sites, going viral rapidly.

## CHAPTER 12

## A SURPRISE CALL FROM LONDON

Nearly dark, as the cabin cruiser approached Portsmouth, creeping through the gentle rippling waters of the Solent. The bright lights were clearly visible along the coastline, highlighting the mismatch of the buildings. The cruiser moved slowly past the concrete gun emplacement, as it rose majestically from the sea from days gone by. Several squatters had taken residence inside, making the place their new safe haven, hidden from the terrapods.

As the cruiser approached the emplacement, Dave shouted over offering help. A large guy with ginger curly hair replied "Keep away from us! This is our sanctuary, find your own and leave us" Not a friendly gentleman, thought the cruiser crew, as they continued on towards the harbour.

As they neared land, the huge body count was clear to see, with many strewn across the beaches, whether young or old. Next, appeared the hovercraft terminal at Southsea, where the doors were wide open. More bodies lay within the building, as well as the outside of the hovercraft landing bay. Many terrapods lay in waiting inside for any victim who inadvertently stumbles across them.

A woman's voice could be heard calling out from within the terminal building. The cruiser crew watched the door, as she came running out, and was bombarded by a waiting wall, of ambushing terrapods. One terrapod jumped up, pulling her body to the ground as yet another victim fell silent.

Pete's eyes, scanned further ahead to a stranded hovercraft, that was perched partially within the sea. Its front was wedged inland, between what was left of the supports, of a small roller coaster. The upturned roller coaster itself, sat precariously above the hovercraft, with its surviving inhabitants under siege, with terrapods pouring into the cars. It was likely the fall had killed many, before the feeding frenzied terrapods had latched onto them. Inside the hovercraft, a multitude of bodies were being feasted on, hinting that the terrapods had attacked the hovercraft crew first, causing the ensuing carnage. The cruiser pushed further along the light tidal waters, as the crew continued searching for a suitable mooring. Everywhere was saturated with terrapods, and no safe place could be found.

They arrived at the ferry port, finding more carnage and plenty of bodies everywhere. Meanwhile, terrapods waited in lines for fresh victims at the quayside. The police and army were fighting furiously against them, but losing the battle and were now retreating. It was not safe to moor here, so they decided to continue westwards, towards Southampton.

Mary pointed towards the helpless figures, wading through the sea water trying to avoid terrapods. No terrapod had ventured into the cold waters for food, they were firmly land bound. The cruiser had no room for extra passengers, so they continued following the coastline inland. They sailed for another forty five minutes, trying to find suitable docking, until they arrived in Southampton.

Terrapods had invaded Southampton in smaller quantities, with many people choosing to hide inside buildings, to avoid them. The cruiser soon came to bear on Ocean Village marina, floating beside the lock gate. They waited several minutes, but no one came to their aid and opened it. They gently reversed back fifty feet, and calmly beached the cruiser on the sand bank, close to the marina.

They scrutinised the area thoroughly, then Pete and Dave disembarked onto the sand bank. They moved swiftly while keeping their wits about them. They soon found themselves on the marina walkway, making haste towards the car park. There, they searched for someone to borrow a car from, but people were a scarce commodity.

They walked across the car park, to a small shopping mall. Inside, they quickly found several dead bodies, being feasted on by parasites. After carefully negotiating two of the bodies, they headed towards a cake shop. Inside it, they found a young female shop assistant, lying on the floor, with a terrapod consuming her shoulder. In her hand was a handbag. Dave moved steadily towards her, and when close enough, he pulled the strap of the bag towards him. It moved easily, until the strap caught on her thumb. He pulled harder, but it was unwilling to budge, so he moved closer, trying to unhook it. The terrapod adjusted itself, moving her body and startling Dave. Inadvertently, he wrenched the strap from her thumb. The movement caused the terrapod to release the woman from its grip, but it soon returned, latching back on her mid rift. Dave pulled away quickly, removing her bag, then he rifled through it, eventually finding a set of keys. He just needed to find her car now!

Both men moved onto the next shop, only to find a well-dressed suited man, lying face down on the floor, with a terrapod enjoying him. Both men gazed at him, before deciding it was too risky to attempt removing his keys. They stepped around him, to search a little further inside. Slumped over the counter, was another smartly dressed man, with no immediate reason why he did not move. No terrapod could be seen on him, and his ailment was a mystery.

Pete slowly crept ever closer, checking him over for hidden terrapods. There was no obvious danger, so he put his hand inside the man's jacket pocket. He removed a set of keys, while staring closely at his face, half expecting him to object. The man was certainly dead, but why thought Pete, was it a heart attack? Pete briefly studied the gentleman once again trying to find a clue to his demise.

Then a loud thunderous bang was heard. The man dropped backwards, revealing a pair of pincers, stuck deep in his stomach. The terrapod had pinned him through the counter, and was devouring him through a hole it had made. However, a second terrapod, had made the noise, by jumping up towards Pete, battering the counter. The counter had split apart, but halted its progress, giving Pete a lucky escape. It was time for Pete and Dave to make a quick exit, so they sprinted back out the shop and exited through the mall entrance.

After leaving plenty of distance between them and the shops, they stopped and began regaining their breaths, whilst searching for the cars matching the keys. They eventually found both cars, then drove them as close to the marina as possible. It would still be a risky journey from the beached cruiser, to the waiting vehicles. The marina itself had been devoid of any parasites so far, so they hoped to get away unhindered.

They disembarked the cruiser, to the relative safety of the cars. Plans were quickly drawn up, so they could continue their arduous journeys. The Ellis family opted to head north to Guildford, avoiding the terrapod problems of the south. Pete, Jan and Bentley would follow then continue onwards another forty miles, to London, where

Jan had friends. They could at least stay there, until the Isle of Wight and the south had been cleansed of all parasites.

They all set off together and headed out of Southampton, avoiding the unwanted pests scattered around the city. After fifteen minutes, they joined the carriageway northwards, and were soon on their way to Guildford, avoiding all major traffic jams and the terrapod infestations.

\*\*\*\*\*\*

Meanwhile, at Newport hospital, terrapods had surrounded the building. All entrances were locked and blocked, for safety. Many people outside had become fodder for the parasites. Inside, an air of despair, had descended on the accident and emergency. There were many injured people inside, looking for treatment, but even more, just seeking protection from the parasites. People held phones to ears, as they checked and warned their loved ones, in nearby towns and villages, causing phone jams.

Inside the hospital lab, Richard and Darren were working hard. Unable to go home, they opted to ride out the invasion inside the hospital, waiting for the army or police to turn up, to rescue them. They continued working with the parasites, trying to find different ways of ridding the island of the beasts, completely unaware of the true extent of the invasion. They knew they were trapped inside the hospital, but assumed the terrapod infestation was confined to an isolated area on the island.

All terrapod samples were under lock and key in the lab, with the exception of one of the smaller creatures, sitting on the bench. They were performing numerous experiments on it. Despite the terrapods being resistant to many substances, they had managed to stop it pouncing, by adding oily substances underneath the subject, or onto the surfaces below. However they were still very puzzled, on how to neutralize the creature completely, but being unable to leave the hospital confines, they decided to work around the clock if required, to combat the terrapod threat.

Richard held the tubed terrapod aloft, and said "Darren, we can get this small one out, then strap it on to the plate over there" He pointed to a smooth steel plate mounted on the bench, with lips protruding upwards on each edge, stopping the terrapod from sliding around or releasing itself. Tough leather straps, sat beneath the lips, with three strong steel fasteners, set at regular intervals used to secure the beast in place. Darren having done it before knew exactly what was being asked of him. He would first use a two foot rod with grabbers at the end, to remove the terrapod. These would securely grab the beast from its prison tube, before giving it a chance to react. Then he would place it on the plate with a thin layer of oil smeared over the surface, reducing its grip and eliminating any danger of it pouncing. This would enable them to control the terrapod, whilst working on it. The only problem they encountered was of keeping the terrapod restrained, by using enough oil beneath it, ensuring it was unable to use its strength to escape its bindings.

First they needed to be very careful, staying at a safe distance from the beast and be ready for any unfortunate mistakes. They were well-rehearsed in the procedure, and extremely careful. They also had a contingency plan in place. This involved a quick dash for the door, locking it securely behind them. Then they would change the code, ensuring no one else could enter, without them knowing.

Darren carefully removed the terrapod from the tube then put it on the plate. Richard duly tightened the first strap around it. Darren then released his grabber tool, enabling Richard to attach the middle and last strap. Darren stood watching, as Richard proceeded with several different chemicals, in a bid to wound or kill the creature. They continued experimenting for an hour until they found themselves hungry. Nothing had worked so far, so they ensured the creature was held securely then Richard said "Do you want some supper now? Then we'll carry on after we've eaten" Darren replied "Yes I wouldn't mind, you eat first and when you're done, I'll eat mine" They were not following hospital rules by eating in the lab, but they wanted to rid the island of the parasites and time was becoming increasingly important.

Richard exited the lab and made his way to the canteen. He ordered fish and chips for the pair of them. After receiving it, he picked up two salt and vinegar sachets, and headed back. He knew they were not supposed to eat in the lab, but these were extreme circumstances, and if they did not find a cure for these parasites, they would likely die inside the lab.

Richard returned to the lab and said "I've got your fish and chips Darren, I'll eat mine first then you go in the clean room, and enjoy yours" Darren smiled and said "Okay, enjoy!" Darren felt very hungry, and could hardly wait for his turn to feast.

Richard finished his food in a rush, coming out feeling very satisfied and said "Your turn Darren!" Darren did not have to be told twice, he shot off quickly for his food. He went in the clean room, got comfortable, quickly tearing open the salt sachet that Richard left him, and pouring it over his food. Darren noticed two sachets of vinegar left for him by his food, because Richard had not used his. He tore one open, allowing the contents to drench his chips, thinking he would sprinkle the other on his fish, but as he poured the contents, his overturned coat sleeve picked the other sachet up, hiding it from view. He soon realised it was missing and quickly searched for it, to no avail. Hunger eventually got the better of him, and he continued eating his food, wondering where the lost vinegar sachet had gone. It did not take him long to finish his supper, and he soon returned to join Richard, in the main lab.

He walked over to Richard, with a full and satisfied belly, and said "What's next Richard" Richard said "Freezing does affect them, but perhaps we need something else alongside the liquid nitrogen" They continued working together, trying several more substances. They froze the creature then applied many different chemicals, until exhausting all supplies and all the ideas they had. They stood away from the terrapod and pondered their lost cause. Richard talking to the terrapod, as if it understood him said "How can we kill you my friend?" Richard said "It's no good we need more things to try Darren. I'll get in touch with the pharmacy, if there's anyone still around" Darren replied "Okay, I'll get the beast back into the tube. If you get yourself in position, we'll put it back, until we get more supplies"

Darren went to the terrapod, but it was now fully defrosted. The oil beneath it was also showing distinct signs of drying out. The terrapod sensed his presence, and suddenly jerked upwards, breaking one of its bindings. Richard manoeuvred the grabbers quickly over the terrapod, and held it tight. Darren thinking it was secure released the other two unbroken straps. Nothing happened to start with, until Richard lifted the beast clear of the plate. The terrapod flattened its back and tried moving towards Darren, with nothing solid beneath it to grip, it failed miserably.

However, Richard dropped the parasite onto the plate, causing Darren to react by moving his arm. The vinegar sachet fell from

Darren's sleeve, straight on to the back of the terrapod. Both men moved backwards out of jumping range of the parasite. They quickly found themselves watching its movements. The terrapod sat silently still for a brief second, before it began attempting to move. It slowly and repeatedly, tried moving up and down, trying to rid itself of the sachet on its back. They studied it for several minutes, watching the contents start to leak over the parasites back. Everywhere the vinegar touched, it scorched the terrapod. Then a pungent burning smell filled the room. When the contents had finished leaking, the terrapod appeared to have severe mobility problems. Although both men were easily within striking distance, it was unable to attack, despite its hapless attempts at moving.

The vinegar began making a large indent in the top of the parasite, and it was clearly in pain. Richard and Darren scrutinised the stricken terrapod, fixating on its apparently melting flesh. Darren said "Looks like you're not the only who doesn't like vinegar Richard!" Richard laughed and said "This gives us fresh ideas on how to conquer the beast, perhaps we could be on to a good thing here. Best I keep some vinegar on me, in case one of these things fancies me as dinner" He added "Well done Darren!" Richard patted Darren on the back then both men decided it was time to get the parasite back, to where it belonged, inside a safe prison tube. Richard immediately rang the pharmacy, sounding very optimistic as he ordered many different types of acidic products to try.

At ten o'clock, several substances duly arrived, so both men set themselves a stern quest, to find out which acidic substances had the strongest effect on the parasites. They were very determined, working through the night, until they had a positive terrapod cure that could be used on a large scale. They found several acidic substances that worked, by subduing and killing the parasites, but by far the best was sulphuric acid. Sulphuric acid destroyed the parasite speedily if used neat, so would mean keeping casualties down to a minimum.

Richard informed the hospital staff of his findings, but without enough acid products inside the hospital, they were unable to go on the offensive against the parasites. The amount of terrapods outside the hospital walls was also unknown, but it could serve as a defence, should terrapods breached the walls. The hospital management informed the local radio station, and many media facilities, in a bid to enlighten people, on how to defend themselves against the parasites.

****** 

The Ellis family, Pete, Jan and Bentley arrived in the Hogg's Back village, near Guildford at ten o'clock. They drove up the stone drive of their house, passing the neatly pruned trees, to a traditional brick built house. The Ellis car pulled up in front of their garage. Pete and Jan's van, followed behind them. Then both parties exited their vehicles, and walked towards the front door. Dave opened it, letting Mary, Joe and Thomas inside then asked Pete, Jan and Bentley to follow them inside.

They were very weary after their journey, so quickly settled down to a warm drink. Meanwhile, Mary took the boys upstairs and prepared them for bed. Bentley followed, because Joe and Thomas called him, until Jan said "Stay Bentley, this is not your house" Mary said "That's okay, he can go up if he wants" Jan allowed Bentley to follow, but said "When they have gone to sleep, send him back down, because we'll be leaving soon" Dave hearing her comment said "Please stay the night, it's been a long day. Sleep here tonight, then leave in the morning" Pete looked at Jan and said "What do you think Jan?" Jan said "That's a good idea, thank you, we'd love to"

The boys, now ready for bed, made their way to the bedroom to settle down for the night. As soon as Joe's head hit the pillow, he drifted off to sleep. Thomas although tired, was frightened and could not sleep. He said "The monsters are coming for me. If I sleep they will get me" Thomas very distressed, wanted someone with him all the time. Mary sat with him for a while, helping him settle, but when she tried leaving, he woke, begging her to stay. Bentley the dog sat outside the bedroom listening, occasionally, putting his head through the open bedroom door. He dare not enter though, because at home, he was never allowed in the bedroom. He roamed Jan's house, allowed in most rooms, but only slept under the stairs, huddled in his warm bed. Thomas's distressed voice, made him stay close to his bedroom. Thomas caught a glimpse of the dog by the doorway, looking in at him. Thomas said "Can Bentley stay with me please mum?" Mary replied "I think he will be leaving with Pete and Jan

138

sometime tonight. I'll ask if he can stay awhile, but Bentley does not know you, he may prefer to be with Jan"

Mary left Thomas's bedside and walked past Bentley, downstairs to have a talk to Jan. On arriving she asked "Jan, Thomas wants Bentley to stay with him tonight, as he is frightened of the monsters. Is it okay?" Jan replied "He usually stays under the stairs at home Mary. You can ask Bentley to stay with Thomas and Joe, he's okay with children, and we are staying tonight" Mary said "Okay, do you want to come up with me, to let Bentley know he can stay" Jan rose to her feet, and they both went upstairs.

They arrived at the top of the stairs, finding Bentley waiting obediently outside the boy's room. Thomas however, had got out of bed and was trying to coax Bentley inside, but the dog would not move, until Jan said "You can go in Bentley" Bentley still unsure, turned and looked at Jan. Jan smiled and said "In you go Bentley, stay with Thomas and Joe tonight" Bentley wagged his tail excitedly, allowing Thomas to pull him inside. Thomas immediately settled into bed then said "I wish you were my dog Bentley" Thomas's eyes closed shut as he drifted off to sleep, while Bentley settled on the floor next to his bed, allowing his head to rest on his front paws, happy to be sharing a room with the boys.

Jan and Mary smiled, whilst quietly leaving the room. Then Mary pulled the door ajar, before both of them quietly descended the stairs, joining Dave and Pete, who were chatting about the day's events. Pete was deciding on the best time to leave in the morning. Pete smiled, as Jan entered the room then said "Are they all settled now?" Jan smiled at the sound of Pete's voice and replied "Yes all three of them are content, especially Bentley, he thinks it is Christmas. He loves company when he sleeps" Pete said "What time do you want to leave in the morning Jan?" Jan replied "I think we ought to leave after rush hour, there's no point driving in busy traffic for several hours. If we leave about nine thirty we should be okay" Then all four continued chatting through the evening.

Mary made the first move to bed, going upstairs to sort out bed linen, for the guest room. She offered Pete and Jan the room, thinking they were a couple. They took the offer, despite it being a little awkward.

Pete, prepared for bed in the bathroom, while waiting for Jan to get ready in the bedroom, like a true gentleman. When returning to the bedroom, Jan was already in bed and he offered to sleep on the floor.

He opened out a sheet, spreading it on the floor, while Jan passed him a pillow, to rest his weary head on. He gently took the pillow, pulling it down to the floor. Jan kept a tight hold on it, as her head followed it downwards, until their eyes met. Pete smiled, and looked deep into her eyes. He watched the glisten of love lighten her brow then felt his heart skip a beat, making him a little light headed. It was clear she felt the same, as together like teenage virgins, they were lost for words. However, no words needed here, as they moved ever closer, until their lips touched, then both gave in to their feelings. A gentle kiss followed, a brief hesitation, before their lips reengaged, kissing passionately, until the pillow dropped to the floor.

After a second long kiss, Pete said "I think we had better settle down to sleep now Jan" Jan replied "Yes, it's a lovely day to fall in love, with a man such as you Pete" Pete said "I never thought I'd find love with such a beautiful lady, in such a strange, mysterious adventure" Then with a twinkle in his eye, he said "We should be going to sleep now" He kissed her one more time, then moved hesitantly away, rearranging his pillow, by fluffing it up. Jan smiled suggestively then said "It's warmer in here!" She pulled the duvet back, revealing her naked body. Pete looked towards her, removed his boxer shorts, and slipped into bed. They romantically embraced, kissing passionately, as Pete slid the cover back over them both.

Morning came, with Pete being the first to wake, with Jan's head, propped gently on his chest. He smiled then kissed her forehead. Jan stirred, looking into his eyes then smiling, she said "I thought I was dreaming" Pete said "No it's not a dream. Meeting you was my dream. I used to see you in town, but never imagined we would find love together" Pete smiled at Jan, causing her face to break into a loving glow. Her arms tighten round him, as she moved closer, then they kissed. After a few seconds Jan said "We should get up, mmmm, but perhaps one more kiss first"

After a cuddle, and several more kisses, Pete got out of bed and dressed himself. He lent over Jan then kissed her and said "I'll see if we can borrow some towels for a shower, I won't be long Jan" Pete reluctantly left Jan, unwilling to stop the moment. Jan then watched him exit the bedroom, and close the door behind. Then she heard his footsteps descend the stairs, until he reached the bottom and entered the kitchen.

Pete returned shortly, with fresh towels, and borrowed clothes. He said "Mary has given us some clothes to wear" He bent down, put his arms around Jan, and kissed her. Jan said "You best get showered Pete, I'll follow you shortly" She then blew him a kiss, Pete smiled, leaving her a towel and some clothes. He picked up Dave's spare clothes, taking them to the shower with him, shaking his rear, as he left the room. Jan smiled then started singing, as she assembled her things together.

Pete returned freshly showered, and smelling clean and Jan grabbed him for a cuddle. She eventually let him go, to have her shower. When she returned, Jan found Pete partially dressed. She immediately went to Pete, for another passionate kiss then hugged him passionately, until her towel slowly, slipped to the floor.

Eventually, Pete and Jan arrived down stairs, finding Dave and Mary in the kitchen, cooking a traditional breakfast. Meanwhile, Joe and Thomas were having fun, playing with Bentley in the dining room. Mary greeted the couple with "Did you sleep well? I've made breakfast for us all. I hope you don't mind, but I've made extra sausages for Bentley Jan" Jan replied "That's good of you, there was no need to worry about us Mary" Mary said "It's no problem Jan, I expect you will want to get off to London, on a full stomach" Jan turned to Bentley and said "Bentley you're a lucky boy, you have sausages for breakfast" Bentley knew the word, and excitedly barked, showing his appreciation. Soon they sat down to breakfast, with Thomas and Joe, feeding Bentley extra sausages from their plates.

After finishing breakfast Pete, Jan and Bentley prepared to leave for their journey to London. It was quite an emotional time, after all that had happened. Everyone knew how lucky they were to escape the island alive. They exchanged phone numbers, vowing to keep in touch. Joe and especially Thomas were also sad to see Bentley leave, as they loved having him nearby, making them feel secure. Pete reversed the car out of the drive, and they waved goodbye to each other, whilst Bentley barked. They headed onwards to London, some forty miles away, to an uncertain future.

\*\*\*\*\*\*

Inside the Royal London hospital, events on the motorway near Portsmouth had come to light. Three consultants, Jacob Wells, Bob

Farmer and Chris Johnston had been assigned the unenviable task, of studying the reports of the invading terrapods. They had viewed video footage, but now wanted the real thing to experiment on.

Jacob's role was to lead the taskforce charged with studying the parasites, and he was now phoning around, trying his best to acquire test subjects. The only known subjects were the examples kept in Newport hospital, in the Isle of Wight. Jacob urged the army to get involved, begging them to try to capture subjects from the motorway incident by Portsmouth, but so far he had not received any reply. The predatory instincts of parasites were all too clear, judging from the motorway incident, making the parasites difficult to apprehend safely.

Jacob called a meeting, to discuss what actions to take in order to acquire a terrapod specimen, and possibly a cure to the parasite problem. They all assembled outside his office, while he asked Stephanie, his secretary to let him know if he had received a reply from the army about acquiring specimens. The team swiftly moved into his office, with Bob being the last one to enter. Jacob closed the door behind them while they found places to sit.

Jacob started the ball rolling with "We know these pests are very resilient. In Portsmouth, firearms were used against them, and this was found to be virtually pointless. Larger firearms damage these beings, but the parasite does have the ability to repair itself, albeit slowly. Does anyone here have anything to add?" Chris said "Fire has little effect on them and they're not as active in the dark of night. How about you Bob?" Bob added "They are mostly invading southern areas, but reports say they are spreading in land very quickly, probably to find a more plentiful food source" He hesitated before adding "us!" Bob continued "How do they reproduce?" Jacob answered "That's a good question! The parasite arrived here on the asteroid fragments that fell around the south coast as small buds. They have matured into pod like creatures over several days. Nobody knows if they are adults yet, there could be another step or even multiple steps in their evolution. They have grown up to two feet at present, but size does vary on their food availability" Bob said "Has anyone captured one? Or are we relying on the army?" Jacob replied "A breakout in Newport in the Isle of Wight, meant some terrapods were initially kept as specimens inside the hospital laboratory, but the hospital has been under siege by the pests for some time. Two men have a large amount of knowledge on these pests, after attempting to remove parasites from victims" Chis said "Would be good to get those specimens here and the possibly those men, if they were prepared to come here. We could use their information, and perhaps come up with a solution to the pests quicker if we worked together" Jacob said "It would be good idea, but we have no way of getting to them. Perhaps the army will get hold of specimens for us. In the meantime, I'll get in touch with both the army and Newport hospital, to see if we can get the men here" Jacob concluded the meeting by asking the team to find out more about the asteroid remnants, that the terrapods had arrived on, in the hope it may give up secrets about the life cycle of the parasite, then aid in their destruction.

Stephanie eventually managed to get Richard Heard in Newport hospital on the phone. She asked him to hold, while informing Jacob he was on the line. After Jacob received the news, he immediately stopped working on his paperwork. He was excited to hear from Richard, who possessed first-hand knowledge of the parasites. Jacob's voice could not hold back the excitement, from the fresh input into his studies of the beasts. Richard gave Jacob guided help in the terrapods behaviour, including how to use acidic products, to disable or kill single parasites. Jacob suddenly became keener to get Richard and Darren to London, to help solve the parasite problem. Richard added that Andy price was also a valuable asset, worthy of bringing to London, if possible. However, Richard insisted that trying to get them out of the hospital at present, would be a suicide mission for anyone. He concluded the call, by saying an army would struggle to get through the many terrapods. Jacob, was desperate to get these men on board the taskforce, so after putting the phone down, he set the wheels in motion to make it happen. Firstly, he let his colleagues know, he had been in touch with Newport hospital, informing them about their findings. Jacob then tried his best to find ways of getting the three men to London.

After the meeting, Jacob asked Stephanie to continually pester the army, requesting troops to be sent to release Newport hospital from its captors. When Jacob's request was turned down, he took it upon himself to pester Field Marshall John Henderson personally, as they knew each other well from their early days, when he trained in the army as a doctor. Jacob, eventually convinced Field Marshall Henderson it was worth sending troops to rescue the three men, and hopefully freeing the hospital.

****** 

Shortly after agreeing to Jacob's request, the Field Marshall received bad news. The contingency of soldiers sent to deal with the motorway chaos near Portsmouth, had been found wanting, and had been forced to retreat from the infested area. They lost fifty per cent of the platoon, in less than an hour, from the hungry multiplying terrapod onslaught, forcing them to withdraw to a two mile safety zone, to avoid any more casualties.

The Field Marshall phoned Jacob, asking him what he wanted, but made it clear it would be unlikely they could rescue everyone else inside the hospital. He was prepared to sanction a quick smash and grab operation, where they would allow two Chinook helicopters to drop soldiers with heavy fire power down to the rooftop, to protect people left trapped inside. They would remove Richard Heard, Darren Kennedy and Andy Price for Jacob, if they were willing. The helicopters would be heavily guarded, as many people would want to use violence to hitchhike a lift out of their predicament. A shoot to kill policy would be enforced.

A plan was quickly hatched to rescue the three important men. It would take several hours to coordinate the troops, and helicopters then inform everyone involved. The rescue was set to take place at eight thirty in the evening, because it would be light enough to see, and would give them a working hour to drop everything, including troops, then pick up the three men safely. Also, the terrapods would be less active when the sun went down, and the temperature was cooler. Richard, Darren and Andy were informed they would depart the hospital from the rooftop via a cage, and lifted up to the helicopter. They would be fast tracked to Biggin Hill airport on the mainland for refuelling then transported on to the Royal London hospital. The Royal London hospital already had a heliport above the building, and here the taskforce would be ready to receive the new recruits.

Two Chinook helicopters flew speedily over the Solent, heading towards Newport on the Isle of Wight. It was filled with many heavily armed soldiers, able to take on parasites outside the hospital walls, but this would not be their job on this occasion. Most would be

144

dropping food supplies to the hospital, while others would stay, in order to give civilians protection against the parasites, if the hospital walls were breached.

After reaching the island they flew over Cowes, where below them terrapods and dead bodies peppered the streets and ferry port. The parasites did not discriminate, whether young or old, trapping people in houses, gardens or work places. They had reduced Cowes to a feasting banquet, of human flesh.

The first helicopter arrived at Newport hospital, as four sultry figures appeared on the flat hospital roof top. They were Richard Heard, Darren Kennedy, Andy Price and Angela, a nurse. The helicopter hovered over the four, with the deafening noise of the rotor blades, making the windows vibrate within their frames.

A door opened at the rear of the helicopter, and a large metal cage with eight armed soldiers was slowly lowered, until resting on the rooftop. The soldiers exited the cage then asked for the identities of the roof dwellers. One soldier told the three men to enter the cage, leaving Angela behind. Andy climbed aboard and Darren followed, struggling awkwardly, as the cage moved around in the helicopter's downdraught.

Suddenly, a terrapod appeared on the rooftop. The soldiers positioned themselves between it, and the remaining two roof dwellers. One soldier, shoved Richard into the cage, then looking straight towards Angela he said "You're not on the list, return to the hospital doorway" Suddenly, the terrapod attacked, launching itself at the soldiers. The soldier to Angela's right was hit, and he fell to ground. Its pincers pieced deep into his head, rendering him paralysed in seconds. The soldier to Angela's left, turned to her then said "Get in the cage now!" Then he shoved her forcefully, into the cage. He locked the cage door, signalling to the helicopter winch man above. He returned to Angela, pointing to the terrapod on the floor, and said "You won't make it back alive" The soldier waved at the winch man, who then started pulling the cage upwards. Both the helicopter and the cage of people rose upwards, leaving the hospital.

Richard, Darren, Andy and Angela could only look on, while they watched soldiers shooting terrapods. Many shots tore through the beasts, but several soldiers fell by the wayside, as they cleared a path to the doorway and the relative safety of the hospital. The last soldier in, watched the cage disappear into the rear doors of the helicopter, before beginning its journey to Biggin Hill airport. He picked off one more terrapod, with a spate of bullets, before casually slipping through the open door and into the hospital. Then he pulled it closed, stopping the parasites from following him.

The second helicopter hovered over the hospital rooftop, in readiness to drop more troops. They waited for a signal from the troops inside the hospital. After receiving it, a battalion of troops made their way down, via a second cage. The door swiftly swung open on the rooftop, civilians poured out, waving and shouting thinking they would be saved and whisked off to safety. They ran up to the cage, trying to climb into it. However, the helicopter troops were only there to supply protection and drop extra supplies.

Many terrapods jumped on the rooftop. Then as civilians stepped clear of the doorway, they were quickly ambushed. The soldiers were forced into protecting them on the rooftop, instead of going on the offensive against the terrapods outside the hospital. Many unsuspecting civilians were picked off, and never made it back to the doorway. Many soldiers died trying to protect people, by putting themselves in the line of fire. Eventually, people stopped trying to board the cage and the helicopter lifted high into the night sky. The strong clung to the cage, as the helicopter powered forward. Most quickly fell to their deaths as the cage swung around in the darkness. More managed to reach the safety of the cage, but the combined weight of the cage and the force of the helicopter flying forward, caused the winch to be torn out of the helicopter. The winch man followed it out the rear of the helicopter, as they both smashed into the descending cage before crashing to ground. The helicopter flew on, leaving the scene with both the troops and civilians at the mercy of the parasites.

The first helicopter arrived at Biggin Hill aerodrome, and was quickly met by a small minibus. It transported everyone back to the terminal building, passing the refuelling truck on the way.

Inside the terminal, they found food and refreshments to hand, while they enjoyed a rest. After the helicopter had been refuelled, the minibus returned everyone to the helicopter. They quickly continued on their journey to the Royal London hospital, expecting to arrive at ten o'clock in the evening.

They duly arrived dead on time, and were greeted by the excited taskforce, charged with the unenviable job of finding a cure for the parasites. The new arrivals were chaperoned into the hospital, while the remaining helicopter troops flew off to their next mission.

After more refreshments, Jacob took Richard, Darren, Andy and Angela to meet the taskforce in the meeting room. When everyone was inside, Jacob's first question was to Richard. He asked if he had any specimens for him to work on. The answer he received was a disappointing "No" Jacob cleared his throat, before addressing the whole taskforce "We still need to acquire specimens, has anyone any ideas on how we could do it safely?" Angela said "We had a patient come in called John McIntire, he had a graze on his arm, from the ferry asteroid. John is still in hospital, as he lost his arm. It might be worth checking for terrapods still left on the asteroid remnants" Jacob said "That's a good idea, thank you Angela" Jacob asked Chris to look into it, after debriefing. Jacob added "We need to know everything about these creatures. Why they are here? Where they have originated from? How many are we dealing with, and most of all, how we can eradicate them? They have the uncanny ability to accommodate our environment well, but there must be a thorn we can push deep into the side of these parasites. If we can't find one, they may change our world as we know it, forever"

They continued talking for an hour, before deciding to let the new recruits leave for a good night sleep. Transport was arranged to escort all the taskforce members to a hotel in Islington. This meant that if anyone suddenly had a brainstorming idea, they would all be in the same place. This way they could run theories past each other, even whilst off duty. This was Jacob's idea as he had used this method successfully on guests in the past with excellent results.

## CHAPTER 13

## A REMARKABLE CREATURE

Eight o'clock in the morning, the taskforce finished eating their hotel breakfast. The talk, quickly turned to terrapods, as they run ideas past each other, proof that Jacob's idea of keeping them together had certainly paid dividends. The conversation was soon broken up, by their transport arriving at nine to return them to the hospital.

Jacob set up two teams, the first to study the creature and its habits, because he thought that if he knew how it behaved, it would allow them to predict its future behaviour patterns, allowing them to find its vulnerabilities. The other team was to study its genetic makeup, then possibly come up with a way to eradicate it, whether using conventional weapons, chemical or perhaps introducing it to a deadly virus. Acids, had impacted positively on the parasites, but these poisonous chemicals would also have a negative impact on the environment.

The first team was made up of Bob Farmer, Richard Heard and Andy Price. The second was Chris Johnston, Darren Kennedy and Angela Jones, and Jacob would work closely with both teams, to ensure all information was shared. First they needed samples and Jacob had begged the army to see if they could help out. He had requested samples the night before, asking if they could get some from the original source on the asteroid, to check their habitat before landing on Earth. He had been pleasantly surprised to hear that there was a piece of asteroid, just around the corner sitting inside London University. Chris was charged with arranging for the asteroid samples to be made available to the team, either with or without terrapods.

Chris organised the transportation of the asteroid remnant, and was excited to hear that there were dead terrapods, still residing on it. It was due at one o'clock in the afternoon, and he could not wait to knock on Jacob's door, to update him with the terrific news.

Inside Jacob's office, Chris had just finished informing him of his good news, when the phone rang. Jacob asked Chris to stay with him until he finished his call. Afterwards, he asked him, to get everyone assembled inside his office to give them Chris's news. He had also received news from the army to add to it.

The army had captured two terrapods, one unfortunately still attached to a soldier's amputated leg. Apparently, it was the only way to save the soldiers life at the time. The soldier had given permission for it to be used to help others, hopefully, saving people from the onslaught of terrapods. The other was apparently acting very strange, and had been found, not on a person or animal, but on a small tree, slowly digesting it. They were due at noon, escorted by army guards and they had advised extreme caution whilst handling both creatures and the asteroid remnant.

The taskforce rushed around, setting up a safe room to hold the terrapods. Inside the safe room, there were three compartments, two for the parasites and another one for the arriving asteroid remnant. Each compartment was separated by thick glass, enabling them to observe and experiment on all three items safely. In the meantime, both teams went to work, collating information, by viewing footage of the parasite behaviour so they could best protect themselves.

Twelve o'clock duly came and as promised, the live terrapods turned up and were delivered to the safe room, ready for observation by the two teams. The two terrapods were segregated and protected from contact with the taskforce, by the thick glass screens. The taskforce were concerned, not just for each other, but also they did not want terrapods reproducing and making more parasites.

They had no sooner finished setting up the two live terrapods, when the asteroid remnant turned up, delivered by the University courier. This was put into quarantine with glass surrounding it, but was more easily accessed, because there no dangerous live terrapods reported to aboard.

Three o'clock arrived, with both teams changing from being excited, to just quietly observing the creatures. Cameras were set up on the live specimens so nothing would be missed. They even set a camera up on the asteroid, despite it being suspected of being lifeless. The teams wondered how the parasites had managed to survive on a piece of dead rock, for the length of time it took to travel to Earth.

Bob Farmer's team took the chance of observing the live terrapod, eating slowly through the remnants of the soldier's leg. It was a grisly sight, but they tried imagining the terrapod consuming it as if it was just food. They wanted to find out if it obeyed any rules of our sacred Earth, such as night resting and slowly digesting its food. Chris Johnston's team observed the other terrapod eating through the tree it was perched on. Both teams planned to study the creatures for two solid hours, before leaving one person observing the parasites on each team. Afterwards, they would take shifts in observing them, until they started tests on the terrapods, at eight o'clock in the evening. Jacob would move between teams, collating information from each one. He would concentrate his attention mainly on the asteroid, while seeking Chris's superior geological knowledge on the rock's makeup.

Two hours passed, as Andy continued watching the first terrapod. He wondered why Jacob had given him a position within the taskforce. He was grateful to Jacob for choosing to bring him to London, because inside the hospital his fate would have been pretty precarious, especially if terrapods had found a way inside. How could he help though? He was a surgeon, not a scientist after all and had never been involved with any research into animals, let alone an alien parasite that had hitched a lift on an asteroid.

He observed the terrapod intensely, noting its behaviour as it consumed the fleshy leg. He viewed the parasites tiny shark like razor teeth, as they vibrating backwards and forwards. The teeth also moved in a sideways motion, resulting in the grinding of flesh into a slippery pulse, allowing it to run freely down a throat like tube, deep into the belly of the beast. Andy knew the only way to find out what it went down into would be to dissect it, but at the moment that was not an option with it being so dangerous. Next, he noticed its two pincers, both with a secure grip on the flesh of the leg. The beast used its pincers to pull itself closer to the fresh uneaten flesh, enabling its teeth to stay in contact with the meat. The larger pincer on the top, was injecting a clear fluid into the flesh and it was clearly leaking out around the puncture wound. The creature showed signs of being a lot stronger than its size would allow you to believe.

Next to Andy, studying the second terrapod was Chris, he observed his specimen doing similar actions on the tree stump it graced. Its pincers were locked deep into the bark, requiring great strength to break through the trunk to push deep into the wood, and keep it attached. The teeth on this terrapod, were much larger than the other terrapod, more akin to grinding through plants and trees, not animal flesh. This led him to believe they were looking at two different species of terrapod. The lack of eyes was very prominently missing on both parasites, along with any hint of ears or a nose. Chris said to Andy "They must know how to find prey, but how Andy? How do they know where food is? Heat may work for the terrapod you have Andy, but mine is a plant eater" Andy said "Some good questions, not sure we can answer them tonight. I'd like to know why I was chosen to join you" Chris said "That one I can answer! You are the only person so far, who has had the opportunity of removing any parasite. You removed one from a live host and lived to tell. A lot of surgeons were asked to, but turned down the job because of the personal risks. I think Jacob wants the opinion of a surgeon when the time comes to dissect one of these beasts" They both continued observing and taking notes for the taskforce, until time came for a shift changeover. Richard and Angela soon took over from Andy and Chris, allowing them to attend the meeting room, to discuss their observations.

In the meeting room, the taskforce were slowly building up a picture of the captured parasites habits. Angela being a nurse was the odd one out, as she was not on the original taskforce list. Darren said "Angela's a very good nurse, would she not be better off working in the hospital Jacob?" Jacob said "Well I hope Angela is good! I certainly did not expect her to be on my list, but circumstances meant she could not be left behind safely. So Angela was brought here by the troops. I believe she also has experience with terrapods. She will have a good eye for changes to the parasites, especially when looking at them as patients, she'll spot differences we miss" Quickly every piece of information collated was put on a shadow board, listing all they knew on one side. Then information required was put on the other side, with how to kill them highlighted. Jacob then said "Tomorrow we'll take samples from our captives and the asteroid, perhaps then we can ascertain what they are made of" He added "I'll be receiving more terrapod behaviour information from the battlefield by the Field Marshall's men. They are able to destroy the parasites using heavy weapons, but although this is fine in large unpopulated open areas it's not acceptable in urban areas. We need to combat these pests, before they get to large cities or possibly London"

Richard and Angela continued observing the terrapods until one o'clock in the morning. After talking to the team, they agreed to continue working through the night, leaving the rest of the team to rest up in the hotel until the next day. Richard and Angela would then go to the hotel and get their rest, returning in the afternoon to resume work. Both teams agreed to take turns working the night shift, because the terrapods could never be left unsupervised, for any reason.

Through the night, Richard and Angela constantly drank coffee, to stay alert. They concluded that both terrapods were not as active during the night, because of the dark and cooler temperatures. During the night they amused themselves, by turning the lights on and off, noting changes within the terrapods behaviour. When the lights were turned off, the terrapods stopped grinding on their food, and rested. As soon as the light was turned on, they resumed grinding on their food source. They turned the temperature down several degrees, leaving the light on and this had a direct effect on the rate the food was consumed. They noted all changes, writing them down along with the temperatures.

Eight thirty in the morning, the rest of the taskforce turned up to work early, guessing Richard and Angela would be extremely tired after being awake twenty four hours. Richard and Angela debriefed inside the meeting room with Jacob. Afterwards, their taxi whisked them off to a warm hotel bed. The rest of the taskforce convened in the meeting room, discussing what was to be done next, except Darren who stayed watching the terrapods.

The meeting started with Jacob, informing the team that they would be extracting biopsies from each terrapod, immediately after the meeting. Then they would test the material, to find out what the terrapods were made of. Jacob would remove a piece of asteroid and study it beneath a microscope, so they could learn more about how the parasites had managed to survive on the asteroid, while travelling to Earth. They would keep an eye on the terrapods, feeding them if needed, then watching how they evolved. They already knew they started out as plant like buds, but he was hoping to find more helpful evidence on the asteroid remnants. After finishing, they set off to meet Darren, inside the quarantine area.

They entered quarantine, with everyone except Jacob, moving close to the glazed walls, keeping the terrapods at bay. Jacob made his way to a small locked cupboard on the wall and removed a key from his pocket, using it to unlock the door. Behind the door on top of a shelf, he found some glass containers with steel lids. Jacob took three containers out, one by one and gave one each to both two teams, keeping one back for himself. Underneath the shelf he removed a long thin tool with jaws protruding out of one end, along with a rotating rubber hand grip and some latex gloves. He handed both teams a pair of gloves, until there was only one pair left for him.

After Jacob fitted his gloves he walked over to the glazed window by the first terrapod. Whilst holding the tool, he opened a small door beneath the main window. Behind it was a recess, with a second door at the end. This door could only be opened by removing a small pin pushed through a bracket, on the inner edge of the door frame. On the inner wall sat several brackets, allowing Jacob's tool to be clipped on to it.

Jacob reached inside the box then slid the pin out, allowing him to open the door to the terrapod prison. He clipped the tool to the brackets and slid the tool into the containment prison, until it touched the outer skin of the terrapod. The terrapod ignored the tool, while continuing to feast on the leg remnant. Jacob said "Now the tool is lined up on the parasite we can use the other end to get a biopsy from the beast" He made sure everyone could see, then twisted the rubber handle anticlockwise and the tool jaws opened outwards. Then he said "Now the jaws are open we push hard against the handle, until it enters the parasite. Then twist the handle clockwise to tighten the jaws, then pull hard on the handle and remove a piece of the terrapod" Jacob did as explained with some degree of difficulty, due to the tough body of the terrapod. He eventually came away with a small piece of the beast.

Jacob requested a glass container with the lid open and put the biopsy inside, by releasing the jaws of the tool. Afterwards, he sealed the container, labelling it with "Substance unknown" He locked the access door to the first terrapod and they all went on to the second terrapod, mimicking the procedure.

Afterwards, Jacob moved on to the asteroid remnant, attempting a similar operation, but this did not work quite as well. The rock smashed open into several pieces, revealing a small hollow area inside the asteroid. Inside, they found three tiny red fully grown dead terrapods. One had an unusual grey substance, beneath its lower pincer, that had run down into the inner asteroid. The sauce like substance had partially dried out below the pincer. However, the further away it was from the pincer, the more it resembled the unformed alien buds. The other two terrapods were dead, but no substance was seen being secreted from them. Instead, there appeared to be long indentations stretching along the centre of the parasites.

This puzzled the team, so they looked closely at the front of both terrapods. One had strange pincers offset from its head, which appeared very out of place. The other was similar in appearance, but instead it had two extra stumps, protruding out of the sides of its head.

The confused team wondered what had happened to the two terrapods and talked about it at length. They assumed these could possibly be mutant terrapods that had died when reaching adulthood. They took a sample of the rock, along with a sample of the secreted substance and put it inside a container. All containers were then taken to the lab by Bob Farmer to be analysed.

It was one o'clock when Richard and Angela returned from the hotel, refreshed and ready for Jacob's update. The others, except for Bob were having lunch and they would be returning to the lab soon, to view the specimens more closely. Bob was left watching terrapods, until Darren returned from rushing his lunch down, giving him a chance to eat. Darren said "Off you go Bob, next time I think we had better get whoever looks after the terrapods something to eat, whilst in here" Bob replied "Sounds good to me Darren" Bob quickly went for his lunch.

After lunch, the remainder of the team found the two missing members gathered inside the meeting room. Jacob, asked Darren to join them. He asked Stephanie to stay with the terrapods, telling her to stand close to the quarantine door, but he made it clear, she was not to enter the room. He informed her, that they would be going to the lab for test results and returning shortly.

The taskforce walked to the lab via a long corridor, while Richard and Angela were being informed of the morning's latest events. They arrived at the lab door and Jacob pushed the buzzer on the wall. A voice was heard checking for identities, before the door clicked and allowed access. Jacob pushed the door open and they walked through and were immediately met by a very tall man, with a large bushy beard. Jacob said "Hi John, have you any results for us please?" John replied "I've some for you, but I'm not sure how it will help. The organic makeup of the terrapods is nothing we don't have on Earth, but it is densely packed together, almost like it has been condensed under pressure. We're still working on the rock sample. It has most of the elements found in our solar system, but it also has other unknown elements, that could possibly be organic. We're just not sure yet" Jacob said "Thank you John, we'll take the readout information with us and work on it. Let me know if you get any more results" The taskforce, thanked John and returned down the corridor, convening once again inside the meeting room.

After a brief chat, they headed off to the quarantine area, where Stephanie was watching over the terrapods. They relieved her, and continued studying the terrapods. Darren wandered over to the asteroid, and scrutinised it very closely. Andy soon followed him and pointed towards the two strange looking terrapods then said "Not sure what has happened there!" Darren said "We think these particular terrapods were mutations, perhaps dying while reaching adulthood" Andy said "They are small adults that is for sure, but what of the substance on that one" He pointed towards the terrapod leaking fluid onto the rock. Andy added "It looks like its reproducing! The further away the substance gets, the more it looks like a maturing bud" Darren said "You could be right!" He looked again at the secreted substance resembling the alien form. He scrutinised both terrapods then said "Andy, I think those other two terrapods are dividing in two, just as a virus or bacteria would do" Andy said "If we're right, there could have been more than one type of terrapod on the asteroid. This might explain why some of them attack each other" Both began pondering their theories.

Both men returned to the team, making their observations known. The others listened then returned to the asteroid, to reassess the terrapods in a different light. They reviewed the possibility that these parasites were actually a basic life form. Andy said "If these are basic beings, they could be space fleas that have hopped on to the asteroid to their next host" They appeared solemn, as Angela said "You don't think something could have put them on the asteroid?" Jacob pondered the thought, before adding "I don't think so they are accidental space hikers" Soon Bob was left looking after the specimens, while the others returned to the meeting room. Richard offered to go to the research lab afterwards and find out if John had come up with any more information, and to offer his assistance.

******

Amongst the motorway body remains, the large terrapods released their pincers from any uneaten flesh, and froze in situ. The centrelines of the terrapods began sinking inwards, leaving a clean vertical indent along their backs. Smaller terrapods, continued feasting on the flesh of their victims, steadily building in size until large enough to follow in the same process. Then the trail of terrapods halted on the roadside, just like a huge roman legion, awaiting orders.

The army arrived on scene standing well back, while watching to see what had occurred to make them stop. There was no obvious reason and there was still a plentiful amount of food to be feasted upon. Perhaps the parasites needed time to digest their food. The army decided it was worth taking advantage of the lull, by safely picking off any loose terrapod.

A large built Sargent, called Reg, signalled to his platoon to cease fire and hold position. He moved swiftly to within fifty yards of a terrapod to attain a better view, while continually talking on his phone to his next in charge Dan. No immediate danger presented itself, so he continued walking until he was ten feet away from the terrapod. The stationary terrapod ignored him, so Reg scanned around and viewed many more frozen parasites. Searching further ahead, he looked at the stationary parasites near the severely burnt helicopter wreckage and the many charred bodies. No one could have survived that carnage, so his gaze was drawn along the line of cars trapped on the carriageway. He checked for any survivors managing to escape the onslaught of terrapods. A deadly hush was apparent, but no sign of life was present.

He peered into a two door yellow mini, inside a young woman occupying the driver's seat, was partially slumped over the passenger seat. A terrapod had gnawed through her right shoulder blade, but the beast was no longer on her. She was dead for sure, likely from blood loss and shock. Reg looked towards front of the car then towards the ground, where a terrapod sat menacingly still.

It possessed two small eruptions on the front left hand side of the creature. At first sight it looked like an injury, until he noticed the parasite was in the process, of what he thought was dividing. The growths resembled a pair of evolving pincers. He informed Dan on the phone, before immediately moving further down the road, scanning more crashed cars by the open barrier. The truck was now a black burnt out shell, with a skeletal frame covering the trailer. He walked towards it, passing several dormant parasites. After arriving at the wreckage, he found hundreds of terrapods sitting behind it along the roadside, separating in a very similar manor to the one he had just viewed. Anyone in this aftermath would have stood no chance against the parasites. He turned his back then said "Dan we'll move back and blast this area to pieces. There's nothing we can do to help anyone here, let's neutralise these pests!" He hurriedly walked back to the yellow car. He looked down at the terrapod and said "The sooner we get rid of you from our planet, the better!" He took several strides back, when suddenly he heard a baby crying, coming from the car. He peered into the car, to where the dead woman was slumped. He heard a cry again so moved ever closer, walking around the rear of the terrapod, in case it woke. He removed his revolver, but knew his best hope would be to run behind the car, if spotted. When at the rear of the car he stared down through the rear window. There was a baby seat, but no baby! He scoured the back of the car trying to find it, but it was nowhere to be found. The baby cried again, this time the sound came from the front of the car. He looked back towards the terrapod surely it was not beneath it! The baby cried again, this time, the sound drew his gaze to the inside of the car. He stepped carefully around the terrapod, keeping his eyes trained on it. Then again he looked into the car at the woman. He glimpsed something moving beneath her arm. It looked like a hand, or perhaps a small foot, as it moved occasionally. He moved his phone up to his ear then said "Dan, I think there's a baby in this car, still alive! I'm going to rescue it from the other side. Can you send in reinforcements to assist, there's a terrapod sitting on the ground close to the car. If it moves kill it! Don't worry about me, if it attaches to me I'm dead anyway, just save the child" Dan said "Craig and Woody will come down and monitor the beast"

Dan ordered Craig and Woody, to quickly march down and assist Reg with the baby. They sprinted down then slowly crept up to the yellow car. Craig waved at Reg, to acknowledge they were ready to cover him. Reg went to the rear of the car, poking his head around the other side slowly, carefully checking for lurking terrapods able to give him a nasty surprise. The area was clear, so he continued on to the passenger door.

On arrival, he tried opening the door, but it was securely locked. He peered inside the car. A baby's head was partially visible covered by a mother's loving arm, whilst it supported her lifeless body. Her arm held her body high enough so as not to crush the small infant. The unfortunate mother had protected the baby, whilst the terrapod attacked. Then the terrapod went into separation, stopping it from consuming her body and moving onto the baby. It was too risky for Reg attempt a rescue from the driver's side with the terrapod in waiting.

Reg waited for the baby's eyes to close, he then smashed the window with the butt of his gun. Then put his hand inside, reached down, and unlocked the car. After opening the door he reached inside checking the woman's neck. No pulse found, so he quickly concluded she had been dead for some considerable time. He then tried pushing her body away from the baby. However, her body protected the baby well, as Reg struggled with his one hand to move her, so eventually, he rested his gun on the car bonnet, and used two hands. He shoved her back hard, until her right leg swung outwards hitting the inside of the car door.

The baby came into full view, wrapped in a cosy warm blanket and clearly hungry. The baby's blue eyes focused directly on Reg's eyes and a tear dropped from its cheek, as it immediately started crying loudly. Reg focused on the job of freeing the baby, despite its crying. He managed to inch towards the child, while wrestling it from its mother embrace. This felt like kidnapping, as it did not seem right taking a baby from its mother, but it was a necessary evil.

Craig and Woody watched the terrapod closely, as two extra pincers erupted violently and the parasite divided very quickly. Just a few inches of flesh held the dividing terrapod together. Woody shouted to Reg "Sir! This thing has nearly separated. I think we need to be making a hasty retreat!" Reg acknowledge the request, but continued with the job in hand.

The last of the flesh divided and the parasite separated, with both new parasites, settling on the roadside close to each other. They appeared timid, so the soldiers were unconcerned as they continued monitoring them both.

Reg, by now had a good hold on the baby, whilst removing it from the vehicle. Once out of the car, Reg held the baby securely in one hand then bent back into the car, taking the woman's handbag from the passenger floor. Rapidly, he made his way to the front of the car, before slowly edging over to the terrapod side. He peered over the front of the car to the floor, immediately spotting the dormant terrapods. Then he continued walking out past the car, heading towards the soldiers. Suddenly, he caught a glimpse of movement. He looked down quickly, to see one of the terrapods flinch. Hastily, he ran and caught the soldiers up then said "Can you take the woman's bag from me. It may give us a clue as to who she was and help track down the baby's father. Be careful of the terrapods near the car!" Craig took the bag and watched Reg walk away, noticing he had forgotten his gun. "Sir, do you want me to pick up your gun?" Reg replied "Oh yes please, I forgot about it, it's on the bonnet" Reg continued walking away with the baby towards the troops.

Craig moved towards the car, quickly passing the dormant terrapods. The nearest terrapod twitched, as he passed it. He picked up the revolver then started to return to his colleague. The twitching terrapod, sprung into life, looking for food. Craig was on its menu! Woody, already having spotted the parasite moving, fired a round of bullets into the beast, forcing it against the car wheel. The parasite was still alive after being knocked off balance, but it allowed Craig to escape safely back to his colleague. Both soldiers then fired off several more quick rounds into the beast, causing the car tyre to burst. Both men then swiftly marched back, eventually catching up with Reg and the baby. When with Reg, they kept their guns trained firmly behind them, ensuring they all reached the sanctuary of the troop's stronghold.

When arriving at the stronghold, Reg met with Dan and said "I'll get the baby safely inside the Land Rover, and Craig can take the baby on to the nearest police station. Perhaps they can trace the baby's father in due time. When the baby's safe Dan, you can saturate the terrapods with heavy mortars" Reg began putting the baby in the Land Rover and was shortly joined by Craig.

Craig had managed to find a child seat, to Reg's amazement. Reg said "Where did you get that from?" Craig replied "One of the lads in B Company left it inside one of the vehicles, from when he borrowed it last weekend" Reg said "Not really allowed on MOD vehicles, but very handy nonetheless, say thanks when you next see him next and be sure its returned" Craig handed the woman's handbag to Reg then they rifled through the contents, finding her driving license and a letter addressed to her. It had both the mother and child's name written inside it. The mother was a Marie Tyler and the baby's name was Paige. Reg returned to Craig, and told him to keep it with the baby, he banged on the Land Rover, urging Craig to drive off and get the baby to a safer place away from the battlefield.

Dan, now back on the frontline, watched the terrapods as they sat patiently after dividing. Only one of the parasites from each pair had become active. Several, had pounced back onto existing prey, continuing their feeding habits. The remaining terrapod, was more pedestrian, ignoring existing prey choosing to turn their attentions towards the soldier's. They began taking large jumps in straight lines, heading for the barricaded troops.

Dan made a decision to use all the firepower at his disposal. He unleashed a hail of bullets, blanketing the terrapod front line. Fifty terrapods were hit on the first wave, but only eight terrapods were torn apart, by the enormous deadly firepower. The rest took the bullets in their stride as the slugs disappeared, deep into the parasites flesh. They continued driving forward forcing Dan to order his troops to retreat then commence a mortar attack.

Ten soldiers came forth and began a barrage of mortars, deep into the heart of the terrapod colony. Heavy mortars, alongside several rounds of machine gun fire, quickly lit up the battlefield. The deafening thunderous roar was to give the terrapods a show of human brute strength.

After a short while, Dan ordered a cease fire, enabling them to check on the carnage from the mortar attack. Many bombardment holes were scattered along the roadside, with several cars burning out of control, including the obliterated yellow mini. Terrapods lay dead and charred along with them. Two hundred or more stricken terrapods could be seen, with their lives ebbing away as soldiers watched them change colour from grey to red. However, hundreds more had survived the massacre and they sprang back to life, jumping over the dead terrapods. Some pounced on the severely injured parasites, feasting on their flesh. Dan watched with horror, before ordering another more thorough attack, insisting they used everything to annihilate the pests. This attack on the surviving terrapods was far stronger in its ferocity, as the troops attempted to destroy all the remaining parasites, outright.

The noise from the artillery eventually came to an abrupt halt and a deadly quiet, enslaved the battlefield. Dan searched the smoking roadside, while waiting for the dust to lift high into the sky, revealing a cratered moonscape scene.

The road was quiet and nothing stirred, until Dan said "Right lads, six of you go down through the craters and kill anything that shows any signs of life. Stay in touch and inform me, when it's clear to march onwards. If clear, we'll get more ammunition, then move on towards the outskirts of Portsmouth" Dan was feeling quite smug, as he wandered back towards Reg giving him his report.

Dan caught up with Reg and said "I think we've blasted those little devils out of here Sir! Six men are checking the wastelands, to ensure nothing is still lurking around" Reg said "Are you sure? One of those parasites, resisted two rounds of ammo, and still returned for more!" Dan and Reg then continued planning their next move, involving gradually cleansing the area, then taking them onto the heart of Portsmouth.

Six soldiers sifted through the decimated roadside, but found nothing alive, save a few terrapods. They were quick to put them to death, by bayonet or by heavy gunfire, cutting them to shreds. The soldiers continued searching through the charred mess and onto the undamaged road behind. No terrapods were present, so they continued onwards a little further. The dead quiet of the road, showed no sign of parasites, as a soldier phoned Dan informing him the route was clear. Dan received the call, while talking to Reg. After they briefly conversed they agreed to move the whole company forward through the carnage.

Reg moved the platoon forward using the grass verges, to avoid the resulting craters, caused by the bombardment. The company arrived a short distance behind the soldiers. They began setting up camp providing protection for the soldiers, as they searched further down the road. Dan promptly ordered the soldiers to move forward again, but this time they had cover, in case any problems arose. The soldier's carefully moved along further, where they approached a nest of terrapods. The soldiers immediately called in the bad news, requesting permission to retreat, to allow a complete bombardment of the local area.

As the soldiers retreated, one noticed several terrapods, surrounding the grass verges behind them. He warned the search party, while giving the order to shoot on sight. Lifting their guns to waist height, they unleashed several rounds into the terrapods, thinking one or two parasites must have escaped the earlier barrage. Terrapods came pouncing out the verges towards them, first one, then two, three, four, five and then a large batch hopped out from a hidden ditch, and headed towards them. One soldier phoned Dan and said "There are hundreds of them, we don't stand a chance!" Dan immediately ordered the rest of the troops to give supporting cover to the soldiers, but it was too late, they were being swallowed up quickly, after being outflanked by the hordes of terrapods. One soldier escaped the terrapods by jumping over the central barrier, only to be caught by parasites waiting for him on the other side in the densely wooded area. All soldiers quickly succumbed to the terrapods, amidst the futility of the covering fire.

This was not what Reg or Dan had envisaged, and they now required more ammunition to take on this large infestation. It was decided to retreat this time, whilst Reg made a call to Field Marshall Henderson on his radio. He requested more fire power and air support, allowing the infantry more protection, as it would be suicide without it.

## CHAPTER 14

## A WARNING IGNORED

News of the goings on near Portsmouth came through to the lab quickly, confirming their worst fears. The terrapods had the ability to divide and multiply, similar to a single celled organism. This was very disturbing, despite shedding light on their reproductive cycle. However, it did not give them a logical reason for the budlike creatures that had been seen. Did the creatures have several ways of multiplying? It was now imperative to find a more potent weapon, other than the gun, perhaps a chemical weapon, that had little effect on life on Earth, but deadly to the alien invaders.

Jacob organised a meeting at eight o'clock in the evening, with everyone present. He had more important information from the land force, engaging the small pockets of terrapods and invaluable knowledge of the bigger picture around the world, it was unfortunately, not good. Jacob was under pressure to produce results, as he proceeded to inform the whole team of his information. At the end of the briefing, he said "Any questions?" He was met by a barrage of questions, but in the end, he began from his left, with Bob. Bob asked "We can use chemical weapons on these beasts, as certain types of acids, are the best option at present, but if these chemicals get into the water supply they would be detrimental to all life. Does the government approve of their use?" Jacob replied "Bob, I have assurances from the top, that if need be, the chemicals are to be used, no matter the consequences on the environment. Safe guards are being put in place for the water system, as we speak. Richard!" Richard asked "We have pockets of these terrapods in the south at the moment, but are they heading this way?" Jacob replied "Yes, is the simple answer, these things are heading to any food source. We are expecting them to arrive in London soon, if they cannot be stopped. We are unsure of the life cycle of a terrapod yet. Do they feed, then rest? Do they feed then multiply, or are they just a relentless parasite, that does not stop, until it reaches a natural death, whenever that may be?" Andy asked "How many other countries are having similar problems?" Jacob replied "I know personally that the Prime Minister was informed by other foreign ministers, that Ireland, France, Germany, Finland, Denmark, Sweden, Holland, Poland, Russia, Ukraine, America and Canada are reporting problems. We think there must be other countries with the infestation as well, but until they admit to it they are unconfirmed" Chris asked "Have they any solutions yet? Are we allowed to share in their information?" Jacob said "Chris, they are in the same position as us, in fact we are more useful to them at present, because the terrapods are more advanced here. We must presume the terrapods will take the same evolutionary pattern all over the world" Darren asked "Has the public been informed?" Jacob answered "They have been informed of a small infestation, under control in the south. We know the public will eventually find out how bad the infestation is then panic will set in. We have to stop the terrapods and so prevent that happening" The last question came from Angela "What if we don't find a cure, can we live with these things?" Jacob replied "I'm not sure! We need to find out how these things exist, so we can at least keep them in check, even if we can't eradicate them" Jacob concluded the meeting and they continued their duties, determined to find a solution.

 They decided to split into two teams, working both day and night, to keep the research on going. Bob, Richard and Andy would come in at seven in the morning, and work until seven in the evening, whilst Chris, Darren, and Angela would take over afterwards. Then after a week they would change shifts, to be fair to each team. Jacob would come in at six in the morning for the handovers, ensuring all information was collated together. Then he would work until nine at night, with important meetings being held at seven when required.

\*\*\*\*\*\*

Nine in the morning at 10 Downing Street, with Prime Minister John Milton keeping abreast of happenings around the south coast, and the ensuing trouble developing inland. Also present are his Foreign

Minister Jeremy Carlton and David Monahan, his Public Relations officer. They were discussing the terrapod invasion and what should be done. John asked "Jeremy, what's the situation in Europe, have they gone public yet?" Jeremy said "No, they're holding back, the French think they can move people away from the infected coastal areas. They are claiming that a train of zoo animals has been derailed and the animals have escaped. I'm not sure how long they will be able to keep that story up. They are only able to get away with it, because the areas infected have only a few isolated small villages. The French army have blocked everything going in and out of the areas" John said "How about Germany, Holland and the other countries?" Jeremy replied "Germany had a small infection, close to the border with Poland. The Germans are claiming that stray wolves from Poland, have ventured into the forests, and have begun attacking people holidaying in the forest and lakes. The Polish are disputing the story, claiming that the Germans had an experiment go wrong, and have created some sort of rabid leech. Both, the Germans and the Polish, are keeping it quiet from the public so far, saying that they are just isolated attacks" John asked "These parasites are getting to be more than a nuisance, can we really hide up the problem Jeremy?" Jeremy answered "Possibly, if the research in the Royal London comes up with a workable solution within the next few days. I think we'll maybe get away with it. We can make up a cover story to hide it" John said "It's my head on the block, if these things get out of control!" He turned to David then asked "David, can we cover this up for two weeks, to give the taskforce a chance to find a cure for these parasites. Then the army could come up with a strategy to defeat them, without too much collateral damage" John added "Field Marshall Henderson has requested, or should I say insisted, that air support is used, to ensure the safety of his ground troops, near Portsmouth. The public will ask why we're sending helicopters into residential areas" David said "Don't worry we'll have the situation under control in a few days. If the papers do pick up on the story, it will blow over after a week or so, when the public lose interest" John said "Okay, we'll run with it, let's see what happens for the moment. We'll inform the public that the helicopters are there for a small outbreak of rabies. Can you let the press pass on the story about the helicopters David? If people mention anything, just say it was rogue foxes that caught rabies, causing an epidemic around Portsmouth. Then tell them, the helicopters are being used to track animals across the countryside" He added "I'll speak to the Royal London personally for an update on the situation. Hopefully, they will have found something to help us through this awkward situation" He concluded the meeting after shaking hands. Then John left the room, soon to be followed by David, then Jeremy.

The Prime Minister walked into his office, sat down, then picked up the phone and rang his secretary. She quickly answered and he said "Carmel, can you get the Royal London Hospital lab on the phone please. A man called Jacob Wells, put him straight through to me Carmel" John then continued viewing reports marked "Urgent" on the current terrapod activities.

Carmel's phone rang and she answered "Prime Minister's office, can I help you?" Jacob replied "I've received a call from your office, requesting I contacted the Prime Minister immediately, my name is Jacob Wells" Carmel said "Yes Sir, he's expecting your call, please hold while I let him know you are on the phone, Mr Wells" "Okay" came the reply. Carmel rang the Prime Minister and said "Sir, I have Jacob Wells on the phone, do you want me to put him straight through?" John answered "Yes please Carmel, I don't want to be disturbed until I've finished the call, thank you" Carmel replied "Okay Sir, I'll put him through now" Carmel returned to Jacob "Mr Wells, I'm putting you through to the Prime Minister now" "Thank you" Replied Jacob. John said "Hi Jacob, have you a cure for me yet?" Jacob answered "No Prime Minister. We know that acidic substances have a negative effect on their health, but you need a lot of it to kill them completely and it would be detrimental to the human population. These parasites are very dangerous and we still don't fully understand their life cycle yet. We know they multiply like a basic life form, but we are confused with the budlike creatures" John said "Thank you Jacob, we intend to keep this matter quiet for now. The terrapods are advancing in land and the army's struggling to hold them. We have sanctioned air power against them, but we are concerned about the casualty count. We're not sure if conventional weapons will be effective on the parasites. We need a chemical weapon quickly Jacob" Jacob replied "Sir, we are working around the clock, but these things are not of this Earth, and have no internal organs as we know! We are doing our best!" John moved the subject on and said "I'm keeping this from the public, just to prevent mass hysteria" Jacob replied "You do need to inform them, or you could be swamped with these things sooner than you think John. At least warn the public, giving them a chance to escape the infected areas" John said "We'll move people from the infected areas and we'll put out warnings, telling people to seek refuge in houses, against the acidic products, if we use them" Jacob said "John, if these terrapods get into the houses the people are as good as dead. You need to move people away from the infected areas. This will starve terrapods of food, then you can wait until nature takes its course, because these parasites need to eat to survive" John asked "Where have they come from and why?" Jacob answered "Not from our universe! We think that they have possibly hitchhiked on the asteroid, then got lucky landing on Earth. I'm not sure we can get rid of these things for good, but we need to warn everyone, of what might be around the corner, if these parasites can't be eliminated" John pondered Jacob's point of view, before he said "No Jacob, I've talked to my advisers. We all think the same we'll keep the terrapods secret, whilst monitoring the situation. If the army can't find a way to keep them in check, I hope I can rely on you to find a solution" Jacob said "Has the outside world found a cure yet?" John answered "No, not yet, don't let us down Jacob!" Jacob said irately "I work on finding cures not miracles John! Tell the public, let them decide" John concluded the call, with "Thank you for keeping us updated Jacob, please let me know if you have any more useful information. The public doesn't need to know, so keep this under your hat, for now. Thanks for now, goodbye Jacob" Jacob, feeling dismissed and with an air of disappointment, said "Okay, good bye John"

******

Two o'clock in the afternoon at the Ellis's house in Guildford. Joe and Thomas were playing in the garden, bouncing on the trampoline. Mary's in the kitchen, clearing up after lunch and Dave was sat on the chair inside the living room, reading the newspaper with the television on in the background. Dave placed the paper on a table next to his chair and began to rise, he moved towards the television, about to turn it off after the boys had left the cartoons on.

Suddenly, the cartoons were cut off and a newsreader appeared on screen, announcing they would be going over to their political editor soon, at 10 Downing Street for an important announcement by the

Prime Minister. Dave thought this must be important coming from the Prime Minister himself, so he sat down and began watching. The picture immediately changed to a view of 10 Downing Street and a smartly dressed blonde woman, holding a microphone. She said "This is Jane McArthur, at 10 Downing Street. We're waiting for the Prime Minister to make an announcement, about reported problems around the south of England" She turned towards the door of 10 Downing Street and the camera zoomed in to the front door. A few seconds later, the policeman moved to the right and the door opened. The Prime Minister exited, with an entourage of ministers. The camera closed in on him, as Jane followed him getting as close as possible. She unceremoniously, shoved her microphone towards him. He said "We have lots of reports of trouble near Portsmouth and Southampton, and we're warning people to stay away from these areas because of a rabies outbreak. Our troops are cleansing the infected areas and will be culling any animal suspected of carrying the infection. There are several fatalities, so we would strongly recommend the area is avoided. The army will stop anyone entering the infected areas. They are using lethal force, along with helicopters, so it is imperative everyone avoids the areas, as there is a risk of death from the rabid animals" He stopped for a while, then said "If you have any questions, I'd be happy to answer them" Jane said "When will the areas be cleared of the infected animals and how dangerous are they?" The Prime Minister replied "We're not completely sure how far it has spread, so we are isolating a large area to keep the public safe. We hope to clear all areas within two weeks, but if it does take longer, we'll let people know" Jane said "What about the people displaced from their homes?" The Prime Minister replied "We're working on that. I've been informed that within a few days, small prefabricated units will be erected near the outskirts of London, this is to house people with nowhere else to go" The Prime Minister added "This is an unusually large infection, that has never been seen on this scale in Britain before" Jane said "Some people have reported seeing grey animals resembling a sort of land ray, have you heard about this?" The Prime Minister said "I've heard the rumours, but there is no truth in it!" The Prime Minister, somewhat flustered along with his entourage, quickly manoeuvred away to his waiting car, avoiding any more awkward questions. Jane concluded the interview with "That was the Prime Minister, commenting on the commotion down south. He denies rumours going around of strange animals, seen near Portsmouth. He has confirmed that rabies was the reason for the strange deaths, in the towns and villages in southern England. Back to you in the studio" The screen quickly changed back to the studio.

Dave finished watching the Prime Ministers stern denial, of any problem. He immediately went to the kitchen and told Mary. Mary said "That's just lies! These things are highly dangerous and not just out of control rabid animals" Dave said "It sounds like these parasites are moving further in land, searching for more food. They could be heading our way" Mary said "We may have to vacate the house and move northwards, if they get nearer" Dave answered "They are thirty miles away from us at the moment, I think we need to find out more, and make a decision on what to do. It's clear the government are hiding up the truth. They haven't even mentioned the Isle of Wight and the problems over there. I'll contact my brother in London to see if we can stay there before the parasites turn up on our doorstep" Mary said "Don't tell Joe or Thomas yet, perhaps the army will sort it out" Dave said "Why don't you check out what's going on near Portsmouth on your tablet, to see if the army have it under control" Mary replied "Okay"

Mary went upstairs and fetched her electronic tablet from the bedroom then returned to the living room, and settling down on the chair that Dave had once sat on. Dave smiled, then commented "Lost that chair then!" He moved closer to Mary, peering over the back of her shoulder, as she typed "Problems near Portsmouth" It wasn't long before disturbing images appeared on screen of people being attacked by terrapods. One image showed a man exiting his car while holding his phone in the air taking pictures, until a terrapod catapulted into his chest. Another image came up of people exiting cars then running into a line of waiting terrapods. A large man was caught by two terrapods. He fell backwards, trapping a woman beneath him. The photographer kept the camera focused on her as she tried escaping, but after eventually managing to break free, a second terrapod pounced on her, embedding itself deep into her face. She slammed back to ground, with blood trickling along the floor from a head wound.

The next video zoomed into a small yellow car where baby Paige was found. Inside, a woman tried frantically to get the baby out of the rear of the car. She managed to free the baby and get her to the front, by manoeuvring her carefully between the head rests. The

171

mother placed the child on the front seat. She then tried reaching backwards into the car, to get a blanket. Suddenly, a terrapod landed beside the car door. Her window was wide open as she watched it prepare to pounce, knowing her fate was likely sealed. Too late to close the window, she chose to lean across the baby, hoping the terrapod would not know baby Paige was there.

The terrapod knew they were both there. It pounced through the open window, landing on the woman. In her last saving effort, she rested her arm over the baby, to conceal and protect baby Paige from any more terrapods, also ensuring she avoided suffocating her from her body weight.

Another phone video, a woman's voice could be heard commentating over the pictures "As I look around, I can see the many fallen victims. These grey ticks, hook on to you, slowly consuming your flesh. None of the people here stood a chance and I'm stuck in the middle. I can't get out, because the parasites are surrounding me. As soon as I move, they will latch on to me" She panned the camera round, showing a grisly picture of the many victims strewn across the roadside, partially eaten, with many smaller adults and children almost completely consumed. The camera then clicked and stopped as it turned off. It shortly resumed, with the camera panning as she spoke "All these people have been eaten after being paralysed, most have seen other victims die first. The fear was plain to see, despite being frozen in time, awaiting their last breath" She panned over to an elderly man, and said "He's nearly gone, the parasite will want more food after finishing him and will come looking for its next meal. If I don't get rescued soon, it will be me!" She panned the camera, showing views of other victims, who were but minor flesh and bone scraps. The camera stayed viewing the haunting remnants, before silently switching off.

Shortly afterwards the pictures returned, this time it was aimed towards a terrapod, sitting ten feet from the photographer as she said "This will more than likely be my last stand. The parasite knows I'm here, it's moved closer to me. I'm keeping quiet, in the hope it won't get me. I will soon make a dash through the gauntlet of flesh eating ticks, probably dying while trying to escape. It does not look like anyone is coming to save me. I've said my goodbyes to loved ones, my name is Julie Walters, please remember me!" The screen went black and fell eerily silent.

Dave looked solemn, as he said "Poor girl, she didn't stand a chance. How can the government hide this up? Where are the army and police?" Mary replied "What if they can't stop these things? They certainly are not rabid animals, more like big fleas" Dave said "I'll contact my brother again I think it is time to leave for London. Clearly the government are hoping it will clear itself up, as if by magic"

******

Seven days passed inside the Royal London hospital, Jacob and his team had manufactured a new weapon, involving acid. Jacob called a meeting at eight o'clock in the evening, to talk about a good way of dispensing the chemical. He did not want to inform the Prime Minister or the army, until they had properly tested it on live subjects. There was also a downside to the chemical that could not be avoided. Everyone convened inside the meeting room, ready for debating several theories, and hopefully the answers.

Jacob started the debate by saying "Richard's idea of using acid against the terrapods is a well-founded one. We already knew the acid would have an effect on the parasites, but did not know which type was the best to use to halt the parasite? There are downsides to consider as well" Jacob looked towards Richard and said "You carry on Richard" Richard continued with "Thank you Jacob, but let's make it clear, this is a united effort we're a team and not everything is crystal clear yet. The creature is sensitive to acids. We tried various types with varying results, all have been positive in at least slowing the creature down. Some will burn into the flesh of the parasite" Darren said "Which one is the best Richard?" Richard replied "Two acids have had the best results, the first being good old vinegar. Acetic acid if strong enough will burn the parasite, impeding its mobility. Unfortunately, you need copious amounts to kill a terrapod outright. The second and most lethal is sulphuric acid, even in low strength it will stop it, but it can recover very slowly over time if allowed to. A medium to high dose will kill the parasite outright, by burning through the flesh turning it into a pungent red liquid, or by burning through the front of the parasite, stopping its ability to feed, thus starving it to death" Chris said "Richard, acetic acid is preferable, but sulphuric acid in strong doses is lethal to humans and plant life. What amount is enough for the beasts, or will we have to accept no go areas in many countries around the world?" Richard answered "This is where hopefully you can help, we need a dosage guide, because the army want to administer the correct amount directly into the heart of the parasitic areas" Angela asked "How will the army do this? That's a lot of acid to administer" Jacob said "Yes, that has to be defined yet, perhaps liaising with the army will help, because just sending missiles into the infected area will work, but it won't guarantee destroying every target completely, even with laser guidance technology" Andy said "Maybe helicopters would be more precise, by administering missiles from a hovering aircraft, because they can get very close to their targets" Angela added "My father was originally a farmer but he retired many years ago. I do remember when he visited an old school friend in California he came back with a fancy idea, for putting insecticides on the crops by using light aircraft. He never used the method, because too many people objected over here and the land he farmed was not considered large enough to warrant it. Surely, using a crop dusting plane, would be a good start in getting a low dosage over a large area, and it could fly slow and low enough, to control the spread" Jacob said "That's a good idea, but it would have some drawbacks, because the acid would not be as lethal in severe rain" Bob Farmer asked "When will we be in position to offer the correct dosage for the army to use? Will the government inform the public, because they deserve to know?" Jacob said "We will work out the dosage over the next week, as for the latter, I'm not sure the Prime Minister and his cabinet will inform the public, unless the parasites end up on their doorstep" Jacob finished up with "We will work hard on the correct dosage together, but there will be no more night shifts. I've arranged for two security staff to watch over the creatures overnight, leaving us fresh and able to work together as a team" Andy said "I can't believe these terrapods just hitch-hiked a lift on the first passing asteroid. Surely, the terrapods would have started out from a planet populated with life of some kind" Jacob answered "I can't answer that, astronomers and scientists on the other side of the pond are working on that question. All we can do is to find a cure for what is in front of us" Darren said "Do you think they were put on the asteroid deliberately?" Jacob said "That's a frightening thought, and one we'll likely never know the answer to" Jacob concluded the meeting with "Let's give the army the right dosage to rid us of these bugs" Then they slowly filter out of the meeting room, with their heads fixated on the job in hand.

Jacob went to his office, closed the door behind him, then sat at his desk, and picked his phone up. He rang Field Marshall John Henderson. The Field Marshall answered "Hi Jacob, how are you? Have you anything for me? We're struggling to keep these pests under control, they've moved to within fifteen miles of Guildford, and they are spreading out along nearby villages. We're having some success destroying them in the open with heavy weapons, but it has decimated the landscape. The problem is, we can't just blow up villages with large populations that are reluctant to move" Jacob answered "I'm good, thanks John. I may have some good news for you, that will at least be less destructive than conventional weapons, but I need to run it past the Prime Minister first, to seek his thoughts. I thought I'd ring you first, as you're in the front line with troops in need of protection" The Field Marshall said "I'm all ears Jacob, what have you? We could do with protection, as I'm losing a lot of troops in close confrontation" Jacob said "Acids! Any type of acid will slow terrapods down, acetic acid even when thinned down, will effectively stop any attacks on an individual trooper, but for a larger more permanent cure, we need to give the terrapods a high dosage of sulphuric acid. Several methods have been proposed on how to administer the lethal dose. We have considered scatter bombs for smaller pockets, but one of my staff has suggested using crop dusters to spray larger areas very quickly. Then you could move in, using spray guns to eliminate any surviving terrapods" The Field Marshall replied "Sounds good to me, it will certainly stop my troops being put at risk in the large areas, but what about built up areas Jacob, will the Prime Minister go for it? It could contaminate the water supply, along with the health of anyone staying in the vulnerable areas" Jacob said "If we do not wipe these things out, they will use us as a food source, and they will keep multiplying until the south is saturated with parasites. After a month, the parasites will move northwards, in search of more food. Then they will move on to the rest of England, Scotland and Wales. Only small pockets in Scotland, the Channel Islands and the Isle of Man, will be left untouched. The rest of the country will be in hiding from parasites, too scared to venture outside, leading to the starving people turning on each other, as survival of the fittest engulfs the nation" The Field Marshall said

"In close up fights, we'll implement the acid for protection as advised and we'll wait for the Prime Ministers reply on the aerial bombardment, although if the situation gets grave, we may have to bypass his permission" Jacob said "Okay John, I'll ring the Prime Minister urgently, hopefully you'll get an answer by today. Best regards John" The Field Marshall said "Good bye" then both men put their phones down.

Jacob immediately rang the Prime Minister's office. The Prime Minister immediately picked up his phone. Jacob said "Hi John, its Jacob here" The Prime Minister replied "Hi Jacob, how are things? Do you have any news for me?" Jacob said "Yes Sir, we have found a weakness in the terrapods armour, and the word is acids!" The Prime Minister was somewhat baffled, as he repeated "Acids! Jacob what do you mean?" Jacob replied "The terrapods weakness is acid. Acetic acid will disable them for short periods, enabling people to escape, or perhaps capture or cull the parasites. Sulphuric acid will destroy them, causing them to disintegrate into a liquid mess. I've talked to Field Marshall Henderson already, we think the best method is to use crop dusters to administer a high dosage, that would be lethal to the parasite" The Prime Minister said "Well that's good to know! Sulphuric acid is a nasty chemical, what about the public?" Jacob said "The public will be at risk from any acid, especially if it gets directly on their skin or into the drinking water. I would suggest that everyone is moved away from the infected areas, before a blanket spreading of acid commences. The army would need to go in afterwards with protective clothing, to kill any surviving parasite" The Prime Minister thought about it for a while, before saying "I'm not sure that would be a good idea. Large areas of the country would be no go areas for up to three years, while a clean-up operation took place, removing all traces of the acids. Can we water the acid down Jacob, so the effects on the environment are less destructive?" Jacob said "Thinning the acids down would not guarantee total eradication of the parasites. I think, keeping the acid neat, is the only way to be sure, otherwise they will invade every part of the land, making it almost impossible to eradicate them. They could wipe out mankind, or even take over as the prime predator on this planet" The Prime Minister thought hard then said "I'll have to put this through parliament to see what the cabinet think. The financial implications are enormous, with the cost of relocating that many people somewhere safer possibly crippling the country" Jacob replied

"There may not be a country if these parasites are allowed to spread up to London's suburbs, then into the city itself. Think of the amount of people inside London alone. The terrapods will use them all as a food source. I beg you to stop them now, before it is too late" The Prime Minister said "I'll get back to you this afternoon and let you know a decision Jacob, but in the mean time I'll sanction the use of local chemicals for personal protection" Jacobs last words were "Okay Sir, let me know, because the army are waiting for the go ahead. Will you tell the public about the parasites?" The prime Minister said abruptly "No, it will only cause mass hysteria and looting in the streets, it's not in their interests. I'll be in touch Jacob, good day" Jacob put the phone down disappointed, because the use of chemicals was not assured. Also, the Prime Minister had chosen not to inform his public, leaving everyone inside the infected areas a potential food source for the parasites.

Two thirty in the afternoon at the lab, with Jacob talking to Chris after spraying a fine sulphuric acid mist onto the first terrapod specimen. The result was clear to see, the parasite melted in front of their very eyes, leaving the two bony pincers lying on the containment floor. The next one was duly sprayed with a watered down version of the acid, resulting in, only a partially melted terrapod.

A live rat was carefully positioned inside the containment area, close to the creature. The terrapod, unable to move, waited for the rat to venture close to it. Then a pincer reflex action, clamped it tight. It soon started gnawing through the rat. The acid damaged area soon began regenerating itself. This was disappointing for the team, along with visual evidence of the need to use neat acid, to be sure of parasite eradication.

Jacob's phone rang, he quickly answered it. It was the Prime Minister. He said "Are you free to talk somewhere private Jacob?" Jacob answered "Wait a minute Sir, I'll go to my office" After exiting the containment area, he stepped into his office, closing the door behind him, then said "I can talk now Sir" The Prime Minister said "We've made a decision. I can see your point of view, but it's hard to convince my cabinet to sanction paying the monumental costs involved in relocating thousands of people for years, away from their homes. We have another solution for you and the army" Jacob was perplexed, because he knew the only way to eliminate terrapods was to use neat sulphuric acid, anything less, would mean parasites

177

regaining their original form, and reverting to killing thousands or possibly millions more people. The Prime Minister said "We agree to the use of sulphuric acid, but we want it watered down to the bare minimum. This will shorten time people are absent from homes" Jacob said "With due respect Sir! You need to use neat acid to kill the parasites! If you water it down, they will recover then continue feeding within a very short period of time" The Prime Minister added "It's not up for debate Jacob, I've informed the army of our decision. The mix will be your choice, but we suggest, no more than fifty per cent of acid is used" Jacob felt as if he was being fobbed off, because he had used eighty per cent acid strength on the second terrapod. It had survived, returning to feast on the rat afterwards. Jacob replied "Sir, it's neat acid, or face the consequences of parasites munching their way to parliament inside a few weeks" The Prime Minister said "If it was up to me, I would opt for your solution, but it is a democratic decision and that's final, unless things change or you come up with another solution. Thank you for your help Jacob" Jacob, unhappy with the decision, said "Thank you Prime Minister, I'll thank my team on your behalf. You are making a grave mistake, but please inform me if things change"

Jacob left his office, with the look of a man who had just received a death sentence. He then entered the containment room, where inside, his team were still busy working. He said "I've just had the Prime Minister on the phone, the government have decided to use sulphuric acid" The team looked pleased, until he added "In a watered down version to reduce the effect on the environment. They need to return people to their homes quickly after the clean-up operation because of the cost implications" The team's optimism, quickly soured and Darren said "The government are making a huge mistake. They will be up to their heads in terrapods, unless they take drastic measures now" Jacob said "I have something personally to say to you all. Thank you for working so hard on this solution, it may be used properly one day, but in the meantime perhaps we can work on making an alternative solution that is more environmentally friendly. Thank you!" He immediately clapped the whole team.

******

The Prime Minister phoned United Kingdom's largest ally, the United States. He called President George Booth, and was immediately put through. The Prime Minister said "Good morning George, how are you and your family?" The president said "We're good here John, how can I help you?" John said "We have a solution to the terrapods here, but how are you coping over there?" George replied "Not good I'm afraid, we're using heavy fire power in the precincts of New York and we have reverted to using the National Guard. We're contemplating removing people from the infected areas and dropping bombs on the highly infected areas" John said "Neat sulphuric acid will destroy the pests best, but we are opting to use it watered down here, in the hope it will have a similar effect. Having strong acid concentrations in towns and cities, would be a disaster with the water supplies, livestock and plant life and totally disastrous for our economy" George said "Good to know we have something that will work, but we think we can contain the terrapods here, our biggest problem is looting and the many property fires erupting everywhere. I've called in the National Guard" John said "The terrapods are more advanced here, as they have been on the ground several hours longer than on your side of the Atlantic, are you sure you can hold them?" George said "Yes, we have several small pockets scattered along a narrow band, stretching across the country" John said "Are you informing the people?" George said "Not at this moment, we're disguising the parasite activity, claiming it's just political rioting erupting everywhere. If we drop bombs on certain precincts, it will be after a full admission of the parasites residing in those areas. We would tell people to get out or take the consequences" John thought it sounded harsh, dropping bombs on populated areas, but he did not imagine it would come to that over here, so said "We won't go that far here, but we'll be using the sulphuric acid in a fifty to fifty mix with water, and evacuating the infected areas. We have reported an outbreak of rabies to the public over here" John concluded the conversation with "I'll be in touch soon George, goodbye" George answered "Be sure and have a good day, and give my best to your family" Both men, put their phones down in unison.

John then made calls to all of United Kingdom's European neighbours, along with the commonwealth nations. Some of the reports he received back were very alarming, with countries destroying whole villages in order to contain the parasites, unfortunately in all of the countries, it was very clear that it had not stemmed the terrapod growth. This led him to believe that there were millions of the pests, many more than ever imagined.

Afterwards, John phoned Field Marshall Henderson, informing him of the latest news. He also told him that the acid manufacturing process had now been started. Pharmaceutical companies would be entrusted to supply all the army's requirements. The government promised to make funds available to aid in the cost. The Field Marshall was given the go ahead to order a squadron of helicopter gunships, along with several light planes to be returned to an RAF base. They would be quickly equipped with crop spraying equipment for the job in hand. The Field Marshall estimated it would take two days for the helicopter modifications. They required brackets to be welded onto the aircraft sides, enabling them to carry the large chemical barrels, and dispensing rails.

After finishing his call to the Field Marshall, the Prime Minister immediately called Jacob, informing him of the finer details of the assaults that were to take place against the parasites near Guildford, Portsmouth and Southampton. The Prime Minister requested that Jacob and his team kept in touch with the army through Field Marshall Henderson. The pharmaceutical companies would ensure chemicals were delivered to the army, and dispersed by the best possible method to all infected areas.

## CHAPTER 15

## ESCAPE TO LONDON

Nearly four o'clock in the afternoon at the Ellis house. Mary removed the last carton of milk from the fridge then made a drink. Then she phoned Dave, who was currently working in Guildford. She asked him to stop off at the supermarket then pick up milk, along with a few other items on the way home. He made a note of the items, then said goodbye. After hanging up, Mary sat down to a hot drink, before starting dinner for when Dave arrived home later.

Dave finished work at five thirty then fetched his belongings, and continued down the lift, to the ground floor. He exited the lift at the bottom, acknowledging the guard as he walked through reception, heading towards the car park. Outside, another security guard said "When will you be getting your car back Dave?" Dave replied "I don't know, possibly, when they allow me back on the Isle of Wight, so I can collect it" In fact, Dave had given up getting his car returned, if truth be known, and was now using Mary's small run around until they had funds to buy another. He soon found Mary's car then got in, setting off towards the supermarket, south of Guildford. It was out of his way, but easier to park there.

After arriving at the supermarket and parking, Dave walked towards the entrance. Suddenly, his attention was drawn to a commotion in the corner of the car park where five people stood, staring at the grass verge beyond the wire fence near the railway tracks. Being curious, Dave moved closer to gain a better view.

He arrived, finding two young youths shouting and waving beside the railway tracks, they were trying to get attention from the onlookers. At first Dave did not see why, and thought they were playing around, but his gaze was quickly drawn further along the track. A third youth was lying face down across the tracks. Dave said to the onlookers "We need to help him or the train will run him over" An old man in front of him replied "Why are they not moving him off the tracks themselves?" He then pointed to a woman and said "The lady over there has rung the services, they will be here soon" Dave moved along the fence, until he was nearly level with the youth lying on the track. He was unable to get any closer, due to several large bushes blocking his path. He wrestled with one of the smaller bushes, before peering over to the man. He could see something on the man's leg. It appeared to look exactly like a terrapod. Dave's worse fears had been realised! The parasites had made it to a large populated city, and more importantly onto the Ellis's doorstep. Dave knew the young man on the tracks was doomed, but the other two men needed to escape the parasites clutches, because more terrapods would be close by.

Dave ran towards the two youngsters then shouted at them to come to the fence and climb over. At first they did not understand, so he tried making hand gestures until they understood his message clearly. They both ran up to the fence and Dave said "There's nothing you can do for him, jump over the fence and get away from the tracks, in case there are more of the parasites lurking. The two young men were distraught and reluctant to leave their friend, but they eventually started to climb the fence.

After climbing over to the supermarket side of the fence, one of the men said "We just wanted to take a shortcut across the train tracks, but we couldn't get through. So we walked further along the line and this thing jumped out of the undergrowth, grabbing Daniel by the leg, then they both fell onto the track. We tried pulling it off, but it made our hands sore" He showed Dave his sore hands. Dave said "You will need hospital treatment for those burnt hands. I'm sorry, but I don't think there is anything that can be done for your friend. We'll see what the police and paramedics say, when they arrive"

The woman, who had minutes earlier phoned the emergency services, said "Has anyone informed the railway, that there is someone on the line?" Everyone shook their heads as she said "I'll find the number, and tell them" A couple of minutes later, she finally got through to a railway employee, and started explaining the situation.

As she talked on the phone, several terrapods appeared beyond the far tracks. They jumped over the tracks, but were unable to breach fence. The woman jumped abruptly and ceased talking in midsentence, whilst rapidly moving away from the fence. After getting her breath back, she continued explaining about the stricken youth, to railway employee. He continued acquiring details, when suddenly she heard the train arriving in the distance. Her voice trembled, as she jumbled her words, until she blurted out "Stop the train now! It's nearly on top of the boy" The man hesitated, before asking her location. She again, with much more urgency, repeated to him "Stop the train now!"

Three onlookers broke rank, and sprinted down the car park, trying to meet the approaching train. They waved frantically at the oncoming train driver. The employee on the phone eventually got the message, and informed the train driver to stop. The driver slammed the brakes on hard. The wheels screeched and smoked, as they gripped the hot steel rails. The occupants were thrown around the carriages, along with their belongings and drinks. Then the train came to a grinding halt, moments from the stricken youth, as he lay motionless across the tracks.

******

The carriage inhabitants slowly rose to their feet and regained their composure. Soon, the internal occupants began questioning the reason for stopping, with many passengers getting very irate. The driver soon calmed the air, by announcing across the speaker system, that there was a young man lying on the train tracks in front of the train. He advised passengers to stay inside the train with the doors closed, until the police and ambulance crew arrived on scene, giving them permission to continue on their journey or to disembark. Many passengers grew impatient and quickly opened the carriage doors and disembarked. The driver repeated his advice, begging passengers to remain inside the train, but many continued ignoring his pleas.

After disembarking the train many opted to walk rearwards, following the train tracks in the knowledge that the last station was only a short distance behind them. Six men however, decided to the walk forward, to check on the young man blocking the train. They past the many passenger carriages, until eventually they arrived at the driver's cab. The first man to arrive looked up at the driver then informed him he was going to remove the boy from the tracks. The driver opened the small side window and said "No, leave him there, let the paramedics deal with him" The man ignored his advice, and continued on to where the youth lay.

He soon found the young man, complete with terrapod on him. He decided to carefully remove the youth from the tracks, avoiding contact with the terrapod. He grabbed the youth and slowly slid him along the ground, until his arm touched the live rail. The young man's body jolted upwards, as electricity surged through him to ground. The terrapods pincers disconnected from the boy's leg, sending the beast hurtling towards the rescuer. Both ended up resting near the car park fence. The man lay motionless on the ground, but still alive. The terrapod flattened its back, launching upwards past the man, coming to rest back on the stricken youth's leg. The sweat poured from the man's forehead, from his near miss with fate. He smiled, as he began pushing his arm downwards on the grassy floor, lifting himself up. His facial expression turned to horror, as he viewed more terrapods in waiting for him. One jumped on him before he could react, his face then kept the distinct look of horror as he slipped quietly back to ground.

The driver, sitting high up in the train cab, watched on as more terrapods appeared menacingly from the grass verges to the right of the tracks. The driver then watched as other men at the front of the train were caught, and picked off by the parasites.

Terrapods, began jumping up at the passenger windows, first breaking the windows, before quickly boarded the train. Once inside, they attacked the trapped and defenceless people, as they desperately tried opening doors to escape. Many escaping passengers were ambushed by parasites, hiding within the bushes.

The driver watched the onslaught, before panicking and moving the train forward. Terrapods, eventually smashed through every carriage window, leaving large chards of glass scattered everywhere inside the compartments. After embarking the carriages, the terrapods went on the rampage attacking all inhabitants. One man manoeuvred past two terrapods as they sat on the floor, but his luck ran out when he literary ran into another perched on the overhead baggage holder. He fell downwards, landing on a protruding chard of glass sticking out of the train seat. The combined weight of him, and the terrapod, caused him to sink slowly downwards, plunging onto the glass, easing the point through his chest, until a small sharp peak protruded from his back, while he gasped his last breath.

The driver continued moving the train slowly, until a thud hit his side window. Looking towards the open window, he found a trapped terrapod, with one pincer caught inside the inner fabric of the cab. He picked up his rucksack with one hand, while continuing to drive the train. He attempted to usher the terrapod away. The parasite was unmoved by his actions, so he remove his other hand from the train lever, enabling him to use both hands. The train came to an abrupt halt, sending the parasite out through the window, and onto the tracks.

A second terrapod slammed into the front screen, causing a large crack. The driver quickly reengaged the power, and the train began pulling forward. The resulting motion, made the terrapod fall to the right of the train, sliding beneath the train and onto the track. The heavy train wheels squashed, then mutilated the parasite. The driver increased the train speed, attempting to escape the infected area. He rapidly passed the supermarket fence, by the many onlookers.

The driver, now feeling relieved, began relaxing, with no more terrapods visible. He bent downwards, resting his bag on the floor, while taking his eye off the scenery for a brief second. When he looked up, a grey coloured object flew up towards the train, smashing through, the already cracked screen. It continued through the glass, perching itself on his face. He slumped forward, whilst gripping the train handle. The train continued accelerating out of control along the tracks, with the snared driver at the helm.

The train eventually arrived at the next station at incredible speed, heading for a stationary train picking up passengers. Many people on the platform heard the oncoming train, and they dived for cover as it sped out of control, ploughing into the standing train.

The speeding locomotive, tore through the stationary train's rear carriage, sending wreckage out all over the platforms, killing several people caught unaware of the impending danger. The rear carriage was instantly peeled open like a banana skin from the force of the train. The speeding train eventually stopped, half way through the following carriage, trapping people inside, leaving the front of the train a tangled mess of twisted metal. The force propelled the stationary train upwards, lifting the driver's cab and the first carriage off the rails, and perched on the platform.

A few minutes later, everything calmed down and all that was left was a deadly silence, with wreckage strewn across several platforms. The dust soon cleared from around the incident area, revealing the true extent of the damage to both trains. The platforms were clear, except for three people, close to where the rear carriage had once stood. A woman in her sixties, unable to escape the wrath of the train, lay on the floor with a piece of steel from the carriage, protruding from her mid rift. Two men in their forties also lay on the floor, both with blood seeping from their chests, but with no obvious reason for their symptoms. They were still alive, but struggling to breathe.

A railway guard entered the platform from the ticket office shouting "Does anyone need help here?" Several people appeared from the front carriage doors of the standing train, letting him know they were mobile, but required help. He quickly advised them to go towards the station ticket office, safely away from the carnage. He quickly turned his attention further down the train, repeatedly asking if help was needed. Three women climbed up onto the platform from the adjacent track. They had jumped underneath the platform, escaping the initial impact and the ensuing airborne wreckage. Their quick reactions had clearly saved their lives. The guard continued downwards until all train carriages had been checked, and cleared of the walking wounded.

The guard shortly began checking the crushed cab, and carriages of the incoming train. Many were mangled beyond recognition, and he felt sure that no one could have possibly survived inside. He peered inside the shredded driver's cab, which was by now embedded within the crumpled rear carriage of the stationary train. The driver was clearly dead inside, with only his blood drenched body parts on show, so he did not dwell too long on the grisly scene. He quickly moved on to the next carriage, this had been crushed into a concertina effect, by impacting the drivers cab at speed. The misshapen carriage sides were intact, but the windows were all broken and lying on the platform floor. At the front of the carriage, many broken bodies had been catapulted forward, and neatly stacked on top of each other.

His eyes turned to the rear of the carriage, there two young lads in their teens, had both hung on to vertical hand bars on impact. They now sat on the floor, looking relatively unhurt from the accident. The guard noticed some grey ray like creatures on both their legs, and the lads appeared very quiet. He moved further along the train, to see if he could help them.

He arrived at the carriage doors by the lads, quickly pushing the exterior door button, in a failed attempt at opening it. He grabbed the manual door handle, forcing one of the doors open, allowing him to squeeze inside. He bent down to the first boy, asking him his name. After receiving no response, he tried shaking his arm to attain a reaction. Several failed attempts later, he felt for a pulse on the boy's neck. After finding a strong pulse, it convinced him, the boy was alive. He surveyed the boy's leg, checking out the strange creature, quickly deciding not to remove it. This was a job for the medical staff, perhaps possibly a surgeon, he thought. He turned his attention to the second boy, who was in a similar position, with yet another creature at home on his leg. He decided it was time to get help for the boys, as quickly as possible.

The guard leaned towards the open carriage door, poking his head outwards searching the platform towards the entrance. He watched several officers running towards him. Then shouted "In here guy's, there are two boys in here with bugs on them!" After they arrived, the guard left the authorities to deal with the two boys, while he moved on to the next carriage.

The guard manoeuvred around the boy's and forced open the connecting carriage door. To his dismay, he found more grisly lifeless souls inside, with creatures feasting upon their flesh. He scoured the internal carriage, finding several creatures sitting on both the floor and the seats of the carriage. Suddenly, his gaze was drawn to the overhead baggage trays, at the rear. There were some very sinister looking creatures in the carriage, ready to pounce, but fortunately he was at a safe distance. Suddenly, a perilous thought dashed through his mind. In the other carriages, many bodies along with their belongings had been launched forward after the crash. They had been left lying neatly stacked up, at the carriage front. He must assume this carriage would be no exception. A cold shiver crawled down his neck. He experienced a strong sense of danger from above. He looked upwards, towards the wire baggage holders. Then discovered two creatures poised, with flattened backs, siting him as their prey. He automatically knew this was not good, and swiftly turned and scampered into the previous carriage. In his haste, he tripped over the boy's feet and fell to the floor.

Immediately, he rose to his feet, running out past the officers and the two boys saying "Watch out, there are more of those creatures in there! Run for your lives!" The police officers dismissed him, thinking he was paranoid, as they continued tending the injured boys.

Soon the officers had a distinct sense of being watched, as they both looked towards the connecting carriage door. A terrapod was perched beside the door. One officer looked at the boys, noting they had the same type of creature on them, and said "Bob! There's one of those things by the door, I think he was right. We need to vacate quickly!" Bob said "Just a second Bernie, we can pull these two out" Bernie said, with an air of panic "No, Bob now!" Before he finished his words, two terrapods appeared from above in the wire trays. Unfortunately, neither of men had seen them. Both terrapods jumped upwards simultaneously, hitting the ceiling with a thud, then fell on to each of the officers in turn, giving them no chance of escape.

More emergency services arrived on the scene, heading down the platform to the damaged carriages. They split into several groups, covering each separate carriage, while searching for anyone still in need of help. Each group entered their individual doors, until a big noise came from the carriage nearest the platform entrance. Paramedics and police, frantically hurried out of the carriage doors, followed shortly by two injured passengers falling to ground, with terrapod infestations.

Everyone on the platform automatically stopped entering the carriages, and stood motionless watching the commotion. They thought twice about entering their allotted carriage. Several seconds passed, before terrapods began leaping from the carriages, via the broken windows. The service men and women were in the line of fire, and easy targets for the parasites. Panic ensued, as everyone ran for safety in the chaos.

Ten minutes later, most escapees were stood by the station entrance, far away from the wreckage. The chief of police ordered a no admittance area on the platforms. The chaos swiftly calmed down, as minor injuries were sent to hospital for treatment. The police chief then waited for army re-enforcements to take over.

******

Back at the supermarket, Dave had watched the terrapods attacking people outside the train. He then viewed the train, as it pulled away with the many terrapods leaping through its windows. However, he had been oblivious to the happenings further down the track, at the station.

Dave searched the tracks, viewing the many stranded victims as they lay on the ground from the terrapod barrage. So far however, the parasites had not made their way into the supermarket car park.

Dave needed to make a decision on whether to continue inside shopping, or to go home and prepare to leave Guildford, as it was no longer a safe haven. The police would soon arrive on the scene, asking questions and possibly keeping him here, while terrapods made their way to his home. He decided to quickly pick up a few items against his better judgement then escape Guildford, until the army arrived and got the situation under control.

He hurried towards the supermarket entrance, removing his phone from his pocket and ringing Mary. Mary answered, and straight away she noticed the anxiety in his voice "Hi Mary, we have problems here! Those creatures have made it to the supermarket, so we are no longer safe" Mary, almost speechless, eventually answered "What shall we do Dave?" Dave replied "We'll go to London and ride things out there until the government admit there is a problem, and sort it out. Can you get things ready there and we'll leave later. I'm getting supplies to take with us, along with anything else you think we need" Mary said "Okay Dave, if you're sure it's the right thing to do" Dave said "It is! We've seen what these things can do. We need to leave before everyone else gets the same idea, or we'll get stuck in the city, at the mercy of these parasites" He paused then added "I'll be thirty minutes, then I'll help pack" He finished the call with "I love you Mary" Then he blew a kiss down the phone. Mary smiled as the phone went quiet, but her returning words of "I love you" fell on deaf ears.

Dave returned the phone to his pocket, while walking through the supermarket entrance, briefly peering back towards the fence by the railway tracks. More terrapods sat poised beyond the fence, but so far they had not found a way of breaching it. Dave made a decision, to quickly get the items needed for their journey to London.

He grabbed a basket on entering, quickly making his way to the first aisle and picking up several items. On the dairy aisle, he collected milk, butter and some cheese, putting them into his basket. He continued shopping, until he had covered everywhere, save the drinks aisle. Dave quickly picked up a bottle of squash and some water then queued at the checkout. Just one woman stood in front of him, as he waited patiently to pay and leave.

A loud shriek came from the entrance to Dave's right, as a young woman shouted "Run, run!" She shrieked again, before a terrapod pounced on her back, then her voice fell silent. Soon the thudding impact of her body hitting the hard floor was heard. A man appearing behind her said "They've torn through the fence, they're heading this way!" As with the woman before, his fate was sealed when a second terrapod latched onto him. People stood stunned, but continued to ignore the warnings signs, being more intrigued than afraid. They gathered around the two victims, until terrapods began appearing through the open entrance.

People, suddenly realised they were in mortal danger, as the creatures caused a mass panicking exodus towards the opposite exit, and they knocked each other over in haste, despite age. Dave watched momentarily, as they passed him to reach the opposite exit. The masses ploughed through the second opening, and were rapidly swallowed up by a gauntlet of terrapods, picking them off at will. Only a few, managed to navigate the terrapods to the safety of their cars, most fell by the wayside. Parasites ambushed anyone brave enough to step through any entrance straight into their clutches.

The woman standing in front of Dave, dropped her shopping bags, and headed towards the door, hoping to sneak out to safety. She failed miserably, as she joined the many casualties. The checkout girl beside Dave jumped from her chair, heading towards the staff exit. She tried opening the door, but found it locked tight. She turned backwards to face the terrapods, as they prepared to prey on her. She momentarily halted and panicked, unsure of what to do next. Dave shouted "Come back here!" The girl, somewhat bewildered, just froze with fear, while awaiting her fate. Dave dropped his basket, dashed to her, and grabbed her hand, quickly leading her back to the checkout. Dave said "Stay away from the entrances and we might escape alive" He was unsure how they would manage it, but he knew the terrapods were only surrounding the entrances. So they might be able to escape through one of the front windows, if they could break through the glass safely.

Dave's eyes scanned the supermarket, until he fixated on a trolley full of canned beers, near the front window. He looked the girl in her eye then said "Stay hidden beneath the checkout if the parasites get in" Shaking and scared, she nodded in acknowledgement.

Dave swiftly moved away from the checkout, grabbing hold of the nearest trolley with the stack of beers. Then he dodged several people as they headed away from the entrances. He then pulled the trolley backwards as far as he could. He squared up to the window. Then with all his might, he launched it directly at the window. The trolley came to an abrupt stop on the protruding ledge beneath the window. The trolley stopped dead, preventing it from crashing through the window. A crate of beers was ejected outwards, with enough force to cause a small vertical crack to appear within the glass. Dave reloaded the trolley then pulled it backwards, for a second attempt. This time, he stacked the beer higher on the trolley, so they protruded over the trolley lip. He thrust it hard and fast, straight into the window again. Again it stopped after hitting the ledge, but its momentum sent the top beer crates crashing into the window, resulting in a three foot hole being made through the glass pane. However, the hole was not large enough for anyone to safely climb through. Dave pulled the trolley backwards again, sliding it along four feet from the first hole. He picked the crates up from the floor, being careful to avoid cutting himself. He quickly replaced them on the trolley. Again, he thrust the trolley through the glass pane, resulting in a larger hole. After a few seconds elapsed, a section of glass between both holes fell onto the pavement outside, in several large pieces.

Dave stood back gingerly, peering through the opening, checking for terrapods. There was none to be seen, so he returned inside to retrieve the checkout girl and make a run for it. Holding her hand tight, he said "We'd best make a run for my car over there" His car was a short distance away through the many parked cars. Terrapods were mostly lurking near the entrances, with the exception of the odd stray. The girl, with tears rolling down her eyes, said "Okay, I'm frightened" Dave said "We have a choice, stay here and hope they don't come in search of us, or run for it and maybe tell your parents about these things. If we survive the parasite gauntlet waiting outside" A smile adorned her face, as she wiped back her tears and said "Let's go!" Dave said "After three we'll go. I'll hold my car keys in my hand, if I don't make it, take them and drive away. I'll do the same" She smiled and said "Okay, we'll make it I'm too young to drive!" Dave said one, two, three go!" He pulled her to her feet then they ran towards the opening, jumping over the window ledge to the other side. They almost slipped on the glass when they landed, as it moved beneath their feet. Both sprinted as fast as they could between the cars, dodging slow moving terrapods, unable to react to them. When they arrived at Dave's car, he pushed the button on the key fob, opening his car. They both clambered into the car quickly, then Dave started the engine, and he began driving them out of the car park.

The road leading out of the supermarket, took them close to the entrance, and the terrapods. They checked to see if anyone else had managed to escape. Several people appeared to be heading safely away from the window opening into the car park.

The checkout girl sat within Dave's car watched two men stood behind the broken window, as they got ready to exit through the gaping window hole. A terrapod sat outside, resting on a piece of the broken glass on the ground, waiting patiently for them by the opening. Both men were unsure whether to jump outside, and make a break for freedom or not. In the end, one of them hesitated briefly, before jumping over, landing behind the terrapod. The glass section slipped forward, taking him onto his knees, causing him to stumble and sprain his ankle. He tried getting up, but his ankle made him fall forward onto his hands, slicing them open on the glass. He glimpsed back towards the terrapod, as it faced the inside of the supermarket. He relaxed, while watching it flatten its back preparing to pounce. He felt safe and relieved, because the parasite seemed to have lost interest in him. He rose slowly, hoping the terrapod would not notice him.

Arriving to his knees, he stared back again towards the terrapod, then quickly back through the window opening. The other man was well within the terrapods sights. He thought, let it pounce, it's him or me. Afterwards, he would be free to escape. So he just waited. He gazed at the fear, gradually mounting within the other man's eyes. Suddenly, the terrapod made its final move, pouncing quickly from the section of glass on the ground. The terrapods actions forced the broken glass to shoot backwards, causing it to miss the man standing inside the supermarket. The glass section beneath the terrapod, was lifted into the air then rapidly sent rearwards, straight into the man behind, slicing into his back, tearing his flesh open and sending him crashing to the pavement.

The man inside the supermarket took his chance. He escaped by running past the terrapod, while the other man lay on the floor, gasping for breath. The man lying bleeding to death on the floor, begged for help, as he faced the wrath of the terrapod. The parasite slowly turned to face his prey, before the inevitable happened.

Inside Dave's car, the young girl began crying, while she explained what was happening. Dave acknowledged the girls tears and tried consoling her, while convincing her of the need to get as far away as possible, to ensure their safety. He drove as fast as he could in the direction of his home. After joining the main road, he asked her "Where do you live?" She answered "Merrow Gate. Thanks for helping me, what's your name?" Dave said "Dave Ellis, I live near you. I'll drop you home then carry on. I suggest you leave here, I've seen these things in action. The government is hiding up their existence. What's your name?" She replied "Jane! I was so frightened back there! I didn't know what to do. I'm going to tell my mother to get us out of here" They continued talking as Jane gradually regained her composure.

They arrived at Jane's house, with her mother watching through the window, looking very worried as Jane exited Dave's car. After opening her front door, her mother ran down to meet her daughter. Jane's mother said "Your supermarket is on the news Jane! There's an incident happening with many fatalities, but they won't say what! I called you at work, but no one answered, I was so worried" Jane replied "Mum these things attacked everyone, they were horrible. I got stuck inside, until Dave managed to get us both out" Jane's mother cuddled her daughter then said "What things? They said it was some sort of isolated incident on the news" Jane said "Mum, we need to leave here. Can we stay at dads please until it has been sorted out" Jane's mother was not keen on seeing her ex-husband in Blackpool, as they had nothing in common, except their daughter Jane, who stayed at his house twice a year for holidays. Jane's mother said "I'm not sure Jane, this will blow over soon. It can't be that bad!" Jane replied "Dave knows more about these creatures. They attack people then eat them. I've seen these things and there are at least a hundred around the supermarket. We won't stand a chance! Can we go to dads for a while, he won't mind" Jane's mother said "He would like you to stay, but he has a new family. I'm not sure I would be as welcome" Dave said "I would advise you both to leave for Blackpool and be safe. If these things reach here, they will kill you" Jane's mother thought about it, then said "Thank you for saving Jane Dave, I owe you a lot. I will think about Blackpool" Dave said "You owe me nothing, just go to Blackpool. These things may make their way to Blackpool anyway if they can't be stopped. Pay me back, by leaving. I have to go now, as I'm leaving for London with my family, that's why I was in the supermarket in the first place" Jane hugged Dave then said "Thank you Dave" Jane's mother again thanked Dave. He quickly returned to his car and drove off, while they waved goodbye to him.

He arrived home, finding Mary rushing out the front door to meet him. She said "Dave, it's all over the news, I thought you might have been killed" Dave said "They were there, but I escaped with a girl at the checkout. I've dropped her off at home, but I left the shopping there, so we'll have to make do" Mary said "I've got everything ready, we just need to put it all inside the car and go. I've done some food, but it won't last us all day" Both of them returned indoors, before loading the car up, leaving Joe and Thomas inside, until the last moment before putting them in the car.

Everyone was assembled inside the car, except Dave, who was ensuring everything, including the house, was safely locked up. He closed the rear of the car then walked back, opening the driver's door. He slid into his seat and got comfortable, then said "Well Mary, we've been here before? Off to London this time!" He put his hand on Mary's knee and smiled as Mary said "The government need to sort this mess out, why are they still pretending it's not happening?" Dave replied "I don't know. The parasites will come to London next" He looked into the back of the car, and said "Okay boys, we're off to London to stay with Uncle James and your Aunt Debra" He started the car then they drove away.

They approached James and Debra's home in Kennington and Dave said "Quiet boys, your mother's phoning Uncle James" Mary, on the phone to James said "We're nearly here James, where can we park?" James answered "Mary I've left room for you on the drive. Tony's on holiday in France for two weeks with his girlfriend and he's taken his car with him" Mary said "Okay, we'll be fifteen minutes, put the kettle on James!" James laughed and said "Okay my love, see you soon"

Dave drove straight into James's drive and parked up. Everyone exited the car, just as James opened the front door. He greeted them with "Don't worry about your stuff! You can sort that out later, come in and have a drink, and let me know what's been going on" After stepping inside, they removed their shoes then settled into the living room with a hot drink. Dave and Mary informed James of their incredible journey to date. He would have thought they were fantasising, but for the incredible news stories, evolving from the media.

Four o'clock arrived, with Debra, James's wife returning home from work. She hurriedly sat down to catch up with the latest news. James decided to leave them to it, while he made dinner.

After dinner, they began chatting some more, along with a few drinks and the time flew past. The television was always on in the background, while they kept an eye out for any updated news coming in from the south. The evening soon drew to a close, with everyone in turn making their way to bed. The boys settled down in Tony's room for their stay, while Dave and Mary used the spare double.

Dave and Mary finally settled in bed to talk about the day's events. Dave said "I do hope Jane and her mother took my advice and moved away from Guildford" Mary replied "If they're watching the news reports they'll leave soon" Dave kissed Mary, then put his arms around her, and they fell peacefully asleep cuddled up together.

## CHAPTER 16

## GLOBAL CRISES ARRIVES

Morning came to Downing Street, and things had taken a turn for the worse, because the promise of a quick cure had not been forthcoming. The Prime Minister thought he would have to go to his public, admitting the problem was not caused by a rabies outbreak. He called an emergency meeting, code named "Operation Cobra" insisting all his top ministers and his top army personnel attended.

They convened inside the war room within 10 Downing Street, with a total of ten ministers, including the Foreign Minister Jeremy Carlton, and the Defence Minister Graham Brookes in attendance. The Prime Minister insisted, his Public Relations consultant David Monahan, Field Marshall Henderson and Jacob wells were also available, to give useful constructive advice.

The Prime Minister said to his Defence Minister "Graham, Jacob has not found an outright cure so far. Have you any ideas on how to stop these parasites, without causing major destruction?" Graham answered "We have tried destroying the terrapods with a muted mixture of acid and water unsuccessfully, but we want to increase the strength to be sure of positive results but…" Graham paused briefly, as the Prime Minister said "But, what Graham?" Graham said "These parasites quickly multiply and we're struggling to hold them. If they multiply in much larger numbers, we won't be able to produce enough acid to neutralise them. They have moved beyond Guildford and are stretching out to both the east and west of the southern counties. I fear it won't be long before they are knocking on our door here in Whitehall" The Prime Minister turned to Jacob and asked "Have you made any progress Jacob?" Jacob said "Sir, we have no option, but to increase the strength of the sulphuric acid. It's the only way we will have a fighting chance against these terrapods, or they will engulf the country and possibly Europe if left unchecked. Will you inform the public?" The Prime Minister said "Jacob, the time has come to tell the public the truth, but the country and I, need a plan to take to them. It will need to include a positive outcome, if more intrusive weapons are to be used and more people are to be displaced from their homes, or left to face chemical and heavy artillery fire" The Foreign Minister Jeremy added "Across Europe, there are clear indications that terrapods are out of control in many areas of France, Germany, Poland, Holland, Russia and the Ukraine. There are, even unconfirmed reports that Spain, Italy and even Africa, have had pockets of marauding terrapods, it also appears they are powerless to stop them. Russia had a town in Oblast destroyed by an aerial assault, killing all the inhabitants in a bid to wipe out the terrapods. It destroyed the village, but terrapods, are still growing in large numbers there" He paused then said "The President of the United States, has said that they are unable to control parasites in several states. They have informed people in the highest infected areas to abandon their homes before the weekend, or face the full force of an army assault" Field Marshall Henderson said "Do I have your permission to use deadly force, alongside the chemical weapons Prime Minister? My troops are protecting the public, but I'm losing many men due to the governments arms embargo in built up areas" The Prime Minister said "After the announcement on television and radio at three o'clock today, you will indeed be permitted to use any deadly force you deem necessary, but you will be required to inform people of the consequences first. So they can escape, or take avoiding action from injury or death" Graham Brookes said "I would like to see as many people as possible in the south, moved up to the relative safety of London. This will allow the army to systematically go through town by town, using chemical weapons to destroy the terrapods outright. The army can then go in afterwards killing every surviving terrapod" The Prime Minister said "How long before the public can move back into their homes?" Jacob answered "Not for several years, it may take up to five years before the south recovers, even longer for certain plant life, but to do nothing, is not an option. If these parasites, rampage through London and beyond, we'll be facing a very different world than the one we know and love" Graham said "I suggest we make temporary housing available in the suburbs, and arrange for make shift sites inside the tube stations to feed and protect the masses. We could encourage families to move up to the midlands or to the north, where there's plenty of space for new settlements to be built. They could opt to stay there afterwards, especially if we keep communities together" The Prime Minister said "It seems to be our best option for now, perhaps they could return home after a two year period and a thorough clean-up operation, if they wanted to. We could offer people a cash incentive to stay" Field Marshall Henderson said "With due respect Sir, if these parasites breach the suburbs and then London's streets, it will be a massacre. These terrapods will have a large food source on their doorstep. You should tell people to go as far north as possible" Jacob said "I agree, take people as far away from the terrapods as possible, and starve them of a food source" The Prime Minister said "I'll give the people the choice, but they will have to leave the most southerly of the counties. Where they go, will be up to them" He turned to his Public Relations consultant then said "David, if you set up a meeting with the press at three o'clock, I'll make an announcement" The Prime Minister continued with "Thank you gentlemen for attending today. If you have any updates for me in the meantime, please let me know. I'll discuss the details now with the rest of my ministers. Then I'll inform the cabinet, before the three o'clock announcement" The Prime Minister allowed everyone to leave, bar his ministers, he then continued with the finer points, before taking the new plan to his cabinet.

Three o'clock came upon the Prime Minister, as he and his advisers, stood inside 10 Downing Street, ready to step outside and face the press. Outside, the press waited patiently with their microphones and cameras at the ready. The door opened, and the Prime Minister walked through first, with his Defence Minister and his Public Relations consultant following closely behind. They past the officer guarding the steps as they walked over to face the multitudes of microphones awaiting them, in front of 10 Downing Street.

The Prime Minister addressed the press through the microphone, and talked about the recent disturbances down south. He announced that there was a suspected alien parasite invasion. He quickly informed the press of the dangerous parasites, called terrapods that were suspected of arriving on Earth, via the recent asteroid fallout. The terrapods were difficult to exterminate, and more drastic action was required to eliminate their presence. The south, along with the Isle of Wight, had been overrun by the parasites, and as a nation they could not afford to allow them to continue on their present path. Both chemical weapons and more drastic military hardware, including possible bombardment of the areas, would now be called upon to halt their progress. At the end of his speech he said "If you have any questions, please ask" A woman shoved a microphone, close to the Prime Minister's face, then said "What will this mean to the people who live in the south? Will they be able to return to their homes afterwards?" The Prime Minister said "They will have to leave their homes, but provision will be made to house them in London's suburbs. People can choose to move to the midlands, or further north, if they so wish and start a new life away from the infected areas" She said "What if they don't want to leave their homes?" He replied "There won't be a choice! If they stay they could end up with serious injuries from the chemicals being sprayed on the terrapods, or the heavy weapons that will be dispensed to subdue these parasites. If we do nothing, there may not be a country. If the terrapods take over everyone will be at their mercy" Another reporter said "What about the rabies scare? Is it still relevant?" The Prime Minister said "The rabies was a cover story used to keep the public away from the infected areas, giving us time to get the situation under control. Unfortunately, terrapods are now out of control as we have failed to contain them" Another reporter asked "What if you still can't contain them? Reports are coming in from Europe and the States, that they are losing the battle. Why were we not informed before?" The Prime Minister said "We can't afford to lose the battle with these parasites, there is far too much for the human race to lose. We're keeping up with the affairs of other countries. We felt it was not in the public's interest to be told due to the panic it would cause" He concluded the press meeting with "Thank you everyone. We'll keep you informed of any changes. Arrangements are being put in place for the expected exodus within the next few days. My Defence Minister will try to answer any more questions you have, thank you" The Prime Minister moved away swiftly and returned to 10 Downing Street, leaving his Defence Minister and Public Relations consultant to deal with a barrage of questions. Afterwards, the media immediately aired the special news broadcast given by the Prime Minister on all television, radio and media channels.

\*\*\*\*\*\*

People in the south, were reluctant to up sticks and move northwards, but as reality set in, along with the gruesome images of terrapods attacking defenceless victims being aired on the media, people began taking notice and moved steadily northwards.

Over the course of seven days, the terrapods came knocking on the door of London's suburbs and the small escaping numbers, quickly turned into droves of fleeing migrants, heading northwards to the midlands and even further to Scotland. Scotland was unable to cope with the mounting numbers of refugees on their doorstep, so they tried policing them. They directed refugees back to the border and resettled them back on the English side, ensuring the financial burden was a cost to England, instead of Scotland. Many people of London's suburbs, followed the government's guidelines in moving, but instead of heading northwards, they opted for the city centre with a promise of the troops destroying all the terrapods hovering outside the suburbs, thus keeping anyone inside the inner perimeter safe.

In Europe and America, the terrapod population exploded out of control. European governments came under ever increasing pressure to rid the countries of their parasites. Many national armies could not cope with the huge numbers of terrapods, and they increasingly looked towards the scientists to save the day. However, the only cure offered was by the London taskforce, of Jacob Wells and his team.

******

Tuesday morning at the Royal London, Jacob called an emergency meeting with everyone present. There was more information on offer from external sources, such as the Greenwich Observatory, because they had recently studied the initial asteroid landings. There was also information from the forensic lab for them to piece together. Another source of information had also arrived from the Arecibo Observatory in Puerto Rico. They supplied more detailed information from the actual asteroid collision, along with earlier pictures of the asteroids original paths as they neared one of the Jupiter's moons.

Jacob said "Good morning everyone! As we know, the army are in deep confrontation with these parasites. We already have a sure fire method of destroying the parasites, but it is limited in the way it can be used in highly populated areas. Bob has studied the asteroid that the terrapods arrived on and has some interesting facts for us. You carry on Bob" Bob stood up then said "We know the parasites came to Earth, via the asteroid, however" He paused then said "I do not think the parasite originated from the asteroid, because the food source on the actual asteroid would not have supported it for a long period. There are three possible theories, to which they may have found their way on the asteroid. The first is that somewhere between Jupiter and Mars's many asteroids and moons, these parasites started out somewhere else and were transferred to the asteroid, via a small collision of some sort. The second possibility is that they were actually on the other asteroid soon to pass by Earth. They could have been transferred onto the asteroid that we have scattered around our planet now" He paused again, before continuing with "The third is an improbable reason, but we can't rule it out. That is, it was put on the asteroid by something, or perhaps someone from outer space" Jacob chuckled as he said "That's an interesting thought, I think very unlikely, but we can't rule it out, I suppose! What else do we know?" Darren said "These things have originated from either a planet, or perhaps a satellite such as a moon, but it would have had a habitable atmosphere similar to ours. I think it would have been a slightly acidic content, making these parasites a little more timid than on our planet. Its digestive system is very basic and very little if any of their prey is wasted, as they grind down the meat to a pulp. Some parasites will consume vegetable matter as well, if there is no animal flesh available. This would indicate that this parasite will, after consuming all animal life, begin consuming plant life, eventually wiping out the planet as we know it, if not stopped" Richard stood to take his turn "The parasite in my opinion, is at a disadvantage on Earth. It's very heavy on our planet and only takes its prey, when cornered or unaware. I think the parasite has originated on a smaller planet, possibly a satellite moon, as said before by Bob. I think it would have been regarded as a flea. If it was on a smaller planet, with a lower gravity it would be a more formidable, faster predator. If it stayed on our planet for several generations, it could adjust to our world. The evolutionary traits from our ancestors and other Earth animals, would suggest it would evolve on our planet. If it did evolve over many decades, we may never be able to eliminate the parasite" Chris stood, and said "I have been in touch with Greenwich Observatory in London, along with the Arecibo Observatory in

Puerto Rico, to see if they could supply us with any more information about the origins of the parasite. I'm hoping to get some early images that were taken long before the asteroids collided, to see if it helps in any way" He sat down, then Angela stood up and said "These terrapods do not have sight, so I think they use a very basic instinct to acquire prey, I think they use vibration or heat to find food. Their digestive system is very basic because they grind food up and break it down in a single pit inside the body of the creature. They mix it with a substance they make, forcing it into their flesh by pressure. This is why when you cut the parasite or a bullet enters its body, the hole is quickly sealed, but the object will stay inside the parasite until it dies. They go red when they die, similar to a lobster when boiled, because of the pigment on their tough flesh. They have a disliking to the cold, so when subjected to extreme cold they will eventually die, but unfortunately it may well be too cold for humans as well. By lowering the temperature to freezing point, it will make the creature less active" Jacob said "The sulphuric acid works well, but as a nation we can't make enough to control the growing parasites. The army is having limited success, but we need to find another weakness to stop them. The cold is a start and can be used to help the Field Marshall and his troops, perhaps to contain small pockets of terrapods. I will pass on the information, I'm sure they will figure a way to utilise it" Bob said "I'll get in touch with the Arecibo Observatory, to see if they can send me more information that may help. I'm interested in the origins of the beast" Jacob said "It would be a good idea to get the original pictures of the asteroids colliding, along with any earlier pictures if they have them from near Jupiter" Jacob soon concluded the meeting and they all went off to their prospective duties.

Three o'clock in the afternoon inside the lab, Bob was on the phone to Rafael at the Arecibo Observatory. He said "Good morning Rafael, I'm Bob Farmer from the taskforce in England. We're trying to acquire information on the two asteroids that recently collided together. We want pictures of the collision itself, or even earlier pictures from when they were near Jupiter, if you have any? Have you any I can view please?" Rafael said "I will see what I can do Bob. I have had many requests for the collision pictures and I've sent many images out on that subject, but you are the first to ask for the earlier pictures. I will send pictures out to you by email" Rafael stopped talking and Bob heard him asking another man for the earlier pictures to be made available to him, so he could send them on. Rafael returned the phone to his ear, then said "Bob, we do have earlier pictures, I'll check them out first and send them over to you in the afternoon. It will be late evening when they arrive to you, if that's okay?" Bob said "That would be perfect Rafael. We can review the collision pictures first then we'll be fresh in the morning, when we look at the earlier images" Bob said "Thanks Rafael" Rafael replied "No problem Bob. I'll check the earlier pictures out myself, you never know we both might come up with something" Bob said "How's the terrapod problem there Rafael?" Rafael answered "They are spreading quickly through some of the poorer areas with no protection from the army. Many people are moving down to the south. We fear we may be overrun in about two and a half months. We're looking at moving people to wetter climes, as terrapods are not so able there. What about where you are Bob?" Bob said "We have a more able army than you, but the result is the same, the terrapods are difficult to stop, sulphuric acid works and extreme cold, but ultimately if we can't wipe them out, they will evolve and we may never be rid of them" Rafael said "Good luck Bob, let's hope the world's finest can come up with solution soon" They said their goodbyes then shortly afterwards, Bob received pictures of the asteroid collision and he began making copies for all taskforce members to study.

Bob, Richard and Darren received the asteroid images first, studying them from start to finish meticulously, trying to work out how the terrapods had survived the cold emptiness of space, on the long journey to Earth. The images showed a large area of grey buds being transported on the asteroid journey, mostly facing into the sun. Some red areas, led Darren to believe that these buds, had indeed died aboard the asteroid, perhaps from being in the colder sections of the asteroid. He noticed that as the asteroid raced through space, it could be keeping the temperature at a reasonably habitable level, probably allowing the buds to live, but not to evolve into the parasites, now gracing the Earth. Also noticeable, was that of Sekhmet's trajectory. It would have normally avoided Earth, but because of the Apophis collision, it had altered its course, causing the apparent accidental entry into Earth's atmosphere. Early pictures appeared to show the asteroid in very close proximity to a large object, by one of Jupiter's moons. He was unsure which moon, but an educated guess would have been Io, but the object intrigued him more as it had a pointed delta shape. After viewing it several times, Darren believed the asteroid had changed course, after nearing the delta shaped object. He decided to seek a second opinion from Richard, Bob and Jacob, just to be sure.

Darren moved onto the next part of the puzzle, the asteroid collision. He thought the collision was at a perfect speed, to change both trajectories, ensuring Sekhmet went to Earth, but where was the other asteroid going? The collision, in his opinion, looked to be premeditated, leaving Darren with many unanswered questions. He phoned Jacob informing him of his theory, quickly asking him to check his findings and assemble the team together, to see if there was any substance to his ideas. Jacob agreed to meet after dinner, after requesting Darren got in touch with Greenwich and Arecibo Observatories to see if more pictures were available, so they could shed more light on Darren's theories.

It was six o'clock when Richard walked into the meeting room, only to find Darren in deep thought, as he scanned the pictures of the initial asteroid course change. He now knew it had occurred by Jupiter's moon Io. Richard said "Darren, there is something not quite right here. It distinctively changes its course between Io, and what I thought was Jupiter's other moon Europa, but I'm assured, it's not Europa! The object is difficult to see, but it's quite large, despite appearing small through the lens. It's reflecting a small amount of light on one side and that's all we can see, leaving the rest a mystery. It could be another asteroid, or possibly a piece of space debris" Darren said "Richard, I'm not sure what it is, but it looks like a delta shape. If you follow these three pictures, the object moves in time with the asteroid and you can see different angles of the object, especially when the light reflects on it" Darren clicked through the pictures several times, while showing Richard. Richard said "You could be right, but at this distance it could be just the light playing tricks, along with us looking for a different reason other than an act of god" Both men continued flicking through the pictures, until the door opened and the rest of the team walked in.

They settled down to a hot drink, as Jacob began informing them of the major events happening around the country. He hinted that Darren may have some interesting news, if proven true. Jacob said "It has not been a good day around the country. I'm afraid the army are losing the battle against the terrapods entering London, even whilst using chemicals. Unfortunately, we can't manufacture enough, to cope with the speed at which these things multiply. We're expecting terrapods to arrive in the city inside two days. The government are advising anyone caught inside the city to remain indoors, or head to underground stations. Many countries have lost the battle against the parasites and are using planes with neat sulphuric acid. We know the sulphuric acid will destroy them, but I have no idea where to get enough to destroy all of the parasites" Bob said "Surely the parasites can be beaten with more potent bombs Jacob" Jacob said "Bob, governments are reluctant to use nuclear weapons, simply because the terrapods have only gone to the areas with a high content of animals and us humans. We know they are like locusts, stripping the food supply namely us, then moving on to the next fertile patch. They multiply first, then they move on to the next killing field" Chris added "As I see it, they are basic animals, perhaps something we would have seen in the early days of Earth. On to you Andy" Andy stayed seated then said "Their flea like muscular bodies, would make them a more formidable creature in their own environment. I think they would have lived in a similar gravity as our moon, enabling them to jump a lot higher than on Earth. I don't think they would have grown to the size they are here, because they appear to be growing to a size that matches their food source. Not good news for us!" Jacob said "We're working on a more potent acid using several different types, because we can't make enough sulphuric acid. There would only have been enough sulphuric acid to eliminate these pests in Earths early days. When Earth, was a far more volcanic and violent place, we as a race would have struggled to live in that type of environment. I fear we are no longer the most feared predator on our blue planet" The air went quiet, as they all ventured into deep thought, pondering the plight of life on Earth.

A few minutes of quiet, was followed by Darren clearing his throat and saying "I have been looking at pictures from the Arecibo Observatory. If you look closely, I think you can see something" He paused momentarily, before continuing with "Something is manipulating the asteroid by Jupiter's moon Io. The asteroid appears to change course while moving past Io. You can see an object very close to where the asteroid changes course. Its course has been altered to collide with the second asteroid, causing it to head towards Earth, eventually entering our atmosphere. The other asteroid Apophis also alters course, but its destination is unknown, I think we should look deeper into this phenomenon" Richard added "I think there is something in it, but I'm no expert it may be worth Rafael from the Observatory looking into it, as he knows what should and shouldn't be in the skies of Jupiter" Jacob nodded his head in confirmation, then said "I think you are right to ask Rafael once again, but no matter what he finds, I fear that as a race we could be doomed in a very short space of time and we may never find out that answer"

******

At 10 Downing Street, the Prime Minister was on the phone inside the war room. All his top ministers were present, waiting for him to connect to the President of The United States of America. Listening in was the Chinese leader Xu Lin, the Indian leader Tashear Khan and the Russian president Vladislav Stepenov, and they were all interested in the events unfolding within the United Kingdom.

The President answered "Hi John, how are you in Britain?" Afterwards, he quickly acknowledged the other world leaders with a simple sentence of "Good afternoon from the USA" The Prime Minister said "Mr President, we are in deep trouble here, terrapods have a strong hold in the south and we are struggling to keep them out of London. Many parasites are moving through the suburbs and heading on towards the midlands virtually unchecked. Each county has been ordered to do what they feel is necessary, to protect their inhabitants. In reality, we think these parasites will overrun the country in a matter of weeks" The other world leaders heard every word being said and despite having their own agendas, they all shared one goal to find a way of securing a permanent cure, or they may eventually revert to the destruction of part, or all of their own countries. Secretly, many countries were also considering the destruction of their neighbour, in order to control the terrapod invasion. China, now in the midst of watching terrapods move through some of their northern villages, had already sanctioned the destruction of many communities in the north, including the deaths of whole towns. Their biggest worry was of terrapods reaching huge cities like Beijing. This was the first time for all the world leaders to be singing from the same hymn sheet. This would be just a start for the world leaders, who were now contemplating a massive meeting of world heads of states, to be held in Brussels at the end of the week. That is, if there was a Brussels to hold it in, but Reykjavik in Iceland was the back-up solution, because terrapods were not fond of the cold and no terrapod had yet been reported on Iceland's lands, making it the logical choice. The meeting lasted about an hour, with the heads of states reporting what they wanted in the way of help, and what they would offer in return. More importantly, was the measures they would go to, to protect the people in their nations. The only thing that was crystal clear was that no single country had been able to keep the terrapods at bay. The British had been the most successful in holding the parasite back from its cities, but they were now thinking of going underground, to keep the terrapods from feeding on their people. They thought that by hiding in the underground tube tunnels, the parasites would simply run out of food and starve, or be so weak they could use conventional weapons, alongside chemical weapons to get the upper hand on them. It was a last resort, but possibly the only way they could win the war.

After they had finished making their demands and offers, the world leaders went back to their waiting public. The Prime Minister this time would hold no punches with his speech. However, before he aired his speech, he would be busy arranging food and supplies to be put in motion for the people who decided to go underground. This alone would not only be a grand operation to arrange, but it would also require many other people staying in the line of fire, to feed the millions that would soon grace the tunnels of London and the other big cities. The Prime Minister and his government had been advised to move up to Scotland and run the country from the Shetland Isles, as they were free of any infection. This was being prepared for him and his cabinet first, as a country cannot run without a government.

## CHAPTER 17

## APOPHIS GOD OF DESTRUCTION ON THE HORIZON

Ten o'clock in the morning, at the Arecibo Observatory in Puerto Rico. A meeting was taking place within the main observatory, with Chad, Rafael and Pedro in attendance. They were discussing the images they had recently sent to London. They were intent on making more in depth studies into the phenomenon that had occurred before the asteroids collided. Rafael was in constant contact with Darren from London and between them they were intrigued by the delta object, close to Jupiter's moon Io. Darren moved his attention to it first, but now Rafael had become obsessed with it, and had blown the pictures up as large as possible, without losing the integrity. Rafael, intrigued by Darren's theory, also found the delta object next to the asteroid. Now, with the pictures blown up, it became clear the strange triangulated object was far larger than Darren had previously thought. The object was in position for a total of twelve hours. Rafael had worked it out by the six hour time period of each picture.

Two consecutive photos showed the object in the same position, with the third, showing the delta object stationary, but the asteroid had clearly moved forward. On the next image, the asteroid had radically changed course and did not correspond to its original expected trajectory that Rafael had plotted. The three men discussed the implications of an object manipulating the asteroid, then changing its original trajectory, causing the collision with Apophis. This would mean the act was likely done by aliens, not only unthinkable, but for what purpose, or was the collision the result of an accident. The men were in two minds about the object. Chad said "Rafael, the object may be alien in design, or it could just a piece of space debris shaped like a delta wing. We can't say for sure it had anything to do with the collision" Rafael said "The object is a perfect delta! What are the odds on it being perfectly shaped like that, unless it was manufactured! The other reason I think it's alien in design, is because it stops when the asteroid continues on its path past Io" Chad said "It's strange I grant you, but it seems to be a farfetched, hopeful way of explaining it" Rafael said "The change of path was so sudden and violent, almost as if it had been forced over by an external source" Pedro added "This object is not a natural thing, it's too smooth and when the light catches the facets, it reflects its perfect triangular shape. I'm sure it's of alien construction, it's like nothing on Earth" Chad said "We'll look at the pictures in more detail, perhaps then we can come up with a logical explanation for the object. I suggest we look at the collision itself to see if that could have been contrived. We do know the first asteroid was carrying the grey buds that have evolved into these dangerous terrapods. However, I think we need to focus on the second asteroid Apophis, because so far we have ignored it. It may be worth keeping a close eye on it to find out where it's heading" Rafael said "If it is indeed aliens that have manipulated the first asteroid, why would they do it, was it an accident or a premeditated act to put these parasites on our planet?" Chad said "You're getting ahead of yourself Rafael. Let's stay with the facts. We'll concentrate on the whole picture. Rafael, keep in touch with Darren in London he seems to be collecting some important information with his eagle eyes" They concluded the meeting then moved onto their duties, putting the asteroid saga to the top of their important to do list, after all the terrapods were heading their way. So far their remoteness had kept them safe, but that could quickly change.

\*\*\*\*\*\*

A new day dawned in London, with Andy having done many autopsies on the terrapods. He had more useful information about the parasites. He went to Jacob's office to speak to him, taking Angela alongside him. Jacob pulled the door closed behind them, before they sat down comparing notes. Andy said "Jacob, these parasites are very adaptable as you already know, but they are able to reproduce in two ways. The quickest, has been seen in the battlefield. They will multiply by dividing in two in front of us, as they don't consider us a major threat" Jacob said "Yes, we know that as we are seeing it in great numbers now" Andy said "They do it that way because there is virtually no gestation period. It's also a quick way to bolster numbers, but it has problems to them as a species. They can't cross breed out any genetic problems that way" Angela said "When we opened up two of the larger terrapods, we found grey buds growing inside. They are not sexed as we know it, but do need spores from other terrapods, to start the life cycle with this method. The spores develop by collecting spores from many different terrapods, just like a fungus. The more spores they collect, the more resilient they appear to be to viruses, or acids, because they all have different tolerances just like humans" Andy added "They will only reproduce using this method, if they have a long time period and a safe environment. They are very vulnerable in this state, despite having a protective membrane over them. I think it's because they could have been a good source of food for something, where ever they have originated from. Perhaps, they were a truffle for some type of animal" Jacob said "That's interesting to know, do you have any more information Andy?" Andy replied "Yes, we have discovered they do not like the cold, so they must have come from a very hot climate, perhaps unbearable for us as a race. This may mean they might only multiply and thrive in warmer climes. They will be able to stomach our cooler climes to a certain extent, but they will not be happy here" Jacob said "What will happen in the winter months to these things Andy?" Andy replied "I'm not sure, they might die or perhaps just hibernate. We won't know until we get there" He added "We have evidence that these terrapods will not seek colder climes, as they will die from hyperthermia. There is conclusive evidence of terrapods venturing into the Alps and once the temperature drops to freezing point, they have all died. This would suggest that the human race would be able to escape and flourish in the colder areas of the world, even if these parasites do take over. It would be survival of the fittest, because wars would be inevitable, as each country made claim to strategic land" Jacob said "I hope it won't come to that, because humans are resilient and can adapt quickly to changes" Angela said "There are other things of interest to consider. They are able to cope with small amounts of moisture in the air and on the floor, but they can't cope with large bodies of water, such as ponds, lakes and the world's oceans. If they enter a large body of water, they simply sink to the bottom unable to ascend to safety. We think they have originated from a small dry planet or satellite. There would have been a much lower gravity. Earth's gravity increases their weight, preventing them from floating in water. They will eventually starve to death, if they encounter the cold oceans and a lack of sunlight" Jacob said "This will be of use to both the army and police, what else do you have Angela?" She answered "I have mentioned light before! If you cut out the light completely for a long period the parasite will die, but it needs to be for a week or more. We can use this knowledge to protect people. By keeping people inside London's underground tunnels, we can use darkened areas to shield them from the outside world. We can make blackout areas inside the entrances, stopping terrapods from breaching the inner station. The tube lines could be utilised to keep inhabitants supplied with all they need for survival, during the winter months. The cold winter months could then be allowed to take their toll on the terrapod population" Jacob said "This is vital information the government can use to save lives, and they have already put some measures in place to realize it. I will be in touch with the Prime Minister immediately after the meeting" Jacob concluded the meeting and they returned to their duties.

Jacob phoned the Prime Minister to brief him with the news from his team. The Prime Minister quickly answered his phone "Good morning Jacob, it's good to hear from you. Have you any good news for me?" Jacob replied "Yes! We have valuable information on the parasites to help you decide the best safety route for the public, and useful information the army can use to defend themselves" The Prime Minister, optimistically said "Good man, tell me please!" Jacob replied "The public can be protected, if they choose to go underground and stay in designated darkened areas. The terrapods have a distaste of the dark. If you set up darkened areas on entering the underground stations, they won't breach the station interiors. The public should be safe, but I suggest you darken the inhabited areas also to confuse the parasites, in case they do manage to breach the stations. The army can use this information to attack terrapods at night, ensuring their casualties are kept to a minimum. Acid works on the parasite very well, but water in large quantities can also make life very difficult for them, but unless it's extremely cold, it won't be lethal" The Prime Minister said "I'll pass this information on to the underground stations. Tunnels will be the arteries, keeping people supplied with food and water. There are also plans for a makeshift sewer system if there's time" Jacob said "The parasites will be less active in the winter with the cold, but that's a long time off yet" The Prime Minister said "Thank you Jacob, I'll pass this information on to the right people, then forward it onto the world leaders. If you acquire more information, please get in touch Jacob" Both men concluded their dialogue.

Meanwhile, Darren was busy studying images of the asteroids. The more he viewed the images by Jupiter's moon Io, the more he was convinced he was witnessing an alien spacecraft. It was getting close to an obsession, but his only saving grace was that, both he and Rafael from the observatory shared his obsessive theory and they were fast becoming good friends, despite the distance between them.

Darren studied the collision image closely, noting the terrapod buds inhabiting the asteroid Sekhmet. Another image came into view and both asteroid trajectories had clearly been altered. He thought the first asteroid had been manipulated, then forced into the asteroid Apophis, but why? Why would aliens manipulate an asteroid to land on Earth, by impacting the asteroid Apophis. They could alter Sekhmet's trajectory without hitting Apophis. It did not make sense, because by making both asteroids collide together, they ran the risk of destroying the asteroid carrying the terrapod buds. Darren was very puzzled and began asking more questions, such as where was the large asteroid heading for now? He knew the images could not give him the answers, but perhaps his friend Rafael could. He decided to phone Rafael later in the afternoon, as it would be morning in the Puerto Rico.

It was four o'clock in the afternoon, when Darren phoned Rafael. Rafael answered "Rafael here" Darren said "Hi Rafael, I've got a few questions you might be able to answer, I know you will be interested in the answers as much as me" Rafael said "What questions do you have Darren?" Darren started with "Do you have more images of the asteroid Apophis and its trajectory" Rafael answered "Yes, we are tracking it now, it will fly past Earth around November, but the day is unclear because the asteroid is very erratic. We think it will be in the second week of November Darren. Why do you want to know?" Darren replied "Like you Rafael, I'm convinced the first asteroid was manipulated towards Earth. Perhaps by aliens, but why would they want to do it? It's beyond me, but I have a question about the collision we can work on" Rafael said "What is it?" Darren said "If say, it was an act by aliens, why would they make Sekhmet collide with Apophis, bearing in mind the colossal size of Apophis. It could have destroyed the smaller asteroid with the parasites living on it" Rafael said "Yes you're right. I'll study the images more closely, to see if it is indeed a spacecraft" Darren said "The other question is, was there another reason for it impacting the larger asteroid?" Rafael said "I will look into the subject, but I'm not sure how long we will be staying here. Our government has declared a national emergency and we may have to escape to the nearest city. Terrapods, are on their way here" Darren said jokingly "You're welcome over here mate, we have a large telescope in Greenwich. Speak to you soon Rafael!" They both hung up then Darren went to see Jacob in his office, giving him his thoughts and theories on the strange spacecraft.

Both men conversed at length in Jacob's office, about the probability of aliens manipulating the asteroid. Jacob, although intrigued said "I can't take a theory to the Prime Minister, only hard facts. To me it could be a craft of some kind, but it would be huge if it was. Judging by its shape, there could be a possibility of it being manufactured. I need hard evidence to convince the Prime Minister, a theory Darren is not enough" Jacob, however mention that he would not rule it out completely and would inform the Prime Minister, albeit off the record. He would leave the Prime Minister to decide if it needed pursuing any further, but Jacob reminded Darren that the Prime Minister had a lot on his plate at the moment, so he informed him not to get his hopes up. After finishing the conversation, Darren left for his lunch, before continuing his studies and conversing with the rest of the team.

******

Inside the Arecibo Observatory, both Chad and Rafael were busy, after having been informed by their President that they will have to vacate the premises by tomorrow lunchtime. This was due to the invading terrapods, swarming around the nearby villages. The observatory would be under siege before the weekend. They were guaranteed a flight to the capital, if they chose to leave tomorrow, but if they delayed, it could mean them making their own way to safety. Chad informed all the staff within the observatory. All, but the engineer Pedro, had decided to take up the offer. Pedro offered to stay as long as Chad and Rafael required him. Chad wanted to speak to Rafael, as he was going to stay inside the main observatory, to study the larger asteroid Apophis. He knew they would never get a chance to watch an asteroid of this magnitude fly by Earth, ever again in their lifetime. Chad said to Rafael "I intend to stay Rafael and observe the asteroid Apophis fly by, to see if we can acquire more information on this monumental asteroid. It will be a magnificent spectacle for us all. The last asteroid, anywhere near this magnitude, landed on Earth sixty five million years ago, wiping out the dinosaurs. This may help us find out more about these parasites gracing Mother Earth. We'll be able to view the collateral damage that the asteroid collision caused to Apophis" Rafael said "Chad, I think there is something you need to know about the asteroid. The asteroid is very erratic, there may be a chance it could end up entering the atmosphere over the Atlantic ocean" Chad said "Even more reason to study it and watch it break up" Rafael said "If it does fly by Earth it will be a wonderful sight, but it could briefly affect the Earth's balance with the moon. There is a chance Apophis could enter Earth's atmosphere, or possibly collide with the moon. It would be catastrophic if either happened" Chad said "Are you sure the asteroid could come our way?" Rafael said "I'm not sure, but it just needs a small change in course and disaster would be upon us" Chad said "Ah well, I had better stay to keep an eye on the asteroid. If it's likely to happen, I think the world will need an early warning, so they can prepare for the worse scenario. I think you should leave tomorrow Rafael, as it does not need two of us here to operate the telescope. I'll pass the images on to America and your friend Darren in England" Rafael said "Two heads are better than one Chad, besides, I calculated that if this asteroid does enter the atmosphere, heading to the capital would not save us from either the ravenous terrapods, or Apophis" Chad said "What do you mean Rafael?" Rafael said "The asteroid is so big it won't break up while entering the atmosphere. It will come to Earth with a very large bang. I think it will land somewhere near Florida in America, or possibly close to the Gulf of Mexico. I would like to study the asteroid trajectory more before I can say for definite" Chad thought hard, then said "When do you think it could happen, if your theory is correct?" Rafael said "Well, I've been speaking to Darren. We estimated it happening in the second week of November, but it's only a guess and as I said, the asteroid might fly by, avoiding us and the moon. It could bury itself into the moon knocking it off its orbit. This would interfere with our tides and many other things related to Earth's eco systems. It could put the moon on a collision course with Earth, a very frightening thought indeed" Chad said "I think you should continue your studies, but include Darren with your findings before leaving the observatory tomorrow. Perhaps go to London just in case your theory turns out to be correct, at least you will be a long way from the landing site" Rafael said "I will stay here as long as you are here Chad" Chad said "No, stay here until tomorrow, then take all the information you need and escape to London, before these parasites come knocking at our door. The knowledge will be shared in two different hemispheres, should anything disastrous happen to either part of the world" Rafael agreed to leave tomorrow, if Chad agreed to come to London later, if his theory had credibility. They both set about their respective tasks, with Rafael telling Chad, he would release more images to the London taskforce for Darren to review.

Rafael continued viewing the latest asteroid images, whilst trying to map out its final trajectory, by extracting information from the previous images. He was finding it extremely challenging, with the huge speed changes and its erratic path. He worked through several images, carefully noting Apophis going into a tank slapping, space wobble straight after the collision. It settled down briefly, until a small flash of light was seen exploding from the right hand side of the asteroids nose. It entered into another violent wobble, before settling down again to a more constant speed. Rafael checked the trajectory, before the flash of light, plotting where it would pass by Earth. Indications showed it would avoid Earth by a very large distance. After the flash however, if the asteroid continued on its current path, it would fly into Earth's gravitational pull ensuring it entered the atmosphere.

Rafael studied the images again and again, but the results were conclusive. He moved onwards, plotting the eventual entry point and touch down area on Earth, it was only then his face dropped. It was a point in the middle of the Gulf of Mexico, so could not have been any worse. A gigantic asteroid impacting this area would leave millions dead in Mexico, Venezuela, parts of Brazil and the lower regions of the United States, depending on the touchdown point. He then struggled with the implications of such huge tidal waves and the large amounts of debris that would be flung up into the atmosphere.

Rafael collated the new images, along with his thoughts and theories then sent them to Darren in London, with a message to phone him. He also took the same information to show Chad, to get his approval and input. He printed the images, along with the projected paths for the asteroid, for before the flash of light occurred and for afterwards. He also added a possible landing point on Earth, for his perusal.

He called Chad over, spreading the images over his desk, as he did so. Chad went to Rafael and sifted through the many images. It was not long before Chad's eye caught the flash of light and the distinct change of path, taken by the asteroid. He said "Rafael I think there are too many coincidences here! I suggest you ask Darren to look at these more closely, let's see if he agrees with your findings. I think you should follow the asteroid daily, until you leave. It might be worth asking Darren and the Greenwich Observatory to check out the area, where the object was last seen. Check Jupiter's moon Io as well, to see if there is any activity there at the moment" Rafael said "Good idea, I didn't think of that" Chad said "It's a long shot, but if both asteroids were manipulated, it would be prudent to find out if it was by the delta object in the images" Chad viewed more images as he visualised the path of Apophis, then said "Apophis, will be caught in the gravitational pull of the moon granted, but I think Earth will narrowly escape an impact, when the asteroid is deflected away from harm's way" He finished his review with Rafael, picked up the images then took them with him to his office, filing them away neatly. He then pursued the asteroid Apophis, checking on its progress hourly.

Morning came to London and Darren was in the meeting room, viewing the fresh images from Rafael. He again looked at the previous pictures, remapping new trajectories and was now convinced he had enough evidence, to prove the asteroids had been manipulated. He concluded, that it was almost certain the second asteroid Apophis was on a direct collision course for Earth. He shouted "Jacob! Everyone, come quick, I have the proof we need to inform the Prime Minister" They all dropped what they were doing, and came running to meet Darren inside the meeting room.

After settling down, Jacob was the first to say something "Darren what have you got?" Darren spread the pictures out along the table and said "Look! The asteroid Sekhmet was manipulated here near Io, and forced to hit Apophis by what looks like some sort of explosive device, planted on the asteroid. Afterwards, it gathers speed before quickly changing course dramatically. It's too much of a coincidence, along with the instantaneous speed gain!" He took a deep breath, then continued "Both asteroids then collide as you see from the before, and after crash images. This action alone alters both asteroid trajectories, causing the smaller asteroid to accelerate and arrive years earlier, than we would have otherwise expected. Normally, we would have expected the action to slow it down but it was accelerated. Why!" He paused for a moment then said "If you view the second asteroid" He moved the images closer to Jacob and Bob, making sure they had the best views and continued with "You can see from the first picture, it slows down briefly from the initial impact, causing a minor space wobble before settling down. If you look at this picture here" He points to the last picture "You can see the tail of the asteroid is longer, because it's actually going faster, but why? I think it received a charge from the impact with the asteroid Sekhmet. It's only an educated theory, but I think the asteroid will speed up, eventually hitting Earth, around the fifteenth of November. If it does happen, it will be a catastrophe that the Earth has not seen, since the age of the dinosaurs!" Darren took a deep breath, while waiting for the others to take in his theory.

Bob was first to acknowledge his theory. He said "The asteroid trajectory of Apophis, may point to it landing on Earth, but as for aliens manipulating one, or both asteroids, it sounds a little farfetched. Let's be honest, we can't manipulate our own weather on Earth! So how could anything, possibly influence a large object such as an asteroid, bearing in mind the speed at which they travel?" Darren said "I thought it impossible, but I'm sure the pictures show otherwise" Both Jacob and Richard viewed the images and Richard said "I thought the delta shape was possibly a trick of the light, but as it has been taken from several different angles, I'm inclined to agree with Darren, but I'm bewildered as to how the object could have altered the asteroids trajectories" Jacob said "I was sceptical, but you may be right Darren. The thought of an asteroid the size of Apophis impacting Earth, is a very frightening thought, but I fear, it could be one, we may not live through" Darren said "Any more questions?" The question appeared to fall on deaf ears as the room went eerily silent for several minutes, until Jacob said "I think we all know what this means, we may have terrapods to contend with at the moment, but if Apophis impacts Earth, we won't have to worry about the terrapods at all. We will have to contend with a very different world, if there is anyone still alive" Darren said "You mean, when Apophis hits Earth Jacob!" Jacob said "Darren, continue with your studies on this new threat, but keep me well informed. I would suggest that Richard and Bob help you, as they have knowledge I think you can utilise. In the meantime, I'll inform the Prime Minister. He won't be happy, but I hope he does take heed of the warning and inform the public of the whole truth, this time" The meeting concluded with everyone, except Jacob and Bob, leaving the room.

When alone, Bob closed the door, leaving him alone with Jacob. He said "Do you realise the consequences of a direct asteroid hit of this magnitude on Earth?" Jacob said "I imagine it will cause colossal damage Bob" Bob said "Depending on where it lands, it could wipe out countries, striking them off the world map. The aftermath would be devastating for us as a race. We're very adaptable, but every country in the world relies on its neighbour in one way or another. It will cause unrest between neighbours, with surviving factions ending up fighting local wars instead of working together. If it hits Europe it could leave a large crater, with a burnt desolate landscape for thousands of miles" Jacob said "Let's hope it does not happen, can you help Darren and find out when this will happen. I'll speak to the Prime Minister now" Bob said goodbye, then left the room. Jacob followed him shortly, then turned and entered his office, closing the door afterwards for privacy.

Jacob immediately called the Prime Minister with the bad news. As expected, the Prime Minister couldn't believe what he was hearing, saying it must be a mistake. However, the gravity of the situation soon sunk in. Then, instead of dismissing the possibility, he found himself asking Jacobs advice on the safest place for people to hide in to survive the impact. The second asteroid impact would happen in two months, but there was still the issue of fending off terrapods. The government now had the added concern of preparing for an impact of devastating proportions. First, he required a definite time and place, so he could make his speech on how to deal with the reality of such a large object colliding with Earth. Secondly, he asked Jacob not to publicise the situation to the rest of the world just yet, as he thought it would be good, if the United Kingdom had a head start in preparing for the worst scenario. Other countries would stockpile goods, such as oil and in particular weapons for the aftermath, of what may be left behind. After all, his allegiance was to his own nation first. He would however, have to tell his cabinet and the opposition, this alone could lead to leaks, but it was a chance he needed to take. The conversation finished and they both returned to work, with the Prime Minister hastily getting in touch with the army, checking how things were going with the terrapod war.

Field Marshall Henderson answered his phone to the Prime Minister, with the noise of gun fire cackling in the background, and several heavy rounds of artillery going off. The outer suburbs looked like a scene from a world war two battlefield. He said "Hello Prime Minister, how are you?" The Prime Minister said "Not so good I'm afraid, but that's a story you will hear about in due time. Have you managed to secure London's suburbs yet?" The Field Marshall said "No Sir, these devils are proving to be very evasive and difficult to do any major damage to because of their sheer numbers. The chemicals work, but unfortunately there are too many of them. If I'm honest, we're fighting a losing battle. Thank Jacob and his team from us! The last piece of information they gave us is at least saving lives for now, but we're in danger of being overrun. If we can't stop them multiplying, it will soon be curtains for London" The Prime Minister said "Be prepared to fall back into the city, leaving just a skeleton crew in the outer limits. I want you and your men to change roles, from attacking terrapods to guarding the key areas of London's underground system. I'll be advising the public to go underground to escape the wrath of these parasites. We'll try to ride the winter out, hoping it will be a harsh one this year, for a change. This will help render the terrapods vulnerable to destruction later" The Field Marshall said "How will the winter help Sir?" The Prime Minister said "The cold should, if the taskforce are right give us an advantage over the winter months, but we will have to grab our chance and make it count. Your role however, will be to protect people against rogue terrapods breaking through defences and to stop the public taking things into their own hands and chaos reigning, instead of common sense" The conversation drew to an abrupt end, as they lost the phone signal.

Three o'clock arrived, with the Prime Minister on air again, this time he spoke with a mellow tone, and a sense of defeatism. He addressed the media outside 10 Downing Street, informing them of what they already knew, and had heard before from his lips. This time however, his body language was of a battered worn down boxer, throwing in the towel. He said "As you probably already know,

London is under siege and it's a war we can't win. Unlike previous world wars, our waters have been breached by a beast, we have named a terrapod. It's an unstoppable parasite, that we haven't seen the likes of on this planet. It's now a worldwide pandemic, and between each nation we'll continue to come up with solutions, but it may take time, possibly even years. It's the opinion of this government that everyone, without exception inside the cities, should take to the underground networks. We'll be able to feed and offer a degree of protection, by using both the army and police against the terrapods, and any rogue gangs, wishing to take the law into their own hands. I think! That is the government think that it is the only solution at present that we can offer. To stay outside the underground stations would be suicide, especially during daylight hours. The underground has been set up to accommodate the capitals inhabitants. Please do not move stations, as there will be plenty of room inside the tunnel networks. Some minor stations will be set up as distribution centres for food and general goods. If you choose to stay away from the underground stations you will have to fend for your selves, as it will be impossible to help you, when terrapods come knocking at our door. We can't afford to commit valuable soldiers to help you when it could cost them their lives trying to save you. If you choose not to go into the underground stations for any reason, you will be able to keep in touch through the telephone network as long as we can keep it running. You will be able to receive news via the radio networks, again for as long as there is a signal" The Prime Minister stopped for a while, then said "Any questions, before I go on to the second part of my speech" Several journalists asked how long conditions would last and was there anywhere else people could go" The Prime Minister's answer was "Initially, we hope it will be until the end of winter, then we might be able to make inroads into beating this parasite, as we believe it will be disadvantaged when the cold graces the country. The only places that will be safe from terrapods, are the colder countries such as the arctic, and the Antarctic, but survival will be difficult there, unless, of course, you were born into those extreme climes!" Questions soon came to a stop after his speech.

The Prime Minister waited briefly for more questions to be launched at him then said "I'm afraid the terrapods are the least of our worries at present as the second part of my speech, is about another catastrophic event that will happen to our planet, with unknown consequences. We think, sorry! We know that another asteroid called Apophis is on its way to Earth. We estimate it will impact Earth in the middle of November, possibly between the tenth, and fifteenth. We're unsure of the exact date, due to the speed it's travelling, but we think, it will happen between these dates. It will enter our atmosphere impacting near the Gulf of Mexico if our estimations are correct, and I have no reason to suspect they are not! This reason is why we think going underground is the right thing to do, because we have no idea of how it will affect us in Britain. This has happened before, when it wiped out the dinosaurs, so it will leave the world a very different and harsher place to live in. It might

even wipe out the human race. There's no plan in place for this catastrophe, we can only hope we survive and can rebuild afterwards. Are there any questions please?" The press was silent as they took in the new statement, but soon found their voice through a female journalist. She said "Jenny Smith, Channel six. Prime Minister, are you sure about the asteroid? Why will it make any difference to anyone in the United Kingdom?" The Prime Minister replied "The asteroid is coming, ignore it at your peril! It will affect the whole world in one way or another. It won't break up while entering Earth's atmosphere, like the first asteroid, it is far too big. It's big enough to cause a deep depression in the Gulf of Mexico. We expect all the countries in that region to be devastated, including parts of the United States. It will likely affect weather systems and the climate in many different regions, including those thousands of miles away from the impact zone. As for other changes, they would only be pure speculation" The Prime Minister waited for more questions, answering as many as he could. Then he concluded the press meeting by saying "I suggest everyone acts quickly, because the deadline for getting into underground stations is August the thirty first. We'll only allow people inside who make their own way to the stations after that date. No help will be given to assist anyone to the stations, because terrapods could be lurking in the streets and outside the entrances. All flights and sea crossings will be suspended on that date, so we can contain any new terrapod outbreaks. Thank you everyone and good luck, we'll keep the public posted as and when we can. There will be one more broadcast on the thirtieth of August, advising everyone to head for the nearest underground station. Best to get into one earlier though, as terrapods will be here sooner than you think" He turned away and returned to the front door of 10 Downing Street.

As he arrived, the door sprung open and his wife met him, with tears in her eyes.

## CHAPTER 18

## GOING UNDERGROUND

By now, the Ellis family had settled into James's house, but things had changed. They heard the newsflash from the Prime Minister and had decided the safest option was to go to their nearest station. It would mean moving once again from a nice comfortable house. It was clear their temporary accommodation was deemed unsafe to stay in. It would also be a lottery driving through London's streets, trying to seek the safer counties of the north. James and Debra disagreed with their decision and decided to head northwards, taking a chance on transportation links and settling near Scotland until normality returned to the country. They would return home after the terrapods were exterminated. Dave argued that there would be no home to return to with the army on the offensive. Homes would be considered collateral damage, in the fight against terrapods. He pointed out that some unscrupulous criminals would also take advantage of the lawlessness, removing valuables and destroying houses, blaming it on the terrapod war.

 James and Debra had decided to leave today and were preparing to do so. They would drive northwards, through the streets of London and head towards the midlands. Then negotiate their way northwards via the coast roads, because the motorways would be jam packed with thousands of people with similar ideas. They would travel in the early morning in the hope the roads would be quieter and the terrapods less active, making the journey safer. Dave and Mary chose to leave for Kennington underground station on the twenty ninth of August, two days before the deadline unless terrapods arrived on their doorstep earlier. They would prepare everything needed in advance, so they were capable of moving at a moment's notice. They could lock the house up, leaving a key hidden inside a small metal box buried beneath the flower bed near the front door. They would leave supplies of canned foods, concealed inside paint containers, within the garage. They hoped to return to the house after the terrapods were under control, if they survived the asteroid impact.

Ten o'clock arrived with Dave, Mary, James, Debra, Joe and Thomas, sat in the living room having a final drink, before saying their goodbyes. Within the hour, James and Debra would heading through London's streets, on their way northwards to an unknown future. Mary was unhappy to see them leave as she hoped they would all stay together, returning as a family unit after surviving the oncoming challenges. James was convinced they would be safer up north. He thought the asteroid collision would not affect the north, giving them a better survival chance.

After finishing their drink and talking about the good times gone James and Debra, placed their final items in their car, and readied to leave. Joe and Thomas said goodbye to James and Debra, not realising this could be the last time they ever see them. Dave kissed Debra on the cheek, then hugged her, while saying goodbye. He then shook James's hand thanking him for his hospitality, while promising to keep in touch.

When it came to Mary's turn, she couldn't hold back her tears, as she hugged James, then Debra for as long as possible. James said "Dave, I've left a message on Tony's answer phone, asking him to look for us in the north, near Carlisle or to seek you in Kennington underground station. Good luck, see you soon" Dave, Mary, Joe and Thomas said "Goodbye" then watched them get in their car and slowly drive away, briefly looking back, at what they were leaving behind.

Mary and the boys stepped back inside the house, while Dave followed on closing the door behind him. Mary sent the boys to bed, leaving Dave and her alone to talk about the finer details of moving to the sanctuary of the underground station.

******

It was now the middle of August, several weeks had passed since the government's announcement, urging people to seek refuge inside the underground network. Pete, Jan and Bentley had decided to take up the offer of refuge, but for now they were lodging in a friend's Victorian house near the Oval cricket ground, in London. The terrapod invasion had not been halted and the army could be heard in the distance, using heavy weapons as the noise ebbed ever closer to them. The gunfire and heavy artillery was quieter at night, but as soon as first light was on London, a barrage of shots could be heard, only stopping briefly, when the air force flew over, dropping their payload of chemicals.

Pete was in the kitchen, when Jan descended the stairs. She arrived at the bottom and Pete said "Good morning Jan" Jan continued into the kitchen straight into Pete's arms, where they kissed and cuddled, before he said "I love you Jan! Strange, but if it wasn't for these parasites, we would never have met. When this is over, will you be my girl?" Jan smiled, as she held Pete tight and said "I would love to" The lovebirds kissed, and hugged for several more minutes.

Suddenly, a long burst of gunfire returned their attentions back to their grim situation. Jan said "What time are we leaving for the underground station?" Pete said "We'll leave at two o'clock then we can settle in by evening. It won't be as comfortable as here Jan" Jan said "But we'll be safe, and we won't get stuck in the mad rush as the deadline draws near" Pete said "I'm not sure what we will find when we get there, but the terrapods will be here soon, along with this second asteroid. Who knows what will be left in its aftermath" Jan said "It won't be a bed of roses in the underground stations. It will be every one for themselves, especially if we are there for a long period and food gets scarce" They had planned the move carefully, being only a short walk from Kennington underground station. If they needed anything before the station was on lock down, they assumed they would be able walk out and fetch it.

Two o'clock arrived, with Pet, Jan and Bentley ready to leave. They collected everything, hiding many food items inside two large suitcases along with their clothes. Jan rested them inside the front door ready to leave, while Pete searched for a supermarket trolley to cart their belongings to the station.

He returned with a trolley then knocked on the door. Jan opened it, and between them, they loaded two large suitcases onto the trolley. Jan went inside fetching two smaller bags, also cramming them on the trolley with some difficulty. Afterwards, they closed the front door and set off down the street, towards Kennington station.

The streets were busy with people heading towards the underground stations, some going to Kennington, whilst others opted for the longer walk to Oval station in the opposite direction. When Pete, Jan and Bentley arrived at the station, they found a long queue with three soldiers checking suitcase contents.

After an hour, it was Pete, Jan, and Bentley's turn to be check into the station. A soldier checked their bags and suitcases thoroughly, asking them if they had any concealed weapons. Jan asked "Why" He replied "This is sanctuary for the inhabitants. We don't want gangs of thugs, robbing and threatening people. You are under military rule now, and we expect you to respect all rules and not take things into your own hands" Jan was shocked and unsure whether it was a good thing or not. She said "If we've forgotten anything, can we go and fetch it" The soldier replied abruptly "You will be given a makeshift tent, with provisions for a short time then allocated your own personal area that will be numbered. If you choose to leave for any reason! You will lose your allocation, and will wait in line to be offered another, if there's room" Pete said "And if you don't have room!" The soldier said "That will be your problem. We won't allow entry if there's no room. We'll tell you where the nearest station is. If you try to enter without authorisation, or because we are full, we'll use deadly force!" Pete, Jan and Bentley now shocked, passed through the checkpoint taking their trolley through then they walked three feet forward, before another soldier said "You can't bring that thing inside, it takes up valuable space someone could live in. Take it back outside please"

Pete and Jan, quickly unloaded their belongings, while Jan stood in line with Bentley. Pete, quickly put the trolley outside. Jan expected the soldier to say Bentley was not allowed in next, because he was a dog, but the soldier stayed silent. Many people walked past her before Pete returned. After he returned, they were directed down the escalator to the lower floor.

When arriving at the bottom of the escalator, another soldier holding tags and an electronic notebook, pointed to a small area with a two man tent. The soldier said "This will be your spot, take this from me" He handed them a laminated piece of paper with the number 1527589 on, then said "I suggest you write your names on it, and on the tent somewhere in case they are stolen. It will be the only way you can prove you have the right to be here" He added "Food for your dog will come out your allowance, so don't ask for extras to feed it" He took note of their names and number, then typed the information into his database.

They settled down, putting their belongings into the tent, whilst removing the things they needed. At the rear of the tent were several cans of food, powdered milk, a can opener, two metal plates and some plastic cups. Jan looked unimpressed with the soldier's reception, and even less happy with their inability to leave the station to acquire extra items needed later, before the expected impact. Inside, they also found two sleeping bags in their makeshift quarters. After settling in they rested and talked about what may happen, when the deadline elapsed.

Now with everything sorted out, they peered outside their tent, curious to see who else was around. There were empty tents on both sides, and the cold tiled station wall behind them. Trains could also be heard running occasionally within the tunnel systems.

A soldier walked by, and they asked if they were able to ride the trains. The answer was a stern "No, only soldiers used them to distribute food, essential goods, and to ferry injured personnel to designated hospital areas. The only way they would be allowed to ride them was in an emergency, such as terrapods, breaching the station" So Pete and Jan, set about making a comfortable home within the tunnel tent world, wondering how long they would be imprisoned, beneath the underground realms.

******

Ten o'clock in the morning on the seventeenth of August, with Jane and her mother, trying to get a train to Euston Station in London, enabling them to head northbound to Manchester and onwards to Blackpool. They were stuck at Wimbledon station and were told there would be no more trains until the following day to Blackpool, due to diverted refugee trains. They made a decision to continue by bus as far as they could, then walk the rest of the journey to Euston station. Then they could continue northwards in the morning, when the trains were reinstated.

The bus terminated at Kennington Park Road, a short distance away from the underground station. Jane and her mother watched the many hordes, moving towards the station entrance, joining the line and waiting to enter. Jane said to her mother "Mum, shall we get on a train here then make our way to Euston?" Her mother pointed to a soldier and said "Okay, we'll check with that soldier over there, perhaps he can help us" They approached him, and Jane asked "Can we get a train to Euston from here" He said "This station is closed! We're only accepting refugees at the moment. I wouldn't advise going to Euston if I was you ladies" Jane's mother replied "Why not?" The soldier replied "Terrapods! They have swarmed the station. A train pulled in at platform three with hundreds of terrapods on board, and all hell broke loose. They're expecting to get them under control tomorrow, if they find them all. It's closed for now though" Jane said to the soldier "Can we stay here for a while and move on in the morning?" He said "If you want to stay here, you'll need to get in line for an allotment on the lower floor, but you won't be able to use the trains they're no longer in service" Jane and her mother quickly discussed their options. Before Jane said "Can we get to Euston by foot?" The soldier answered "It would be suicide by foot! You'll have to wait until the terrapods have been cleared from within the station then enter by train. If it was me, I would ride both the terrapod infestation and the asteroid impact out here. At least, if you go inside now, you'll get a place. If you leave it any longer, you may not get a place" Jane turned to her mother then said "Best we stay here mum!" Her mother replied "Okay Jane, let's get in line" They promptly thanked the soldier, and moved in line.

Two hours later, they found themselves checking in through the underground entrance, and heading down the escalator. They were quickly placed in a tent next to Pete and Jan. Inside their tent they found basic provisions, along with sleeping bags. Next to them, Pete and Jan looked on, as they settled in.

After getting comfortable, Jan introduced herself to Jane and her mother, attempting to make them feel at home, as they were likely to be neighbours for a long time. Jane explained about the events that had happened to her inside the supermarket. She also informed them of a man who had helped her escape the terrapod onslaught. Pete and Jan, told Jane about their narrow escape from the Isle of Wight and how they made their way to Guildford, then onwards to Kennington. Eventually deciding to go underground, to wait out the asteroid, in the hope they could survive both the impact, and the parasites.

****** 

Meanwhile, a young girl joined the Kennington underground refugee queue. She was a familiar face to several people, but they could not place her. Some thought, she may have been a star once, but she was dressed in scruffy worn out clothes. Most were unsure, so avoided approaching her. She appeared quiet, almost shell-shocked, and it was clear she had been through an extremely difficult journey in order to reach the station.

She finally arrived at the front of the queue and was greeted by a soldier. He said "Hello love, can I check your bag please?" She gave him her bag, but said nothing. He checked it, then said "What's your name" She muttered "Julie" He said "Julie, please go through and see that soldier over there" He pointed to a tall soldier, who was checking for space on the floor below. He found a small area with a tent fit for two and another one suitable for four, and he was busy trying to allocate them to refugees.

Julie slowly walked towards him, as he said "You on your own love?" Julie nodded in acknowledgement then he led her down the escalator, to a spot in front of Jane and her mother. He issued her a laminated number and asked for her name. She replied "Julie" He replied "Julie what?" Quietly spoken, she said "Julie, I can't remember my last name" The soldier said "That won't do! I have to put something down" So he typed in Smith, and said "Smith! Your name is Julie Smith for now, until you remember your real name" He informed her about the accommodation rules, before leaving her alone.

Jane said "Are you okay Julie?" Julie acknowledged them though she was reluctant to speak. Bentley stuck his head out of the tent opening, to see who had moved in. After a while, he moved nearer to Julie, sniffing her. Stealthily, he moved back to the edge of Pete and Jan's allotted area, but stayed as close as he dared to Julie's space, before relaxing. Julie relaxed beside him, putting her hand towards Bentley's head, as he peered up at her. He pushed his head closer to her hand, allowing his head to be stroked. Julie stroked it gently, as Bentley rested his head on the floor feeling content, only moving occasionally, to nudge her hand when she stopped stroking him.

Julie soon relaxed whilst leaning against her bag, and slowly drifting off to sleep. Bentley moved in closer, resting his head on her hand, until they both fell into a deep sleep.

Two hours later, Julie woke up finding Bentley huddled up beside her. She rubbed her eyes, while focusing on the many tent peaks, set out neatly in blocks making up the numerous mini communities. There was one vacant tent left in their set of ten, with enough room for a maximum of four. Julie's tent however, could sleep two so she luckily had plenty of room inside.

Jan, realising Julie was awake, said "My name's Jan! It looks like Bentley has taken a shine to you" Julie said "My name's Julie, he's a lovely dog" Jan introduced Pete, Jane and her mother Sarah to Julie, and finally Bentley. Then Jan said "How did you end up here Julie?" Julie replied "I was trapped on the roadside, watching people being slaughtered from terrapods, when I was cornered. I remember rising from my hiding place behind a car after being spotted by a terrapod. I remember running afterwards, dodging two terrapods and hiding behind an open car door. I waited several minutes, until the terrapod settled down then I made a break for the terrapod front line, between me and the soldiers. I reached the terrapod line, but I must have tripped, knocking myself out near the soldier's barricade. I woke up, finding a soldier carrying me in his arms and putting me into a jeep. I was driven back here and left by the roadside, and told to come here to seek a safe place to stay. That's how I ended up here" Pete said "Who was the soldier that came to your aid" Julie said "I heard someone call him Craig, but I did not get a chance to thank him" They continued talking until the day drew to a close, and the flow of refugees stopped.

Morning arrived, with Jane chasing around, asking the soldier's if the way to Euston station had been cleared, and whether they could continue on their journey. She eventually found the officer in charge, and his answer was brief and to the point. He said "Euston station has been overrun by terrapods. All tunnel entrances into the station have been sealed up and no trains are running in or out of it. You won't get out of London, terrapods are running amok everywhere. We're expecting more refugees to arrive within the next two days, and we are already close to the limit. If I was you, I'd think yourself lucky and learn to love your tent, as you could be here for some considerable time" Jane knew escaping London looked hopeless now. She returned to her mother, then after a short conversation, they decided to stay.

******

Nine thirty arrived on the morning of the twentieth of August, with Dave and Mary, watching the mass migration, as it headed towards the underground station. They thought it was time for them to follow. This was mainly because, newsflashes were advising people to head to underground stations as they were filling up fast. Many were stretched to their limits, with many refusing new admissions. Euston station was now closed, so people from that area had moved further afield, to get a placement inside other underground stations. This caused a knock on effect with people having to move further and further away from their nearest station, putting them ever closer to the terrapods invasion, and the army's activity.

Dave thought, that if they left going to an underground station until the end of the month, they would be unable to secure a place. Dave said "Mary we're ready to leave now! We need to get a place at Kennington underground station. We can't get any sleep now anyway, with the army trying to blow these parasites away. If these things were in a secluded area they would probably have used nuclear weapons by now, despite the danger to the odd person" He paused, then added "I can't believe we're going underground, just like a colony of ants" Mary answered "Better ants, than parasite fodder. You're right, we'll leave today and secure our place before they all go" Dave said "Okay, we have our belongings packed. We just need some minor items, then we can go" Mary said "You get the boys ready then we'll leave" so Dave, did as he was asked.

Ten o'clock arrived, with the Ellis family assembled outside the front door, holding their luggage. Mary checked Joe and Thomas were present then said "If you're ready Dave, let's go!" Dave was ready, so he locked the house door then they all made their way towards the underground station.

They arrived outside the underground station, and duly joined the huge queue. A soldier greeted them with "It will be a long wait, if you're trying to get in here. We're expecting to close our doors later, as we're rapidly running out of space. You could try your luck at the Oval station, if you can't get in here"

The sun beat down on the queuing refugees, as Dave worried that the long wait, would make Joe and Thomas restless, and possibly run off, getting lost. He said "Mary, Shall we go down the road?" Mary said "No, the soldier's would have told everyone the same thing, so lots of people will try to get inside the Oval. The queue will move from here over to there. We're better off staying here and waiting"

The Ellis family stayed in line, whilst watching the line slowly move along. Many people, decided to leave to try the Oval station, only to return later complaining the Oval station had been closed, as it was out of space.

Meanwhile, other people started yelling obscenities at the soldiers, urging them to hurry up. Occasional scuffles broke out between the people queuing. A gang of men, tried pushing in, until eventually a soldier walked up to them and said "Get in line at the rear, if you want a place in here, then you might just get in" One man said "There are five of us mate, we could easily take you out!" The soldier replied "Maybe three of you may get past me, perhaps even four, but with permission to kill. At least one of you won't make it past me, and my colleagues will make short work of the rest of you. This is military law here, not gang law!" The man thought better of it, quickly apologising with "Sorry mate, it's the stress" The men quickly returned to the end of the queue.

Three thirty arrived, with the Ellis family finally reaching the underground entrance. The soldier in front of them shouted to his colleague, standing within the doorway "How many more can we fit in Ben?" A voice came back "We can fit four in one tent, and six at the rear, by the tube train entrance" The soldier near the Ellis family said "You're good to go, follow that soldier over there" He pointed to the soldier by the escalator. They wandered over to the soldier, who then took them down the escalator and led them to the four man tent next to Julie.

At the tent they were handed their number, then gave the soldier their information, whilst putting their belongings inside the tent. They thanked the soldier and began making the best of the situation.

Outside, the soldier announced they had only six places available, and he would allocate those places to families with children. He also added that there was additional shelter being erected at the Oval cricket ground, just a short walk away. Then he pointed back down the road, towards his right.

The mood quickly turned nasty, as the five men, who had earlier been ordered back to the end of the queue came forward, confronting the soldier once again. The soldier repeated "The first two families with children will be allowed inside, but the rest of the people here will have to seek shelter at the cricket ground, where there is plenty of room for everyone. Cover has been erected to protect everyone, who goes there" The soldier was joined by two extra soldiers with guns, clearly loaded and showing a sign of strength. Calm appeared as the soldier quickly chose two families. The two families disappeared inside the station and were duly given their allocation.

Outside however, the five men began fighting between other men, using knifes. All hell broke loose with the street erupting into violence. Many people with children went running for safety, inside the nearby shops and houses. The three soldiers shouted over to the men, asking them to stop, but it fell on deaf ears. One soldier shot a round of bullets into the air, to cool the situation down. The men briefly stopped to look around, then one man said "If we stay out here we're dead anyway, so I might as well die by your gun" He ran straight towards the soldier, in an attempt to disarm him, but was met by hail of bullets from a second soldier, cutting him down and killing him stone dead. Two more men attempted running at the soldiers. They also met a hail of bullets, killing one, while injuring the second, bringing him to his knees.

Two civilians, within the station confines, obviously knew the dead men, so decided to attack the soldiers from behind. One met a swift death from a single shot to the head by a soldier. The other, managed to take down the soldier with a can opener, stabbing it deep into his neck, rupturing his main artery. The soldier fell to his knees then watched in disbelief, as his blood squirted downwards, soaking his kit, before trickling to ground. After thirty seconds, he fell to the floor, while his fellow soldiers watched the life ebb from his eyes. The attacker reached for the dead soldier's gun, as the remaining soldiers put several rounds of bullets into him, ensuring he no longer presented a threat.

A deadly hush became apparent, as people moved away from the entrance, avoiding conflict with the soldiers, and the remaining fighters. Most, made a hasty beeline towards the Oval cricket ground, pushing people over along the way. A soldier standing inside the station, stared defiantly behind him, as he said "If there's anyone else, who does not want to abide by the rules, please leave now! As there will be no exceptions if you break them!" No answer was forthcoming.

After a two minute silence, a second soldier appeared from the floor below. Between them they quickly began removing the lifeless bodies. They rested them a hundred yards away from the entrance, in garden undergrowth. After returning to the station one said "I know he was a fellow soldier, but we can't help him now. We do not want to give terrapods any reason to come knocking on our door" Both soldiers picked up their fallen colleague, picked him clean of weapons, and one of the soldiers removed his wallet with his identity card. He threw his wallet away along with his money, then muttered "That's of no use where we're headed" They continued lifting his body, placing it with the two dead civilians.

While placing his body on the ground one of the soldiers looked upwards. He spotted a man with two young two boys, crouched inside a doorway. They looked stunned and frightened, as the soldier said "I thought you would have gone to the Oval shelter" The man answered "We'll take our chance in these empty houses, it looks a safer bet than going into the cricket ground with the likes of those thugs, you've just disposed of" The soldier said "Is it just you three?" The man said "Yes!" The soldier looked towards his colleague, then said "We have three dead bodies here" The other soldier said "I see what you're saying, we can't help them, but we have room for these people" The soldier looked back towards the man, and said "There are three dead bodies here, which means somewhere inside, there are three empty beds. You can come inside the station if you like, their loss is your gain" The man thought hard about the offer then looked at his children, knowing they were safer inside and said "Yes, we would like to, thank you" The soldier said "Follow us back, Jim here, will check you for weapons. If you leave the station for any reason, you won't be allowed to return" Together, they all returned to the station. Jim checked them as promised, before they found the spot, where the two dead men had once resided. Jim issued the dead soldier's sleeping bag to them, as the three of them settled down for some well needed sleep.

Downstairs, Pete and Jan were talking to Jane's mother Sarah, she was explaining how the supermarket had been involved in an incident, and how she had been worried for her daughter's safety.

Mary stuck her head out the tent opening, after hearing voices. She peered towards Pete and Jan then said "Is that you Jan?" Jan replied "Yes, I don't believe it! We didn't think we'd see you again. How are you?" Mary said "We're good, Dave, Joe and Thomas are here as well" Jan said "I'm glad you're safe, Pete's here, and we've been here for quite a while now" Dave poked his head out the tent and said "Good to see you Pete! Hi Jan, it's nice to meet you Sarah, looks like we could be here until the winter breaks, if the media's right" Jane sitting inside the tent, recognised the voice outside, and putting her head outside said "Hi Dave" Dave said "Hello Jane, good to see you again" He added "It's unbelievable, we've all met up again inside the station after going our different ways" Julie moved towards them and was about to introduce herself, but was beaten to it by Mary, when she said "Hi Julie, I know you from the internet" Julie said "What do you mean?" Mary said "You were on the roadside, making a video diary of a terrapod attack, while you uploaded pictures to the internet. You said your name was Julie Walters, we were sure you had been killed by terrapods" Julie said "I'm Julie Walters! Thank you, I'd forgotten my name due to a fall. I was rescued by a soldier, but I don't know where he went. I presume, he's still fighting the parasites, or possibly dead" They all settled down, retelling their individual stories, while gradually getting reacquainted once again. Meanwhile, Julie pondered what had happened to the brave soldier, who had rescued her.

\*\*\*\*\*\*

It was now eleven o'clock, on the thirty first of August. Kennington underground station was full to capacity. Many people, unable to enter inside, had been diverted towards the cricket ground. However, some chose to stay outside, within fifty feet of the entrance. Any closer and the soldiers would have to implement a shoot to kill policy, due to government orders. This was to give the inhabitants who had the right to stay, protection against outsiders removing them forcefully, and taking their places. The soldiers promised that if any one died while inside, their body would be removed, and the next person on the list would be allowed to enter. Many scuffles had broken out some attempting to attain entry, but most were from the lack of food and water.

The government used planes to drop supplies into designated areas for people unable to get shelter. However, large gangs had taken over the drop zones, taking full advantage of the situation by extorting money, goods or favours for the exchange of life saving provisions. Hence, fights and gang warfare was now rife. Most civilians, too frightened to venture out during the night, stayed hidden inside derelict houses, until the daylight hours in order to remain safe. Others began growing their own plants inside houses, hiding it in the roof cavities or secret compartments, in case the gangs got wind of it. There was however, no escaping the terrapods heading their way, and they were now nearly on top of them. Whether they were rich man, poor man, soldier or a gang leader the parasites did not differentiate, as they were all meat for the grinder.

The first sign of terrapods arriving at Kennington was from a soldier, as he sprinted towards a group of people gathered outside the entrance talking. He shouted "Run to the cricket ground, they are coming! The terrapods are on their way, run!" He stood in the middle of the road, aiming his automatic weapon down towards the end of the street then shouted "If you are quick, you can still make the shelter! Go now!" Many people picked their bags up and slowly began making their way past the soldier, heading towards the cricket ground. It was too pedestrian for the soldier's liking, so he shouted "Quickly, unless you want to die here!" Many walkers meandered slowly down the road, while they watched even more soldiers running towards them.

When at a safe distance, the soldiers turned and opened fire into a long wave of terrapods in the road behind. It was then, that the gravity of the situation grabbed the walker's fears, as they burst into a sprint. Any fallers were left for dead amidst the stampeding hordes. The critically injured, would be fodder for the terrapods to feast upon later. Many failed to make the cricket ground and were cut off by terrapods, pouncing from the nearby gardens.

When the fortunate runners did reach the cricket ground, they tried to negotiate the turnstiles, before reaching the relative safety of the ground and the protective line of soldiers. Terrapods trapped many people as they tried entering through the turnstiles. The turnstiles soon turned into a human food jam for terrapods. As people realised there was no way through, they turned backwards only to find their pathway blocked by the oncoming charge of people, seeking refuge inside the cricket ground. Terrapods picked them off at will, as the masses ground to a standstill, unsure of which way to run.

People returned towards the safety of the soldiers and gunfire was riffled off, as troops tried holding back the marauding terrapods. The soldiers were slowly driven backwards amidst the onslaught, until they found themselves camped outside Kennington underground station. One soldier shouted to his comrades guarding the underground station "We can't protect you any longer, pull down the steel shutters and keep the parasites out. We're falling back, good luck!" The soldiers retreated, leaving behind the underground inhabitants.

Any human stragglers close to the cricket ground were quickly swallowed up, by the relentless terrapods as they followed the retreating soldiers and any lucky escapees.

The station soldier pulled the shutter down, closing it tightly from the outside world. Quickly, the floor outside of the entrance became carpeted in hungry terrapods, leaping up at the shutter, in a pointless effort to attach to the soldiers standing safely inside. It served only to make the soldiers jump with fear, behind their steel safety shield. A soldier peeking at the terrapods through a small gap in the shutter, with his gun aloft said "God works in mysterious ways, but these little devils, make no bones as to their intent!"

## CHAPTER 19

## THE JOURNEY TO LONDON

Several months passed and it was now the second of November, terrapods had overrun most of the inhabited land. Only a few pockets had survived the rapidly growing parasite population. The Royal family had escaped to the remoteness of Scottish highlands. The government had chosen to settle on the Shetland Isles. The terrapods had not reached the remote highlands, tending to stay near highly populated areas with a good food source. The only other areas avoiding parasite contact were the remote islands off the mainland, or small mainland farms with a minimal labour force for harvesting crops mostly in East Anglia and Wales.

All hospitals in large cities, moved into underground stations capable of supporting the huge workforce and equipment required to run them. These buildings were purpose built and strengthened, with many troops protecting them from terrapods and the local gangs. The Royal London hospital, along with the taskforce had been moved into Waterloo station, along with the staff from King's and St Bart's hospitals. The human population had shrunk somewhat from terrapods consuming the multitudes of people. It now made better sense to amalgamate all three hospitals, keeping all the medical expertise under one roof. Other regions, both inside and outside London had followed suit.

The war on terrapods raged around the country, as fierce battles ensued. Protective buildings were erected inside the underground stations using darkened entrances, to halt the parasites passage. Then at night when terrapods were less active, the army along with civilian factions used terrorist type tactics, to destroy large areas of dormant parasites. They also marked areas with flares to guide planes into non populated areas, to flatten them, using missiles or chemicals. These tactics impacted the terrapod population, but served only to keep the status quo.

Outside the country, many nations used differing methods to keep terrapod numbers down, with the United States choosing conventional weapons. America protected huge volumes of people inside large sports stadiums, along with the underground networks inside the larger cities. They used chemical weapons to keep the terrapods at bay outside the large populated areas, resulting in no go areas due to the contamination.

The American President hid inside Area 51, sending out weekly broadcasts to let every citizen know, he was looking after their interests. However, many people were collateral damage from the chemicals being systematically deployed by soldiers, in order to kill terrapods. Amongst the chaos, people were now taking matters into their own hands, blaming their president for running away and hiding to save his own skin. As soldiers became terrapod victims, it led to a plentiful supply of weapons, so large gangs broke out in the populated areas, taking what they wanted by force. If you crossed them you were either killed or fed to the local terrapod population, if it was considered a worthy enough crime in their eyes. The National Guard did nothing to stop them, because their hands were tied fighting off terrapods. Many had families in the ganglands, so they decided to throw in the towel against the terrapods, choosing to look after their own families from marauding gangs. Others chose to make their own gangs in the guise of vigilantes. They used the National Guard badges to extinguish the worst gang members in their areas, claiming they were the law in a lawless state. The United States had returned to "The Wild West Syndrome" as some people put it.

Several South American countries under siege from the parasites, begged neighbouring countries to allow refugees to cross their borders. They were flatly refused, forcing people back into the clutches of terrapods and a certain death. These acts were common, in vain attempts to stop the infestation. They proved futile because terrapods found many ways to infiltrate countries, either through poorly guarded borders, or by travelling with refugees on board ships.

Rio was wiped off the map, as terrapods made short work of the highly populated shanti towns, before continuing on to the more affluent areas. The only escape route was by sea using boats to move on to the next town, then waiting for the inevitable expanding terrapod population to catch them up, to restart the cycle again. The mountains were a place where terrapods dare not venture. They would climb to the tree line, but no further, as they could not deal with the cold. Many farmers took advantage making nearby mountains habitable, but it was a hard life and many first time city farmers failed to feed themselves sufficiently on the hillsides, and became victims of the harsh way of life.

Europe followed the United Kingdom, with the exception of the mountainous areas, where small villagers used tunnels with cave like cut outs inside to protect themselves. The terrapods avoided these areas, due to the cold of winter approaching and the cooler climes as you reached high into the hills. Instead, terrapods chose to pick off villagers lower down and quietly wait, biding their time for the rest.

Moving onto China, there was a dense population of terrapods settling inside Beijing. The authorities told everyone to move out the city, giving them a thirtieth of October deadline, then at eight minutes past eight o'clock in the evening, they flattened the city with a huge aerial onslaught, leaving nothing and no one alive amongst the ruins. Russia chose to move people northwards, as close to Siberia as possible, then in the densest concentration of terrapods they dropped a small nuclear bomb on the areas, to the disgust of China.

North and South Vietnam turned on each other, in a huge conflict. The North decided to bombard the border between the two countries, to ensure terrapods spotted within the controlled area, did not reach the lower realms of North Vietnam. It was a futile gesture, as terrapods found different routes to enter the country and rampage through the poorest areas. This act of violence inflamed the South Vietnamese, pouring petrol on an already smoking fire. Total war broke out between the two nations, with terrapods enjoying unenviable free fodder from the fallen victims.

Australia was the only country to survive any major terrapod infestation, partly because of the strict nature of their border controls, and because as soon as the world admitted to a problem, their Prime Minister Anne Carter shut up shop. She refused to allow foreign goods and migrants into the country, avoiding the risk of cross infection. It however came at a huge cost with all but one country in the world, severing ties to them. Only their neighbour New Zealand would support them. The North Island of New Zealand was inhabited by terrapods so everyone uprooted, moving down to the South Island with help from the Australians.

\*\*\*\*\*\*

Chad stayed with Pedro working at the Arecibo Observatory, and they were now trapped by terrapods. They knew their days were numbered, because it was only a matter of time before the parasites discovered a way into the main telescope chamber. However, they were able to contact the outside world using the internet. They survived on food from the Observatories kitchenette, but knew they would run out of food by the eleventh of November, when the asteroid Apophis was due to touch down. It appeared pointless asking for food to be dropped to them as death was assured anyway, and their request would likely be ignored with the world thinking about their own plights.

Chad looked into the night sky through the telescope lens, quickly finding Apophis, as it sped to Earth. He looked intensely at the large celestial body while using the telescopes computer, to estimate the impact time with Earth. The mammoth asteroid was so close now he could estimate touchdown to within a few hours. Chad said "It will impact Earth north-west of us, in the Gulf of Mexico. It will wipe us off the map, along with parts of South America and the Southern States of America. The Tsunami will destroy many nearby islands to!" Chad paused, then said "Pedro, I'm sorry you are stuck here with me. Apophis will hit Earth on the eleventh of this month, between eight and ten o'clock in the evening. The choice we have will be to die at the hands of parasites, or wait to be pounded by the might of Apophis" Pedro said "If I was not here I would have gone home, and would likely have died as terrapod food days ago. I think I'll wait for the asteroid and become part of one of Earth's biggest historic event" Chad said "We'll work on the asteroid and give the world as much information as possible, at least whilst we're able to Pedro. We can't stop it and it will wipe us out, but it will have a huge impact on the terrapods as well. It will at least reduce their numbers" Pedro said "I'm prepared to die, but do you think Rafael got away?" Chad said "I sent him an email a little while back, but I have not received a reply yet so we must assume the terrapods got to him"

Both men looked sad as they wondered how Rafael had met his grisly death. They continued working, knowing in nine days they would be turned to dust by Apophis.

\*\*\*\*\*\*

The President of the United States, now set up in Area 51, replaced his phone after finishing his call with the British Prime Minister. Together, they knew precisely when the asteroid would impact the planet. Both began gathering different estimates on the collateral damage that would occur around the world. The American experts estimated it would plunge into the sea causing huge tsunamis, affecting an area of five hundred miles around the impact point. The British however, claim the area affected could be more like a thousand miles or even further, with large plumes of scalding sea water being launched skywards, eventually falling back to Earth with other minerals and elements. The British thought, the Americans were being too cautious of the destructive power of the asteroid, but many nations preferred the American point of view on the predicted outcome.

\*\*\*\*\*\*

Meanwhile, at Waterloo station the taskforce had been reformed, after moving from the Royal London hospital. They were working on ways of destroying terrapods, but the focus had been altered to accommodate the thoughts of the incoming asteroid. They would check predictions of the asteroid impact first then pick up the terrapod problem afterwards, if they survived.

Darren had been in touch with Rafael after he had abandoned the Arecibo Observatory. He begged him to come to London and join them in their studies, as he thought his asteroid knowledge would be invaluable for the taskforce in their fight against the parasites. Rafael had agreed to make his way to London, but the last time Darren had heard from him, was when he was turned away from Puerto Rico's International airport, because all flights were grounded. Rafael said he would try to come by ship, but that was three days ago. Nothing had been heard from him since.

******

Rafael had managed to convince a fisherman with a small boat, to aid his escape to America and hopefully avoiding the asteroid impact. The fisherman took Rafael's money, promising to take both Rafael and his girlfriend Maria, to Key West in the United States. Afterwards, the fisherman would continue navigating his way further northwards to New York. Both Rafael and Maria's parents were keen for them to leave Puerto Rico, because staying would mean a certain death. Unfortunately, they could not afford to go with them.

The fishing vessel neared Key West and the fisherman offered to take the couple on to Miami, if they paid him more money. They only had fifty dollars, but he wanted another five hundred for the extra journey. They could not afford any more, so they asked him to leave them in Key West. The fisherman then quickly asked if they had any valuables he could have instead. When the answer was no, his mood changed and he said "The Keys are thirty miles from here, I think you should pay me the extra fifty dollars or I'll leave you here!" An irate Rafael said "We gave you enough money to take us to the Keys and that is what you will do!" The fisherman said "This is my boat and I can do what I like, if you give me the fifty dollars, then I might let you off at the Keys" Rafael and Maria did not trust him now and said emphatically "No!" The disgruntled fisherman answered them by pulling a long knife out from his pocket that he used for gutting fish. He said "The money or I'll gut you Rafael, then your girlfriend" Rafael put his hand in his pocket, pulling out all the money he had. The fisherman snatched the cash and said "Both of you sit down!" He removed a length of rope from the side of his boat, insisting Maria tied Rafael's hands.

Maria reluctantly tied Rafael's hands, while watching the fisherman closely. She then asked "What are you going to do?" He replied "I want you to go into the cabin with me. If you don't do as I ask, I'll gut your boyfriend and feed him to the sea life" Maria immediately realised, rape was on the fisherman agenda and began crying. Maria looked towards Rafael, as she moved into the cabin, and waited. The fisherman followed her inside then said "Undress for me!" Maria slowly undone the button on her blouse, but the fisherman wanted her to speed up and said "Hurry, or we'll be in Miami before I get pleasure from you" Maria moved in closer to him, until her breasts were on show for his eyes. The fisherman stood beside her, sliding his sharp blade onto her neck. He said "You don't need him, you'll learn to be my girl" She started trembling uncontrollably as his hand touched her breast. Maria shoved his hand away, and said "No! I'll never want you!" The fisherman replied "If that's how you want it! I'll carve up Rafael and still keep you for myself, or you can take your chance on the kindness of the sea!" Maria's tears flowed, as she said "Will you let Rafael live, if I let you?" The fisherman said "Okay, only if you stay with me" Maria cried, while thinking about his offer. She finally agreed this time, then allowed the fisherman to get close, until again, he held the knife to her throat and said "He can live, but he'll be bobbing about in the beautiful sea" He laughed out loud, as Maria tried pushing him away, but his grip tightened this time. Then he quickly forced her face down onto the boats control panel. Then with the other hand, he pulled down on her underwear and said "Be a good girl now! Think of your boyfriend" His unshaven face, touched her cheek, as the edge of his blade slowly released her throat. He then prepared to take Maria.

Suddenly, Rafael's hand grabbed the fisherman's arm, pulling the knife away. Rafael's other hand, grabbed the fisherman's head, while forcing his thumb, deep into his eye socket. The fisherman now partially blinded, and stunned, fell backwards away from Maria. He lashed out wildly with his knife, slicing into Rafael's arm, causing a red line of blood to trickle from the wound. The fisherman said "Well then, I planned to finish you off and dump you overboard anyway!" He regained his balance lunging forward, whilst swinging the knife at Rafael. He missed again then moved backwards. Again, he steadied himself, and readied for a second attack. He looked Rafael in the eye and said "Take your last breath Rafael!" He launched towards Rafael, with a wild slash of his knife. Rafael fell backwards, tripping over the fishing net lying on the deck. He fell downwards then joined the netting. The fisherman smiled, as he moved in for the kill.

Maria came darting out of the cabin, hitting the fisherman hard with the ships log, directly on the crown of his head. He fell sideways, ending up leaning, precariously over the side of the boat. Rafael, quick as a flash, rose to his feet and ploughed into the fisherman, causing him to lose his grip and fall over the edge of the boat. The fisherman, whilst still holding his knife, again lashed out, catching his own hand. He sliced it open, causing blood to gush out. Then he continued downwards, hitting the water with a big splash.

After a minute, the fisherman tried swimming back to the boat, but it was travelling faster than he could swim, leaving him bobbing in the sea alone. He shouted to Rafael and Maria "You can't leave me here! I'll die. You need me to navigate to the Keys" Maria shouted back "Land is on the horizon, we don't need your help, you scumbag. You have a knife! That's more than you were prepared to leave Rafael!" She then spat into the water towards the fisherman, as they sailed on towards the Keys.

The fisherman floated in the blue waters, looking to his left. He spotted land, albeit a very long way off. He put his knife in mouth, while checking on his blood soaked hand. He cursed Rafael and Maria, before beginning to swim towards the distant shoreline. After several strokes, he noticed his blood discolouring the sea water behind him. Then felt like he was no longer alone. He stopped swimming and spun round quickly, to find two fins circling behind him. They ebbed ever closer as he watched the striped colouring of the unmistakeable Tiger shark. He panicked and began swimming for his life, whilst heading for the shore. The sharks followed menacingly behind, biding their time while waiting for him to get tired, so they could end the chase.

The fishing vessel navigated around Key West as Rafael and Maria looked for somewhere to drop anchor, but there was nowhere suitable. They moved along coast, only to find a man violently waving a rifle in the air. He shouted "Go to the mainland! Go to Miami, you're not safe here" He immediately turned his back on them and focused behind.

Maria searched the shore, watching the hundreds of terrapods, littering the roadside. Quickly she turned towards the man, then shouted "Swim to us, we'll take you with us" He shouted back "No! I've lost everything, my wife and my children go!" He shot into the air, warning them off. Then turned his gun towards a terrapod, shooting its top pincer clean off. Realising escape was impossible, he removed his right shoe, and sock, then he rested the rifle handle on the floor, and put his chin over the barrel. Then with one swift manoeuvre of his big toe, he pulled the trigger downwards. A loud bang sounded and his life was extinguished. He slumped to the ground, while Maria cried "No!" She then pushed her head deep into Rafael's arms, hiding from the horror.

Rafael continued watching, as the terrapods leapt on his warm body. Swiftly he took Maria into the cabin to comfort her. He then powered the boat away from the shoreline, and into deeper waters. He navigated northwards using the ships compass on the instrument panel.

Two hours quickly passed, with Rafael pondering why they had not spotted land. He checked the compass, but to his dismay he found it was stuck on north. This was not good, because he did not have clue where they were headed. He told Maria the bad news, her reply was "Better out here than on land, especially if it is covered by those terrapods" Rafael looked skywards trying to use the relative sun position, to estimate where they were headed. Then he continued heading on to where he thought was north.

An hour later, a large cruise liner appeared on the horizon. Rafael tried getting in touch with the liner using the international distress call. After receiving no answer on the boat's original channel, he tried using several different channels, in the hope of reaching the liner.

He eventually received a reply from a male voice "This is the Winds of Time cruise ship who are you?" Rafael did not know his boats name, because it was hidden by the fishing nets, so he replied "This is Rafael and Maria from Puerto Rico. We've been stranded on this vessel since the captain fell overboard, while navigating to Miami. Can you help us?" The voice came back with "This is Mark Johnston, you're a long way from Miami and for your information, I would not advise you, I repeat do not continue on to Miami, as it has been engulfed by terrapods. A thousand of us, including the crew have stolen this ship and we're sailing to England. We believe it will be the safest place to be when the asteroid hits Earth" In Rafael's eyes this was excellent news, as it was where he and Maria wanted to go. Rafael decided to ask for help and to see if they could board the ship, and get a ride to England. Rafael said "We want to go to England, can we board your ship and travel with you?" Mark replied "Everyone on ship has paid to travel except the crew, so how will you pay for your ride?" Rafael asked Maria how much cash the fisherman had left behind. She answered "Nine hundred dollars, see if that will do!" Rafael said hopefully "We have nine hundred dollars for our passage, is that enough?" Rafael heard Mark discussing their plight to the ship's Captain, in the background. Mark replied "Nine hundred pounds is not enough to slow the ship down, to pick you up then return back up to full speed Rafael. What else do you have to offer?" Rafael said "I was the first to spot both asteroids and tell the world they would hit Earth. My colleague Chad is still working inside the Arecibo Observatory studying the phenomena, and I can get in touch with him if you have internet connection. I can check on the latest news" Mark talked to his Captain then shortly said "Rafael and Maria, welcome aboard the Winds of Time, we'll slow down then intersect with your course about a mile in the direction you are holding. We'll throw you a line and pull your vessel in, so you can board us. We'll tow your vessel alongside, so we can use it to ferry people onto dry land when we arrive at Ramsgate, if you've no objection?" Rafael said "That sounds good to me!" A relieved Rafael continued through the waves and eventually linked up with the liner. Meanwhile, Maria sorted out what little belongings they had.

After boarding the liner, Rafael and Maria settled into a first class cabin with all the luxuries they could need, with the exception of food as it was rationed. They soon received a message from the Captain requesting that Rafael visited the bridge. Rafael sorted his belongings then agreed to go to the bridge, as long as Maria could accompany him.

Rafael and Maria arrived on the bridge, finding a large man in his sixties wearing the Captains hat and jacket. He obviously was not the original ship's Captain. He said "Hello Sir, I'm Captain Paul Dawson, I was retired until being somewhat hijacked and asked to sail this vessel to London" Rafael said "Where's the original Captain?" The Captain replied "He returned to Miami to save his family" He paused, before continuing with "To cut a long story short he lost his family and his life to the parasites, poor chap! I'm the reserve" Rafael said "Have you sailed a ship this size?" The Captain replied "Not a cruise liner this size, but I was in the Royal Navy until retiring ten years ago. I captained a light weight frigate, for thirty years and I must admit if you ignore the electronic aids on the bridge, they are beautiful ships" Rafael was somewhat impressed as he said "So what would you like to speak to me about" The Captain replied "Well Rafael, we'll be going to Ramsgate in England, but because of the liner's size we won't be able to dock, because there's only an old disused hovercraft base there. I that is, the committee on board, would like to know if the ship will be safe if it stays on the water when the asteroid impacts Earth, or would we be better off going ashore" Rafael said "I think either option is viable. The terrapods won't be able to board the ship, but in the long term you will need to seek land to replenish supplies and perhaps grow food" The Captain said "I would like to know the exact time the asteroid will impact Earth. Also, will any following tsunamis reach London?" Rafael said "The asteroid will hit on the eleventh between eight and ten o'clock in the gulf area, but it's, only an estimate. If you have internet connection, I can email my friend Chad, to see what he has to say. He could tell us where to hide" The Captain said "We do have internet access at the moment. It would be useful to know thank you Rafael. I'll get someone to show you the internet connection. Best do it sooner rather than later, in case we lose it" The Captain concluded the conversation, by requesting his number two accompanied Rafael to the recreation area, to access the internet.

Rafael sat in the ships recreation area emailing his friend Chad at the Observatory. After several minutes, he eventually received a reply. He was ecstatic to hear from his friends, but guessed Chad and Pedro would obviously die inside the Observatory from the asteroid impact, as they had no way of escaping it. Chad was relieved to hear Rafael had managed to sail away from the impact zone, and now had a chance of escaping the consequences of the monumental major disaster on the horizon. They both emailed at length updating each other with their adventures.

After receiving the information he required from Chad, Rafael had mixed emotions. It was good to hear from Chad and Pedro, but he was saddened they would not escape the asteroid consequences. Both men emailed their goodbyes, with Rafael promising to keep in touch with them every day. When finished, he wondered how the two brave men would meet their deaths, by terrapod or by asteroid impact.

\*\*\*\*\*\*

The tenth of November arrived, it was now a day before the impact and the cruise liner sailed serenely past Southampton and on to Portsmouth, it was clear, terrapods had decimated the inhabitants. The only survivors were living on board small boats, just off the shoreline, or barricaded high up inside buildings. The liner crept slowly along the gentle waters, while the crew searched for communities untouched by parasites. It quickly became clear that some areas had seen major battles, with buildings in ruins, many fires and no visible signs of life to be found. This was echoed around the coastline, until they arrived at their destination.

At Ramsgate the Captain dropped anchor and ordered a meeting to be held in the ships theatre. He asked everybody to decide what they wanted to do. The choices were simple, they either disembarked via the fishing vessel taking their chances on land, or they stayed aboard the liner awaiting their fate amongst the uncertain aftermath of the asteroid. A contingency plan was also on offer, this was to sail northwards to Scotland and settle there, if England was uninhabitable. Each person or family chose their own path, with the Captain promising to honour all decisions. He informed everyone that the ship would only be anchored in Ramsgate for two days, unless they did not survive the impact. If unable to find provisions they would leave on the second day and head to Scotland. Anyone wishing to travel with them could do so, if they made it back to the ship in time. Unloading of people from the ship would begin as soon as the meeting finished. Guns and supplies would be given to anyone who required them to help defend themselves against terrapods. However, they would be rationed to one per party, along with the ammunition.

Rafael and Maria thanked the Captain, and the many people they befriended on their journey to England. They boarded the fishing vessel with one of the sailors at its helm. They were relieved to see the fishing vessel being used to ferry people to the safety of dry land.

Rafael and Maria waved back at the crew standing on the bridge, glimpsing the Captain removing his hat, whilst returning the wave. They smiled as the boat moved serenely away from the liner, heading for shore. Rafael wondered how many would survive their uncertain future.

The boat arrived to shore then tied up to a small jetty, allowing the passengers to disembark. Quickly they set about their journeys ahead. The bulk of the migrants headed in land by foot. Many going to the railways, in the hope they would still be running and would take them to safety. They had not realised the true extent of the terrapod invasion, thinking it was confined to a few small pockets in England. They waited in empty railway stations, only to find their grisly final destinations feet away, when terrapods jumped up from the tracks and on to the platforms.

Rafael and Maria decided to head to Waterloo station in the heart of London, because Darren in the British taskforce had told him in their last communication he would be heading there. Rafael knew Waterloo station was on the river Thames by a bridge, so he thought the best way to get there would be by car, following the coast line heading northwards. They would then follow the river in land, checking every station along the way until they found the station.

Rafael and Maria immediately set out following the coastline to the north, checking abandoned cars along the roadside, looking for keys still left inside. Keeping close to the shoreline was a good idea, because terrapods were not in abundance due to the freezing breeze coming in from the North Sea. It was a very desolate lonely walk, with no life to be seen but by far the safest option.

They soon arrived at an old disused hovercraft terminal, originally used for the channel crossings for many years. The workshop next door looked as if it was still being used. Rafael and Maria decided to look inside, to see if any cars had been left unattended or if anyone was still around to help them.

They cautiously approached the workshop entrance then Rafael knocked on the door, and shouted "Is anyone there?" No answer was forthcoming, so he repeated his request and waited briefly, before trying to open the door. He slowly, but carefully pushed the door ajar, expecting to bump into a preying terrapod. No parasites were visible so he fully opened it, allowing him to see into the workshop. In front of him sat two boats, both were thirty foot long. One sat high in the air supported by a wooden jig, with part of its wooden hull missing whilst in a state of renovation. The other was resting on a truck with its mast severely damaged.

Rafael and Maria stepped inside and moved towards the truck. On arrival to the cab, they slowly opened its door finding keys in the ignition barrel. Rafael climbed inside the cab and tried starting it. The engine turned, but did not start. Suddenly, a man's voice said "Hey! That's my truck! You won't start it without fuel!" The man was sitting within the suspended boat and only became visible, when he peered out from behind the lower part of its hull. Rafael and Maria jumped and it took a few seconds, before Maria answered "Sorry! We thought no one was here! We need to get to Waterloo station in London" The man said "Not in my truck! Why do you want to go there?" Maria said "We need to meet a man there and escape the second asteroid" The man said "No point running away, what will be, will be!" Rafael said "It's important we get there and meet up with the British taskforce. We need to help exterminate the terrapods" The man said "Terrapods have left me alone here. It's secluded here and hidden away from busy town. The closure of the port meant everyone left here years ago, searching for work elsewhere. I took over the maintenance bay, fixing up some of the local boats. You won't get to London by car or rail, your best bet is by boat using the river. Then docking next to one of the many pleasure cruise jetties" Rafael said "Is there anywhere we can hire a small boat from to get us there?" The man said "Well, you'll find many discarded boats along the river, but that's thirty miles away. However, you'll need to negotiate your way inland first. I wouldn't advise it!" Rafael said "Does anyone around here have a boat they can loan us?" The man said sarcastically "I don't have a boat, but if you promise to look after her, I have something you could borrow" Rafael said "Anything that will get us to Waterloo station will do!" The man said "follow me!" They followed him to a large roller door at the rear of the workshop. He lifted the door, revealing a concrete landing pad leading directly down into the sea and extending out to the left side of the bay.

There, sat a mini red hovercraft all by itself. He said "This was a toy of mine fifteen years ago. A company specialising in making scale models sold it to me. I removed the cabin and put a small turbine on the back, making it a full working hovercraft. It does work, but I've not used it to travel as far as London before" Rafael looked it over quickly then said "This is a cool piece of kit, can we use it?" The man said "Yes, if you want to, but you'll need a few flying lessons" Maria said "Thank you Sir, what's your name?" The man said "It's Stanley, but don't forget this is a toy! I'm not sure how it will cope in the open sea, it will be rough out there but it won't sink" Rafael said "I'd rather trust the sea, than a gauntlet of terrapods anytime"

After checking the hovercraft over, they started it up and to Stanley's surprise, it ran beautifully. Stanley quickly set about teaching Rafael how to fly the beast, using the beach to show Rafael how to manoeuvre it. Rafael found manoeuvring it a little tricky to begin with, but eventually mastered the basics. Stanley said "The hovercraft will take two people at best, anymore and it will likely sink in rough seas or struggle to go anywhere. It will still be quicker than any boat, but it will be very thirsty on fuel. You'll need extra diesel on board in case you run out in the middle of the river, but it will float, albeit leaving you stranded" Rafael said "Will you come with us Stanley?" Stanley replied "I won't leave here, I'm safe here from the parasites and as I said, the craft will only hold two" Rafael said "I've studied the asteroid that's on its way to Earth. I suggest you move to higher ground when the sea level rises from the multiple tsunamis. You could go out to sea and ride the wave literally on your boat" Stanley said "Thanks for the advice, I'll finish the boat by tomorrow and take my chance on the sea as you say"

Rafael and Maria put their belongings into the hovercraft then started it up. Stanley strapped an extra fuel can to the rear of the crafts plastic panelling, then shook Rafael's hand and kissed Maria on the cheek. He said "Good luck, perhaps we'll meet again, when you return my hovercraft!" Rafael pulled the throttle back and the hovercraft lifted its skirt and turned seawards. Maria waved back to Stanley as they glided out of sight, heading northwards towards the Thames estuary.

The journey to Waterloo Bridge took two long hours, with the craft requiring refuelling on the fly. They searched the banks of the Thames, finally finding a safe place to dock near Waterloo Bridge.

Leaving the hovercraft tied up to a pleasure craft jetty, Rafael and Maria clambered out. They climbed up several sets of stairs, before reaching the top of the embankment. They arrived on the north side of Waterloo Bridge, peering across the span towards the station on the south side. The London eye sat to right looking truly magnificent, except for the many discarded bodies littering the landmark. They needed to cross the bridge, but it was covered in prowling terrapods, many still digesting the unfortunates. Other car dwellers had stopped on the bridge, as terrapods breached their cabins and slayed them. However, there was a narrow winding passage running through the terrapod colony on the bridge, but it would mean certain death if attempted by foot.

Maria scanned the roadside along the Strand, viewing the many waiting terrapods. However, there was a slim glimmer of hope. An abandoned black taxi sat just twenty feet away, with the driver's door open. The driver lay on the opposite side of the road, being disposed of by a large terrapod. Maria nudged Rafael, to gain his attention then pointed towards the taxi. Cautiously, they walked towards the taxi watching for lurking parasites. After reaching it they looked inside, checking for any nasty surprises. The taxi was empty, but there was no sign of any keys in the ignition either. Rafael gazed back at the driver on the floor. He noticed his keys on the ground next to him, so Rafael sneaked towards the dead man and began picking up his keys. The keys jangled as he lifted them. The terrapod flinched, immediately turning to face Rafael. Rafael said "I think I've been spotted Maria!" He threw the keys into Maria's hands, enabling her to catch them cleanly. She caught them, then distressed, watched as the terrapod flattened its back. It catapulted towards Rafael, only to be intersected by a second terrapod taking it back to ground. Then it began feasting on the beast, giving Rafael a narrow escape.

Rafael, quickly scampered back to the Maria, and they both climbed into the taxi. Maria reversed the taxi over several terrapods, before driving towards Waterloo Bridge. They entered the bridge and Maria gradually navigated through the terrapod army, along with the many chaotically abandoned cars. Only then, did they witness the full horror of the terrapods munching through the people of London. As they drove along Rafael watched something very strange. He viewed terrapod eating terrapod, perhaps from the lack of food.

After negotiating the bridge, Maria drove the taxi to the front of Waterloo station. Where many terrapods had gathered, blocking the entrance. Rafael peered into the entrance curious as to why terrapods had not ventured inside the building, despite the lack of a barrier to hinder them.

Maria sneaked the car a little closer and it soon became apparent, the station was in complete darkness. She approached the entrance, running over several terrapods in the process. Rafael said "There's only way we'll get inside safely. We'll have to drive through the entrance. There are too many terrapods in front of us to simply walk in" Maria said "Okay, let's hope no one is standing inside when we arrive" She slammed the accelerator pedal down hard, sped forward and mounted the pavement. The taxi bounced up several steps, running over many more terrapods, then ploughed into the open entrance. The front suspension broke, and a tyre burst, but its momentum, propelled it beyond the darkened entrance, with sparks spewing out of the underside of the taxi, until it ground to a halt inside the station.

They vacated the taxi, rapidly running deeper into the station, only to find a brightly lit area with soldiers holding automatic weapons at them. Darren of the taskforce immediately ran over to the soldiers, trying to find out what the commotion was all about. A soldier, pointing his gun at the couple said "We should shoot you for that! Who are you?" Rafael said "This is Maria and I'm Rafael from Puerto Rico!" The soldier, somewhat bewildered was about to ask them to leave, until Darren said "Rafael! Rafael, from the Arecibo Observatory! I didn't think you would make it. Welcome to London and the taskforce" The soldier, somewhat perplexed, said "Do you know him Sir?" Darren said "Yes, he's on our team. He's been working with us from Puerto Rico" Darren put his arms around Rafael and Maria then led them quickly away from the soldiers saying "You must come down and meet the rest of the team" The soldiers, still a little bemused, began clearing up the mess from the taxi's ungracious entrance.

The taskforce now had a new employee, who could maybe shed light, not just on the parasites, but also on the oncoming asteroid Apophis. Rafael was quizzed about the size and speed of the asteroid, along with the exact impact position. When they found out Rafael was going to lose his best friend and colleague Chad from the asteroid impact, the mood went very sombre. Jacob promised to do his best to get a Skype link to his friend Chad and his engineer Pedro, so they could at least see a familiar face before they took their last breath on this world.

## CHAPTER 20

## THE ARRIVAL OF THE APOCALYPSE

The sun rose high above the Arecibo Observatory, on the eleventh of November. Chad and Pedro were sipping a cold beer together, wishing each other the best. Pedro said "This will be our last day, gracing this blue planet of ours and we'll be in prime position to watch something that has not happened on this Earth, for sixty five million years" Chad said "We'll watch the events unfold above us until eight o'clock tonight when Apophis lands. Ours will be a quick and glorious death. Unlike the other poor souls around the globe" Pedro said "It's been an honour working with you. It's good Rafael has a fighting chance of surviving the asteroid" Chad said "He's a good lad, I hope he remembers us" Pedro said "Yes, so what shall we do on our last day?" Chad said "Pedro, you have been our engineer for twenty years, but you have never witnessed first-hand, the view through the lens. How would you like to see Apophis and view our new god of destruction for yourself" Pedro said "I would so enjoy the chance to see it. I can't think of anyone better to show me than you Chad" Chad said "We'll spend the day watching Apophis as it makes its way to us. Then we can drink the champagne I've kept for a special occasion. After all, we don't want the champagne going to waste. I can't think of a more special occasion than Apophis" Pedro laughed then said "The champagne won't last 'til tomorrow, either way!" Both men laughed together while sipping their beers.

Chad and Pedro continued watching the asteroid until nine o'clock in the morning. Chad then recalculated the impact time. The asteroids close proximity to Earth, made it easy to precisely estimate the impact time. Chad said "Pedro I've calculated the impact time. Before, I estimated the impact time to be eight o'clock tonight, but with the speed increase, it will happen at eleven o'clock in the morning" Both men continued monitoring the speed and direction of the asteroid over the next hour, confirming the new impact time to the world.

******

It was two thirty in the afternoon inside Kennington underground station. The Ellis family and Julie Walters were conversing about their good fortunes, within their small commune. They were commenting about the chance coincidences, ensuring they all met up again. Mary and Julie decided to leave the rest talking, as they headed up the escalator to check on the terrapods scattered outside the station entrance.

When arriving at the top, they walked to the entrance, where five soldiers met them. The first fifteen feet of the entrance, had been darkened, forming a tunnel as it entered into the station. Mary said "Why have you not blocked the entrance off, surely terrapods can still get inside? A strong door would keep them out better?" The nearest soldier said "We have been assured by experts within the taskforce, that this is a safest way of keeping the parasites out. The parasites are less active in the dark, so it's easy for us to eliminate any single stray terrapod. Any parasite finding itself inside the blackened area freezes and slowly dies of starvation, without danger to civilians or the army. This is by far the safest way to protect ourselves against the beasts, without confrontation" Mary and Julie looked unconvinced, but the soldiers seemed to know what they were doing.

Suddenly, there was a crack of gunfire, it came from outside as several automatic guns were heard, edging closer and closer to the station entrance. One soldier said "That's our troops shooting!" The soldiers pushed past the women, proceeding to guard the blackened entrance. Two soldiers moved into the blacked out area. Then one soldier shouted "Clear of terrapods Sir, shall we go out?" The soldier beside Mary shouted back "Stay there and guard the entrance, only soldiers are allowed to pass through. If anyone else tries, shoot to kill!" Mary was shocked by the soldiers order and said "The soldiers may have civilians with them, will you allow them through?" The soldier said "I'm only authorised to allow soldiers inside. Civilians, must stay outside, unless anyone leaves the sanctuary of the station, allowing them to take their place" The soldier inside the blackout area said "There are two men, one's in uniform, the other is a civilian branding an army issue gun. They have a young boy and baby with them. Can I allow them in Sir?" The soldier replied "Allow the soldier to pass through" The blackout soldier shouted over to the soldier outside "You can come in, but only you!" The soldier begged for all to be allowed in. After being turned down for the second time, he spoke to the civilian holding the baby, informing him that he was not allowed inside the station with the children. It quickly became apparent that both men were extremely unhappy. The civilian immediately thrust the baby into the soldier's arms. The soldier quickly took the baby and entered the station. He handed the baby to a soldier standing inside the blackout area.

After briefly conversing with the soldier, he returned to the waiting civilian, giving him his jacket to wear. The civilian put on the soldier's jacket then shouted back, we're both soldiers, you don't have the right to leave a three year old child outside at the mercy of these terrapods. The soldier near Mary heard him, then said "We don't have room inside" Then he turned to the officer in charge and said "Sir, the terrapods are closing in on them, can I allow them through?" The officer in charge could not make his mind up and clammed up. Mary said "The boy can take my place" The officer said "No, you must stay here to look after your family" He struggled with his conscience, as the terrapods closed in on the three outside. Then he blurted out "Let them in! I won't have a child's death on my conscience. We'll manage somehow" The blackout soldier shouted "Get in, we'll cover you!" The two men with child entered the station, protected by a barrage of bullets, cutting through the menacing terrapods behind.

The two soldiers, the boy, and the baby were reunited, after going through the entrance. The officer in command said to the soldier, wearing the army trousers "You're very lucky! Who are you?" He replied "I'm Corporal Craig Healey and the other man is Private David Dean or Deano as most call him. The young boy is my son Michael and the baby girl, was saved by my commanding officer from terrapods near Portsmouth. They were at my house with my babysitter, until it was overrun by terrapods. We only managed to get back in time to protect and save the children" The soldier said "Why is Deano not in uniform" Craig said "He was off duty when I asked him to go to my house to protect the children, because he was nearer than me" The soldier said "You best find somewhere to put your things both of you. I'm sure the children will be well looked after" The officer was now thankful they had been allowed inside.

Craig and Deano carried the children past the officer, then approached Mary and Julie. Julie immediately recognised Craig. He was the trooper who had carried her to safety on the roadside. Craig and Julie's eyes met, and she smiled and said "Hello Craig!" Craig looked at Julie, thinking this beautiful girl knows me, but how? He stared into her eyes and then at her facial expression, then it dawned on him. She was indeed the girl he had rescued from the terrapods, near Portsmouth. He smiled then said "You look a lot different from the last time I saw you Julie!" Julie was impressed that Craig knew her name and that he had also recognised her. They talked briefly, as Julie told Mary about Craig, the man who had saved her life.

Realising both the men and children, had nowhere to rest, Julie offered to squeeze them all into her tent, but after attempting it, they discovered it was a far too tighter squeeze for them all. Deano soon found sleeping quarters with other soldiers and returned and said "Two soldiers over there have offered to put me up in their four man tent. I'll sleep there when I need to. We can work around the shift patterns for now" Craig and Julie continued conversing and it soon became apparent they were getting on very well indeed.

\*\*\*\*\*\*

Three thirty arrived at Waterloo station, as the taskforce gathered together within their new meeting room. Jacob and Richard finally managed to reach Chad and Pedro using a Skype link. Rafael was pleased to be talking to his friends in the Observatory. Chad and Pedro were a little tipsy after drinking the champagne, but in good spirits, despite knowing they had but a short time left on this Earth.

After the initial greetings, Chad and Pedro informed the taskforce of the new asteroid impact time. They had moved the touchdown time forward and it was now thirty minutes until impact. Chad said "Hope you're ready for it over there, when we go it will make for a huge firework display for thousands of miles" Rafael said "I think they should rename Apophis in your memories, immortalising you both forever" Laughter followed, until Chad broke it with "It's been a pleasure knowing you Rafael" Then Chad quickly checked the telescope and found Apophis then said "Nearly here boy's, best hold on tight, it's going to be a rough ride on this hellcoaster" They continued talking using Skype, with all the taskforce managing to speak to the men in the Observatory.

******

Eleven o'clock came quickly to the Observatory, as the asteroid lightened up, even the daylight sky. It sped along leaving a huge trailing tail behind it, soring towards its final resting place on Mother Earth. The Earth's serenity, hid the fact that she was a sitting, unprepared duck, compared to the angry Apophis moving in for the kill at tremendous speed. Apophis approached Earth at forty thousand miles an hour. The moon appeared, to gracefully move out of the asteroids path, allowing it free passage to the blue planet. One more minute and it would be upon Earth and negotiating the atmosphere. However, there was one more satellite to dispose of before entering the atmospheric shell.

The vulnerable Space Station stood in the asteroids path, with spacemen and women from all nations, watching inside in awe of the magnificent monster approaching. Their admiring thoughts turned to horror, as they realised the asteroid was about to plough straight through them. The Space Station, one of man's technological marvels, took decades to design and build and was about to pulverised by Apophis in a single second. The astronauts aboard had nowhere to run from this incomprehensible emergency. Several headed for escape capsules, but only two of the unfortunate twelve made it.

The asteroid ploughed through half of the station, pulverising it, before the ensuing heat trail melted through the remnants left behind, causing it to break in two. One section was dragged unceremoniously along with the asteroid like a rag doll. Four faces peered out of the tiny windows, as it was towed violently through space, taking them to their deaths on entry to the atmosphere. Another section was sent spinning out of control, and left on an erratic orbit. Every now and then two faces could be seen inside, trying to sneak a peek at the colossal asteroid, whilst awaiting their own fates.

Apophis hit the atmosphere like a hammer, causing a loud sonic boom to be heard all over Africa. People looked skywards, watching the space station remnants disintegrate in the sky. It continued zooming across the bright blue sky, clear to see by the naked eye. Onlookers watched in awe as the huge plume of smoke exited its tail.

Apophis was far bigger and more powerful than the first asteroid, and Earth's atmosphere was powerless to stop this monumental heavenly slice of history, from entering the clear blue air of the third planet from the sun. It fought its way through the thin air, pushing it aside with a second sonic boom. Apophis, did not escape unscathed for its crime, as large chunks of rocks were flung from its body and thrown all over the African continent.

Most people watched the asteroid as it tore through the sky, but they ignored the large chunks of rocks being spewed out, until they lit up the skies with a bright white light and exploded. Most came to rest over the nations of Africa, causing impact fires and flattening bushes, trees and buildings alike, and killing unsuspecting people on the ground.

A few seconds later, the main asteroid disappeared from sight and another sonic boom sounded. A pulsating shockwave duly followed, flattening everything on the ground within a two hundred mile radius of the explosion. Buildings, bridges, trees and a huge build-up of sand was launched upwards then released back down over a township, completely burying all the inhabitants. While the main part of the asteroid continued on its journey towards the Gulf of Mexico, oblivious of its destructive power.

At the Observatory, Chad and Pedro were looking through the telescope lens. They abruptly lost sight of the asteroid, but continued conversing to Rafael on Skype, whilst sipping champagne. Chad said "That's it Rafael, it's been a pleasure to work with you. The asteroid will be somewhere inside the atmosphere heading our way. We have, but a few seconds now. Good bye my friend" Pedro said "Good bye Rafael, good luck for the future. Help those guys beat those dam terrapods and…" The link was abruptly cut off.

Darren put his hand on Rafael's shoulder then said "I'm sorry Rafael, the asteroid's blocking the signal, they have only a few seconds before impact" Rafael began crying and Maria put her comforting arms around him, as tears rolled down both their cheeks.

Jacob said "The beast is here! We had better be ready for it! It will be a long hard winter ahead, if we survive!"

******

Above the Gulf of Mexico, the asteroid screamed across the sky at astronomical speed, whilst lighting up the sky with its deadly vapour trail. The Gulf was now in the asteroids sights, and it is but a few seconds from its final resting place. The loud deafening boom made the inhabitants of the Caribbean islands, hold there bursting ear drums, as blood trickled from them.

Apophis shrieked down into the heart of the Gulf, crashing deep into the sea and pulverising the seabed. The superheated asteroid melted into the rock causing a huge indent, deep into the Earth's crust. The rush of superheated air, shot outwards in a boiling raging ring to the shores of the Gulf countries. A fire ring followed, rapidly engulfing the local islands, including the Arecibo Observatory in Puerto Rico. It reduced them to a singed barren desert landscape, within a fraction of a second. Boats sailing the sea, were set alight as the supercharged heat, instantly reduced them to scorched charcoaled wrecks.

Survivors of the fire ball, witness in awe a large body of water being sucked into the air like a water spout, then it quickly spread out towards them. The island survivors ran for the protective safety of the indoors. Many more watched in astonishment, as superheated water, came funnelling down at high velocity towards them. It arrived, cooking them instantly where they stood. People jumped into the equally boiling sea, in a bid to escape, but many scalded lifeless bodies soon floated to the surface.

The ensuing fire ball, sped away from the impact area like a large expanding halo, sent from the devil himself to burn everything inside a thousand miles. Mexico, Florida, the northern countries of South America, and even parts of California were not spared. The displaced water from the impact area left a huge void around the impact area. The sea water finally returned to fill it, by draining the surrounding coastal areas of millions of gallons of sea water. When completely full, it returned the water outwards in a one hundred foot tsunami that reached out in all directions. This was the first of many to come. The coastal towns of the Gulf area took the initial tsunami shock wave, as it quickly engulfed roadways then swept buildings, cars and even trains two miles inland. It eventually halted, depositing them neatly in a long trail upon the hillsides. All of the Gulf islands, Jamaica, Trinidad and even as far away as Bermuda were drained of life, as the water flooded all but the highest ground. To the north the tsunami swallowed half of the state of Florida, as it flowed up along the rest of the Gulf areas and expanded out through the low line river networks. The Keys were cleansed of buildings and the connecting bridge was left battered, and detached from the mainland. The everglades disappeared, swamped with high water, ensuring it joined the Gulf sea waters. The Mississippi had a huge tidal wave running the length of the delta, flooding areas hundreds of miles inland, wiping out towns and villages along its flood plains. The Panama Canal was widened by fifty feet, as the tidal flood water went through destroying locks and upending ships, before settling continuing into the ocean beyond.

The tsunami wave, rode the Atlantic eastwards going unseen for a considerable amount of time. It took several hours to reach the northern coasts of Africa, sending waves of a hundred feet high crashing onto fishing villages on the western coasts, with devastating consequences. Thousands of unprepared people were caught out by the tsunami coming to land, especially when the asteroid had landed thousands of miles away in the Gulf of Mexico. The tsunami's wave, forced its way into the Mediterranean Sea with a reduced height of sixty feet, as it negotiated the narrow causeway. However, it still destroyed many low lying seaside resorts, with its increased speed. The worse hit was Venice, when it tore out its foundations from underneath it, leaving the city beneath the sea like a modern Atlantis.

The wave continued northwards to Spain and France, and onto England causing flooding to western coastlines and river estuaries. Even London on the east coast of England, had its share of flooding, with the Thames barrier closing, to stop most of the flood waters. The barrier worked, but at the price to many areas north of London. It forced the extra water up the eastern coastline. The sea water made short work of destroying coastal defences, already stretched to their limits. It washed the frugal defences away and rolled inwards hundreds of miles, reclaiming land that had once belonged to the sea, leaving several hill cities cut off from the mainland. Holland also found itself with big problems, as the low level container ports were wiped off the map, and instantly returned back to the sea.

******

Beneath the sea of the impact area, the pulverised bedrock left behind small voids, allowing hot volcanic lava to gradually seep up from beneath the Earth's crust. Seismic disturbances frequently increased as each day passed. Earthquakes, within the states of California Oregon and Washington increased in intensity. Volcanoes, such as St Helens began making very short and sharp eruptions, sending dust clouds high into the sky. Many people, chose to escape northwards, worried in case of full eruptions occurred. Gradually, more volcanoes of western America began showing increased volcanic activity, sending plumes of ash careering skywards, getting thicker and higher day by day.

On the fifteenth of November beneath the impact area, lava reacted with the sea water in huge quantities, causing a large rift to open within the seabed. It exploded violently, throwing up monstrous amounts of molten rock, containing massive amounts of sulphur into the sea. A huge eruption followed, cutting through the boiling sea water and heading skywards, before exploding into minute particles. The fine dust steadily continued spreading outwards, held in suspension as it slowly circled the globe. This was joined by the ever thickening ash clouds, from the volcanic activity in western America.

The asteroid impact had a knock on effect with the world's tectonic plates, causing earthquakes in South America, Japan and Indonesia and many volcanoes erupted frequently near the fault lines. Over two weeks, the world was consumed by a dirty brown ash cloud, delivered by the pollutants of the frequent volcanic eruptions. The dust clouds blocked eighty per cent of the sunlight, sending the world into devilish darkness, not seen for millions of years. Smog gradually tainted the world's air, along with a pungent smell of sulphur.

The effect on the terrapods was immediate, rendering them sluggish and not the terrifying predator they had once been. This enabled people to venture out from their protective sanctuaries. The lack of light was subduing the terrapods, but death was soon to be on the horizon for them. The volcanic activity supporting the ungodly ash clouds and the blackening of the atmosphere, promised two race saving secrets. One in the way of sulphur, the other was the rich nitrogen. When the rain began falling on Mother Earth, it fell as rancid acid rain. When the rain fell on the terrapods, they were disposed of very quickly. Their tough flesh resisted weapons, by swallowing deadly bullets, but the rain ate through their acid sensitive flesh, rendering them into a molten mess. This quickly removed the threat to humanity from the deadly parasites.

******

In Waterloo station, both soldiers and refugees, ventured out the entrance and back into the light again. They watched the terrapods dying on Waterloo Bridge, as the acid rain flushed their melting flesh into the river. Any surviving stray terrapod, received a dose of freshly collected rain from onlookers.

Inside the station, the taskforce had been reassembled and asked to continue their work. They needed to find a better cure for the parasites. This was just in case there should be another outbreak in the near future, or if the rain did not exterminate all the parasites.

Inside Kennington underground station, inhabitants had been told to remain inside until all local terrapods were confirmed dead by troops. They received the all clear after two weeks then people began coming out to face a new world, with no clue on how to start rebuilding.

The Ellis family along with Pete, Jan and Bentley the dog, ventured outside, to check on their new surroundings. Many houses had sustained major damage, and not one single house had been spared from damage by bullet. Whole streets had been levelled, leaving only their foundations. It was apparent the army had used acids in their bid to destroy terrapods, as many burnt stricken parasites lay dying inside homes. Down towards the Oval underground station, many troops and civilian body parts were strewn about, clearly having lost the fight against terrapods. It was not a pretty sight, so Dave and Mary hid the horror from their children's view. Dave said to Mary "Who would believe a natural disaster, would bring these parasites here and a similar disaster would bring them to their knees, wiping them out and saving humanity!" Mary said "It was a high price to pay. We don't know the extent of the damage from the second asteroid yet, nor what price civilisation has paid" Dave said "I'm sure all will unfold in good time, but for now we must find out if we still have a home to return to" Dave continued with "It won't be easy, but after the last several months, it will be a huge relief to live outside the underground prison"

Craig, his son and Julie holding baby Paige, appeared from inside the station entrance then approached Dave. Dave acknowledged them and said "What are your plans?" Julie replied "I don't know, I lived in Portsmouth with my parents, but they died when the parasites overrun the estate. I managed to escape using my father's car. I doubt there is a house to go back to now, just bad memories" Craig said "My ex-wife sent my son to live with me because of the terrapod infestation. I begged her to stay, but she declined the offer and the terrapods engulfed the area taking her life. I now need to find the father of little baby Paige. He may be alive somewhere" Mary said "Let's hope you can find him"

Jane and her mother Sarah ventured out the entrance, looking shocked and bewildered. They walked up to their new friends and Jane said "It's such a waste of life, how do we repair this mess?" Jane's mother said "We rise to the occasion, it may take time, but we will survive and prosper. We're not dinosaurs, and we can and will work as one, to solve this problem. After all, nothing stays the same. We must find a way to cope together then move on" They all took heart in her words, even though it was not going to be a walk in the park. Pete and Jan said "We'll find our way back to the Isle of Wight and find out who managed to survive"

Ray and Kira appeared outside the station entrance and looked around at the chaos. Kira said "It's good to taste the fresh air. Where do we go from here Ray?" Ray replied "I don't know! Do we go home or perhaps we could make a new start somewhere else! Kira said "Let's leave London and head west, away from the massacred masses" Ray replied "Sounds good to me, the quiet is a welcome relief after the continuous gunfire" Ray put his arm around Kira and they began walking away from the station, acknowledging the Ellis family as they passed them.

A soldier quickly began moving body parts to the side of the road, ready for burning. A lone man said to him "What are you doing?" The reply came back "We have to burn the bodies of the fallen, before they become a serious health hazard" The man said "I see what you mean, are you identifying them first" The soldier said "If they have anything on them to identify them with. We're keeping them in the hope that people will ask about them later. It might give relatives closure on their loved ones, but I fear whole families may have perished" The man said "I've nothing to go home to, do you mind if I help?" The soldier said "I presume you lost people as well. I lost all of my family. I'd be grateful for some help, thank you Sir" The two men worked together, clearing the area and making a healthier environment.

******

Around the world, the terrapods were extinguished, leaving a very different world. The human race was once a huge dominant force on the planet, but there numbers had since dwindled to a mere quarter of what they were six months ago, before the arrival of the terrapods, and the coming of the second asteroid. The asteroid left both South and North America, with large areas decimated by the destructiveness of the impact. The African coast had been battered by the multiple tsunami waves, and inland many bush fires caused by burning asteroid shrapnel had wiped out crops and plant life. Droughts followed, as many people began slowly dying of starvation. This time there would be no help from western countries, as they were struggling with their own turmoil. More was to come as the huge ash clouds that had engulf the skies saving humanity from the terrapods, would have a nasty sting in its tale. It removed the sunlight, leaving a dark chilling impact winter that would ultimately, have a lasting impact on worldwide crop growth.

Many people the world over, returned to their homes to pick up the pieces. In the United Kingdom there was a north and south divide, with the north only having been partially touched by the destructive wrath of the army, as it made war against the terrapods. Many southerners decided, heading northwards was their only option, so they uprooted and moved. People of the north were very accommodating, until large numbers of refugees started migrating to the big cities, causing overcrowding and food shortages. Violence became rife as guns were freely available, from the many fallen soldiers who lost their lives doing their duty during the terrapod war.

Weapons were picked up by passing strangers, no matter what their intent.

Across the world, food was hard to come by and even countries like Russia, China and America, struggled feeding the people left and many died hungry. America, a country in ruins, who had once been a super nation with a big say in the world affairs, was found wanting. Southern states were flooded and uninhabitable, with many millions dead. The western seaboard had many active, unpredictable volcanoes with eruptions spewing out thick ash debris, covering vital lifesaving crop fields. Many people had either travelled eastwards, away from the volcanoes or had previously headed northwards to settle in Alaska, where terrapods had avoided going to, because of the colder climes.

In large American cities, gangs broke out with both the army and the police looking the other way, while they attempted cleaning up the many corpses left by the terrapods. By the time they thought about restoring order, the authorities found themselves swamped by gang warfare and unable to reinstate marshal law.

The only areas of the world saved from major problems, were the Arctic Circle, the Antarctic, Greenland and Iceland, but even Iceland noticed more activity within their range of active volcanoes. Australia another country untouched by most events, was now feeling the adverse effects from the ash cloud, as it crept over the country, blackening the northern territories.

The ash clouds had slowly spread around the world with its greyish brown tinge. The first countries to experience what this really meant, was Mexico, North and South America and Canada. It blackened their skies, removing light within a few days, then the temperature plummeted to minus five degrees, bringing with it an extremely cold harsh winter. Many people perished from the cold and the ever decreasing food supplies. Hot tropical countries were poorly prepared for arctic conditions. Countries in the northern hemisphere were hit hardest, with temperatures plummeting to minus fifty in places, making it impossible to venture outside. Many northern rivers froze, along with the river fish stocks. The sea was also severely hit by the high acidity levels from the acid rain. The world's ecosystem quickly began changing, as certain species unable to adjust to the acid levels, quickly became extinct either directly from the acidity, or because the food they fed on died. This meant a glut of food to start, then nothing at all, leaving them to starve.

Within a month, three quarters of the Earth was covered by a thick dust cloud, leaving only part of the Arctic Circle, the Antarctic and southern Australia receiving any lifesaving light from the sun. The rest of the Earth was shrouded in darkness, with only the occasional small ray of light sneaking through, when high winds allowed. The Earth's average temperature dropped six degrees. The deserts of Africa, cooled enough to allow plants to grow, where light slipped through the clouds. Places such as Scotland, and the north of England had bitterly cold temperatures of minus twenty five. The south of France was so cold, rivers and lakes froze allowing people to skate on them. Siberia in Russia had an unusual temperature increase by five degrees and was having its mildest winter ever. Unlike the rest of Russia, Ukraine and Georgia, where they were experiencing a three degree drop in temperature with an extremely harsh winter. The worst of the cold was felt in the Gulf of Mexico, where tropical weather was traded in for freezing acid rain, and snowball sized hailstones.

Up through the west of America, where volcanic activity was at its strongest, many electrical storms continually revolved around the active volcanoes, causing rain to turn to ice when touching the ground.

Australia was having problems with winds up to a hundred and fifty miles an hour in the south, causing wide scale damage to property. Meanwhile in the north, they had already witness two hurricanes called Jack and Jill hitting the barrier reef, sucking up ships and fish alike, then violently depositing them inland seventy miles.

In London, the cloud blackened the sky, lowering temperatures to a cool minus ten degrees, warm compared to the northern areas of the country. The taskforce decided to stay inside the underground station, sheltered from the cold of winter. Jacob, Richard, Darren and Rafael discovered that nitric and sulphuric acid mixed together in small amounts was deadly to the terrapods. However, it was of no use to them now, when the terrapods were presumed to have been swiftly wiped out by the second asteroid. They now changed their focus to the impact winter that was now upon them. It was obvious the cold weather would last for several months. How long, would depend on Mother Earth's ability to clear the debris from her skies and for her ecosystem to recover. They guessed it would be June of next year, before the light would return once again, and shine brightly through the murky brown blanket masking the sun.

Many surviving governments were powerless to govern their countries after being cut off from their people. Others such as the British government had frozen to death in the wintry tundra, after heading northwards. Countries governed by dictators found their subjects revolting against their controlling oppressors. Many deliberately chose to leave the dictators and their families, to their freezing fates.

\*\*\*\*\*\*

The Ellis family, returned to their home in Guildford, finding their home still standing, but in a mess from where the soldiers had broken the locks then gone through everything checking for terrapods. Pete and Jan decided to stay with the Ellis family for a while, as no ferries were running to the Isle of Wight. They had been informed that soldiers were working their way to the ferry port, and would be in touch when safe to use the ferries. Jane and her mother could not go home, because their home had been completely destroyed by the aerial bombardment from the Royal Air Force, as they tried keeping terrapods at bay. They temporarily moved in next door to the Ellis family, with permission of the owners who had gone northwards. At least until normality returned to the country, and they were able to return from the north. Craig and Julie returned to Craig's house, with his son and baby Paige. They found themselves looking after baby Paige, while Craig continued looking for her missing father.

Although temperatures were freezing, the biggest problems they all faced were of acquiring fresh uncontaminated water. They could at least survive on canned foods, and bottled water from abandoned supermarkets and shops for a while, but ultimately they needed fresh foods to be grown in the near future.

The surviving inhabitants of the new colder Earth gradually adapted to the impact winter, scavenging food after fresh foods ran out. Many stayed underground, seeking the safety of the tunnels from the cold climes, and the large street gangs, that roamed topside unchecked.

The soldiers began clearing the way to most of the islands around the United Kingdom, finding small pockets of survivors. Pete and Jan eventually received news from the Isle of Wight of people having escaped the attentions of the terrapods. It looked like the only survivors that had made it, were situated inside the hospital at Newport and the local police station.

******

The world entered its second mini ice age, with an uncertain future ahead. Around the world, people adapted or died trying. Animals struggled with the cold and many reptile species became extinct, but some animals did thrive such as bears, wolves, penguins, sharks and even certain whales. Many species of both animals and plant life would perish, while others flourished, but which ones?

Humans are very resourceful, yet still retain a degree of animal instinct when in harsh unforgiving environments. Most of all, humans can adapt whilst working together, so they might just be able to ride out the cold wilderness of the impending impact winter. Dinosaurs were the last dominant predator to conquer Earth, some sixty five million years previous, but they lost the fight against the last asteroid impact, sending them into extinction.

**What lay ahead for Earth, and its many diverse inhabitants?**

# The End

**Terrapods
The
Invasion Begins**

**By
G T Philips**